WHERE THE SHADOWS LIE

WHERE THE SHADOWS LIE

MICHAEL RIDPATH

CORVUS

First published in the UK in 2010 by Corvus,
an imprint of Grove Atlantic Ltd.

9 8 7 6 5 4 3 2 1

A CIP catalogue record for this book is available from the British Library.

ISBN: 978-1-84887-397-1 (hardback)
ISBN: 978-1-84887-398-8 (trade paperback)

Printed in Great Britain by the MPG Books Group

Corvus
An imprint of Grove Atlantic Ltd
Ormond House
26-27 Boswell Street
London WC1N 3JZ

www.corvus-books.co.uk

for Barbara, as always

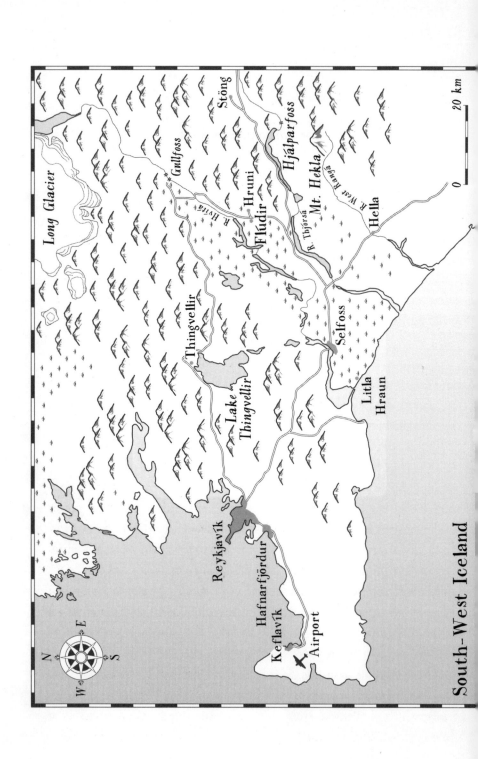

South-West Iceland

CHAPTER ONE

PROFESSOR AGNAR HARALDSSON folded the letter and slipped it back into its small yellowing envelope.

He glanced again at the address inscribed in an upright, ornamental hand: Högni Ísildarson, Laugavegur 64, Reykjavík, Iceland. The stamp bore the profile of a beardless British king, an Edward or a George, Agnar wasn't certain which.

His heart thumped, the envelope performing a tiny dance in his shaking hand. The letter had arrived that morning enclosed within a larger envelope bearing a modern Icelandic stamp and a Reykjavík postmark.

It was all that Agnar could have hoped for. It was more than that; it was perfect.

As a professor of Icelandic at the University of Iceland, Agnar had been privileged to handle some of the oldest manuscripts of his country's sagas, copied out by monks with infinite care on to sheaves of calf skins using black bearberry juice for ink, and feathers from the left wings of swans for pens. Those magnificent documents were Iceland's heritage, Iceland's soul. But none of them would cause as great a stir in the outside world as this single sheet of paper.

And none of them was his discovery.

He looked up from his desk over the serene lake in front of him. It glittered a rare deep blue in the April sunshine. Ten minutes before it had glinted steel grey, and in a few more minutes it would do so again as dark clouds from the west chased after those

1

disappearing over the snow-topped mountains across the lake to the east.

A perfect location for a summer house. The cabin had been built by Agnar's father, a former politician who was now in an old-people's home. Although summer was still some time away, Agnar had escaped there for the weekend to work with no distractions. His wife had just given birth to their second child, and Agnar had a tight deadline to get through a pile of translation.

'Aggi, come back to bed.'

He turned to see the breathtakingly beautiful figure of Andrea, ballet dancer and third-year literature student, naked as she glided across the bare wooden floor towards him, her blonde hair a tangled mess.

'I'm sorry, darling, I can't,' he said nodding towards the mess of papers in front of him.

'Are you sure?' She bent down to kiss him, and ran her fingers under his shirt and through the hair on his chest, her mane tickling his nose. She broke away. 'Are you really sure?'

He smiled and removed his spectacles.

Well, perhaps he would allow himself one distraction.

CHAPTER TWO

SERGEANT DETECTIVE MAGNUS Jonson trudged along the residential street in Roxbury towards his car. He had a load of typing to do back at the station before he could go home. He was tired, so tired: he hadn't slept properly for a week. Which was perhaps why the smell had hit him so badly.

It was a familiar smell: raw beef a week past its sell-by date tinged with a metallic edge. He had experienced it many times in his years with the Boston Police Department's Homicide Unit.

Maria Campanelli, white female, twenty-seven.

She had been dead thirty-six hours, stabbed by her boyfriend after an argument and left to decompose in her apartment. They were out looking for him now, and Magnus was confident he would be found. But to be certain of a conviction they needed to make sure they got the paperwork one hundred per cent accurate. A bunch of people to be interviewed; a bunch of forms to be filled out. The department had suffered a scandal a few years back with a series of slip-ups in the chain of evidence, documents misfiled, court exhibits lost. Since then defence lawyers had jumped on any mistakes.

Magnus was good at the paperwork, which was one of the reasons he had recently been promoted to sergeant. Perhaps Colby was right, perhaps he should go to law school.

Colby.

For the twelve months they had been living together she had gradually turned up the pressure: why didn't he quit the department and go to law school, why didn't they get married? And then,

3

six days ago, when they were walking arm in arm back from their favourite Italian restaurant in the North End, a Jeep had driven past with its rear window wound down. Magnus had thrown Colby to the sidewalk just as a rapid succession of shots rang out from a semi-automatic rifle. Maybe the shooters thought they had hit their target, maybe there were too many people around, but the Jeep had driven off without finishing the job.

That was why she had kicked him out of her apartment. That was why he had spent sleepless nights in the guest room of his brother's house in Medford. That was why the smell had gotten to him: for the first time in a long time the smell of death had become personal.

It could have been him splayed out on the floor of that apartment. Or Colby.

It was the hottest day of the year so far, which had, of course, made the smell worse, and Magnus was sweating in his suit jacket. He felt a touch on his elbow.

It was a guy of about fifty, Latin, bald, short and overweight, unshaven. He was wearing a large blue shirt which hung out over jeans.

'Detective?'

Magnus stopped. 'Yeah?'

'I think I saw something. The night the girl was stabbed.' The man's voice was gruff, urgent.

Magnus was tempted to tell the guy to beat it. They had a witness who had seen the boyfriend come, another who had seen him leave six hours later, three who had heard a loud argument, one who had heard a scream. But you could never have enough witnesses. Another statement to type up when he got back to the station.

Magnus sighed as he reached for his notebook. There were still several hours to go before he could go home and take the run and shower he needed to get the smell out of his system. If he wasn't too exhausted for a run by then.

The man looked nervously up and down the street. 'Not here, I don't want nobody to see us talking.'

Magnus was about to protest – the victim's boyfriend was a cook at the Boston Medical Center, hardly someone to be scared of – but then he shrugged and followed the man as he hurried down a small side street, between a dilapidated grey clapboard house and a small red-brick apartment building. Little more than an alley, with some kind of construction site with a high wire fence at the end. A heavily tattooed kid with a yellow T-shirt stood at the street corner. He smoked a cigarette, his back to Magnus.

As they entered the alleyway, the bald guy seemed to speed up. Magnus lengthened his stride. He was about to yell to the guy to slow down, when he stopped himself.

Magnus had been asleep. Now he was awake.

Among the forest of tattoos on the kid's arms, Magnus had noticed a small dot above one elbow, and a pattern of five dots above the other. One five, fifteen, the tattoo of the Cobra-15 gang. They didn't operate in Roxbury. This kid was way outside of his territory, by at least three miles, maybe four. But the Cobra-15 were customers of Soto's operation, local distribution agents. The guys in the Jeep in the North End had been working for Soto, Magnus was sure.

Magnus's instinct was to straighten up and turn, but he forced himself not to break his stride and alert the kid. Think. Think fast.

He could hear footsteps behind him. Gun or knife? The sound of a gun would be risky this close to the crime scene – there were still one or two cops milling around. But the kid knew Magnus was armed and no one brings a knife to a gunfight. Which meant gun. Which meant the kid was probably pulling it out of the waistband of his pants right then.

Magnus dived to the left, grabbed a garbage can and threw it to the ground. As he hit the ground he rolled once, reached for his gun and pointed it towards the kid, who was raising his own weapon. Magnus's finger curled around the trigger, and then his training kicked in. He hesitated. The rule was clear: don't fire if there is a chance of hitting a civilian.

In the mouth of the alleyway stood a young woman, grocery

5

bags in both arms, staring at Magnus, her mouth open. She was wide, real wide, and directly behind the kid in the yellow T-shirt in Magnus's line of fire.

The hesitation gave the kid time to raise his own gun. Magnus was looking straight down the barrel. A stand off.

'Police! Drop your weapon!' Magnus shouted, even though he knew the kid wouldn't.

What would happen next? If the kid fired first, he might miss Magnus, and then Magnus could get away his own shot. Although he was six foot four and weighed over two hundred pounds, Magnus was lying prone on the street, partially hidden by the dislodged trash can, a smallish target for a panicked kid.

Perhaps the kid would back off. If only the woman would move. She was still rooted to the spot, her mouth open, trying to scream.

Then Magnus saw the kid's eyes flick upwards and behind Magnus. The bald guy.

The kid wouldn't have taken his eyes off Magnus's gun if the bald guy was holding back. He would only risk that if the bald guy was relevant to the situation, if he was his saviour, if he had his own gun and was approaching Magnus from behind. Hold off for a couple of seconds until the bald guy shot Magnus in the back, that was the kid's plan.

Magnus pulled his trigger, just once, not the twice he had been trained. He wanted to keep the numbers of bullets flying towards the fat woman to a minimum. The kid was hit in the chest; he jerked and fired his own gun, missing Magnus.

Magnus reached out to the trash can and flung it behind him. He turned to see the empty container hitting the bald guy in the shins. The man was reaching under his belly for his own gun, but doubled over as he tripped on the can.

Magnus fired twice hitting the guy each time, once in the shoulder and once in the bald crown of his head. A mess.

Magnus pulled himself to his feet. Noise kicked in. The fat woman had dropped her groceries and was screaming now, loud, very loud. It turned out there was nothing wrong with her lungs. A police siren started up somewhere close. There was the sound of shouting and running feet.

The bald guy was still, but the kid was sprawled on his back on the ground, his chest heaving, his yellow T-shirt now stained red. His fingers were curled around his gun as he tried to summon up the strength to point it towards Magnus. Magnus stamped hard on his wrist and kicked the gun out of the way. He stood panting over the boy who had tried to kill him. Seventeen or eighteen, Hispanic, close-cropped black hair, a broken front tooth, a scar on his neck. Taut muscles under swirls of ink on his arms and chest, intricate gang tattoos. A tough kid. A kid his age in Cobra-15 could already have several dead bodies to his name.

But not Magnus's. At least not today. But tomorrow?

Magnus could smell gunpowder and sweat and fear and once again the metallic bite of blood. Too much blood for one day.

'I'm taking you off the street.'

Deputy Superintendent Williams, the chief of the Homicide Unit, was firm. He was always firm, that was one of the things Magnus appreciated about him. He also appreciated that he had come all the way from his office on Schroeder Plaza in downtown Boston to make sure that one of his men was safe. They were in an anonymous motel room in an anonymous motel somewhere off I-91 between Springfield, Massachusetts and Hartford, Connecticut, chaperoned by FBI agents with Midwestern accents. Magnus hadn't been allowed back in the station since the shooting.

'I don't think that's necessary,' Magnus said.

'Well, I do.'

'Are we talking Witness Protection Programme?'

'Possibly. This is the second time someone has tried to kill you within a week.'

'I was tired. I let my guard down. It won't happen again.'

Williams raised his eyebrows. His black face was deeply lined. He was small, compact, determined, a good boss, and honest.

That was why Magnus had gone to him six months before when he had overheard his partner, Detective Lenahan, talking on his cell phone to another cop about tampering with evidence in a homicide investigation.

They were on a bullshit stakeout. Magnus had gone for a walk and was returning to the car when he stopped in the fall sunshine just behind the passenger window. The window was open a crack. Magnus could hear Lenahan clearly, wheedling, cajoling and threatening a Detective O'Driscoll to do the right thing and smudge the fingerprint evidence on a gun.

Magnus and Lenahan had not been partners for long. At fifty-three, Lenahan was twenty years older than Magnus. He was experienced, smart, popular, and he seemed to know everyone in the Boston Police Department, especially those with Irish last names. But he was lazy. He used his three decades of experience and knowledge of police methods to do as little work as possible.

Magnus saw things differently. As soon as he had closed one case he was eager to move on to the next; his determination to nail the perp was legendary within the department. Lenahan thought there were good guys and there were bad guys, there always were and there always would be. There was not very much that he or Magnus or the whole Boston police force could do about that. Magnus thought that every victim, and every victim's family, deserved justice, and Magnus would do his very best to get it for them. So the Jonson–Lenahan partnership was hardly made in heaven.

But until that moment, Magnus had not imagined that Lenahan was crooked.

There are two things that a cop hates more than anything else. One is a crooked cop. Another is a cop who rats on one of his colleagues. For Magnus the choice was easy – if people like Lenahan were allowed to get away with destroying evidence of a homicide, then everything he had devoted his career towards was worthless.

Magnus knew that most of his colleagues would agree with him.

But some would turn a blind eye, convince themselves that Magnus had misheard, that good old Sean Lenahan could not be one of the bad guys. And others would think that if good old Sean got himself a little retirement nest egg by taking money off one bad guy who had just killed another, then good luck to him. He deserved it after serving the citizens of Boston so loyally for thirty years.

Which is why Magnus had gone straight to Williams and only Williams. Williams had understood the situation. A couple of weeks later Magnus's promotion came through and he and Lenahan were split up. An undercover team from the FBI was brought in from out of state. A major investigation was launched and Lenahan was linked with two other detectives, O'Driscoll and Montoya. The Feds discovered the gang that was paying them off; it was Dominican, led by a man named Pedro Soto, who operated out of Lawrence, a faded mill town just outside Boston. Soto supplied cocaine and heroin wholesale to street gangs all over New England. The three crooked detectives were arrested and charged. Magnus was billed as the star witness when the case eventually came to trial.

But the FBI hadn't yet amassed enough evidence to charge Soto. He was still out there.

'Your guard slips once, it can slip again,' said Williams. 'If we don't do something you'll be dead within two weeks. They want your ass and they'll get it.'

'But I don't see why they want to kill me,' Magnus said. 'Sure, my testimony will nail Lenahan, but I can't point to Soto or the Dominicans. And you said Lenahan isn't cooperating.'

'The FBI thinks it's figured out Lenahan's angle. The last thing he wants is to wind up in a maximum-security prison with a bunch of convicted killers, no cop would want that, he'd be better off dead. But without your testimony, he'll walk. Our guess is that he has given the Dominicans an ultimatum: they get rid of you or he'll give them to us. And if he doesn't, his buddy Montoya will. If you die, Lenahan and the other two go free, and Soto's operation continues as if nothing has happened. But if you live to testify,

Lenahan does a deal with the FBI, and Soto and his boys will have to close down business and head home to the Dominican Republic. If we don't get to them first.'

Williams looked Magnus right in the eye. 'Which is why we have to figure out what to do with you.'

Magnus saw Williams's point. But full witness protection would mean starting up a new life with a new identity on the other side of the country. He didn't want that. 'Got any ideas?' he asked Williams.

'Matter of fact, I do.' Williams smiled. 'You're an Icelandic citizen, right?'

'Yes. As well as US. I have dual.'

'Do you speak the language?'

'Some. I spoke it as a child. I moved here with my dad when I was twelve. But I haven't spoken it since he died.'

'Which was when?'

'When I was twenty.'

Williams allowed a brief pause to express his sympathy. 'Well, I guess you speak it better than most of the rest of us, then.'

Magnus smiled. 'I guess so. Why?'

'An old buddy in the NYPD called me a couple months ago. Said he'd heard I had someone who spoke Icelandic in my unit. He'd just had a visit from the National Police Commissioner of Iceland. He was looking for the NYPD to loan him a detective as an advisor. He didn't necessarily want someone senior, just someone experienced in the many and varied crimes that our great country has to offer. Apparently, they don't get many homicides in Iceland, or at least they didn't until recently. Obviously, if that detective happened to speak Icelandic, that would be a bonus.'

'I don't remember anybody telling me about this,' Magnus said.

Williams smiled. 'They didn't.'

'Why not?'

'Same reason I'm telling you now. You're one of my best detectives and I don't want to lose you. Except now I would rather have you alive in an igloo in Iceland than dead on a sidewalk in Boston.'

Magnus had given up long ago telling people that there were no igloos in Iceland. Nor were there any Eskimos, and only very rarely polar bears. He hadn't been to Iceland since just after his father's death. He had his doubts about going back, severe doubts, but at that moment it seemed like the least bad option.

'I called the Icelandic Police Commissioner an hour ago. He's still looking for an advisor. He sounded very excited by the idea of a detective who speaks the language. So, what do you think?'

There really was no choice.

'I'll do it,' Magnus said. 'On one condition.'

Williams frowned. 'Which is?'

'I take my girlfriend with me.'

Magnus had seen Colby angry before, but never this angry.

'What do you think you are doing, getting your goons to kidnap me? Is this some kind of joke? Some kind of weird romantic gesture where you think I'm going to take you back? Because if it is, I can tell you right now it's not going to work. So tell these men to take me back to the office!'

They were sitting in the back seat of an FBI van in the parking lot of a Friendly's restaurant. Two agents had cruised by the offices of the medical-equipment company where Colby was in-house counsel and whisked her away. They were gathered around their car fifty feet away, with the two agents who had driven Magnus.

'They tried to kill me again,' Magnus said. 'Almost succeeded this time.'

He still couldn't believe how stupid he had been, how he had let himself be led off the main street down an alley. Since the shooting he had been interviewed at great length by two detectives from the Firearm Discharge Investigative team. They had been told they would only have one chance to talk to him, so they had been very thorough, focusing especially on his decision to pull the trigger when there was an innocent civilian in the line of fire.

Magnus didn't regret that decision. He had traded the near

certainty of his own death for a small probability that the woman would be harmed. But he had a better answer for the detectives. If the gangsters had shot him, they would probably have shot the woman next, as a witness. The Firearms Discharge guys liked this idea. They were careful not to ask him whether he had thought of that before or after he had pulled the trigger. They were going to do things by the book, but they were on his side.

This was the second time he had shot and killed someone while on duty. After the first, when he was a rookie patrol officer in uniform two months into the job, he had suffered weeks of guilt-filled sleepless nights.

This time he was just glad to be alive.

'Too bad they failed,' muttered Colby. Two tiny red dots of anger sizzled on each cheek; the corners of her brown eyes glistened with fury. Her mouth was set firm. Then she bit her lip, pulling strands of dark curly hair back behind her ears in a familiar gesture. 'I'm sorry, I didn't mean that. But it's got nothing to do with me. I don't want it to have anything to do with me, that's the whole point.'

'It already does have to do with you, Colby.'

'What do you mean?'

'The chief wants me to go. Leave Boston. He doesn't think the Dominicans will stop until they've killed me.'

'That sounds like a good idea.'

Magnus took a deep breath. 'And I want you to come with me.'

The expression on Colby's face was a mixture of shock and contempt. 'Are you serious?'

'It's for your own safety. If I'm gone they might go after you.'

'What about my work? What about my job, dammit?'

'You'll just have to leave that. It'll only be for a few months. Until the trial.'

'Was I right the first time? Is this just some weird way for you to get me back?'

'No,' said Magnus. 'It's because I'm worried for you if you stay.'

Colby bit her lip again. A tear ran down her cheek. Magnus reached out and touched her arm. 'Where would we go?'

'I'm sorry, I can't tell you until I know you will say yes.'

'Will I like it?' She glanced at him.

He shook his head. 'Probably not.' They had discussed Iceland many times during their relationship, and Colby had been consistent in her distrust of the country, its volcanoes and its bad weather.

'It's Iceland, isn't it?'

Magnus just shrugged.

'Wait a minute, let me think.' Colby turned away from him and stared out over the parking lot. A large family of four waddled out to their car carrying tubs of ice cream, smiles of anticipation on their faces.

Magnus waited.

Colby turned and stared him right in the eye. 'Do you want to get married?'

Magnus returned her stare. He couldn't believe she was serious. But she was very serious.

'Well?'

'I don't know,' Magnus hesitated. 'We could talk about it.'

'No! I don't want to talk about it, we've talked about it for months. I want to decide right now. You want me to decide to drop everything and go away with you. Fine. I'll do it. If we get married.'

'But this is totally the wrong way to make a decision like that.'

'What do you mean? Do you love me?'

'Of course I love you,' Magnus replied.

'Then let's get married. We can go to Iceland and live happily ever after.'

'You're not thinking clearly,' Magnus said. 'You're angry.'

'You bet I'm angry. You've asked me to commit to going away with you, and I'll do it if you commit to me. Come on, Magnus, decision time.'

Magnus took a deep breath. He watched the family climb into the car which sagged on its axles. They pulled out past the other FBI vehicle, the one that had picked up Colby. 'I want you to come with me for your own safety,' he said.

'So that's a no, then?' Her eyes bored into his. Colby was a determined woman, that was one of the things Magnus loved about her, but he had never seen her this determined. 'No?'

Magnus nodded. 'No.'

Colby pursed her lips and reached for the door handle. 'OK. We're done here. I'm going back to work.'

Magnus grabbed her arm. 'Colby, please!'

'Get your hands off me!' Colby shouted and threw open the door. She walked rapidly over to the four agents standing around the other car and muttered something to them. Within a minute the car was gone.

Two of the agents returned to the van and climbed in.

'I guess she's not going with you,' said the driver.

'I guess she's not,' said Magnus.

CHAPTER THREE

MAGNUS LOOKED UP from his book and out of the airplane window. It had been a long flight, made longer by the five-hour delay in their departure from Logan. The plane was descending. Beneath him was a blanket of coarse grey clouds, torn only in a couple of places. As the aircraft approached one of these Magnus craned his neck to try to get a glimpse of land, but all he could see was a patch of crumpled grey sea, flecked with white caps. Then it was gone.

He was worried about Colby. If the Dominicans did come after her it would unequivocally be his fault. When he had first told her about Lenahan's conversation she had counselled against going to Williams. She claimed she had always thought law enforcement a stupid profession. And if he had agreed to marry her in the parking lot of Friendly's, she would be in the seat next to him on her way to safety, instead of in her apartment in the Back Bay, waiting for the wrong guy to knock at the door.

But Magnus had had to do what was right. He always had and he always would. It was right to go to Williams about Lenahan. It was right to shoot the kid in the yellow T-shirt. It would have been wrong to marry Colby because she forced him to. He had never been sure why his parents had gotten married, but he had lived with the consequences of that mistake.

Perhaps he was too nervous, perhaps the Dominicans would ignore her. He had demanded that Williams organize some police protection for her, a request that Williams had reluctantly agreed to; reluctantly because of her refusal to go to Iceland with Magnus.

But if the Dominicans did catch her, would he be able to live with the consequences of that? Perhaps he should just have said yes, agreed to whatever she wanted just to get her out of the country. That's what she had been trying to force him into. He hadn't allowed himself to be forced. And now she might die.

She was thirty, she wanted to get married and she wanted to marry Magnus. Or a modified Magnus, a successful lawyer pulling down a good salary, living in a big house in Brookline or maybe even Beacon Hill if he was really successful, driving a BMW or a Mercedes. Perhaps he would even convert to Judaism.

She hadn't cared that he was a tough cop when they had first met. It was at a party given by an old friend of his from college, also a lawyer. The mutual attraction had been instantaneous. She was pretty, vivacious, smart, strong willed, determined. She liked the idea of an Ivy League graduate walking the streets of South Boston with a gun. He was safe but dangerous, even his occasional bad moods seemed to attract her. Until she started to view him not as a lover but as a potential husband.

Who did she want him to be? Who did *he* want to be? For that matter, who was he? It was a question Magnus often asked himself.

He pulled out his electric-blue Icelandic passport. The photograph was similar to the one in his US passport, except the Icelander was allowed to smile, whereas the American was not. Red hair, square jaw, blue eyes, traces of freckles on his nose. But the name was different. His *real* name, Magnús Ragnarsson. His name was Magnús, his father's name was Ragnar, and his grandfather's name was Jón. So his father was Ragnar Jónsson and he was Magnús Ragnarsson. Simple.

But of course the US bureaucracy could not cope with this logic. A son could not have a different last name to his father *and* his mother, whose name was Margrét Hallgrímsdóttir, and still have the government computers accept him as part of the same family. Obviously it couldn't cope with the accents on the vowels, and it didn't really like the non-standard spelling of Jonsson either. Ragnar had fought this for a few months after his son arrived in the country and then thrown in the towel. The twelve-year-old Icelandic boy Magnús Ragnarsson became the American kid Magnus Jonson.

He turned back to the book on his lap. *Njáls Saga*, one of his favourites.

Although Magnus had spoken very little Icelandic over the past thirteen years, he had read a lot. His father had read the sagas to him when Magnus had moved to Boston, and for Magnus they had become a source of comfort in the new confusing world of America. They still were. The word *saga* meant literally *what is said* in Icelandic. The sagas were the archetypal family histories, most of them dealing with the three or four generations of Vikings who had settled Iceland around 900 AD until the coming of Christianity to that country in 1000. Their heroes were complex men with many weaknesses as well as strengths, but they had a clear moral code, a sense of honour and a respect for the laws. They were brave adventurers. For a lone Icelander in a huge Junior High School in the United States, they were a source of inspiration. If one of their kinsmen was killed, they knew what to do: they demanded money in compensation and if that was not forthcoming they demanded blood, all strictly according to the law.

So when his father was murdered when Magnus was twenty, *he* knew what to do. Search for justice.

The police never found his father's killer, and despite Magnus's efforts, neither did he, but he decided after leaving college to become a policeman. He was still searching for justice, and despite all the murderers he had arrested over the last decade, he still hadn't found it. Every murderer was his father's murderer, until they were caught. Then the quest for just retribution went on, unsatisfied.

The plane descended. Another gap in the clouds; this time he could see the waves breaking against the brown lava field of the Reykjanes Peninsula. Two black stripes bisected the barren stone and dust: the highway from Reykjavík to the airport at Keflavík. Wisps of cloud, like smoke from a volcano, drifted over an isolated white house in a puddle of bright green grass, and then Magnus was over the ocean again. The clouds closed in beneath the airplane as it began its turn for the final approach.

He had the feeling, as Iceland came nearer and nearer, that he was moving towards solving his father's murder, or at least *re*solving it. Perhaps in Iceland he could finally place it in some kind of perspective.

But the airplane was also bringing him closer to his childhood, closer to pain and confusion.

There was a golden period in Magnus's life before the age of eight, when his family all lived together in a little house with white corrugated-metal walls and a bright blue corrugated-metal roof, close to the centre of Reykjavík. It had a tiny garden with a white-painted picket fence and a stunted tree, an old whitebeam, on which to clamber. His father went off to the university every morning, and his mother, who was beautiful and always smiling then, taught at the local secondary school. He remembered playing soccer with his friends during the long summer nights, and the excitement of the arrival of the thirteen mischievous Yuletide elves during the dark cosy winters, each dropping a small present in the shoe Magnus left beneath his open bedroom window.

Then it all changed. His father left home to go and teach mathematics at a university in America. His mother became angry and sleepy – she slept all the time. Her face became puffy, she got fat, she yelled at Magnus and his little brother Óli.

They moved back to the farm on the Snaefellsnes Peninsula where his mother had been brought up. That's where the misery started. Magnus realized that his mother wasn't sleepy all the time, she was drunk. At first she spent most of her time away in Reykjavík, trying to hold down her job as a teacher. Then she returned to the farm and a series of jobs in the nearest town, first teaching and then working cash registers. Worst of all Magnus and Óli were left for long periods in the care of their grandparents.

Their grandfather was a strict, scary, angry man, who liked a drink himself. Their grandmother was small and mean.

One day, when Magnus and Óli were at school, their mother had drunk half a bottle of vodka, climbed into a car and steered it straight into a rock, killing herself instantly. Within a week, amid acrimony of nuclear proportions, Ragnar had arrived to take them both away to Boston with him.

Magnus returned to Iceland with his father and Óli on an annual basis for camping trips in the back country and to spend a couple of days in Reykjavík to see his grandmother and his father's friends and colleagues. They had never gone near his mother's family.

Until a month after his father died, when Magnus made the trip to try to effect a reconciliation. The visit had been a total disaster. Magnus had recoiled in stunned bewilderment at the strength of the hostility from his grandparents. They didn't just hate his father, they hated him too. For an orphan whose only family was a mixed-up brother, and with no clear idea of which country he belonged to, that hurt.

Since then he had never been back.

The plane broke through the clouds only a couple of hundred feet above the ground. Iceland was cold and grey and windswept. To the left was the flat field of volcanic rubble, grey and brown covered with russet and green moss, and beyond that the paraphernalia of the abandoned American airbase, single-storey sheds, mysterious radio masts and golf balls on stilts. Not a tree in sight.

The plane hit the runway, and manoeuvred up to the terminal building. Improbably cheerful ground staff battled their way out into the wind, smiling and chatting. A windsock stuck out stiff and horizontal, as a curtain of rain rolled across the airfield towards them. It was 24 April, the day after Iceland's official first day of summer.

Thirty minutes later Magnus was sitting in the back of a white car hurtling along the highway between Keflavík and Reykjavík. Across the car was emblazoned the word *Lögreglan* – with typical stubbornness Iceland was one of the very few countries in the world that refused to use a derivation of the word 'police' for its law-enforcement agency.

Outside, the squall had passed and the wind seemed to be dying down. The lavascape, undulating mounds of stones, boulders and moss, stretched across towards a line of squat mountains in the distance, still not a tree in sight. Thousands of years after the event this patch of Iceland hadn't recovered from the devastation of a massive volcanic eruption. The thin layers of mosses nibbling at the rocks were only just beginning a process of restoration that would take millennia.

But Magnus wasn't looking at the scenery. He was concentrating hard on the man sitting next to him, Snorri Gudmundsson, the National Police Commissioner. He was a small man with shrewd blue eyes and thick grey hair brushed back in a bouffant. He was speaking rapidly in Icelandic, and it took all Magnus's powers of concentration to follow him.

'As I am sure you must know, Iceland has a low per-capita homicide rate and low levels of serious crime,' he was saying. 'Most policing involves clearing up the mess on Saturday and Sunday mornings once the partygoers have had their fun. Until the *kreppa* and the demonstrations over this last winter, of course. Every one of my officers in the Reykjavík area was tied up with those. They did well, I am proud of them.'

Kreppa was the Icelandic word for the credit crunch, which had hit the country particularly badly. The banks, the government and many of the people were bankrupt, drowning under debt incurred in the boom times. Magnus had read of the weekly demonstrations which had taken place in front of the Parliament building every Saturday afternoon for months, until the government had finally bowed to popular pressure and resigned.

'The trend is worrying,' the Commissioner went on. 'There are more drugs, more drug gangs. We have had problems with Lithuanian gangs and the Hells Angels have been trying to break into Iceland for years. There are more foreigners in our country now, and a small minority of them have a different attitude to crime to most Icelanders. The yellow press here exaggerates the problem, but it would be a foolish police commissioner who ignored the threat.'

He paused to check if Magnus was following. Magnus nodded to indicate he was, just.

'I am proud of our police force, they work hard and they have a good clear-up rate, but they are just not used to the kind of crimes that occur in big cities with large populations of foreigners. The greater Reykjavík area has a population of only a hundred and eighty thousand, the entire country has only three hundred thousand people, but I want us to be prepared in case the kinds of things that happen in Amsterdam, or Manchester, or Boston for that matter, happen here. Which is why I asked for you.

'Last year there were three unsolved murders in Iceland, all related. We never knew who committed them until he volunteered himself at police headquarters. He was a Pole. We should have caught him after the first woman was killed, but we didn't, so two more died. I think with someone like you working with us, we would have stopped him then.'

'I hope so,' said Magnus.

'I've read a copy of your file and spoken to Deputy Superintendent Williams. He was very flattering.'

Magnus raised his eyebrows. He didn't know Williams did flattery. And he knew there were some serious black marks in his record from those times in his career when he hadn't always done exactly what he had been told.

'The idea is that you will go through a crash course at the National Police College. In the mean time you will be available for training seminars and for advice should something crop up that you can help us with.'

'A crash course?' said Magnus, wanting to check that he had understood correctly. 'How long would that take?'

'The normal course is a year, but since you have so much police experience, we would hope to get you through in less than six months. It's unavoidable. You can't arrest someone unless you know Icelandic law.'

'No, I see that, but how long did you ...' Magnus paused as he tried to remember the Icelandic word for 'envision' '... see me being here?'

'I specified a minimum of two years. Deputy Superintendent Williams assured me that would be acceptable.'

'He never mentioned that kind of timeframe to me,' said Magnus.

Snorri's blue eyes bored into Magnus's. 'Williams did, of course, mention the reason why you were so eager to leave Boston on a temporary basis. I admire your courage.' His eyes flicked towards the uniformed police driver in the front seat. 'No one here knows about it apart from me.'

Magnus was about to protest, but he let it drop. As yet, he had no idea how many months it would be until the trial of Lenahan and the others. He would go along with the Police Commissioner until he was called to testify, then he would return to Boston and stay there, no matter what plans the Commissioner had for him.

Snorri smiled. 'But, as luck would have it, we have something to get your teeth into right away. A body was discovered this morning, in a summer house by Lake Thingvellir. And I am told that one of the initial suspects is an American. I am taking you straight there now.'

Keflavík Airport was at the tip of the peninsula that stuck out to the west of Reykjavík into the Atlantic Ocean. They drove east, through a tangle of highways and grey suburbs to the south of the city, lined with small factories and warehouses and familiar fast-food joints: KFC, Taco Bell and Subway. Depressing.

To his left, Magnus could see the multicoloured metal roofs of little houses that marked the centre of Reykjavík, dominated by the rocket spire of the Hallgrímskirkja, Iceland's largest church, rising up from the top of a small hill. No sign of the clusters of skyscrapers that dominated the downtown areas of even small cities in America. Beyond the city was Faxaflói Bay, and beyond that the broad foot of Mount Esja, an imposing ridge of stone that reached up into the low cloud.

They passed though bleak suburbs of square squat blocks of flats to the east of the city. Mount Esja rose up ever larger ahead of them, before they turned away from the bay and climbed up Mosfell Heath. The houses disappeared and there was just heath land of yellow grass and green moss, bulky rounded hills and cloud – low, dark, swirling cloud.

After twenty minutes or so they descended and Magnus saw Lake Thingvellir ahead of him. Magnus had been there several times as a boy, visiting Thingvellir itself, a grass plain that ran along the floor of a rift valley at the northern edge of the lake. It was the spot where the American and European continental plates split Iceland in two. More importantly for Magnus and his father, it was the dramatic site of the Althing, Iceland's annual outdoor parliament during the age of the sagas.

Magnus remembered the lake as a beautiful deep blue. Now it was dark and foreboding, the clouds reaching down from the sky almost low enough to touch the black water. Even the hump of a small island in the middle was smothered by the dense blanket of moisture.

They turned off the main road, past a large farm with horses grazing in its home meadow, down to the lake itself. They followed a stone track to a row of half a dozen summer houses, protected by a stand of scrappy birch trees, not yet in leaf. The only trees in sight. Magnus saw the familiar signs of a newly established crime scene: badly parked police cars, some with lights still flashing unnecessarily, an ambulance with its back doors open, yellow tape fluttering in the breeze and figures milling about in a mixture of dark police uniforms and white forensic overalls.

The focus of attention was the fifth house, at the end of the row. Magnus checked the other summer houses. It was still early in the season, so only one, the second, showed signs of habitation, a Range Rover parked outside.

The police car pulled up next to the ambulance and the

Commissioner and Magnus got out. The air was cold and damp. He could hear the rustle of the wind and a haunting bird call that he recognized from his childhood. A curlew?

A tall, balding man with a long face, wearing forensic overalls, approached them.

'Let me introduce Inspector Baldur Jakobsson of the Reykjavík Metropolitan Police CID,' the Commissioner said. 'He is in charge of the investigation. Lake Thingvellir is covered by the police at Selfoss to the south of here, but once they realized this could be a murder investigation they asked me to arrange for assistance from Reykjavík. Baldur, this is Sergeant Detective Magnús Jonson from the Boston Police Department...' He paused and looked at Magnus quizzically. 'Jonson?'

'Ragnarsson,' Magnus corrected him.

The Commissioner smiled, pleased that Magnus was reverting to his Icelandic name. 'Ragnarsson.'

'*Good afternoon,*' said Baldur stiffly, in halting English with a thick accent.

'*Gódan daginn,*' replied Magnus.

'Baldur, can you explain to Magnús what's happened here?'

'Certainly,' Baldur said, his thin lips showing no smile or other sign of enthusiasm. 'The victim was Agnar Haraldsson. He is a professor at the University of Iceland. This is his summer house. He was murdered last night, hit over the head in the house, we think, and then dragged down into the lake. He was found by two children from the house just back there at ten o'clock this morning.'

'The house with the Range Rover out front?' asked Magnus.

Baldur nodded. 'They fetched their father and he dialled 112.'

'When was he last seen alive?' Magnus asked.

'Yesterday was a holiday – the first day of summer.'

'It's Iceland's little joke,' said the Commissioner. 'The real summer is a few months off yet, but we need anything we can get to cheer ourselves up after the long winter.'

Baldur ignored the interruption. 'The neighbours saw Agnar arrive at about eleven o'clock in the morning. They saw him park his car outside his house and go in. They waved to him, he waved back, but they didn't speak. He did receive a visitor, or visitors, that evening.'

'Description?'

'None. They just saw the car, small, bright blue, something like a Toyota Yaris, although they are not precisely sure. The car arrived about seven-thirty, eight o'clock. Left at nine-thirty. They didn't see it, but the woman remembered what she was watching on TV when she heard it drive past.'

'Any other visitors?'

'None that the neighbours know of. But they were out all afternoon at Thingvellir, so there could have been.'

Baldur answered Magnus's questions simply and directly, his long face giving an air of serious intensity to his responses. The Commissioner was listening closely, but let Magnus do the talking.

'Have you found the murder weapon?'

'Not yet. We'll have to wait for a post-mortem. The pathologist might give us some clues.'

'Can I see the body?'

Baldur nodded and led Magnus and the Commissioner past the side of the house down a narrow earth pathway to a blue tent, erected on the edge of the lake, about ten metres from the house. Baldur called for overalls, boots and gloves. Magnus and the Commissioner put them on, signed a log held by the policeman guarding the scene and ducked into the tent.

Inside, a body was stretched out on the boggy grass. Two men in forensic overalls were preparing to lift it into a body bag. When they saw who had joined them they stopped what they were doing and squeezed out of the tent to give their senior officers room to examine the corpse.

'The paramedics from Selfoss who responded to the call dragged him out of the lake when they found him,' Baldur said. 'They thought he had drowned, but the doctor who examined the body was suspicious.'

'Why?'

'There was a blow on the back of his head. There are some rocks on the bottom of the lake and there was a chance that he might have struck one of them if he had fallen in, but the doctor thought the blow was too hard.'

'Can I take a look?'

Agnar was, or had been, a man of about forty, longish dark hair with flecks of grey at the temples, sharp features, stubble of the designer variety. Under the bristle, his face was pale and taut, his lips thin and a bluish-grey colour. The body was cold, which was no surprise after spending the night in the lake. It was also still stiff, suggesting he had been dead more than eight and less than twenty-four hours, which meant between four o'clock the previous afternoon and eight o'clock that morning. That was no help. Magnus doubted whether the pathologist would be able to come up with anything very precise about time of death. It was often difficult to be certain of a drowning, whether the victim had died before or after immersion in water. Sand or weed in the lungs was a clue, but that would have to wait for the autopsy.

Gently Magnus parted the professor's hair and examined the wound at the back of his skull.

He turned to Baldur. 'I think I know where your murder weapon is.'

'Where?' Baldur asked.

Magnus pointed out to the deep grey waters of the lake. Somewhere out there the rift between the continental plates at Thingvellir continued downwards to a depth of several hundred feet.

Baldur sighed. 'We need divers.'

'I wouldn't bother,' said Magnus. 'You'll never find it.'

Baldur frowned.

'He was hit by a rock,' Magnus explained. 'Something with jagged edges. There are still flecks of stone in the wound. I have no idea where the rock came from, possibly the dirt road back there, some of those stones are pretty big. Your lab could tell you. But my guess is the killer threw it into the lake afterwards. Unless he was very stupid – it's the perfect place to lose a rock.'

'Do you have forensic training?' Baldur asked, suspiciously.

'Not much,' said Magnus. 'I've just seen a few dead people with dents in their heads. Can I see inside the house?'

Baldur nodded. They walked back up the path to the summer house. The place was getting the full forensics treatment, powerful lamps, a vacuum cleaner, and at least five technicians crawling around with tweezers and fingerprint powder.

Magnus looked around. The door opened directly into a large living area, with big windows overlooking the lake. Walls and floor were soft wood, the furniture was modern but not expensive. Lots of bookshelves: novels in English and Icelandic, history books, some specialist literary criticism. An impressive collection of CDs: classical, jazz, Icelanders Magnus had never heard of. No television. A desk covered with papers occupied one corner of the room, and in the middle were chairs and a sofa around a low table, on which was a glass half filled with red wine, and a tumbler containing the dregs of what looked like Coke. Both were covered in a thin film of smudged fingerprint powder. Through one open door Magnus could see a kitchen. There were three other doors that led off the living room, presumably to bedrooms or a bathroom.

'We think he was struck over here,' said Baldur, pointing towards the desk. There were signs of fresh scrubbing on the wooden floor, and a few inches away, two chalk marks surrounded tiny specks.

'Can you do DNA analysis on this?'

'In case the blood came from the murderer?' Baldur asked.

Magnus nodded.

'We can. We send it to a lab in Norway. It takes a while for the results to come back.'

'Tell me about it,' said Magnus. In Boston the DNA lab was permanently backed up; everything was a rush job and so nothing was. Somehow Magnus suspected that the Norwegian lab might treat its neighbour's lone request with a bit more respect.

'So we think that Agnar was hit on the back of the head here as he was turning towards the desk. Then dragged out of the house and dumped in the lake.'

'Sounds plausible,' said Magnus.

'Except ...' Baldur hesitated. Magnus wondered if he was wary about expressing doubts in front of his boss.

'Except what?'

Baldur glanced at Magnus, hesitating. 'Come and look at this.' He led Magnus through to the kitchen. It was tidy, except for an open bottle of wine and the makings of a ham and cheese sandwich on the counter.

'We found some additional specks of blood here,' Baldur said, pointing to the counter. 'They look like high-velocity blood spatter, but that makes no sense. Perhaps Agnar hurt himself earlier. Perhaps he somehow staggered in here, but there are no other signs of a struggle in here at all. Perhaps the murderer came in here to clean himself up. Yet if that were the case, you would expect the spatters to be much bigger.'

Magnus glanced around the room. Three flies were battering the window in a never-ending attempt to get out.

'Don't worry about it,' he said. 'It's the flies.'

'Flies?'

'Sure. They land on the body, gorge themselves, then fly into the kitchen where it's warm. There they regurgitate the blood – it helps them to digest it. Maybe they wanted some of the sandwich for dessert.' Magnus bent down to examine the plate. 'Yes. There's some more there. You'll be able to see better with a magnifying glass, or Luminol if you have any. Of course it means that the body must have been lying around in here long enough for the flies to have their feast. But that's only fifteen, twenty minutes.'

Baldur still wasn't smiling, but the Commissioner was. 'Thank you,' was all the inspector could manage.

'Footprints?' asked Magnus, looking at the floor. Footprints should show up well on the polished wood.

'Yes,' said Baldur. 'One set, size forty-five. Which is odd.'

It was Magnus's turn to look puzzled. 'How so?'

'Icelanders usually take their shoes off when they enter a house. Except perhaps if they are a foreign visitor and don't know the customs. We spend as much time looking for fibres from socks as footprints.'

'Ah, of course,' said Magnus. 'Anything in the papers on the desk?'

'It's mostly academic stuff, essays from students, draft articles on Icelandic literature, that kind of thing. We need to go through it more thoroughly. There was a *fartölva* which the forensics team have taken away to analyse.'

'Sorry, what is a *fartölva*?' asked Magnus, who was unfamiliar with the Icelandic word. He knew the difference between a halberd and a battleaxe, but some of the newer Icelandic words threw him.

'A small computer you can carry around with you,' explained Baldur. 'And there is a diary with an entry; it tells us who was here last night.'

'The Commissioner mentioned an American,' Magnus said. 'With size forty-five feet, no doubt?' He had no idea what that was in US shoe sizes, but he suspected it was quite large.

'American. Or British. The name is Steve Jubb and the time is seven-thirty yesterday evening. And a phone number. The number is for the Hótel Borg, the best hotel in Reykjavík. We're picking him up now. In fact, if you'll excuse me, Snorri, I have to go back to headquarters and interview him.'

Magnus was struck by the informality of Icelanders. No 'Sir', or 'Commissioner Gudmundsson'. In Iceland everyone called everyone else by their first names, be it a street sweeper speaking to the president of the country, or a police officer speaking to his chief. It would take a little getting used to, but he liked it.

'Be sure to include Magnús in the interviews,' the Commissioner said.

Baldur's face remained impassive, but Magnus could tell that he was seething inside. And Magnus couldn't blame him. This was probably one of Baldur's biggest cases of the year, and he would not appreciate doing it under the eyes of a foreigner. Magnus might have more experience of homicides than Baldur, but he was at least ten years younger and a rank junior. The combination must have been especially irritating.

'Certainly,' he said. 'I'll get Árni to look after you. He'll drive you back to Headquarters and get you settled in. And by all means come and chat to me about Steve Jubb later on.'

'Thank you, Inspector,' Magnus said, before he could stop himself.

Baldur's eyes flicked towards Magnus, acknowledging the evidence of this faux pas that Magnus wasn't a real Icelander after all. He called over a detective to escort Magnus, and then left with the Commissioner back to Reykjavík.

'Hi, how are you doing?' said the detective in fluent American-accented English. 'My name's Árni. Árni Holm. You know, like the Terminator.'

He was tall, painfully thin, with short dark hair and an Adam's apple that bobbed furiously as he spoke. He had a wide friendly grin.

'Komdu saell,' said Magnus. 'I appreciate you speaking my language, but I really need to practise my Icelandic.'

'All right,' said Árni, in Icelandic. He looked disappointed not to be showing off his English skills.

'Although I have no idea what "the Terminator" is in Icelandic.'

'Tortímandinn,' said Árni. 'Some people call me that.' Magnus couldn't resist a smile. Árni was on the weedy side of wiry. 'OK, not many, I admit,' said Árni.

'Your English is very good.'

'I studied Criminology in the States,' Árni replied proudly.

'Oh. Where?'

'Kunzelberg College, Indiana. It's a small school, but it has a very good reputation. You might not have heard of it.'

'Uh, I can't say I have,' said Magnus. 'So where to next? I'd like to join Baldur for the interview of this Steve Jubb.'

CHAPTER FOUR

THE FIRST THING Magnus noticed was that Steve Jubb wasn't American. He had some kind of British accent, from Yorkshire, it transpired; Jubb was a truck driver from a town called Wetherby in that county. He was unmarried, living alone. His passport confirmed he was fifty-one.

Magnus and Árni were watching the interview on a computer screen down the hall. All the interview rooms in Reykjavík police headquarters were installed with tape recorders and closed-circuit television.

There were four men in the interview room: Baldur, another detective, a young Icelandic interpreter and a big, broad-shouldered man with a beer belly. He was wearing a denim shirt open over a white T-shirt, black jeans and a baseball cap, under which peeked thin greying hair. A neat little grey beard on his chin. Magnus could just make out the green and red swirls of a tattoo on his forearm. Steve Jubb.

Baldur was a good interviewer, relaxed and confident and more approachable than he had been with Magnus earlier. He even smiled occasionally, an upward twitch of the corners of his lips. He was using the traditional cop's technique, taking Jubb backwards and forwards through his story. Trying to get him to slip up on the details. But it meant Magnus was able to catch up on what Jubb had done that evening.

The interview was slow and stilted; everything had to be translated back and forth by the interpreter. Árni explained that this wasn't just because Baldur didn't speak good English – it was a requirement if anything said in the interview was to be admitted in court.

Jubb had plenty to explain, but he explained it well, at least at first.

His story was that he had met Agnar on a holiday to Iceland the previous year and had arranged to look him up on this trip. He had hired a car, the blue Toyota Yaris, and driven out to Lake Thingvellir. Agnar and he had chatted for a little over an hour and then Jubb had driven straight back to the hotel. The receptionist remembered his return. Since her shift ended at eleven, his timing was corroborated. Jubb hadn't seen anything or anyone suspicious. Agnar had been friendly and talkative. They had discussed places in Iceland that Jubb should visit.

Jubb confirmed that he had drunk Coca-Cola and his host red wine. He had kept his shoes on in the summer house: his shoe size was ten and a half under the UK measurement system. Jubb wasn't sure what that was in Continental sizes.

After half an hour of this Baldur left the room and found Magnus. 'What do you think?' he asked.

'His story holds up,' Magnus replied.

'But he's hiding something.' It was a statement, not a question.

'I think so too, but it's tough to tell from in here, I can't really see him. Can I speak to him face-to-face? Without the interpreter? I know anything he tells me won't be admissible, but I might loosen him up. And if he lets something slip, you can zero in on it later.'

Baldur thought for a moment and then nodded.

Magnus wandered into the interview room and took the chair next to Jubb, the one that had been occupied by the interpreter. He leaned back.

'Hey, Steve, how's it going?' Magnus said. 'You holding up OK?'

Jubb frowned. 'Who are you?'

'Magnus Jonson,' Magnus said. It seemed natural to slip back into his American name when he was speaking English.

'You're a bloody Yank.' Jubb's Yorkshire accent was strong and direct.

'Sure am. I'm helping these guys out for a spell.'

Jubb grunted.

'So, tell me about Agnar.'

Jubb sighed at having to repeat his story yet again. 'We met a year ago in a bar in Reykjavík. I liked the bloke, so I looked him up when I came back to Iceland.'

'What did you talk about?'

'This and that. Places to visit in Iceland. He knows the country pretty well.'

'No, I mean what did you talk about that made you want to see him again? He was a university professor, you're a truck driver.' Magnus remembered Jubb's unmarried status. 'Are you gay?' Unlikely, but it might provoke a reaction.

'Course I'm not bloody gay.'

'Then what did you talk about?'

Jubb hesitated, then answered. 'Sagas. He was an expert, I'd always been interested in them. It was one of the reasons I came to Iceland.'

'Sagas!' Magnus snorted. 'Give me a break.'

Jubb shrugged his broad shoulders and folded his arms over his belly. 'You asked.'

Magnus paused, assessing him. 'OK, I'm sorry. Which one is your favourite?'

'The *Saga of the Volsungs*.'

Magnus raised his eyebrows. 'Unusual choice.' The most popular sagas were about the Viking settlers in Iceland during the tenth century, but the *Saga of the Volsungs* was set in a much earlier period. Although written in Iceland in the thirteenth century, it was a myth about an early Germanic family of kings, the Volsungs, who eventually became the Burgundians: Attila the Hun had a role in the story. It wasn't one of Magnus's favourites, but he had read it a few times.

'OK. So what was the name of the dwarf who was forced to give his gold to Odin and Loki?' he asked.

Jubb smiled. 'Andvari.'

'And Sigurd's sword?'

'Gram. And his horse was called Grani.'

Jubb knew his stuff. He might be a truck driver, but he was a well-read man. Not to be underestimated. 'I like the sagas,' Magnus said with a smile. 'My dad used to read them to me. But he was Icelandic. How did you get into them?'

'My grandfather,' Jubb said. 'He studied them at university. He used to tell me the stories when I was a lad. I was hooked. Then I found some of them on tape and I used to play them in the wagon. Still do.'

'In English?'

'Obviously.'

'They are better in Icelandic.'

'That's what Agnar said. And I believe him. But it's too late for me to learn another language now.' Jubb paused. 'I'm sorry he's dead. He was an interesting bloke.'

'Did you kill him?' It was a question Magnus had asked all sorts of people during his career. He didn't expect an honest answer, but often the reaction the question provoked was useful.

'No,' said Jubb. 'Of course I bloody didn't!'

Magnus studied Steve Jubb. The denial was convincing, and yet … The lorry driver was hiding something.

At that moment the door opened and Baldur burst in, followed by the interpreter. Magnus couldn't conceal his irritation; he thought he was beginning to get somewhere.

Baldur was clutching some sheets of paper. He sat at the desk and laid them in front of him. He leaned over and turned a switch on a small console by the computer. 'Interview recommences at eighteen twenty-two,' he said. And then, in English, staring at Jubb: 'Who is Isildur?'

Jubb tensed. Both Baldur and Magnus noticed it. Then he forced himself to relax. 'I've no idea. Who is Isildur?'

Magnus asked himself the same question, although he thought the name sounded familiar from somewhere.

'Take a look at these,' Baldur said, returning to Icelandic. He pushed three sheets of paper towards Jubb and handed another three to Magnus. 'These are printouts of e-mails taken from Agnar's computer. E-mail correspondence with you.'

Jubb picked up the sheets of paper and read them, as did Magnus. Two were simple messages confirming the visit Steve had suggested on the phone and arranging a date, time and place to meet. The tone was more businesslike than an informal arrangement to meet up for a chat with an acquaintance.

The third e-mail was the most interesting.

From: Agnar Haraldsson
To: Steve Jubb
Subject: Meeting 23 April

Dear Steve

I'm looking forward to seeing you on Thursday. I have made a discovery that I think you will find very exciting.

It is a shame that Isildur can't be there as well. I have a proposal for him that it would be good to discuss in person. Is it too late to persuade him to come?

Kind Regards,

Agnar

'So – who is Isildur?' Baldur asked once again, this time in Icelandic. The interpreter translated.

Jubb sighed heavily, tossed the papers on to the desk and crossed his arms. He said nothing.

'What was the proposal Agnar wanted to discuss with you? Did he discuss it with you?'

Nothing.

'Did he tell you what the discovery was?'

'I'm not answering any more questions,' said Jubb. 'I want to go back to my hotel.'

'You can't,' said Baldur. 'You're staying here. You are under arrest.'

Jubb frowned. 'In that case, I want to speak to someone from the British Embassy.'

'You are a suspect in a murder inquiry. We can inform the British Embassy that we are holding you, but you don't have the right to see them. We can get you a lawyer if you wish.'

'I do wish. And until I've seen him, I'm not saying anything.' And Steve Jubb sat in his chair, a big man, arms folded tightly across his chest, lower jaw jutting out, immovable.

CHAPTER FIVE

BALDUR RAN A brisk morning meeting, brisk and efficient. Half a dozen detectives were present, plus Magnus, the assistant prosecutor – a young red-haired woman called Rannveig – and Chief Superintendent Thorkell Holm, the head of the Reykjavík Metropolitan Police CID. Thorkell was in his early sixties, with a round jovial face and shiny pink cheeks. He seemed at ease with his detectives, happy to blend into the background and listen to Baldur, who was in charge of the investigation.

There was an air of expectancy around the table, enthusiasm for the task ahead. It was a Saturday morning. A long weekend of work to come for everyone, but they seemed eager to start.

Magnus felt himself caught up in the excitement. Árni had driven him back to his hotel the night before. He had grabbed something to eat and gone to bed – it had been a long day, and he was still exhausted from the shooting in Boston and its aftermath. But he slept well for once. It was good to be out of reach of Soto's gang. He was eager to get a message to Colby, but he would have to arrange access to a computer for that. In the meantime the investigation into the professor's murder intrigued him.

And he intrigued the detectives around him. They stared at him when he entered the room: none of the smiles you would expect from a group of Americans welcoming a stranger. Magnus didn't know whether this was the typical initial reserve of Icelanders, a reserve that was usually replaced by warmth within ten minutes, or if it was something more hostile. He decided to ignore it. But he was glad of the uninhibited friendly smile of Árni sitting next to him.

'Our suspect is still saying nothing,' Baldur said. 'We've heard from the British police: his criminal record is clean apart from two convictions for possession of cannabis in the 1970s. Rannveig will take him before the judge this morning to get an order to keep him in custody for the next few weeks.'

'Do we have enough evidence for that?' Magnus asked.

Baldur frowned at the interruption. 'Steve Jubb was the last person to see Agnar alive. He was at the scene of the crime at about the time the murder was committed. We know he was discussing some kind of deal with Agnar but he won't tell us what he was doing there. He's hiding something, and until he tells us otherwise, we're going to assume it's a murder. I'd say we have enough to hold him, and so will the judge.'

'Sounds good to me,' said Magnus. And it did. In the US what they had would not be nearly enough to hold a suspect, but Magnus could learn to like the Icelandic system.

Baldur nodded curtly. 'Now, what have we got?'

Two detectives had interviewed Agnar's wife, Linda, at their house in Seltjarnarnes, a suburb of Reykjavík. She was devastated. They had been married seven years and had two small children. It was Agnar's second marriage: he was divorced when they met – like his first wife, Linda had been one of his students. He had gone to the summer house to catch up on some work – apparently he had a deadline looming for a translation. He had spent the previous two weekends there. His wife, stuck alone with the children in Seltjarnarnes, had not been too happy with that.

Agnar's laptop had not revealed any more interesting e-mails to Steve Jubb. There was a jumble of Word files and Internet sites visited, all of which would be analysed. There were piles of working papers in his office at the University and at the summer house which would be read through.

Forensics had found four sets of fingerprints in the summer house: Agnar's, Steve Jubb's and two others as yet unidentified.

None from Agnar's wife, who had stated that she had not visited the summer house yet that year. There were no prints on the passenger door of Jubb's rented Toyota, confirming his claim that he had visited Agnar alone.

They had also found traces of cocaine use in the bedroom, and a one-gram bag of the drug hidden in a wardrobe.

'Vigdís. Any luck with the name Isildur?' Baldur asked.

He turned to a tall elegant black woman of about thirty, who was wearing a tight black sweater and jeans. Magnus had noticed her as soon as he had walked into the room. She was the first black person Magnus had seen since he had arrived in Iceland. Iceland didn't do ethnic minorities, especially blacks.

'It seems that Ísildur, with an "í", is a legitimate Icelandic name.' She pronounced the Icelandic letter with a long "ee" sound. 'Although it is very rare indeed. I have searched the National Registry database, and only come up with one entry for that name in the last eighty years, a child named Ísildur Ásgrímsson. Born 1974, died 1977 in Flúdir.' Flúdir was a village in the south-west of Iceland, Magnus dimly remembered. It was pronounced *Floothir*, the 'd' being the Icelandic letter 'đ'.

Vigdís had a perfect Icelandic accent, Magnus noticed. It sounded very odd to him, he had worked with plenty of black female detectives in Boston, and he was half expecting a laconic Boston drawl, not a lilting Icelandic trill. 'His father, Ásgrímur Högnason, was a doctor. He died in 1992.'

'But no sign of anyone alive today with that name?'

Vigdís shook her head. 'I suppose he might be a *vestur-íslenskur*.' She meant a Western Icelander, one of those Icelanders, predecessors of Magnus himself, who had crossed over the Atlantic to North America a century before. 'Or he could live in England. If he was born overseas he won't be on our database.'

'Anyone heard of an Ísildur?' Baldur asked the room. 'It does sound Icelandic.' No one said anything, although Árni, who was sitting next to Magnus, seemed about to open his mouth and then thought better of it.

'All right,' said Baldur. 'This is what we know. It's clear that Steve Jubb went to the summer house for more than a chat with an acquaintance. He was doing some kind of deal with Agnar, something involving a man named Ísildur.'

He stared around the room. 'We need to find out what it is that Agnar had discovered, and what deal they were negotiating. We need to find out a lot more about Agnar. And most of all we need to find out who the hell this Ísildur is. Let's hope Steve Jubb will begin to talk once he realizes that he is going to spend the next few weeks in jail.'

When the meeting was over, Chief Superintendent Thorkell asked Magnus for a word. His office was big and comfortable, with a magnificent view of the bay and Mount Esja. The clouds were higher than the day before; far out into the bay a patch of sunlight reflected off the water. Three photographs of small fair-haired children were positioned on the chief superintendent's desk so that both Thorkell and his visitors could see them. A couple of primitive paintings, probably by the same kids, hung on the wall.

Thorkell sat down in his big leather desk chair and smiled. 'Welcome to Reykjavík,' he said.

At least he, like Árni, seemed friendly. Magnus couldn't see any physical similarity between them, but they shared the same last name, Holm, and so they were probably related. A small minority of Icelanders used the same family naming system as the rest of the world. They were often from wealthier families, descendants of young Icelanders who had travelled abroad to Denmark to study and given themselves family names while they were there.

But then all Icelanders were related. The society was more of a gene puddle than a gene pool.

'Thank you,' Magnus replied.

'You will be part of the National Police Commissioner's staff, but when you are not at the Police College you will have a desk here, with us. I very much support the Commissioner's initiative in requesting you, and I think you will be a great help to us in the current investigation.'

'I hope so.'

Thorkell hesitated. 'Inspector Baldur is an excellent detective, and very successful. He likes to use tried and tested techniques that work in Iceland. It boils down to the fact that in such a small country someone always knows someone who knows the criminal. But as the nature of crime changes in this country, so must the methods of fighting it, which is why you are here. Flexibility is perhaps not Baldur's strong point. But don't be afraid to voice your opinion. We want to hear it, you will have my assurance of that.'

Magnus smiled. 'I understand.'

'Good. Now, someone from the Commissioner's office will be in touch with you this morning about salary and accommodation and so on. In the meantime, Árni will set you up with a desk, a phone and a computer. Do you have any questions?'

'Yes, one. Can I carry a gun?'

'No,' said Thorkell. 'Absolutely not.'

'I'm not used to being on duty without one,' Magnus said.

'Then you will become used to it.'

They stared at each other for a moment. A cop needed a badge and a gun, as far as Magnus was concerned. He appreciated the difficulties with the badge. But he needed the gun.

'How do I get a licence to carry?'

'You don't. No one has guns in Iceland, or not hand guns. They have been banned since 1968, after a man was shot dead.'

'You're telling me there are no police officers with firearms training?'

Thorkell sighed. 'We do have some firearms officers in the Viking Squad – it's what we call our SWAT team. You may be able to practise on the indoor range at Kópavogur, but we cannot permit you to carry a weapon outside it. That's just not the way we do things here.'

Magnus was tempted to say something about flexibility and voicing his opinion, but he appreciated the chief superintendent's support and didn't want to antagonize him needlessly, so he just thanked him again and left.

Árni was waiting outside. He led Magnus to an office stuffed with small screened-in cubicles, with the sign *Violent Crimes* on the door. Two or three of the detectives that Magnus had seen at the meeting were on the phones or their computers, the others were already out interviewing people. Magnus's desk was right opposite Árni's. The phone worked, and Árni assured him that someone from the IT department would set him up with a password that morning.

Árni disappeared to the coffee machine and returned with two cups. The boy had promise.

Magnus sipped his coffee and considered Agnar. He didn't yet know much about the professor, but he did know that he was someone's husband, the father of two children. Magnus thought of those kids growing up with the knowledge that their father had been murdered, of the devastated wife struggling to come to terms with the destruction of her family. They needed to know who had killed Agnar and why, and they needed to know that the murderer had been punished. Otherwise – well, otherwise they would end up like Magnus.

The familiar urge returned. Even though Magnus had not yet met them, might never even meet them, he could promise them one thing: he would find Agnar's killer.

'Have you decided where you are going to stay in Reykjavík?' Árni asked, sipping from his own cup.

'No, not really,' Magnus replied. 'The hotel's OK, I guess.'

'But you won't be able to stay there the whole time you're with us?'

Magnus shrugged. 'I don't know. I guess not. I've no idea how long that will be.'

'My sister has a spare room in her apartment. It's a nice place, very central, in Thingholt. You could rent that. She wouldn't charge much.'

Magnus hadn't begun to think about money, accommodation, clothes, living expenses; he was just pleased to be alive. But operating out of a suitcase in a hotel room would soon get tiresome, and Árni's sister might provide a quick easy solution to a problem he hadn't even begun to address yet. And cheap. That might be important. 'Sure, I'll take a look at it.'

'Great. I'll show you around this evening, if you like.'

The coffee wasn't bad. Icelanders lived on many cups of coffee a day – the whole society was fuelled by caffeine. Perhaps that was one of the reasons why they never sat still for long.

'I'm sure I've heard this name Ísildur somewhere,' Magnus said. 'Maybe it was a kid at school. But that would have shown up on Vigdís's search.'

'Probably just the movie,' Árni said, sipping from his own cup.

'The movie? What movie?'

'*The Fellowship of the Ring*. Haven't you seen it? It's the first of *The Lord of the Rings* trilogy.'

'No, I haven't seen the movie, but I did read the book. So Ísildur's one of the characters, right? What is he, some kind of elf?'

'No, he's a man,' said Árni. 'He wins the ring at the beginning of the movie and then loses it in a river somewhere. Then Gollum finds it.'

'Árni! Why didn't you mention this at the meeting?'

'I was going to, but then I thought everyone would just laugh at me. They do that sometimes, you know. And it obviously doesn't have anything to do with the case.'

'Of course it does!' Magnus just stopped himself from adding the words 'you idiot!'. 'Have you read the *Saga of the Volsungs*?'

'I think I did at school,' said Árni. 'It's about Sigurd and Brynhild and Gunnar, isn't it? Dragons and treasure.'

'And the ring. There's a magic ring. It's an Icelandic take on the *Nibelungenlied* which Wagner based his *Ring Cycle* on. I bet Tolkien read it too. And it's Steve Jubb's favourite saga – it's probably the only saga he *has* read. He's a *Lord of the Rings* nut and he has a friend who is another *Lord of the Rings* nut whose nickname is Isildur.'

'So Isildur isn't Icelandic at all?'

Magnus shook his head. 'No, he's probably another truck driver from Yorkshire. We need to talk to Baldur.'

A look of panic flashed across Árni's face. 'Do you really think this is important?'

'I do,' Magnus nodded. 'It's a lead. In a murder investigation you take every lead you get.'

'Um … Perhaps you should see Baldur by yourself.'

'Oh, come on Árni. I won't tell him you knew all along who Isildur was. Let's go.'

They had to wait an hour for Baldur to return from the courthouse on the Laekjargata, but he looked happy. 'We can detain Steve Jubb for three weeks,' he said when he saw Magnus. 'And I have a search warrant for his hotel room.'

'Didn't he make bail?' Magnus asked.

'There's no chance of bail in Iceland for a murder suspect. We usually get three weeks to pursue our investigation before we have to hand over evidence to the defence. Once we have finished with him here, Jubb will be taken to the prison at Litla Hraun. That will make him think.'

'I like it,' Magnus said.

'Strange thing is, he has a new lawyer. We gave him a kid a couple of years out of law school, but he's already fired him and hired Kristján Gylfason, who is about the most experienced criminal lawyer in Iceland. Someone must be helping him; finding the lawyer and paying for him. Kristján doesn't come cheap. And for that matter, neither does the Hótel Borg.'

'Isildur?' Magnus asked.

Baldur shrugged. 'Maybe. Whoever he is.'

'We think we have an idea about that.'

Baldur listened to Magnus's theory, a frown crossing the dome of his forehead. 'I think we need to have another word with Mr Jubb.'

CHAPTER SIX

STEVE JUBB'S NEW lawyer, Kristján Gylfason, was smooth: intelligent face, prematurely silver hair, an air of calm competence and wealth. His very presence seemed to give Jubb comfort. Not good.

There were now five men in the interview room: Jubb, his lawyer, Baldur, Magnus and the interpreter.

Baldur flung an English copy of *The Lord of the Rings* onto the desk. There was silence in the room. Jubb's eyes flicked down to it. Árni had rushed out and bought it from the Eymundsson bookshop in the middle of town.

Baldur tapped the book. 'Ever read this before?'

Jubb nodded.

Baldur slowly and deliberately opened the book at chapter two and passed it over to Steve Jubb. 'Now, read that and tell me you don't know who Isildur is.'

'It's a character in a book,' Jubb said. 'That's all.'

'How many times have you read this book?' Baldur asked.

'Once or twice.'

'Once or twice?' Baldur snorted. 'Isildur is a nickname, isn't it? He's a friend of yours. A fellow *Lord of the Rings* fan.'

Steve Jubb shrugged.

Magnus glanced at the lower extremity of a tattoo peeking out beneath Jubb's sleeve. 'Take off your shirt.'

Steve Jubb shrugged and removed the denim shirt he had been wearing since his arrest. He revealed a plain white T-shirt, and on his forearm a tattoo of a helmeted man with a beard wielding an axe.

46

A man? Or perhaps a dwarf.

'Let me guess,' said Magnus. 'Your nickname is Gimli.' He remembered that Gimli was the name of the dwarf in *Lord of the Rings*.

Jubb shrugged again.

'Is Isildur a buddy from Yorkshire?' Magnus asked. 'You meet in a pub every Friday, have a few beers and talk about old Icelandic sagas?'

No answer.

'You get cop shows in England?' Magnus asked. '*CSI*, *Law and Order*?'

Jubb frowned.

'Well, in those shows the bad guy gets to remain silent while the good guys ask all the questions. But it doesn't work that way in Iceland.' Magnus leaned forward. 'In Iceland if you keep quiet we think you've got something to hide. Isn't that right, Kristján?'

'My client's decision not to answer your questions is his own,' the lawyer said. 'I have explained the consequences.'

'We *will* find out what you are hiding,' Baldur said. 'And your failure to cooperate will be remembered when it comes to trial.'

The lawyer was about to say something, but Jubb put a hand on his arm. 'Look, if you two are so bloody clever, you'll eventually figure out that I had bugger all to do with Agnar's death, and then you'll have to let me go. Until then, I'm saying nowt.'

The arms folded, the jaw jutted out. Steve Jubb didn't utter another word.

Vigdís was waiting for them outside the interview room.

'There's someone from the British Embassy to see you.'

Baldur swore. 'Damn it. He's only going to waste my time. But I must speak to him, I suppose. Is there anything else?' Baldur could tell from the look of suppressed excitement on Vigdís's face that there was.

'Agnar had a lover,' Vigdís said, with a small smile of triumph.

Baldur raised his eyebrows. 'Did he indeed?'

'Andrea Fridriksdóttir. She is one of Agnar's Icelandic literature students at the university. She came forward as soon as she heard he had been killed.'

'Where is she?'

'Downstairs.'

'Excellent. Let's go and talk to her. Tell the man from the British Embassy I will be with him as soon as I can. But I want to speak to this Andrea first.'

Realizing that he was not invited, Magnus returned to his desk, where a woman from the National Police Commissioner's office was waiting for him. Cell phone, bank account, daily allowance, payment of salary, cash advance, even the promise of a car in a few days, she had it all prepared. Magnus was impressed. He was quite sure that the Boston Police Department could never match her for efficiency.

She was followed by a man from the IT Department. He gave Magnus his password, and spent a few minutes showing him how to use the computer system, including how to access e-mail.

Once the man had gone, Magnus stared at the screen in front of him. The time had come. Magnus could put it off no longer.

It had turned out that the FBI agents who had escorted Magnus in his last days in Massachusetts were out of the Cleveland Field Office. One, Agent Hendricks, had been designated his contact man. Magnus had agreed never to use the phone to the United States, even to Deputy Superintendent Williams. Especially to Deputy Superintendent Williams. The fear, that was never articulated but which was in the minds of Magnus, the FBI and Williams himself, was that the three police officers who had been arrested were not alone. That they had accomplices, or perhaps just friends in the Boston PD, friends for whom tracing Magnus's whereabouts would all be in a day's work.

So the idea was that the only form of communication would be e-mails. Even those Magnus could not send directly, but via Agent Hendricks in Cleveland. That was the method that Magnus would have to use if he wanted to contact Colby.

And he needed to contact Colby. It had become clear to him that he couldn't take the risk that she would be attacked or killed on his account. She had outmanoeuvred him, and he had to accept that.

He stared at the screen for several minutes more, trying out arguments, justifications, explanations, but he knew Colby, and he was aware of the danger of giving her the opportunity to complicate things. So in the end he kept it simple.

The answer to your question is yes. Now please come with me. I am very worried about you.

With all my love

Magnus.

Not very romantic – hardly the right way to start a life together. Although he was attracted to Colby, loved her even, the more he got to know her the more sure he was that they shouldn't get married. It wasn't just his fear of commitment, although Colby was absolutely right that he did suffer from that. He just knew that if there was a woman out there somewhere that he could spend the rest of his life with, it wasn't Colby. Her latest high-stakes ploy was an example of why.

But he had no choice. She had given him no choice.

He composed a brief report to Williams, telling him he was safe and in e-mail contact should Williams learn anything about the trial date.

He thought of writing to Ollie, as his brother now called himself, but decided against it. The FBI had informed Ollie that Magnus was disappearing, and an agent had taken his stuff from the guestroom in Ollie's house. That would have to be enough – the less Magnus had to do with Ollie the better. He realized that it wasn't just Colby who was at risk from the Soto gang, his brother might be too.

Magnus closed his eyes. Nothing he could do about that now except hope that the gangsters would ignore them all.

Oh, God. Maybe Colby was right. Maybe he should just have pretended that he hadn't heard Lenahan's conversation.

Of course, in his beloved sagas, the heroes always did their duty. But then most of their relatives came to a bloody end before the story was finished. It was easy to be brave with your own skin, much harder with other people's. He felt more like a coward than a hero, safe in Iceland when his brother and his girlfriend were in danger.

But then the ancient Icelandic reaction kicked in. If they touched a hair of Colby's or Ollie's head, he would make the bastards pay. All of them.

Baldur held another conference at two o'clock that afternoon. The team were still fresh and enthusiastic.

He began with the initial findings from the autopsy. It looked likely that Agnar had drowned; there was some mud found in his lungs, which suggested that he was still breathing when he hit the water. As Magnus had suspected, the fragments of stone in the victim's head wound were from the dirt road rather than the lake floor.

There were small traces of cocaine in the victim's blood, and some alcohol, but not nearly enough to cause intoxication. The pathologist's conclusion was that the victim was struck on the back of the head with a stone, fell unconscious and was dragged into the lake where he drowned. No surprises there.

Baldur and Vigdís had interviewed Andrea. She had admitted that her affair with Agnar had been going on for about a month. She was besotted with him, she had spent most of the previous year trying to seduce him, and had finally succeeded after a drunken student party to which he had been invited. She had spent one weekend with him at the summer house. Her finger-prints were indeed one of the two sets that remained unidentified.

Andrea said that Agnar had seemed terrified that his wife would discover what had happened. He had promised her after she had caught him with a student four years before that he would remain faithful, and until Andrea he had kept his word. Andrea's impression was that Agnar was scared of Linda.

Magnus outlined the theory that Isildur was a nickname for a *Lord of the Rings* fan, and that Steve Jubb was one himself. One or two of the faces around the table looked a little uncomfortable. Maybe Árni wasn't the only one to have seen the *Lord of the Rings* movie.

Baldur handed round the list of entries from Agnar's appointments diary. Dates, times, and the names of people he had met, mostly fellow academics or students. He had been away on a two-day seminar at the University of Uppsala in Sweden three weeks before. And one afternoon the previous week was blocked out with the word 'Hruni'.

'Hruni is near Flúdir, isn't it?' Baldur said.

'Just a couple of kilometres away,' Rannveig, the assistant prosecutor, said. 'I've been there. There's nothing but the church and a farm.'

'Perhaps the entry refers to the dance rather than the place,' Baldur said. 'Something collapsing that afternoon? A disaster?'

Magnus had heard of Hruni. Back in the seventeenth century the pastor of Hruni was notorious for the wild parties he held in his church at Christmas. One Christmas Eve the devil was seen hanging around outside, and the following morning the whole church and its congregation had been swallowed up by the earth. Since then the phrase 'Hruni dance' had slipped into the language to mean something that was falling apart.

'The little boy who died young came from Flúdir,' said Vigdís. 'Ísildur Ásgrímsson. And here's his sister.' She pointed to a name on the list of appointments. 'Ingileif Ásgrímsdóttir, sixth of April, two-thirty. At least, I'm pretty sure that she was the boy's sister. I can check.'

'Do that,' said Baldur. 'And if you are right, track her down and interview her. We're assuming that Isildur is a foreigner but we need to keep an open mind.'

He picked up a sheet of paper on the conference table in front of him. 'We have searched Steve Jubb's hotel room and the forensics people are examining his clothes. We found a couple of interesting text messages that had been sent on his mobile phone. Or we think they might be interesting, we just don't know. Take a look at the transcriptions.'

He passed around the sheet, on which two short sentences had been typed. They were in a language that Magnus didn't recognize, didn't even begin to recognize. 'Does anyone know what this is?' Baldur asked.

There were frowns and slowly shaking heads around the table. Someone tentatively suggested Finnish, someone else was sure it wasn't. But Magnus noticed that Árni was shifting uncomfortably again.

'Árni?' Magnus said.

Árni glared at Magnus, and then swallowed, his Adam's apple bobbing. 'Elvish,' he said, very quietly.

'What?' Baldur demanded. 'Speak up!'

'They might be in Elvish. I think Tolkien created some Elvish languages. This might be one of them.'

Baldur put his head in his hands and then glared at his subordinate. 'You're not going to tell me the *huldufólk* did this, are you now Árni?'

Árni shrank. The *huldufólk*, or hidden people, were elf-like creatures who were supposed to live all over Iceland in rocks and stones. In everyday conversation Icelanders were proud of their belief in these beings, and, famously, highways had been diverted to avoid removing rocks in which they were known to live. Baldur did not want his murder investigation to be derailed by the most troublesome of all Iceland's many superstitions.

'Árni could be right,' said Magnus. 'We know Steve Jubb and Isildur, whoever he is, were doing a deal with Agnar. If they needed to communicate with each other about it they could have used a code. They are both *Lord of the Rings* fans: what better than Elvish?'

Baldur pursed his lips. 'All right, Árni. See if you can find someone in Iceland who speaks Elvish, and ask them if they recognize what this says. And then get them to translate it.'

Baldur glanced around the table. 'If Steve Jubb won't tell us, we need to find out who this Isildur is ourselves. We need to get in touch with the British police in Yorkshire to see if they can help us with Jubb's friends. And we need to check all the bars and restaurants in Reykjavík to find out if Jubb met anyone else apart from Agnar. Perhaps Isildur is here in town; we won't know until we ask around. And I am going to interview Agnar's wife.' He doled out specific tasks for everyone around the table, except Magnus, and the meeting was over.

Magnus followed the inspector into the corridor. 'Do you mind if I join Vigdís to interview the sister of the kid who died?'

'No, go ahead,' said Baldur.

'What do you think so far?' Magnus asked.

'What do you mean, what do I think?' Baldur said, stopping.

'Oh, come on. You have to have a hunch.'

'I keep an open mind. I gather evidence until it points to one conclusion. Isn't that what you do in America?'

'Right,' Magnus said.

'Now, if you want to help, find me Isildur.'

CHAPTER SEVEN

INGILEIF ÁSGRÍMSDÓTTIR OWNED an art gallery on Skólavördustígur, which was a bit of a mouthful, even for an Icelander. New York had Fifth Avenue, London had Bond Street and Reykjavík had Skólavördustígur. The street led up from Laugavegur, the busiest shopping street in town, to the Hallgrímskirkja at the top of a hill. Small stores lined the road, part concrete, part brightly painted corrugated metal, selling art supplies, jewellery, designer clothes and fancy foods. But the credit crunch had made its mark: some premises were discreetly empty, displaying small signs showing the words *Til Leigu*, meaning *For Rent*.

Vigdís parked her car a few metres below the gallery. Above her and Magnus the massive concrete spire of the church thrust upwards. Designed in the nineteen thirties, it was supported by two great wings that swept up from the ground; it looked like Iceland's very own intercontinental ballistic missile, or possibly a moon rocket.

As Magnus climbed out of the car, he was almost knocked over by a blonde girl of about twenty dressed in a lime green sweater with a short leopard-skin skirt and a two foot tail hurtling down the hill on a bicycle. Where were the traffic cops when you needed them?

Vigdís pushed open the door to the gallery and Magnus followed her in. A woman, presumably Ingileif Ásgrímsdóttir, was speaking to a tourist couple in English. Vigdís was about to interrupt them, when Magnus touched her arm. 'Let's wait until she's finished.'

So Magnus and Vigdís examined the objects on sale in the gallery, as well as Ingileif herself. She was slim with blonde hair that came down in a fringe over her eyes and was tied back in a ponytail. A quick broad smile beneath high cheekbones, a smile which she was using to maximum effect on her customers. An English couple, they had begun by picking up a small candle holder made of rough red lava, but had ended up buying a large glass vase and an abstract painting that hinted of Reykjavík, Mount Esja and horizontal layers of pale grey cloud. They spent tens of thousands of krónur.

After they had left the store, the owner turned to Magnus and Vigdís. 'Sorry to keep you waiting,' she said in English. 'Can I help you?'

Her Icelandic accent was delicious, as was her smile. Magnus hadn't appreciated that he looked so obviously American; then he realized it was Vigdís who had prompted the choice of language. In Reykjavík, black meant foreigner.

Vigdís herself was all business. 'Are you Ingileif Ásgrímsdóttir?' she asked in Icelandic.

The woman nodded.

Vigdís pulled out her badge. 'My name is Detective Vigdís Audarsdóttir of the Metropolitan Police, and this is my colleague, Magnús Ragnarsson. We have some questions for you relating to the murder of Agnar Haraldsson.'

The smile disappeared. 'You'd better sit down.' The woman led them to a cramped desk at the back of the gallery and they sat on two small chairs. 'I saw something about Agnar on the news. He taught me Icelandic literature when I was at the university.'

'You saw him recently,' Vigdís said, checking her notebook. 'On the sixth of April, at two-thirty?'

'Yes, that's right,' said Ingileif, her voice suddenly hoarse. She cleared her throat. 'Yes, I bumped into him in the street, and he asked me to drop in on him some time at the university. So I did.'

'What did you discuss?'

'Oh, nothing, really. My design career, mostly. This gallery. He was very attentive, very charming.'

'Did he say anything about himself?'

'Not much had changed really. He had married again. He said he had two children.' She smiled briefly. 'Difficult to imagine Agnar with kids, but there you are.'

'You come from Flúdir, don't you?'

'That's right,' said Ingileif. 'I was born and brought up there. Best farmland in the country, biggest courgettes, reddest tomatoes. Can't think why I ever left.'

'Sounds like quite a place. It's near Hruni, isn't it?'

'Yes. Hruni is the parish church. It's three kilometres away.'

'Did you meet Agnar at Hruni on the afternoon of the twentieth of April?'

Ingileif frowned. 'No, I didn't. I was in this shop all day.'

'It only takes a couple of hours to drive there.'

'Yes, but I didn't go there to meet Agnar.'

'He met someone in Hruni that day. Doesn't it strike you that it's a bit of a coincidence that he should go to Flúdir, the village where you grew up?'

Ingileif shrugged. 'Not really. I have no idea what he was doing there.' She forced a smile. 'This is a small country. Coincidences happen all the time.'

Vigdís looked at her doubtfully. 'Is there anyone who could confirm that you were in the shop that afternoon?'

Ingileif thought a moment. 'That was Monday, wasn't it? Dísa in the boutique next door. She dropped in to borrow some tea bags. I am pretty sure that was Monday.'

Vigdís glanced at Magnus. He realized that she was holding off on pushing Ingileif directly on her relationship with Agnar, and so he decided on a different tack. They could always come back to Agnar later. 'You had a brother, named Ísildur, who died young?'

'Yes,' said Ingileif. 'It was several years before I was born. Meningitis, I think. I never knew him. My parents didn't speak about him much. He was their first child, it hit them badly, as you can imagine.'

'Isn't Ísildur an unusual name?'

'I suppose it is. I hadn't really thought about it.'

'Do you know why your parents gave him that name?'

Ingileif shook her head. 'No idea.' She seemed nervous and was frowning slightly. Magnus noticed a V-shaped nick above one of her eyebrows, partly hidden by her fringe. Her fingers were fiddling with an intricate silver earring, no doubt designed by one of her colleagues. 'Except that Ísildur was my great-grandfather's name, I think. On my father's side. Maybe my dad wanted to honour his own grandfather. You know how names recur in families.'

'We'd like to ask your parents,' Magnus asked. 'Can you give us their address?'

Ingileif sighed. 'I'm afraid they are both dead. My father died in 1992, and my mother last year.'

'I'm sorry,' Magnus said, and he meant it. Ingileif appeared to be in her late twenties, which would mean she had lost her father at about the same age Magnus was when he lost his mother.

'Were either of them fans of the *Lord of the Rings*?'

'I don't think so,' said Ingileif. 'I mean, we had a copy in the house so one of them must have read it, but they never mentioned it.'

'And you? Have you read it?'

'When I was a kid.'

'Seen the movies?'

'I saw the first one. Not the other two. I didn't really like it. When you've seen one orc you've seen them all.'

Magnus paused, waiting for more. Ingileif's pale cheeks blushed red.

'Have you ever heard of an Englishman named Steve Jubb?'

Ingileif shook her head firmly. 'No.'

Magnus glanced at Vigdís. Time to get back to Ingileif and Agnar. 'Ingileif, were you having an affair with Agnar?' she asked.

'No,' Ingileif replied angrily. 'No, absolutely not.'

'But you found him charming?'

'Yes, I suppose so. He always was charming, and that hasn't changed.'

'Have you ever had an affair with him?' Magnus asked.

'No,' said Ingileif, her voice hoarse again. Her fingers drifted up towards her earring.

'Ingileif, this is a murder investigation,' Vigdís said slowly and firmly. 'If you lie to us now then we can arrest you. It will be a serious matter, I can assure you. Now, once more, did you ever have an affair with Agnar?'

Ingileif bit her lip, her cheeks reddening again. She took a deep breath. 'OK. All right. I did have an affair with Agnar when I was his student. He was divorced from his first wife then, it was before he remarried. And it was hardly an affair, we slept together a few times, that was all.'

'Did he finish it, or did you?'

'I suppose it was me. He did have a real magnetism for women then, in fact he still had it when I last saw him. He had this way of making you feel special, intellectually interesting as well as beautiful. But he was sleazy, basically. He wanted to sleep with as many girls as he could just to prove to himself what a good-looking guy he was. He was deeply vain. When I saw him the other day he tried to flirt with me again, but I saw through it this time. I don't mess around with married men.'

'One last question,' said Vigdís. 'Where were you on Friday evening?'

Ingileif's shoulders lowered marginally as she relaxed, as if this was one difficult question she could answer. 'I went to a party for a friend who was launching an exhibition of her paintings. I was there from about eight until, maybe, eleven-thirty. There were dozens people there who know me. Her name is Frída Jósefsdóttir. I can give you her address and phone number if you want.'

'Please,' said Vigdís, passing her her notebook. Ingileif scribbled something on a blank page and handed it back.

'And afterwards?' asked Vigdís.

'Afterwards?'

'After you left the gallery.'

Ingileif smiled shyly. 'I went home. With someone.'

'And who would that be?'

'Lárus Thorvaldsson.'

'Is he a regular boyfriend?'

'Not really,' said Ingileif. 'He's a painter: we've known each other for years. We just spend the night together sometimes. You know how it is. And no, he's not married.'

For once in the conversation, Ingileif seemed completely unembarrassed. So did Vigdís for that matter. She obviously knew how it was.

Vigdís passed the notebook across again and Ingileif scribbled down Lárus's details.

'She's not a very good liar,' Magnus said when they were back out on the street.

'I knew there was something going on between her and Agnar.'

'But she was convincing that that was all in the past.'

'Possibly,' said Vigdís. 'I'll check her alibi, but I expect it will hold up.'

'There must be some connection with Steve Jubb,' Magnus said. 'The name Isildur, or Ísildur is significant, I know it. Did you notice she didn't seem surprised we were asking about her long-dead brother? And if she saw the *Lord of the Rings* movie the name Isildur would have jumped out at her. She didn't mention that connection at all.'

'You mean she was trying to downplay the Ísildur name?'

'Exactly. There's a connection there she's not talking about.'

'Shall we bring her in to the station for questioning?' Vigdís suggested. 'Perhaps Baldur should see her.'

'Let's leave it a while. Let her relax, drop her guard. We'll come back and interview her again in a day or two. It's easier to find the hole in a story second time around.'

They checked with the woman who owned the boutique next door. She confirmed she had dropped into Ingileif's gallery one afternoon earlier that week to borrow some tea bags, although she wasn't absolutely sure whether it was the Monday or the Tuesday.

Vigdís drove up the hill past the Hallgrímskirkja. Magnus peered up at a large bronze statue on a plinth in front of the church. The first *vestur-íslenskur*, Leifur Eiríksson, the Viking who had discovered America a thousand years before. He was staring out over the jumble of brightly coloured buildings in the middle of town to the bay to the west, and on towards the Atlantic.

'Where are you from originally?' Magnus asked. Although his Icelandic was already improving rapidly, he was finding it tiring, and there was something familiar about sitting in a car with a black partner that tempted him to slip back into English.

'I don't speak English,' Vigdís replied, in Icelandic.

'What do you mean you don't speak English? Every Icelander under the age of forty can speak English.'

'I said I don't speak English, not I can't speak it.'

'OK. Then, where are you from?' Magnus asked again, this time in Icelandic.

'I'm an Icelander,' Vigdís said. 'I was born here, I live here, I have never lived anywhere else.'

'Right,' Magnus said. A touchy subject, clearly. But he had to admit that Vigdís was an incontrovertibly Icelandic name.

Vigdís sighed. 'My father was an American serviceman at the Keflavík airbase. I don't know his name, I've never met him, according to my mother he doesn't even know I exist. Does that satisfy you?'

'I'm sorry,' said Magnus. 'I know how difficult it can be to figure out your identity. I still don't know whether I am an Icelander or an American, and I just get more confused the older I get.'

'Hey, I don't have a problem with my identity,' said Vigdís. 'I know exactly who I am. It's just other people never believe it.'

'Ah,' said Magnus. A couple of raindrops fell on the windscreen. 'Do you think it will rain all day?'

Vigdís laughed. 'There you are, you *are* an Icelander. When in doubt discuss the weather. No, Magnús, I do not think it will rain for more than five minutes.' She drove down the other side of the hill towards the police headquarters on Hverfisgata. 'Look, I'm sorry, I just find it easier to straighten out those kind of questions up front. Icelandic women are a bit like that, you know. We say what we think.'

'It must be tough being the only black detective in the country.'

'You're damn right. I'm pretty sure that Baldur didn't want me to join the department. And I don't exactly blend in when I'm out on the streets, you know. But I did well in the exams and I pushed for it. It was Snorri who got me the job.'

'The Commissioner?'

'He told me my appointment was an important symbol for Reykjavík's police force to be seen as modern and outward looking. I know that some of my colleagues think a black detective in this town is absurd, but I hope I have proved myself.' She sighed. 'The problem is I feel like I have to prove myself every day.'

'Well, you seem like a good cop to me,' Magnus said.

Vigdís smiled. 'Thanks.'

They reached police headquarters, an ugly long concrete office block opposite the bus station. Vigdís drove her car into a compound around the back and parked. The rain began to fall hard, thundering down on the car roof. Vigdís peered out at the water leaping about the parking lot and hesitated.

Magnus decided to take advantage of Vigdís's direct honesty to find out a bit more about what he had got himself into. 'Is Árni Holm related to Thorkell Holm in some way?'

'Nephew. And yes, that is probably why he is in the department. He's not exactly our top detective, but he's harmless. I think Baldur might be trying to get rid of him.'

'Which is why he dumped him on me?'

Vigdís shrugged. 'I couldn't possibly comment.'

'Baldur isn't very happy with me being here, is he?'

'No, he isn't. We Icelanders don't like being shown what to do by the Americans, or anyone else for that matter.'

'I can understand that,' Magnus said.

'But it's more than that. He's threatened by you. We all are, I suppose. There was a murderer on the loose last year, he killed three women before he turned himself in.'

'I know, the Commissioner told me.'

'Well, Baldur was in charge of the investigation. We failed to find the killer and there was a lot of pressure on Snorri and Thorkell to do something. People wanted heads to roll. Moving Baldur on would have been the easiest thing to do, but Snorri didn't do that. I'd say Baldur isn't out of the woods yet. He needs to solve this case and he needs to do it himself.'

Magnus sighed. He could understand Baldur's position, but it wasn't going to make his life in Reykjavík easy. 'And what do you think?'

Vigdís smiled. 'I think I might learn something from you, and that's always good. Come on. The rain is easing off, just like I said it would. I don't know about you, but I've got work to do.'

CHAPTER EIGHT

INGILEIF WAS SHAKEN by the visit of the two detectives. An odd couple: the black woman had a flawless Icelandic accent, whereas the tall red-haired man spoke a bit hesitantly with an American lilt. Neither of them had believed her, though.

As soon as she had read about Agnar's death in the newspaper, she had expected the police. She thought she had perfected her story, but in the end she didn't think she had done very well. She just wasn't a good liar. Still, they had gone now. Perhaps they wouldn't come back, although she couldn't help thinking that somehow they would.

The shop was empty so she returned to her desk, and pulled out some sheets of paper and a calculator. She stared at all the minus signs. If she delayed the electricity bill, she might just be able to pay Svala, the woman who made the glass pieces in the gallery. Something in her stomach flipped, and an all-too familiar feeling of nausea flowed through her.

This couldn't go on much longer.

She loved the gallery. They all did, all seven women who owned it and whose pieces were sold there. At first they had been equal partners: her own skill was making handbags and shoes out of fish skin tanned to a beautiful luminescent sheen of different colours. But it emerged that she had a natural talent for promoting and organizing the others. She had increased sales, jacked up prices and insisted on concentrating on the highest quality articles.

Her breakthrough had been the relationship she had developed with Nordidea. The company was based in Copenhagen, but had shops all over Germany selling to interior designers. Icelandic art fitted well into the minimalist spaces that were so highly fashionable there. Her designers made glassware, vases and candleholders of lava, jewellery, chairs, lamps, as well as abstract landscapes and her own fish-skin leather goods. Nordidea bought them all.

The orders from Copenhagen had grown so fast that Ingileif had had to recruit more designers, insisting all the time on the best quality. The only problem was that Nordidea were slow payers. Then, as the credit crunch bit in Denmark and Germany, they became even slower. Then they just stopped paying at all.

There were repayments on a big loan from the bank to be made. On the advice of their bank manager the partners had borrowed in low-interest euros. The rate may well have been low for a year or two, but as the króna devalued the size of the loan had ballooned to the point where the women had no chance of meeting their original repayment schedule.

More importantly for Ingileif, the gallery still owed its designers millions of krónur and these were debts that she was absolutely determined to meet. The relationship with Nordidea had been entirely her doing; it was her mistake and she would pay for it. Her fellow partners had no inkling of how serious the problem was, and Ingileif didn't want them to find out. She had already spent her legacy from her mother, but that wasn't enough. These designers weren't just her friends: Reykjavík was a small place and everyone in the design world knew Ingileif.

If she let all these people down, they wouldn't forget it, and neither would she.

She picked up the phone to call Anders Bohr at the firm of accountants in Copenhagen that was trying to salvage something from Nordidea's chaotic finances. She telephoned him once a day, using a mixture of charm and chastisement in the hope of badgering him into giving her something. He seemed to enjoy talking to her, but he hadn't cracked yet. She could only try. She wished she could afford a plane ticket to have a go at him in person.

A hundred kilometres to the east, a red Suzuki four-wheel-drive pulled up outside a cluster of buildings. There were three structures: a large barn, a large house and a slightly smaller church. A big man climbed out of the car – he was well over six feet tall, with dark hair greying at the temples, a strong jaw hidden by a beard, and dark eyes glittering under bushy eyebrows. He looked more like forty-five than his real age, which was sixty-one.

He was the pastor of Hruni.

He stretched and took a deep gulp of cool, clear air. White puffs of clouds skittered through a pale blue sky. The sun was low, it never rose very high at this latitude, but it emanated a clear light that picked out in shadow the lines of the hills and mountains surrounding Hruni.

Far to the north the sunlight was magnified white on the smooth horizontal surface of the glacier which filled the gaps between mountains. Low hills, meadows that were still brown at this stage of spring, and rock surrounded the hamlet. The village of Flúdir, while just on the other side of the ridge to the west, could have been twenty kilometres away. Fifty kilometres away.

The pastor turned to look at his beloved church. It was a small building with white-painted corrugated sides and a red-painted corrugated roof, standing in the lee of a rock-strewn ridge. The church was about eighty years old, but the gravestones around it were gnarled weather-beaten grey stone. Like everywhere in Iceland, the structures were new, but the places were old.

The pastor had just come back from ministering to one of his flock, an eighty-year-old farmer's wife who was terminally ill with cancer. For all his forbidding presence the pastor was good with his congregation. Some of his colleagues in the Church of Iceland might have a better understanding of God, but the pastor understood the devil, and in a land that lay under constant threat of earthquake, volcano or storm, where trolls and ghosts roamed the countryside, and where dark winters suffocated isolated communities in their cold grip, an understanding of the devil was important.

Every one of the congregation of Hruni was aware of the awful fate of their predecessors who had danced with Satan and been swallowed up into the ground for their sins.

Martin Luther had understood the devil. Jón Thorkelsson Vídalín, from whose seventeenth-century sermons the pastor borrowed heavily, understood him. Indeed, at the farmer's wife's request, the pastor had used a blessing from the old pre-1982 liturgy to ward off evil spirits from her house. It had worked. Colour had returned to the old lady's cheeks and she had asked for some food, the first time she had done that for a week.

The pastor had an air of authority in spiritual matters that gave people confidence. It also made them afraid.

In years gone by, he used to perform an effective double act with his old friend Dr Ásgrímur, who had understood how important it was to give his patients the will to heal themselves. But the doctor had been dead nearly seventeen years. His replacement, a young woman who drove over from another village fifteen kilometres away, put all her faith in medicine and did her best to keep the pastor away from her patients.

He missed Ásgrímur. The doctor had been the second-best chess player in the area, after the pastor himself, and the second most widely read. The pastor needed the stimulation of a fellow intellectual, especially during the long winter evenings. He didn't miss his wife, who had walked out on him a few years after Ásgrímur's death, unable to understand or sympathize with her husband's increasing eccentricity.

Thoughts of Ásgrímur reminded the pastor of the news he had read the previous day about the professor who had been found murdered in Lake Thingvellir. He frowned and turned towards his house.

To work. The pastor was writing a major study of the medieval scholar Saemundur the Learned. He had already filled twenty-three exercise books with longhand writing: he had at least another twenty to go.

He wondered whether his own reputation would ever match that of Saemundur's, that a future pastor of Hruni would write about *him*. It seemed absurd. But perhaps one day he would be called upon to do something that the whole world would notice.

One day.

CHAPTER NINE

Árni was having trouble locating Elvish speakers in Iceland, especially on a Saturday.

The couple of professors at the university he called were dismissive of his request. Tolkien was not a subject of serious study, and the only person who had any interest in the British author had been Agnar himself, but his colleagues doubted that he spoke any Elvish. So Magnus suggested that Árni dive into the Internet and see what he came up with.

Magnus himself decided to make use of the Internet to try to track down Isildur. Isildur was clearly the senior partner in the relationship with Steve Jubb and probably the one putting up the money. If Steve Jubb wouldn't tell them anything about the deal he was discussing with Agnar, maybe Isildur would. If they could find him.

The more Magnus thought about it, the less likely it seemed to him that Isildur would be a friend of Jubb's from Yorkshire. That kind of nickname was more common in the online world than the physical one.

But before he got to work, there was an e-mail waiting for him, forwarded by Agent Hendricks, who fortunately seemed to be working on a Saturday.

It was from Colby.

Magnus took a deep breath and opened it.

Magnus

The answer must be no. I can tell you don't really mean it, so don't pretend you do.

Don't bother sending me any more e-mails, I won't reply to them.

C.

Magnus felt a rush of anger. She was right, of course, he didn't really want to marry her, and there was no chance that he would be able to persuade her that he did. But he *was* worried about her safety. He typed rapidly.

Hi Colby,

I am very worried about you. I need to get you to safety. Now. If you don't want to come with me then I will try to arrange something else. So please get in touch with me, or if not me, with the FBI, or with Deputy Superintendent Williams at Schroeder Plaza. If you do contact him, speak to him directly and only him.

Please do this one thing for me,

Love

Magnus

It probably wouldn't work, but it was worth a try.

Magnus spent the rest of the afternoon in the murky waters of the Internet, feeling his way around forums and chat rooms. There were an awful lot of *Lord of the Rings* fans out there. They seemed to split into the amateurs and the obsessives. The amateurs were mostly thirteen-year-old boys who couldn't spell and had seen the movies and thought the Balrogs were really cool. Or they were thirteen-year-old girls who couldn't spell and had seen the movies and thought that Orlando Bloom was really hot.

These brief posts were outweighed by mighty articles from the obsessives, who wrote thousands of words on obscure aspects of Middle Earth, Tolkien's invented world. There were disputes about whether those Balrogs had real wings or metaphysical ones, or about why there were no young ents, or about exactly who or what was Tom Bombadil.

Magnus hadn't read *The Lord of the Rings* since he was thirteen himself, and he had only a vague recollection of all these characters. But it wasn't just the obscurity of the arguments that surprised him, it was the passion and occasionally vitriol that accompanied them. To a great many people all over the world, *The Lord of the Rings* was clearly very, very important.

After two hours he found a posting from a man named Isildur. An obsessive. It consisted of several paragraphs commenting on a long academic article by someone called John Minshall on the nature of the power of the One Ring in *The Lord of the Rings*.

There are a number of rings of power in Tolkien's book, all made by elves, except for the greatest of them, the One Ring to rule them all, which was made by Sauron, the Dark Lord. Long before the events of the book took place a desperate battle was fought between the evil Sauron and an alliance of men and elves; a battle which was won by the alliance. The ring was cut off the Dark Lord's hand by a man named Isildur. But afterwards, on his march home, the victorious Isildur and his men were waylaid by orcs. As Isildur tried to escape he jumped into a river, where the ring slipped off his finger and was lost. Soon afterwards the orcs caught him and he was shot through with arrows.

The ring lay at the bottom of the river for centuries until it was discovered by a hobbit-like creature named Déagol who was fishing there with his friend Sméagol. Sméagol was overwhelmed with desire for the beautiful glittering ring, and when his friend refused to give it to him, he strangled him and put the ring on his own finger. Over time Sméagol was consumed by it, becoming a slithering, obsessive creature called Gollum, until eventually, centuries later, the ring was taken from him by Bilbo Baggins, the hero of Tolkien's first book, *The Hobbit*.

The ring has all kinds of powers. The keeper of the ring does not grow old, but eventually he becomes weary and fades away. If the holder wears the ring, he becomes invisible to normal mortals.

Over time, the ring exerts a power over its keeper, causing him to lie, cheat or even kill to maintain possession of it. Wearing it becomes an addiction. But most importantly, Sauron, the Dark Lord, is searching for the ring. When he finds it he will gain total domination of Middle Earth. The only way the Ring can be destroyed is if it is taken to Mount Doom, a volcano in the centre of Mordor, Sauron's own country, and thrown into the 'Crack of Doom'. This becomes the quest for Bilbo's nephew, a hobbit named Frodo.

Minshall argued that the powers of the ring showed that Tolkien had been inspired by Wagner's *Ring Cycle* of operas, in which the gods compete to take control of the Ring and dominate the world.

This idea seriously upset the present-day Isildur.

He quoted Tolkien himself who denied that there was a connection, claiming that 'both rings are round, and there the resemblance ceases'. Then Isildur launched on a long discourse quoting from the *Saga of the Volsungs* and the *Prose Edda*, both written in Iceland in the thirteenth century. He claimed that Tolkien had read the *Volsung Saga* when he was still a schoolboy and that it had inspired him for the rest of his life.

Both these sources describe how three gods, Odin, Hoenir and the trickster god Loki, were travelling when they came upon a waterfall where a dwarf named Andvari was fishing in the shape of a pike. Loki caught him, and stole some gold from him. Andvari tried to keep back a magic ring, but Loki spotted it, and threatened to send the dwarf to Hel, who was Loki's daughter, the goddess of death, unless he gave the ring to Loki. Andvari laid a curse on the ring and disappeared into a rock. During the rest of the saga the ring passes from person to person, creating mayhem wherever it goes. Isildur seemed to believe that both J.R.R. Tolkien and Richard Wagner had read the *Saga of the Volsungs*, which explained the similarity between the two stories.

There followed a series of ever more heated postings back and forth, until a third commentator appeared calling Tolkien a liar and a plagiarist. This seemed to unite Minshall and Isildur in defence of their hero, and the subject was laid to rest there.

Magnus strongly suspected that this was the same Isildur who was Steve Jubb's partner: both of them shared an interest in the *Volsung Saga*. Fortunately the web page included a link to the e-mail address of the people posting the commentaries. Isildur's address indicated an Internet Service Provider from the US. The question was, how could Magnus find out who he was?

There was a small chance that sending him an e-mail asking him to help the Reykjavík police with a murder inquiry would elicit a response. There was a much greater chance that it would tip Isildur off that the police were on to him, and he would go quiet.

The previous year Magnus had been involved in the investigation of the rape and murder of a woman in the middle-class suburb of Brookline. She had received anonymous e-mails from a stalker. With the help of a young technician named Johnny Yeoh in Computer Forensics, Magnus had tracked down the IP address of the computer from which the e-mails had been sent, despite all kinds of ploys the sender had used to disguise it. It turned out he was the woman's next-door neighbour. He was now serving life in Cedar Junction.

Magnus had Isildur's e-mail address. All he needed to do was provoke an e-mail response from him, which would include a 'header' divulging the IP address of Isildur's computer.

He thought for a minute and then tapped something out.

Hi Isildur,

I found your comment about the Saga of the Volsungs very interesting. Where can I get a copy?

Matt Johnson

A simple, if slightly dumb question which would take Isildur only a few seconds to respond to, with luck not enough time to worry about the e-mail address from which it was sent. Worth a try.

The problem with e-mail correspondence was that you never knew how long a reply would take to arrive. It could be a minute, an hour, a day or a month. While he was waiting, Magnus checked how Árni was doing. He had made some progress: he had found a lecturer in Linguistics at the University of New South Wales who claimed to be an expert on Tolkien's invented languages, of which there were supposed to be fourteen. Like Magnus, he had sent an e-mail inquiry and was waiting for a response.

Árni had also found traces of an Isildur. There was someone using that nickname who seemed to be trying to build an online translation service into and out of Quenya, which was one of Tolkien's most detailed Elvish languages. Whether it was the same Isildur or some other *Lord of the Rings* obsessive using that name, they could not be certain.

Magnus went back to his own computer. He was in luck. There was a brief e-mail from Isildur.

Hi Matt

You should be able to get a copy from Amazon. There is a good Penguin Classics edition. It's well worth reading. Enjoy.

Isildur

Magnus hit a few keys on his computer, and a string of codes and numerals was revealed, the e-mail header.

Pay dirt.

'Árni. Do you know anyone in your Computer Forensics department who could check out an e-mail header for me?'

Árni looked doubtful. 'It's Saturday. They'll be at home. I could try to get hold of someone, but it will take a while. We might have to wait until Monday.'

Monday was no good. Magnus checked his watch. It was about lunch time in Boston. Johnny Yeoh was a civilian, not a police officer, but he was the kind of geek who would drop everything to be helpful if he was interested. Magnus and he had gotten on well, especially since Magnus had made sure that Johnny had received plenty of credit for his work in tracking down the Brookline killer. This would be just the kind of task to get Johnny's juices flowing.

Magnus tapped out a quick e-mail, cutting and pasting the header from Isildur's message. He made sure that there was nothing in the text of the e-mail that might suggest that he was anywhere but some city in the heart of America. He considered sending it to Johnny's Boston PD address via Agent Hendricks. The problem was Johnny wouldn't get it till Monday. Magnus needed a result more quickly than that.

Magnus could remember Johnny's home e-mail address – he had used it enough times the previous year. He weighed the risks. There was no way that anyone would be monitoring Johnny Yeoh for a contact with Magnus. And although Lenahan had lots of buddies throughout the police department, Johnny was about the least likely person to be one of them.

He tapped out Johnny's address and pressed send.

With any luck, by morning they would know who Isildur was.

CHAPTER TEN

THINGHOLT WAS A jumble of brightly coloured little houses in the central 101 postal district of Reykjavík, clinging to the side of the hill below the big church. It was where the artists lived, the designers, the writers, the poets, the actors, the cool and the fashionable.

It wasn't really a cop's neighbourhood, but Magnus liked it.

Árni drove him along a quiet street just around the corner from the gallery Magnus had visited earlier that afternoon, and stopped outside a tiny house, probably the smallest in the road. The walls were cream concrete, and the roof lime-green corrugated metal, out from which jutted a lone window. Paint on walls and roof was peeling and the grass in the tiny yard at the side of the building was straggly and trampled down. Yet it reminded Magnus of the house he had grown up in as a child.

Árni rang the doorbell. Waited. Rang the bell again. 'She's probably asleep.'

Magnus checked his watch. It was only seven o'clock. 'She's in bed early.'

'No, I mean she hasn't got up yet.'

Just then the door opened, and there stood a very tall, black-haired girl, with a pale face, wearing a skimpy T-shirt and shorts. 'Árni!' she said. 'What are you doing waking me up at this hour?'

'What's wrong with this hour?' Árni said. 'Can we come in?'

The woman nodded, a slow droop of her head, and stood back to let them in. They went through the hallway into a small living room, in which was a long blue sofa, a big TV, a couple of bean bags on the polished wooden floor and a bookcase heaving with books. The walls were panelled in wood; the longest had been painted in swirls of blue, green and yellow, giving an impression of a tropical island.

'This is my sister, Katrín,' Árni said. 'This is Magnús. He's an American friend of mine. He was looking for a place to stay in Reykjavík and so I suggested here.'

Katrín rubbed her eyes and tried to focus on Magnus. Her top was more of a singlet than a T-shirt, one of her small breasts peeked out. She looked quite a lot like Árni, tall, thin and dark, but where Árni's features were weak, hers were strong, white face, angled cheekbones and jaw, thick short black hair, big dark eyes.

'Hi,' she said. 'How are you?' She spoke in English, with a British accent.

'I'm doing good,' Magnus replied. 'And you?'

'Yeah. Cool,' she mumbled.

'Shall we sit down and have a chat?' Árni asked.

Katrín focused on Magnus, staring him up and down. 'No. He's cool. I'm going back to bed.' And with that she disappeared into a room off the hallway.

'Looks like you passed,' said Árni. 'Let me show you the room.' He led Magnus up some narrow stairs. 'Our grandparents used to live here. It belongs to both of us now, and we rent out the room on the first floor. Here we are.'

They emerged into a small room with the basic furniture: bed, table, a couple of chairs and so on. There were two windows, pale evening light streamed in through one, and through the other Magnus could see the spire of the Hallgrímskirkja swooping high above the multicoloured patchwork of metal roofs. 'Nice view,' he said.

'Do you like the room?'

'What happened to the previous tenant?'

Árni looked pained. 'We arrested him. Last week.'

'Ah. Narcotics?'

'Amphetamines. Small-time dealer.'

'I see.'

Árni coughed. 'I would appreciate it if you could keep an eye on Katrín while you're here. In a low-key way, of course.'

'Will she mind that? I mean, is she happy sharing a place with a cop?'

'There's no need to tell her what you do, is there, do you think? And I wouldn't let Chief Superintendent Thorkell know you are staying here.'

'Uncle Thorkell wouldn't approve?'

'Let's just say that Katrín isn't his favourite niece.'

'How much is the rent?'

Árni mentioned a figure that seemed very reasonable. 'It would have been twice that a year ago,' he assured Magnus.

'I believe you.' Magnus smiled. He liked the little room, he liked the tiny house, he liked the view, and he even liked the look of the weird sister. 'I'll take it.'

'Excellent,' said Árni. 'Now let's go and get your stuff from your hotel.'

It didn't take long to ferry Magnus's bag back to the house, and once Árni had made sure that Magnus was installed, he left him. There was no sound from Katrín.

Magnus stepped out on to the street. Consulting a city map, he walked one block down the hill and one block across. The sky had cleared, apart from a single thin slab that covered the top of the ridge of stone and snow that was Mount Esja. Magnus was beginning to spot a pattern: the base of the cloud moved up and down the mountain several times a day, depending on the weather. The air was clear and crisp. At eight-thirty it was still light.

He found the street he was looking for and made his way slowly along, examining each house as he went. Perhaps he wouldn't recognize it after all these years. Perhaps they had changed the colour of the roof. But as he followed the road over a hump he saw it: the small house with the bright blue roof of his childhood.

He stopped outside it and stared. The old whitebeam was still there, but a rope had been added to one of the branches. A good idea. A deflated football lay in a bed of daffodils, just about to bloom. He was glad there were still children there; he guessed most of the houses in that neighbourhood were now inhabited by young couples. A large Mercedes SUV stood proudly outside, containing two child seats. A far cry from his father's old VW Beetle.

He closed his eyes. Above the murmur of the traffic he could hear his mother calling Óli and him inside for bed. He smiled.

Then the front door began to open and he turned away, embarrassed that the current owners would see a strange man leering at their house.

He made his way down the hill towards the centre of town. He passed a group of four men and a woman unloading equipment from a van. A band getting ready for Saturday night. The girl with the leopard-skin miniskirt and tail zipped past on her bicycle. In Reykjavík, he realized, you could expect to see the same person on the streets several times in one day.

He stopped at Eymundsson's bookstore, an all-glass jewel on Austurstraeti, where he picked up the last English copy of *The Lord of the Rings*, and a copy of the *Saga of the Volsungs*, in Icelandic.

He headed over towards the Old Harbour and another memory from his childhood, a small red kiosk, *Baejarins beztu pylsur*. He and his father used to go there every Wednesday night, after handball practice, for a hot dog. He joined the line. Unlike the rest of Reykjavík, *Baejarins beztu* hadn't changed over the years, except there was now a picture outside of a grinning Bill Clinton tucking into a large sausage.

Munching his hot dog, he strolled through the harbour area and along the pier. It was a working harbour, but at this time of the evening it was peaceful. On one side were trawlers, on the other, sleek whale-watching vessels and small inshore fishing boats. There was a smell of fish and of diesel, although Magnus passed a squat white hydrogen fuel pump. He paused at the end, a respectful distance from a fisherman fiddling with his bait in a bag, and surveyed the stillness.

Beyond the harbour wall, the black rock and white snow of Mount Esja was reflected in the steel-grey water. A seagull wheeled around him, looking for a discarded morsel, but after a few seconds abandoned him with a disappointed cry. An officious looking motor boat cut through the harbour entrance on some mission of nautical bureaucracy.

Iceland had changed so much since the disruptions of his childhood, but what he recognized of Reykjavík brought back the early years, the happy years. There was no reason to visit his mother's family; they need never even find out he was in the country. He was pleased with the way his Icelandic seemed to be coming back so well, although he was aware that he spoke with a touch of an American accent: he needed to work on rolling those 'r's.

Reykjavík was a long way from Boston, a long way north of Boston. Twenty-five degrees of latitude. It wasn't just the cold air or the patches of snow that told him this – Boston Harbor could be cold and bleak enough – it was the light: clear but soft, pale, thin. There was a subtle warmth to the greys of the harbour in Reykjavík, compared with its harsher Boston counterpart.

But he would be glad when the trial date came up and he could go back. Although the Agnar case was an interesting one, he missed the violent edge of the streets of Boston. At some point over the last ten years, sorting out the day-to-day procession of shootings, stabbings and rapes, finding the bad guys and bringing them to justice, had become more than a job. It had become a need, a habit, a drug.

Reykjavík just wasn't the same. Toytown.

He felt a pang of guilt. Here he was safe, thousands of miles from that teeming city of drug gangs and police-corruption trials. But Colby wasn't. How could he get her to listen to him? He had the feeling the harder he pushed it, the more obstinate she would become. But why? Why did she have to be like that? Why did she have to use this issue, of all issues, to try to resolve the question of their relationship? If he were more emotionally subtle, if he were Colby herself, for example, he would be able to figure out a way of manipulating her to come with him. But as he tried to think of a plan, his head began to spin.

He sighed and turned back to the city. As he walked back up the hill along Laugavegur he looked out for a likely bar for a quick beer. Down a side street he spied a place called Grand Rokk. From the outside it looked a bit like a scruffy Boston pub, but with a tent covering tables at which a dozen people were smoking as they drank. Inside, the place was about a quarter full. Magnus eased his way past a group of regulars lined up along the bar and ordered himself a large Thule from the shaven-headed barman. He found a stool in the corner and sipped his beer.

The other drinkers looked as if they had been there a while. Quite a few had shot glasses containing a brown liquid crouching next to their beers. A line of tables along one wall were inlaid with the squares of chessboards. There was a game in progress. Magnus watched idly. The players weren't that good, he could beat them easily.

He smiled when he remembered challenging his father, a formidable player, night after night. The only way Magnus could ever beat the clever strategist was by aggressive assaults on his king. They nearly always failed, but sometimes, just sometimes he would break through and win the game, to the pleasure of both father and son. Magnus knew that although his father would never dream of giving him a break, he was rooting for Magnus, always rooting for Magnus.

Too often, Magnus saw his father only through the dreadful prism of his murder, and forgot the simpler times before his death. Simpler, but not simple.

Ragnar was a very clever man, a mathematician with an international reputation, which was why he had been offered the position at MIT. He was also humane, the saviour who had whisked Magnus and his little brother away from misery in Iceland when they had feared that he had abandoned them. Magnus had many fond memories of his father from his teenage years: not only playing chess and reading the sagas together, but also hiking in the

Adirondacks and in Iceland, and long discussions through the evening about anything that Magnus was interested in – sparring matches in which his father always listened to Magnus and respected his opinion, yet also tried to prove him wrong.

But there was one aspect of his father's life that Magnus had never understood: his relations with women. He didn't understand why Ragnar had married his mother, or why he left her. He certainly didn't understand why he had then gone on to marry that awful woman Kathleen. She was the young wife of one of the other professors at MIT, and Magnus realized later that they must have been having an affair even when Magnus joined his father in Boston. Although outwardly charming and beautiful, Kathleen was a controlling woman who resented Magnus and Ollie. Within a few months of their marriage she seemed to resent Ragnar too. Why his father hadn't seen that coming, Magnus had no idea.

Eighteen months after that dreadful occasion, Ragnar was dead, found stabbed on the floor of the living room at the house they were renting for the summer in Duxbury, on Boston's South Shore.

Magnus had had no doubt who was the chief suspect. The detectives investigating the case listened to his theories about his stepmother with sympathy at first, and then with irritation. After an initial couple of days where they seemed to pursue her vigorously, they let her drop. This made no sense to Magnus, since they didn't have another suspect. Months went by and the police couldn't come up with a better idea than that a total stranger broke into the house, stabbed Ragnar, and then disappeared into the ether, leaving no trace other than a single hair, which the police had been unable to identify, despite DNA testing.

It was only the following year, when Magnus devoted his summer vacation from college to making his own inquiries, that he discovered that his stepmother had had a cast-iron alibi: she was in bed with an air-conditioning engineer in town at the time of the killing. A fact that stepmother and policemen had conspired to keep from Magnus and his brother.

The bar was filling up with a younger crowd, overwhelming some of the earlier drinkers who staggered out into the dusk. A band set up, and within a few minutes began to play. The music was too loud for a contemplative beer, so Magnus left.

Outside, the streets, so quiet earlier, were full, teeming with the young and not-so-young dolled up for a night on the town.

Time for bed, Magnus thought. As he opened the door of his new lodgings, he passed Katrín on her way out, dressed in black gothic finery, her face powdered white and improbably studded with metal.

'Hi,' she said with half a smile.

'Have a good evening,' said Magnus in English. Somehow that seemed the correct language in which to speak to Katrín.

She paused. 'You're some kind of cop, aren't you?'

Magnus nodded. 'Kind of.'

'Árni's such an arsehole,' Katrín muttered, and disappeared into the semi-darkness.

Diego took his time breaking into the ground-floor apartment in Medford. The apartment was the bottom half of a small clapboard house in a quiet road, and the good news was that the yard was obscured by trees. No one would see him, so he could focus on not making a noise.

He climbed through the kitchen window and padded into the living room. The bedroom door was open and he could hear gentle snoring. He sniffed. Marijuana. He smiled. That should slow his target down nicely.

He slid into the bedroom. Noted the lump on the bed, and the bedside light. He drew his gun, a Smith and Wesson .38 revolver. Then he switched on the light, pulled back the covers and cocked his weapon. 'Sit up, Ollie,' he barked.

The man sat bolt upright, his eyes blinking, his mouth open in surprise. He matched the photograph Diego had studied earlier: about thirty years old, skinny, light brown curly hair, blue eyes that were now puffy and bloodshot.

'Yell, and I blow your head off! You got me?'

The man swallowed and nodded.

'All right. Now, I got one simple question for you. Where's your brother?'

Ollie tried to speak. Nothing came out. He swallowed and tried again. 'I don't know.'

'I know he stayed with you here last week. Where did he say he was going to when he took off?'

Ollie took a deep breath. 'I have no idea. He was here one day and gone the next. Just grabbed his stuff and left without saying goodbye. Typical of my brother. Hey, man,' Ollie seemed to be waking up, 'can we come to some arrangement here? Like, I give you some money and you leave me alone?'

Diego grabbed Ollie's head by his hair with his left hand and shoved the revolver into his mouth with his right. 'The only arrangement we come to is you tell me where he is. You don't know where he is that's tough for you 'cause you die.'

'Hey, man, I don't know where he is, I swear!' Ollie's words were muffled as he tried to speak with metal in his mouth.

'You ever played Russian roulette?' said Diego.

Ollie shook his head and swallowed.

'It's real easy. There are six chambers in this revolver. One of them holds a bullet. You and I don't know which one. So when I pull the trigger, we don't know whether you gonna die. But you let me pull the trigger six times, you dead for sure. Get it?'

Ollie swallowed and nodded. He got it.

Diego let go of Ollie's hair, he didn't want to shoot his own hand, after all, and then he pulled the trigger.

A click. The chamber rotated.

'Oh, God,' said Ollie.

'You might think it's just you that's taking the risk,' went on Diego. 'But in point of fact it's me too. 'Cause if I blow your head off and you ain't told me what I wanna know, then I lose, see? Makes the game kinda fun for the both of us.' He smiled at Ollie. 'So, once more, where's your brother at?'

'I don't know, man, I swear I don't know!' Ollie shouted.

'Hey, quiet!' Diego narrowed his eyes. 'You know, I still don't believe you.' He pulled the trigger again.

Click.

Ollie cracked. 'Oh God, don't shoot me, please don't shoot me! I'd tell you if I could, I swear I would! Some guys from the FBI came to get his stuff. I asked where they were taking him, but they wouldn't tell me.'

Diego heard a low hissing sound and smelled warm urine. He glanced down at the rapidly spreading dark patch on Ollie's boxers. In his experience, once they pissed themselves, they were usually telling the truth.

But he pulled the trigger for the third time, just for the hell of it. Click.

He'd discussed this situation with Soto. There were two schools of thought. One was you waste every relative and associate of the witness to send a clear message to him and anyone else who might be tempted to follow his lead. But when the witness was a cop, that wasn't such a good idea. You'd be declaring a major war on a heavily armed and well-organized opposition. The most successful drugs businesses operated under the radar, making as little fuss as possible, keeping business conditions nice and calm.

Ollie didn't know where Magnus was. There was no point in stirring things up.

'OK, man, I'm gonna quit this game now,' Diego said. 'Let's call it a tie. But don't you go to the cops telling them I'm looking for your bro', you know what I'm saying? Otherwise we don't play no games, I just blow you away with the first shot.'

'All right, man. All right. That's cool.' Ollie sobbed as tears streamed down his face.

Diego leaned over and turned out the light. 'You go back to bed now. Sweet dreams.'

CHAPTER ELEVEN

MAGNUS FOLLOWED THE stocky frame of Officer O'Malley towards the bright lights of the 7-Eleven. His fingers twitched an inch or so above his gun.

O'Malley turned and smiled. 'Hey. Loosen up, Swede. Keep your eyes open but don't get too tense. If you're tense, you make mistakes.'

O'Malley had decided to call Magnus 'Swede' in honour of his Scandinavian ancestry, and an old Swedish partner he had worked with twenty years before. Magnus hadn't set him straight: if his training officer wanted him to be Swedish, he would be Swedish. He'd been on the streets for only two weeks, but already he had a great respect for O'Malley.

'Looks quiet,' O'Malley said. They had been given no information by the dispatcher as to the nature of the disturbance at the convenience store.

Magnus saw a thin figure move towards them from out of the shadows. O'Malley hadn't seen him. The figure was making a direct line for O'Malley. Magnus tried to reach for his gun, but his arm wouldn't move. The figure raised his own weapon, a three fifty-seven Magnum, and pointed it at O'Malley. In a panic Magnus managed to get his fingers around his own gun, but he couldn't lift it. Try as he might, it was too heavy. Magnus opened his mouth to shout a warning to his partner, but no sound came.

The man turned to Magnus and laughed, still pointing his gun at O'Malley. He was young, scrawny and looked as if he hadn't washed for a week. His eyes were bloodshot and unfocused, he had bad teeth and his complexion, lit up by the light emanating from the convenience store, was like wax. It was if he were dead already, some kind of walking zombie.

O'Malley still hadn't seen him.

Magnus tried to shout, tried to lift his gun. Nothing. Just an eerie cackle from the gunman.

Then there was a shot. Two. Three. Four. They went on and on.

Finally, O'Malley fell to the ground. Magnus's gun arm responded. He raised his weapon and fired into the laughing face of the dopehead. He fired and fired again, and again and again ...

Magnus woke up.

There was noise outside his window. Reykjavík 101 at play on a Saturday night: laughter, accelerating cars, shrieks, singing, vomiting, and underneath it all, the persistent bass rumble of powerful amplifiers.

The chunky volume of *The Lord of the Rings* lay open on the floor where he had let it drop a couple of hours earlier. It smothered the slimmer edition of the *Saga of the Volsungs*.

He checked his watch. 5.05 a.m.

It was an old familiar dream: it had disturbed his nights for two years after that first shooting. Of course the reality had differed from the dream, the dopehead had only fired two shots into O'Malley before Magnus dropped him. But during those long nights Magnus had debated pointlessly with himself whether he could have fired sooner and saved O'Malley, or delayed longer and saved the dopehead.

That was a long time ago. Magnus thought he had taken the second shooting much better than the first, now that he was an experienced cop. Maybe he had thought wrong. His subconscious demanded time to deal with it, and there was nothing he could do about it, however tough a cop he was.

Bummer.

*

Reykjavík Metropolitan Police Headquarters was a busy place early on Sunday morning. Exhausted uniformed police led pale and shaky citizens along the corridors, taking them through the later stages of the weekly Saturday-night arrest cycle.

As soon as Magnus arrived at his desk, he turned on his computer. He smiled as he saw the e-mail from Johnny Yeoh. The kid had come up with the goods.

At the morning meeting, Baldur looked as if he hadn't slept much either. Dark bags drooped under his eyes, and his cheeks were sunken and grey. Magnus surveyed his fellow detectives around the table; they had lost a lot of their earlier bounce.

Baldur began with the latest reports from forensics. With Agnar, Steve Jubb and Andrea, three of the four sets of fingerprints in the house were accounted for. The footprints were confirmed as Steve Jubb's. But there were no bloodstains on any of Jubb's clothes, not even the tiniest spatter.

Baldur asked Magnus if it would be difficult to smash someone over the head and then drag them out of the house and twenty metres down to the lake without getting any blood on your clothes. Magnus had to agree that it would be difficult, but he contended it was not impossible.

'I spoke to Agnar's wife yesterday,' Baldur said. 'She's an angry woman. She had no idea of the existence of Andrea. She believed her husband had kept his promise to be a good boy.

'Also she has been through Agnar's papers and discovered that he was in a much deeper financial hole than she had realized. Debts, big debts.'

'What has he been spending the money on?' Rannveig, the assistant prosecutor asked.

'Cocaine. She knew about the cocaine. And he gambled. She estimates he owed about thirty million krónur. The credit-card companies were beginning to complain, as was the bank that held the mortgage on their house. But now he's dead, a life insurance policy will take care of that.'

Magnus did a quick mental calculation. Thirty million krónur was a bit over two hundred thousand dollars. Even by the standards of Iceland's debt-addicted citizens, Agnar owed a lot of money.

'All in all, Linda had a motive to kill her husband,' Baldur continued. 'She says she was alone with her young children on the Thursday night. But she could easily have slung them in the back of the car and driven to Thingvellir. It's not as if they could tell us, one's a baby and the eldest isn't even two yet. We need to keep her in the frame. Now, Vigdís. Did you speak to the woman from Flúdir?'

Vigdís ran through the interview with Ingileif. She had checked out Ingileif's alibi: she had indeed been at her artist friend's party until eleven-thirty on the evening Agnar was murdered. And with her 'old friend' the painter afterwards.

'She might have been telling the truth about that, but we think she was lying about other stuff,' said Magnus.

'What other stuff?'

'She was very coy about Agnar,' said Vigdís. 'My hunch is there was more going on there than she let on.'

'We'll go back and talk to her in a couple of days,' said Magnus. 'See if her story sticks.'

'Any progress on Isildur?' Baldur asked.

'Yes,' said Magnus. 'I found someone calling himself Isildur on a *Lord of the Rings* forum on the Internet. I got hold of his e-mail details and asked a buddy of mine in the States to check him out.'

'Are you sure it's the same one?'

'We can't be absolutely sure, but it looks highly likely to me. This man is obsessed with magic rings and Icelandic sagas, just like Steve Jubb.'

Baldur grunted.

Magnus went on. 'His name is Lawrence Feldman and he lives in California. He has two houses, one in Palo Alto and one in Trinity County, which is two hundred and fifty miles north of San Francisco. That's where the e-mail message came from.'

'Two houses?' said Baldur. 'Do we know if he is wealthy?'

'He's loaded.' Although Johnny hadn't been able to pull the

police files on Feldman, if indeed there were any, he had found plenty of stuff on the Internet about him. 'He was one of the founders of a software company in Silicon Valley, 4Portal. The company was sold last year, and each of the founders walked away with forty million bucks. Feldman was only thirty-one. Not bad going.'

'So he could easily afford an expensive lawyer,' said Baldur.

'And a room at the Hótel Borg for Steve Jubb.'

'OK. We need to get this guy's police record, if he has one,' said Baldur. 'Can you do that?'

'I could, but it's probably easier if the request came from the Reykjavík police,' said Magnus. 'More official, fewer favours called in.'

'We'll organize that,' said Baldur.

'But I could go see him,' Magnus said.

'In California?' Baldur looked doubtful.

'Sure. It would take a day to get there, a day to get back, but I might get him to tell me what he and Jubb are up to.'

Baldur frowned. 'We don't know for sure that this is the same Isildur that Steve Jubb is working for. And anyway, he won't talk. Why should he? Steve Jubb isn't saying anything, and we have him in custody.'

'Depends how I ask him.'

Baldur shook his head. 'It will cost money. I'm not sure I can get authorization for a trip that will probably be a waste of time. Haven't you heard of the *kreppa?*'

It was impossible to spend more than a few hours in Iceland without hearing about the *kreppa*. 'Just an economy fare and perhaps one night in a motel,' Magnus said. He looked at the bodies around the table. 'You're putting a whole lot of resource into this investigation. An airplane ticket won't make much difference.'

Baldur glared at Magnus. 'I'll think about it,' he said, giving Magnus the distinct impression that he wouldn't.

'OK,' Baldur continued, addressing the group. 'It looks like someone calling himself Isildur was behind the negotiations with

Agnar. If this Lawrence Feldman was that man, he had the cash to back a significant deal.'

'But what could they have been negotiating over?' said Vigdís.

'Something to do with *The Lord of the Rings*?' Magnus said. 'Or the Saga of the Volsungs, maybe. I read it again last night. A magic ring plays an important part in both books. There's a theory that Tolkien was inspired by the *Volsung Saga*.'

'All the old copies of the saga will be in the Árni Magnússon Collection at the University of Iceland,' said Baldur. Árni Magnússon was a Danish-educated antiquarian who travelled around Iceland in the seventeenth century gathering up all the sagas he could find. He transported them to Denmark, but they were returned to Iceland in the 1970s, where they were housed in an institute bearing the great collector's name. 'Are you saying Agnar had stolen a copy?'

'He might have switched it for a facsimile,' suggested Vigdís.

'Perhaps,' said Magnus. 'Or perhaps he had some wacko theory that he was selling to Isildur. Maybe he was going to do some research for him.'

Baldur frowned and shook his head.

'It could be narcotics,' Rannveig said. 'I know it's boring, but in Iceland, if it's an illicit deal, it's nearly always drugs.'

There was silence for a moment around the table. The assistant prosecutor had a point.

'Was there anything in Agnar's papers suggesting what this deal could be?' Rannveig asked.

'No, I checked most of them myself,' Baldur said. 'Apart from those e-mails on his computer, there is nothing about a deal with Steve Jubb. And the files on his laptop are all work related.'

'What was he working on?' Magnus asked.

'What do you mean?'

'I mean what was he researching when he died?'

'I'm not sure he was researching anything. He was marking exam papers. And translating a couple of sagas into English and French.'

Magnus leaned forward. 'Which sagas?'

'I don't know,' Baldur said, defensively. He clearly didn't appreciate being interrogated in his own meeting. 'I didn't read through all his working papers. There are piles of them.'

Magnus restrained himself from pushing the point. He didn't want to put Baldur's back up any more than he had to. 'Can I take a second look? At his working papers, I mean.'

Baldur stared at Magnus, making no attempt to hide his irritation. 'Of course,' he said drily. 'That would be a good use of your time.'

There were two places to look: Agnar's room at the university, or the summer house. There would be more papers at the university, and it was closer. On the other hand, if Agnar had been working on something relevant to Steve Jubb it was likely to be at the summer house where it would be available for his meeting.

So Árni drove Magnus out to Lake Thingvellir. 'Do you think Baldur will let you go to California?' he asked.

'I don't know. He didn't seem excited by the idea.'

'If you do go, can you take me with you?' Árni glanced at Magnus sitting in the passenger seat and noticed his hesitation. 'I did my degree in the States so I am familiar with US police procedures. Plus, California is my spiritual home.'

'What do you mean?'

'You know. The Gubernator.'

Magnus shook his head. Árni would be demanding a personal interview with Arnold Schwarzenegger next. Besides, Magnus would rather approach Lawrence Feldman in his own way without his Icelandic puppy at his heels. 'We'll see.'

Deflated, Árni drove over the pass beyond Mosfell Heath and down towards the lake. It wasn't actually raining, but there was a stiff breeze that ruffled the surface. Their approach was watched by a posse of sturdy Icelandic horses from the farm behind the cottages, their long golden forelocks flopping down over their eyes.

Magnus noticed a boy and a girl playing by the shore of the lake – the boy was about eight, the girl much smaller. Again, only the one summer house with the Range Rover was occupied. Agnar's property was still a crime scene, with yellow tape fluttering in the wind and a police car parked outside, in which sat a solitary constable reading a book. *Crime and Punishment* by one F.M. Dostojevskí, it transpired. Magnus smiled. Cops everywhere liked to read about crime; it wasn't surprising that the Icelanders had a more literary approach to it than their American counterparts.

The policeman was glad of the company and let Magnus and Árni into the house. It was cold and still. Fingerprint dust covered most of the smooth surfaces, adding to the sense of desolation, and there were chalk marks around the traces of blood on the floor.

Magnus examined the desk: drawers full of papers, most of them printouts from a computer. There was also a low cupboard just to the left of the desk, in which more reams of paper lay.

'OK, you check out the cabinet, I'll check out the desk,' Magnus said, slipping on a pair of white latex gloves.

The first bundle he examined was a French translation of the *Laxdaela Saga*, on which were scribbled comments in French. These only covered the first half of the manuscript. Magnus had learned some French at school, and he guessed that Árni had been correcting or commenting on the work of another translator, probably an Icelandic-speaking Frenchman.

'What have you got, Árni?'

'*Gaukur's Saga*,' he said. 'Have you ever heard of it?'

'No,' said Magnus. That wasn't necessarily a surprise. There were dozens of sagas, some well-known, some much less so. 'Wait a minute. Wasn't Gaukur the guy who lived at Stöng?'

'That's right,' said Árni. 'I went there when I was a kid. I was scared out of my wits.'

'I know what you mean,' said Magnus. 'My father took me there when I was sixteen. There was something really creepy about that place.'

Stöng was an abandoned farm about twenty kilometres north of the volcano, Mount Hekla. It had been smothered in ash after a massive eruption some time in the middle ages, and had only been rediscovered in the twentieth century. It lay at the end of a rough track which wound its way through a landscape of blackened destruction: mounds of sand and small outcrops of lava twisted into grotesque shapes. When Magnus read of the apocalypse, he thought of the road to Stöng.

'Let me take a look.'

Árni handed the manuscript to Magnus. It was about a hundred and twenty crisp, newly printed pages, in English. On the cover were the simple words: 'Gaukur's Saga, translated by Agnar Haraldsson'.

Magnus turned the page, scanning the text. On the second page he came upon a word that brought his eyes to an abrupt halt.

Ísildur.

'Árni, look at this!' He flicked rapidly through more pages. Ísildur. Ísildur. Ísildur. Ísildur.

The name cropped up several times on each page. Ísildur wasn't a bit player in this saga, he was a main character.

'Wow,' said Árni. 'Shall we take it back to headquarters to get forensics to look at it?'

'I'm going to read it,' Magnus said. 'Then forensics can take a look.'

So he sat down in a comfortable armchair, and began to read, passing each page carefully to Árni as he finished with it.

CHAPTER TWELVE

ÍSILDUR AND GAUKUR were two brothers who lived at a farm called Stöng. Ísildur was strong and brave with dark hair. He had a hare lip and some people thought he was ugly. He was a skilled carver of wood. Gaukur, although two years younger than Ísildur, was even stronger. He had fair hair and was very handsome, but he was vain. He was an expert with a battleaxe. Both brothers were honest and popular in the region.

Their father, Trandill, wanted to pay a visit to his uncle in Norway and to go on Viking raids. Their mother had died when the boys were small, so Trandill sent them to a friend, Ellida-Grímur of Tongue, to be fostered. Ellida-Grímur agreed to manage the farm at Stöng in Trandill's absence. Ellida-Grímur had a son, Ásgrímur, who was the same age as Ísildur. The three boys became fast friends.

Trandill was away for three years, spending the summers raiding and trading in the Baltic and in Ireland, and the winters with his uncle, Earl Gandalf the White, in Norway.

One day a traveller returning to Iceland from Norway arrived at Tongue with a message. Trandill had been killed in a fight with Erlendur, Earl Gandalf's son. Gandalf was willing to pay the compensation that was due to Trandill's sons, and to hand over the inheritance if one of the brothers would come to Norway to collect it.

When Ísildur was nineteen, he decided to travel to Norway to visit his great uncle and claim his inheritance. Gandalf and his son

Erlendur welcomed him with great warmth and hospitality. Gandalf said that Erlendur had killed Trandill in self-defence when Trandill had attacked him in a drunken rage. The other men at the court who had witnessed Trandill's death agreed that this was the case.

Ísildur decided to spend the summer on Viking raids with Erlendur. They went to Courland and Karelia in the East Baltic. Ísildur was a brave warrior and won much booty. After many adventures, he returned to the house of Gandalf a wealthy man.

Ísildur told Gandalf that he wanted to return to Iceland. Gandalf gave Ísildur the compensation he was owed for his father's death, and also Trandill's treasure. But the night before Ísildur was due to set sail, Gandalf said he had something else to give him. It was locked in a small chest.

Inside was an ancient ring.

Gandalf explained that Trandill had won the ring on a raid in Frisia when he had fought the famous warrior chieftain, Ulf Leg Lopper. Ulf Leg Lopper was ninety years old, but he appeared to be no older than forty and he was still a fearsome fighter. After a long struggle, Trandill felled him. He saw the ring on Ulf Leg Lopper's finger and chopped the finger off.

Despite the fact that he was dying, Ulf Leg Lopper smiled. 'I give you thanks for relieving me of my burden. I found this ring in the River Rhine seventy years ago. I have worn it every day since then. During that time I have won great victories and wealth in battle. Yet although I wear the ring, I feel that the ring owns me. It will bring you great power, but then it will bring you death. And now I can die, in peace at last.'

Trandill examined the ring. Inside were inscribed in runes the words 'The Ring of Andvari'. He was going to ask Ulf more about the ring, but when he looked down, Ulf was dead, a smile on his face, no longer a great warrior, but a wrinkled old man.

Gandalf told Ísildur the legend of the ring. It had belonged to a dwarf named Andvari, who used to fish by some waterfalls. The ring was seized from Andvari, together with a hoard of gold, by

Odin and Loki, two ancient gods. Andvari laid a curse on the ring, saying it would take possession of its bearer and use the bearer's power to destroy him, and would continue to do so until it was taken home to Hel. [Translator's footnote: Hel was the domain of Hel, the goddess of death and Loki's daughter.]

Odin, foremost of the gods, reluctantly gave the ring to a man named Hreidmar as compensation for killing his son. The ring had drawn great power from Odin. In the following years the ring fell into the possession of a number of keepers, each of which was corrupted, including Hreidmar's son Fafnir, who became a dragon; the hero Sigurd; the Valkyrie Brynhild and Sigurd's sons Gunnar and Hogni. Everywhere it went it left a trail of treachery and murder in its wake, until finally it was hidden by Gunnar in the Rhine so that his father-in-law Atli could not get hold of it.

There it lay for centuries until it was found by Ulf Leg Lopper.

When Trandill returned to Norway he was a changed man: secretive, cunning and selfish. He constantly taunted Erlendur and one evening, in a drunken rage, he attacked him. Erlendur killed him with a lucky blow.

Erlendur was going to take the ring, but Gandalf laid claim to it. That evening he put it on. At once he felt different: stronger, powerful, and also greedy.

Later that evening a Sami sorceress from the North knocked at the door of Gandalf's house seeking shelter. She saw that Gandalf was wearing the ring. She was overcome with terror and tried to leave into the night, but Gandalf stopped her. He demanded to know what she had seen.

She said that the ring had a terrible power. It would consume all who owned it, until a man so powerful wore it that he would rule the world and destroy everything good in it. The world would be plunged into eternal darkness.

Gandalf was concerned. He could feel the effect that the ring was having on him, but he was not yet in its power. He took off the ring at once and told the sorceress that he would destroy it. She said that the only way the ring could be destroyed was as

Andvari had prophesied; it must be thrown into the mouth of Hel.

'Tell me, woman, where is Hel?'

'It is a mountain in the land of fire and ice,' the sorceress replied.

'I know where she means,' said Erlendur. 'Trandill told me of it. It is Hekla, a great volcano near his farm at Stöng.'

So Gandalf decided never to wear the ring again and to keep it safe for Trandill's sons. He told Ísildur to take the ring to Hekla in Iceland and throw it into the volcano.

That night Ísildur had a dream that he was leading a glorious raiding party through England and he won a hoard of gold. He woke up before it was light and put on the ring. Immediately he felt taller, stronger, invincible. And he was determined to earn an even greater fortune overseas.

He went to Gandalf and demanded that the earl give him a ship and permit him to lead a raiding party to England. Gandalf saw he was wearing the ring and ordered him to take it off. Ísildur felt a surge of anger shoot through him. He took up an axe and was just about to split Gandalf's skull when Erlendur grabbed him from behind.

As they struggled, Erlendur shouted: 'Stop, Ísildur. You don't know what you are doing! It is the ring! You will make me have to kill you just like I killed your father!'

Ísildur felt a burst of strength course through his veins and he threw Erlendur off him. He raised his axe high above the defence-less Erlendur. But when he looked down on his cousin and his friend with whom he had shared so many adventures that summer, he stopped himself. He threw down the axe and pulled the ring off his finger. He replaced the ring in its box and left for Iceland immediately.

He returned home to Iceland with the ring and his treasure. Gaukur had taken over the management of the farm at Stöng, and was betrothed to a woman named Ingileif. When Ásgrímur heard that Ísildur had returned he travelled to Stöng to meet his foster-brother. Ísildur told his brother and his foster-brother about his adventures in Norway and the Baltic. Then he told them all about Andvari's Ring, and Earl Gandalf's instruction that he toss it into Hekla. He described the immense sense of power he had felt when he put on the ring, and the constant temptation to try it on again. He said that he intended to take the ring up the mountain the very next day and he asked Gaukur and Ásgrímur to accompany him to make sure that he went through with the quest.

Hekla had a fearsome reputation and no one had climbed it before. But the three men were brave and undaunted, so early the next morning they set off for the volcano. On the second day, they were most of the way up the mountain when Ásgrímur slipped down a gully and broke his leg. He could not continue further, but he agreed to wait until the brothers returned from the summit.

He waited until nearly midnight before he heard the sound of footsteps scrambling down the mountain. But there was only one man, Gaukur. He told Ásgrímur what had happened. He and his brother were standing by the crater at the top of the mountain. Ísildur took the ring from its box and was about to toss it into the crater, but he seemed unable to do so. He said that the ring was very heavy. Gaukur urged him to throw it, but Ísildur became angry and put the ring on his finger. Then he turned and before Gaukur could grab him, he leaped into the crater.

'At least the ring is destroyed,' said Ásgrímur. 'But at a very high price.'

In the years afterwards, Gaukur changed. He became vain and quarrelsome, cunning and greedy. But he was even stronger and braver in battle and had a fearsome reputation. Despite all this, his foster-brother Ásgrímur remained steadfast in his loyalty. He frequently supported Gaukur in the various disputes Gaukur was involved in at the annual gathering of the Althing in Thingvellir.

Gaukur married Ingileif. She was a wise woman and beautiful. She had a strong temper, but she was usually quiet. She noticed the change in Gaukur and she did not like it. She also noticed that

Gaukur spent much time at Steinastadir, the farm of his neighbour Ketil the Pale.

Ketil the Pale was a clever farmer, wise and peaceful and a gifted composer of poetry. He was popular with everyone, except perhaps his wife. Her name was Helga. She had fair hair and long limbs and was contemptuous of her husband, but admired Gaukur.

There was a marsh between the two farms, on Ketil the Pale's land. It was waterlogged in winter, but in spring it produced very sweet grass. One spring Gaukur decided to graze his own cows on the land and chased Ketil the Pale's cows away. Ketil the Pale protested, but Gaukur brushed him off. Ketil the Pale did nothing. Helga scolded her husband for being so weak.

After midsummer, when Gaukur was returning from the Althing at Thingvellir, he passed by Ketil the Pale's farm. He came across a slave of Ketil the Pale who was slow to get out of his way. So Gaukur chopped off his head. Once again, Ketil the Pale did nothing.

Helga was again contemptuous of Ketil the Pale. She scolded him from morning until night, vowing never to share his bed again until he had demanded compensation from Gaukur.

So Ketil the Pale rode over to Stöng to speak to Gaukur.

'I have come to demand compensation for the unlawful killing of my slave,' Ketil said.

Gaukur snorted. 'His killing was perfectly lawful. He blocked the way back to my own farm and would not let me pass.'

'That is not my understanding of what happened,' said Ketil.

Gaukur laughed at him. 'You understand very little, Ketil. Everyone knows that every ninth night you are the woman to the troll of Búrfell.'

'And they know that you could not sire anyone because you were gelded by the troll's daughters,' Ketil replied, for at that time Gaukur and Ingileif had no children.

Whereupon Gaukur picked up his axe and after a brief struggle chopped off Ketil the Pale's leg. Ketil dropped down dead.

Afterwards Gaukur made even more visits to Ketil the Pale's

farm, where Helga was now the mistress. Ketil's brother's demanded compensation from Gaukur, but he refused to pay, and his foster-brother Ásgrímur supported him loyally.

Ingileif was jealous, and determined to stop Gaukur. She spoke to Thórdís, Ásgrímur's wife and told her a secret. Ísildur had not jumped into the crater of Hekla while wearing the ring. He had been killed by Gaukur, who had taken the ring, and then pushed his brother into the crater. Gaukur had hidden the ring in a small cave watched over by a troll's hound.

Thórdís told her husband what Ingileif had said. Ásgrímur did not believe her. But that night he had a dream. In his dream he was with a group of men in a great hall and an old Sami sorceress pointed to him. 'Ísildur tried and failed to destroy the ring and was killed in the process. Now it is up to you to find the ring and to take it to the mouth of Hel.'

Killing a man without reporting it was a great crime. Although Ásgrímur was convinced by his dream, he had no proof with which to accuse Gaukur, and Gaukur was not the man to accuse without proof. So Ásgrímur went to his neighbour Njáll, a great and clever lawyer, to help him. Njáll admitted that it would be impossible to prove anything at the Althing. But he suggested a trap.

So Ásgrímur told Thórdís who told Ingileif that Ísildur had given him a helm in secret when he had returned from Norway. The helm belonged to Fafnir, the son of Hreidmar, and it was famous in legend. Ásgrímur had hidden it in an old barn on a hill at the edge of his farm at Tongue.

Then Ásgrímur stood watch, hiding in the roof of the barn to ambush Gaukur, if he should come looking for the helm. Sure enough, on the third night, he caught Gaukur entering the barn, looking for the helm. Ásgrímur confronted Gaukur who drew his sword.

'Would you kill me in order to steal what is not yours, just as you killed your brother?' Ásgrímur asked.

In answer Gaukur swung his sword at Ásgrímur. They fought. Although Gaukur was the stronger and the better warrior, he was overconfident and Ásgrímur was fired with anger at the betrayal by the foster-brother whom he had always supported so loyally. He ran Gaukur through with a spear.

Ásgrímur searched for the ring but never found it and Ingileif would not tell him where it was hidden. She said that the ring had already caused enough evil and should be left to rest.

Six months after Gaukur's death, Ingileif gave birth to a son, Hogni.

But the ring did not lie quietly. A century later there was an enormous volcanic eruption and Hekla smothered Gaukur's farm at Stöng in ash, to be lost for ever.

The ring is still hidden somewhere in the hills near Stöng. One day it will emerge, just as it emerged out of the Rhine at the time of Ulf. When it does, it must not fall again into the hands of an evil man. It must be tossed into the mouth of Mount Hekla, as the Sami sorceress decreed.

Until that time this saga shall be kept secret by the heirs of Hogni.

Magnus handed the last page to Árni, who still had several pages to go, which was fair enough since English was not his first language. Magnus stared out over the lake at the two small islands in the middle.

He tried to control his excitement. Could the saga be real? If it was, it would be one of the greatest finds in Icelandic literature. More than that, its discovery would reverberate around the world.

He was quite certain that if it was genuine, it was previously unknown. There were no doubt plenty of minor sagas that Magnus had never heard of, but this was no minor saga. The Ring of Andvari, and the fact that the main character was Gaukur, the owner of Stöng, would have ensured that the story would have become widely known within Iceland and beyond. Magnus recognized a couple of the characters from his beloved *Njáls Saga*: Njáll himself and Ásgrímur Ellida-Grímsson.

But was it genuine? It was difficult to be sure in translation, but the style looked authentic. Icelandic sagas had none of the poetic flourishes of medieval tales from the rest of Europe. At their best they were terse, precise and down to earth, more Hemingway than Tennyson. Unlike the rest of Europe, the ability to read in medieval Iceland was not confined to the clergy and books were not restricted to Latin. It was a nation of scattered farms, and there was a need for farmers isolated from village priests to be able to read the Bible for themselves and their households during the long winter nights. The sagas were historical novels written to be read by, not simply recited to, a mass audience.

If the saga was real, Gaukur's descendants had done a wonderful job of keeping it secret over the centuries. Until now, when a two-bit professor of Icelandic had taken it upon himself to show it to the wider world. Magnus had no doubt that this is what Agnar wanted to sell to Steve Jubb and the modern-day Isildur.

The links to *The Lord of the Rings* in *Gaukur's Saga* were obvious, much stronger than the *Saga of the Volsungs*. For one thing, the 'magic' of the ring was more powerful and more specific. Although there was nothing about invisibility, the ring took over the character of its keeper, corrupting him and causing him to betray or even kill his friends. And it extended his life. Ísildur's quest to throw the ring into Mount Hekla had obvious parallels with Frodo's quest to fling Sauron's Ring into Mount Doom.

The *Lord of the Rings* Internet chat rooms would be buzzing for years once they saw the saga. If they ever saw it. Perhaps the modern Isildur's plan was to hoard it somewhere, his very own Viking booty.

Magnus was not surprised he was prepared to pay so much.

But this was an English translation. There must be an Icelandic original, or more likely a copy of it, from which Agnar had made his translation. Magnus was sure that Baldur would have noticed an original saga written on eight-hundred-year-old vellum, but he could easily have missed a modern-day Icelandic copy.

While Árni finished reading the last few pages, Magnus searched through Agnar's other papers.

Nothing.

'Perhaps it's in Agnar's office at the university?' Árni suggested.

'Or maybe someone else has it,' said Magnus, thinking.

He looked out of the window over the lake towards the low snow-topped mountains in the distance. Then it came to him.

'Come on, Árni. Let's get back to Reykjavík.'

CHAPTER THIRTEEN

THE GALLERY ON Skólavördustígur was only open for a couple of hours on Sundays and by the time Magnus and Árni got there it was closed. But, peering in through the window, Magnus could see a figure working at the desk at the back of the shop.

He rapped on the glass door. Ingileif appeared, looking irritated. The irritation increased when she saw who it was. 'We're closed.'

'We didn't come here to buy anything,' Magnus said. 'We want to ask you some questions.'

Ingileif saw the grim expression on his face and let them in. She led them back to her desk which was covered in number-strewn papers, weighted down with a calculator. They sat facing her.

'You said your great-grandfather's name was Ísildur?' Magnus began.

'I did.'

'And your father's name was Ásgrímur?'

Ingileif frowned, the nick appearing above her eyebrow. 'Obviously. You know my name.'

'Interesting names.'

'Not especially,' said Ingileif. 'Apart from perhaps Ísildur, but we discussed that.'

Magnus said nothing, let silence do its work. Ingileif began to blush.

'Anyone in your family named Gaukur?' he asked.

Ingileif closed her eyes, exhaled and leaned backwards. Magnus waited.

'You found the saga, then?' she said.

'Just Agnar's translation. You should have known we would. Eventually.'

'Actually, Gaukur is a name we tend to avoid in our family.'

'I'm not surprised. Why didn't you tell us about it?'

Ingileif put her head in her hands.

Magnus waited.

'Have you read it?' she asked. 'All the way through?'

Magnus nodded.

'Well, obviously I should have told you, I was stupid not to. But if you have read the saga, you might understand why I didn't. It's been in my family for generations and we have successfully kept it a secret.'

'Until you tried to sell it.'

Ingileif nodded. 'Until I tried to sell it. Which is something I deeply regret now.'

'You mean now that someone is dead?'

Ingileif took a deep breath. 'Yes.'

'And this saga was really kept a secret for all those years?'

Ingileif nodded. 'Almost. With one lapse a few hundred years ago. Until my father, knowledge of the saga had only been passed on from father to eldest son, or in a couple of instances, eldest daughter. My father decided to read it to all us children, something my grandfather was not very happy about. But we were all sworn to absolute secrecy.'

'Do you still have the original?'

'Unfortunately, it wore out. We only have scraps left, but an excellent copy was made in the seventeenth century. I made a copy of that myself for Agnar to translate; it will be in his papers somewhere.'

'So, after all those centuries, why did you decide to sell it?'

Ingileif sighed. 'As you can imagine, people in my family have always been obsessed by the sagas, and by our saga in particular. Although my father became a doctor, he was the most obsessed of the lot. He was convinced that the ring mentioned in the saga still existed and he used to go on expeditions all around the valley of the River Thjórsá, which is where Gaukur's farm was, to look for it. He never found it, of course, but that's how he died. He fell off a cliff in bad weather.'

'I'm sorry,' said Magnus. And although Ingileif had lied to him, he was sorry.

'That put the rest of us off *Gaukur's Saga*. My brother, who until then had been brainwashed by Dad to a level of obsession that matched his, wanted nothing more to do with it. My sister was never very interested. I think my mother had always found the saga a little weird and held it responsible for Dad's death. Of all of them, I was perhaps the least put off: I went on to study Icelandic at university. So when I found I needed money desperately, it seemed to me that I was the only one who would really care if we sold it.

'The gallery is going bust. It is bust really. I need money badly – a lot of money. So when my mother died last year I spoke to my brother and my sister about selling the saga. Birna, my sister, couldn't give a damn, but my brother Pétur argued against it. He said we were custodians of the saga, it wasn't ours to sell. I was a bit surprised, but eventually Pétur relented as long as it could be sold privately, with a secrecy clause. I think he might have his own money problems. Everyone does these days.'

'What does he do?'

'He owns bars and clubs. Do you know Neon?'

Magnus shook his head. Ingileif frowned at his ignorance. 'It's one of the most famous clubs in Reykjavík,' she said.

'I'm sure it is. I haven't been here very long,' said Magnus.

'I know it,' Árni chipped in.

'I could see you were a party animal,' Ingileif said.

Now it was Árni's turn to blush.

'So, once you had decided to sell it, why did you approach Agnar?' Magnus asked.

'He taught me at university,' Ingileif said. 'And, as I told you, I knew him quite well. He was sleazy enough to agree to sell the saga on the quiet away from the Icelandic government, but he liked me well enough not to rip me off totally. And it turned out he knew just the right buyer. A wealthy American *Lord of the Rings* fan, who was willing to keep the purchase private.'

'Lawrence Feldman? Steve Jubb?'

'I didn't know his name. You mentioned the name Steve Jubb before, didn't you? But you said he was English.'

'That's why you said you had never heard of him?'

'I hadn't heard the name before. But I admit I wasn't very helpful. I was desperately trying to keep the saga secret. As soon as I had told Agnar about it, I had second thoughts. I even told him that I wanted to take it off the market and keep it in the family.' She pursed her lips. 'He told me that it was too late. He knew all about it, and unless I went through with the sale, he would tell.'

'He blackmailed you?' Magnus said.

'I suppose you could call it that. I deserved it. And it worked. I thought it would be better all round to sell the saga secretly and split the proceeds between Pétur, Birna and myself, than allow Agnar to broadcast its existence to the whole world.'

'How much did he say it would bring?'

'He was in the process of negotiating the price. He said it would be millions. Of dollars.'

Magnus took a deep breath. 'And where is this saga now?'

'In the gallery safe.' She hesitated. 'Do you want to see it?'

Magnus and Árni followed her through to a store cupboard at the back of the shop. On the floor was a combination safe. Ingileif twiddled the knobs. She pulled out a leather-bound volume, and placed it on the desk.

'This is the seventeenth-century copy, the earliest complete copy.' She opened up the book at a random page. The pages were paper, covered in a neat black handwriting, clear and easy to read. 'You know when you asked me whether the saga had been kept a secret, I said there was one lapse?'

Magnus nodded.

'Well, this was copied from an earlier version that was bought from one of my ancestors by Árni Magnússon, the great saga collector. The rest of the family was furious that he had sold it. Árni Magnússon took it with all the others to Copenhagen, and it was one of those that was destroyed in the terrible fire of 1728, before it was catalogued. There is only one mention of *Gaukur's Saga* in existence today, to our knowledge, with no details as to what it contains. The majority of the collection went up in smoke, especially the paper copies. Within the family, we believe there was a reason the fire started.'

'Arson? Someone wanted to destroy it?'

Ingileif shook her head. 'That's not what they meant, although knowing how obsessive my family were, I wouldn't have been surprised. No it was more bad luck, fate, call it what you will.'

'The power of the ring,' said Árni.

'Now you are beginning to sound like my father,' said Ingileif. 'But when Agnar was murdered, I couldn't help seeing the parallels.' She turned back to the safe. 'And then there is this. The original, or what's left of it.'

She carefully extracted a large old envelope, lay it on the desk, and slipped out two layers of stiff card, between which, separated by tissue paper, were perhaps half a dozen sheets of brown vellum. She pulled back the tissue so that they could see one of the sheets closely.

It was faded, torn at the edges, and covered in black writing. This was surprisingly clear: the initial letters of chapters were decorated in fading blues and reds. Magnus could make out the word 'Ísildur'.

'Amazing,' Magnus said. And indeed it was. Any doubts he had had about the authenticity of the translation he had read in Agnar's summer house were dispelled. He had gawped at the old sagas in the Árni Magnússon exhibition, but he had never seen one this close. He couldn't resist reaching out with his fingertip to touch it.

'It is, isn't it?' Ingileif said, a note of pride in her voice.

'Do you know who wrote it?' Magnus asked.

'We think it was someone called Ísildur Gunnarsson,' Ingileif said. 'One of Gaukur's descendants, of course. We think he lived in the late thirteenth century, right when most of the major sagas were written.'

'But if this was such a great family secret, how did Tolkien ever see it?' Magnus asked. 'I mean, the links to the *Lord of the Rings* are so strong, it can't just be coincidence. He must have read it.'

Ingileif hesitated. 'Wait a minute.' She returned to the safe, and returned a moment later.

She placed a small, yellowing envelope on the desk in front of Magnus.

'May I look?'

Ingileif nodded.

Magnus carefully pulled out a single sheet of paper, folded once. Magnus unfolded it and read:

20 Northmoor Road
Oxford

9 March 1938

My dear Ísildarson

Thank you so much for sending me the copy of Gaukur's Saga, which I have read with great pleasure. It is almost fifteen years now, but I remember very clearly that meeting of the Viking Club in the college bar at Leeds when you told me something of the saga, although I had no idea that the saga itself would prove to be such a wonderful story. I look back on those evenings fondly – a repertoire of Old Icelandic drinking songs is something that no student of Anglo-Saxon or Middle English should be without!

I am very glad you enjoyed the book I sent you. I have recently begun a second story about Hobbits set in Middle Earth, and I have written the first chapter, entitled 'A long-expected party', with which I am very pleased. But I expect that this book will be a much darker work than the first, more grown up, and I have been searching for a means of linking the two stories. I think perhaps you might have given me that link.

Please forgive me if I borrow some of the ideas from your saga. I can promise absolutely that I will continue to respect your family's wish that the saga itself should remain secret, as it has done for so many hundreds of years. If you do object, please let me know.

I will return the copy of the saga to you next week.

With best wishes,
Yours sincerely,

J.R.R. Tolkien

Magnus's heart was pounding. The letter would double the value of the saga, treble it. It was an astounding discovery, the key to what had become one of the most pervasive legends of the twentieth century.

A wealthy *Lord of the Rings* fan would pay a fortune for the two documents.

Or kill for them.

Magnus had read the first two chapters of *The Lord of the Rings* only the night before. The first was indeed 'A Long-Expected Party', which celebrated Bilbo Baggins's eleventh-first birthday, a jolly affair full of hobbits and food and fireworks at the end of which Bilbo put on his magic ring and disappeared. In the second, 'The Shadow of the Past', the wizard Gandalf returned to lecture Bilbo's nephew Frodo on the strange and evil powers of the ring, and to give him the task of destroying it in the Crack of Doom.

It was clear that between the first and the second chapters lay *Gaukur's Saga*.

'Can I see?' said Árni.

Magnus exhaled – he hadn't even realized he had been holding his breath. He handed the letter to him.

'You showed this to Agnar?'

Ingileif nodded. 'I let him have it for a few days. He wanted anything I could find to authenticate the saga. He was pleased with this. He was convinced it would help us get a better price.'

'I'll bet he was. So Högni Ísildarson was your grandfather?'

'That's right. His father, Ísildur, founded a furniture store in Reykjavík at the end of the nineteenth century. Then, as now, many Icelanders travelled abroad to study, and in 1923 Högni went to England, to Leeds University, where he studied Old English under J.R.R. Tolkien.

'Tolkien made a big impression on my grandfather, he inspired him. I remember him telling me about him.' Ingileif smiled. 'Tolkien wasn't really that much older than my grandfather, only in his early thirties, but apparently he had an old-fashioned air about him. As if he lived in a time before industrialization, before big cities and smoke and machine guns. They corresponded on and off for as long as Tolkien was alive. My grandfather even arranged for one of his nieces to work for Tolkien in Oxford as a nanny.'

'It would have been a good thing all around if you had shown me this the last time I was here,' Magnus said.

'Yes, I know,' said Ingileif. 'And I'm sorry.'

'Sorry isn't really good enough.' Magnus looked straight at her. 'Do you have any idea why Agnar was killed?'

This time she held his gaze. 'No. I told myself that all this was irrelevant to his death, which is why I had no need to tell you about it, and I know of no connection.' She sighed. 'It's not my job to guess, but doesn't it seem likely that these people you were talking about thought that they could get hold of the saga without paying Agnar?'

'Unless you killed him,' Magnus said.

'And why would I do that?' She returned his gaze defiantly.

'To shut him up. You told me yourself that you wanted to withdraw the sale of the saga and he threatened to tell the world about it.'

'Yes, but I wouldn't kill him for that reason. I wouldn't kill anyone for any reason,' Ingileif said.

Magnus stared hard. 'Maybe,' he said. 'We'll be in touch.'

CHAPTER FOURTEEN

MAGNUS LET THE hundred and twenty pages of *Gaukur's Saga* fall on to Baldur's desk with a thump.

'What's this?' Baldur asked, glaring at Magnus.

'The reason Steve Jubb killed Agnar.'

'What do you mean?'

Magnus reported what he and Árni had found at the summer house and his subsequent interview with Ingileif. Baldur listened closely, his long face drawn, lips pursed.

'Did you get this woman Ingileif's prints?' Baldur asked.

'No,' said Magnus.

'Well, bring her in and take them. We need to see if those are the missing set at the scene. And we should get this authenticated.' He tapped the typescript in front of him.

He raised his fingers into a steeple and touched his chin. 'So, this must be the deal they were discussing. But that still doesn't explain why Agnar was killed. We know that Steve Jubb didn't get a copy of the saga. We didn't find it in his hotel room.'

'He could have hidden it,' Magnus said. 'Or mailed it the next morning. To Lawrence Feldman.'

'Possibly. The Central Post Office is just around the corner from the hotel. We can check if anyone remembers him. And if he sent it registered mail, there will be a record of it, as well as the address it was sent to.'

'Or perhaps the deal went bad? They had a fight about the price.'

'Until they had the original saga in their possession, Feldman and Jubb would want Agnar alive.' Baldur sighed. 'But we are getting somewhere. I'll have another go with Steve Jubb. We'll get him back from Litla Hraun tomorrow morning.'

'May I join you?' Magnus asked.

'No,' said Baldur, simply.

'What about Lawrence Feldman in California?' Magnus said. 'It's even more important to speak to him now.' Magnus could feel Árni stiffening in anticipation behind him.

'I said, I would think about it, and I will think about it,' said Baldur.

'Right,' said Magnus, and he made for the door of Baldur's office.

'And Magnus,' Baldur said.

'What?'

'You should have reported this *before* you saw Ingileif. I'm in charge of the investigation here.'

Magnus bristled, but he knew that Baldur was right. 'Right,' he said. 'Sorry.'

Árni went to fetch Ingileif and bring her in to the station to be fingerprinted. Magnus called Nathan Moritz, a colleague of Agnar's at the university who had been interviewed earlier by the police. Moritz was at home, and Magnus asked him to come into the station to look at something. The professor sounded doubtful at first, but when Magnus mentioned it was an English translation of a lost saga about Gaukur and his brother Ísildur, Moritz said he would be right over.

Moritz was an American, a small man of about sixty with a neat pointed beard and messy grey hair. He spoke perfect Icelandic, which wasn't surprising for a lecturer on the subject, and explained that he was on a two-year secondment to the University of Iceland from the University of Michigan. They slipped into English, when Magnus admitted that he was operating under a similar arrangement.

Magnus fetched him a coffee and they sat down in an interview room, the typescript from the summer house in front of Magnus. Moritz had brought his own exhibit, a big hardback book. He was so excited he could barely sit still, and he ignored his coffee.

'Is that it?' he said. '*Gaukur's Saga?*'

'We think so.'

'Where did you get it?'

'It seems to be an English translation that Agnar made.'

'So that's what he was working on!' Moritz said. 'He was beavering away at something for the last few weeks. He claimed that he was commenting on a French translation of the *Laxdaela Saga*, but that sounded strange. I've known Agnar for years, worked with him on a couple of projects, and he was never one to bother himself unduly over deadlines.' Moritz shook his head. '*Gaukur's Saga.*'

'I didn't know it existed,' said Magnus.

'It doesn't. Or at least we didn't think it did. But it used to. Look.'

Moritz opened up the book in front of him. 'This is a facsimile of the *Book of Mödruvellir*, from the fourteenth century, one of the most important collections of the sagas. There are eleven of them in all.'

Magnus walked around the table and stood behind Moritz's shoulder. Moritz leafed through the book, each brown page a faithful copy of the vellum of the original manuscript. He paused at an empty page on which were written only a couple of faded lines. Indecipherable.

'There is a big gap between *Njáls Saga* and *Egils Saga*. No one could read this line until the invention of ultra-violet light. Now they know what it says.' Moritz quoted from memory. '"Insert here *Gauks Saga Trandilssonar*; I am told that Grímur Thorsteinsson Esq has a copy."' He turned to Magnus and smiled. 'We knew that there once was a *Gaukur's Saga*, but we thought it had been lost, like so many others. Gaukur is mentioned once, very briefly in *Njáls Saga*; that he was killed by Ásgrímur.'

'When you read the saga, you will find out how,' said Magnus with a smile, returning to his seat. The *Book of Mödruvellir* must have been the instance of the saga's existence that Ingileif had mentioned.

'The other place he crops up in is extraordinary,' Moritz said. 'There are some Viking runes in a tomb in Orkney, graffiti really, which were discovered in the nineteenth century. The runes claim that they were carved by the axe once owned by Gaukur Trandilsson of Iceland. So the man really did exist.'

Moritz looked at the sheaf of papers in front of Magnus.

'And that's the English translation? May I read it?'

'Yes. Although you will have to use gloves and you will have to read it here. We need to give it to our forensics people before it can be copied.'

'Do you know where the original is?'

'Yes, I do. There are only scraps of the original vellum, but there's an excellent seventeenth-century paper copy. We can show it to you tomorrow. Of course, we can't be sure what we've found is genuine. We need you to authenticate it.'

'With pleasure,' said Moritz.

'And keep this confidential. Don't say a word to anyone.'

'I understand. But don't let your forensic people handle either document without my supervision.'

'Of course,' said Magnus. 'If the saga *is* genuine, how much would it bring?'

'It's impossible to say,' Moritz replied. 'The last medieval manuscript on the market was sold by Sotheby's in the nineteen sixties to a consortium of Icelandic banks. It had belonged to a British collector. Of course this time around the banks haven't got any money, nor has the Icelandic government.' He paused. 'But for this? If it is authentic? There will be plenty of willing buyers outside Iceland. You're talking millions of dollars.'

He shook his head. 'Many millions.'

*

As Magnus returned to his desk, Árni was waiting for him, looking excited.

'What is it? Did Ingileif's fingerprints match?'

'No. But I've heard back from Australia.'

'The Elvish expert?'

Árni handed Magnus a printout of an e-mail.

Dear Detective Holm,

I have been able to translate most of the two messages you sent me. They are in Quenya, the most popular of Tolkien's languages. The translations are as follows:

1. *I am meeting Haraldsson tomorrow. Should I insist on seeing the story?*
2. *Saw Haraldsson. He has (??). He wanted much more money. 5 million. We need to talk.*

Note – I could not find a translation for the word 'kallisar-voinen', which I have marked (??).

It has been a pleasure to find that my knowledge of Quenya has finally been of practical assistance to someone!

Kind Regards

Barry Fletcher
Senior Lecturer
School of Languages and Linguistics
University of New South Wales

'Well, the first message is pretty clear. The second was sent at eleven p.m., the night of the murder, right?' Magnus said.

'That's right. As soon as Jubb got back to the hotel having seen Agnar.'

'No wonder he needed to talk, if he had just pushed a dead body into the lake.'

'I wonder what the kallisar— whatever-it-is word means?' Árni asked.

Magnus pondered it for a moment. 'Manuscript? "He has the manuscript." That would make sense.'

'I don't know,' said Árni.

'What do you mean?'

'That doesn't sound right to me. It sounds as if Agnar has something *else*. Something he wants more money for. That Jubb wants to speak to Isildur to discuss whether he should pay for it.'

Magnus sighed. His patience was running low. 'Árni! We know Agnar died that night. This message explains he was holding out for a lot more money. So Jubb killed him and he needed to speak to the boss once he had done it. Simple. Happens in drug deals back home all the time. Now, let's show this to Baldur. He's going to want to discuss this with Jubb.'

Árni followed Magnus to Baldur's office. It didn't seem quite that simple to him, but Árni was used to being wrong on police matters. He had learned the important thing was not to make too much of a fuss over his mistakes, and not to let them get him down.

Vigdís drove up the winding road to Hruni. It had taken her nearly two hours to get there from Reykjavík; a long way to go just to tick off a name on a list. But Baldur had insisted that every appointment in Agnar's diary should be investigated, and so now it was time to check the mysterious entry *Hruni*.

She passed two or three cars coming the other way, and then she rounded a bend and came upon the valley in which Hruni nestled. As Rannveig had said there was nothing there apart from a church and a rectory beneath a crag. And a view over the meadows to distant mountains.

The Sunday service must just have finished. There were three cars parked on the gravel apron in front of the church. Two of them drew away as Vigdís came to a stop. In front of the church two figures, one very large, one very small, were in deep discussion. The pastor of Hruni and one of his parishioners.

Vigdís hung back until the conversation had finished and the old lady, her cheeks flushed, hobbled rapidly to her small car and drove off.

The pastor turned towards Vigdís. He was a big block of a man, with a thick beard and dark hair flecked with grey. For a moment she felt a flash of fear at his sheer size and power, but she was re-assured by the clerical collar around his neck. Bushy eyebrows rose. Vigdís was used to that.

'Vigdís Audarsdóttir, Reykjavík Metropolitan Police,' she said.

'Really?' said the man in a deep voice.

Vigdís sighed and took out her identification. The pastor examined it carefully.

'May I have a word with you?' she asked.

'Of course,' said the pastor. 'Come into the house.' He led Vigdís into the rectory through to a study cluttered with books and working papers. 'Please sit down. Would you like a cup of coffee, my child?'

'I'm not a child,' said Vigdís. 'I'm a police officer. But yes, thank you.'

She moved a pile of yellowing journals off the seat of a sofa and on to the floor. As she waited for the pastor to return, she examined his study. Open volumes sprawled over a large desk and books lined the walls. Any bare patches were adorned with old prints of various scenes from Icelandic history: a man on the back of a seal or a whale in the sea; a church tumbling down, no doubt Hruni itself; and three or four etchings of Mount Hekla erupting.

Through the window Vigdís could see the modern-day church of Hruni, red and white, spick and span, nestled among ancient gravestones and scrappy trees.

The pastor returned with two cups of coffee, and lowered himself into an old chintz armchair. It creaked with his weight. 'Now, how can I help you, my dear?' His voice was deep and he was smiling, but his eyes, deep-set and dark, challenged her.

'We are investigating the death of Professor Agnar Haraldsson. He was murdered on Thursday.'

'I read about it in the papers.'

'We understand that Agnar visited Hruni quite recently.' Vigdís checked her notes. 'The twentieth. Last Monday. Did he come to see you?'

'He did. It was in the afternoon, I think.'

'Did you know Agnar?'

'No, not at all. That was the first time I had met him.'

'And what did he want to discuss with you?'

'Saemundur the Learned.'

Vigdís recognized the name, although history had not been her strongest subject at school. Saemundur was a famous medieval historian and writer. Come to think of it, it was Saemundur who was on the back of the seal in the print on the wall of the study.

'What about Saemundur the Learned?'

The pastor didn't answer for a moment. His dark eyes assessed Vigdís. She began to feel uncomfortable. This wasn't the usual discomfort she felt when Icelanders stared at her as a black woman, that she was used to. This was something else. She was beginning to wish that she had brought a colleague to accompany her.

But Vigdís had been glared at by all kinds of unsavoury characters before. She wasn't going to let a mere priest disconcert her.

'Do you believe in God, my child?'

Vigdís was surprised by the question, but was determined not to show it. 'That has no relevance to this inquiry,' she said. She didn't want to cede control of the interview to this man.

The pastor chuckled. 'I'm always amazed by how officials always avoid that simple question. It's almost as if they are ashamed to admit they do. Or perhaps they are ashamed to admit they don't. Which is it in your case?'

'I'm a police officer. I am asking the questions,' Vigdís said.

'You're right, it's not directly relevant. But my next question is this. Do you believe in the devil, Vigdís?'

Despite herself, Vigdís answered. 'No.'

'That surprises me. I thought your people would be comfortable with the idea of the devil.'

'I think if there is part of me that is superstitious, it's the Icelandic half,' said Vigdís.

The pastor laughed, a deep rich rumble. 'That's probably true. But it's not superstition, or at least it's more than that. The way people believe is different in Iceland than in other countries, it has to be. We can see good and evil, power and peace in the country-side all around us. Not just see it, we hear it, smell it, *feel* it. There is nothing quite like the beauty of the midday sun reflecting off a glacier, or the peace of a fjord at dawn. But as a people we have also experienced the terror of volcanic eruption and earthquake, the fear of becoming lost in a winter blizzard, the bleak emptiness of the lava deserts. You can *smell* the sulphur in this country.

'Yet even in the most barren lava fields we notice those first little signs of life through the ice and the ash. The mosses nibbling at the lava, breaking it down into what will become fertile earth in a few millennia. This whole land is creation in progress.'

The pastor smiled. 'God is right here.' He paused. 'And so is the devil.'

Despite herself, Vigdís was listening. The slow deep rumble of the pastor's voice demanded her attention. But his eyes unsettled her. She felt a surge of panic, a sudden desire to bolt out of the study and run as far and as fast as she could. But she couldn't move.

'Saemundur understood the devil.' The pastor nodded to the print on the wall. 'As you know, he was taught by Satan at the School of Black Arts in Paris. According to legend, he tricked the devil on many occasions, once persuading him to change into the shape of a seal and carry him back from France to Iceland. Yet he was also Iceland's first historian, perhaps its greatest historian. Although the work itself has been lost we know the saga writers used and admired his history of the Kings of Norway. A fine man. I have devoted my life to studying him.'

The pastor indicated a row of twenty or so thick exercise books on a shelf right next to the desk. 'It's a long, slow process. But I have made some interesting discoveries. Professor Agnar wanted me to tell him about them.'

'And did you?' Vigdís managed to ask.

'Of course not,' said the pastor. 'One day all this will be published, but that day is still many years away.' He smiled. 'But it was gratifying that at last a university professor recognized that a mere country priest could make a contribution to this nation's scholarship. Saemundur himself was a priest at Oddi, not far from here.'

'How long did this conversation take?'

'Twenty minutes, not more.'

'Did Agnar mention an Englishman named Steve Jubb to you?'

'No.'

'What about a woman named Ingileif Ásgrímsdóttir? She comes from Flúdir.'

'Oh, yes, I know Ingileif,' the pastor said. 'A fine young woman. But no, the professor didn't mention her. I didn't know he knew her. I believe she studied Icelandic at the university, perhaps she was one of his students?'

Vigdís knew that there were one or two more questions she really should ask, but she was desperate to get out of there. 'Thank you for your time,' she said, getting to her feet.

'Not at all,' said the pastor. He stood up and held out his hand.

Before she could stop herself, Vigdís took it. The pastor held her hand tightly in both of his. 'I would love to speak to you more about your beliefs, Vigdís.' His voice was both calm and authoritative at the same time. 'Up here at Hruni you can begin to understand God in a way that is impossible in the big city. I can see that you have an unusual background, but I can also see that you are an Icelander at heart, a true Icelander. It's a long drive back to Reykjavík. Stay a while. Talk to me.'

His large hands were warm and strong, his voice was soothing and his eyes were commanding. Vigdís almost stayed.

Then summoning a strength of will from somewhere deep within herself, she pulled her hands away, turned and stumbled out of his house. She hurried to her car at just short of a run, started it and accelerated away from Hruni back towards Reykjavík, breaking the speed limit all the way.

CHAPTER FIFTEEN

COLBY ADMIRED HER new summer dress in the mirror in the bedroom of her apartment in the Back Bay. She had bought it at Riccardi's on Newbury Street the previous Sunday. A splurge but it looked good. Simple. Elegant. Classy. It looked especially good with the earrings. Earrings that Magnus had given her for her last birthday.

Magnus.

No matter how hard she tried, and she tried real hard, she kept on thinking of Magnus.

Where was he now? In Iceland? Stuck in the rain in some godforsaken rock in the middle of the North Atlantic. He had been ridiculous to think that she would give up her job for weeks, possibly months, to join him there.

As if he would give up his job for the couple of hours it would take to go see a movie with her.

But at least he was safely out of the country. She knew that he lived in a dirty, dangerous world, but that world had never imposed itself on her until the other evening in the North End when they had been shot at. Magnus had claimed that they were both still in danger. But she was sure that the more distance she put between him and her the safer she would be.

She fingered the earrings. Sapphires ringed with diamonds. Big-ticket items for a cop's salary. They really were beautiful.

Of course she had nearly made a mistake, a big mistake, in pressing him to marry her. She was very glad he had said no.

It wasn't that she didn't find him attractive. Quite the contrary. She loved to pull herself tightly into his broad chest. She loved the sense of latent power and danger that hovered around him. He could be frightening when he lost his temper, but she even loved that about him. He was smart too, a great listener, and she could spend all evening just talking to him. He wasn't Jewish, but she could deal with that, even if her mother had problems with it.

The trouble was, he was a loser. And he always would be.

It was the job, of course. With his degree from Brown he could have done much better than police work, as she had frequently pointed out to him. But he never would. He was obsessed with the job, with solving the murder of one deadbeat after another. Often Magnus was the only person anywhere who cared who had shot whom. She knew it all had to do with his father, but all that knowledge did was make her realize how hard it would be to change him.

Not hard. Impossible.

Her friend Tracey had told her it was a waste of time to try to change boyfriends. An even bigger waste of time to go into a marriage with the aim of changing your husband. It just didn't work.

His decision to tell his Chief about the crooked detective was the last straw. It was all very honest and honourable, but it was dumb. Boston wasn't nearly the nest of corruption it had been twenty years before, but people who took on the city establishment would never find themselves a part of it.

In her own company, a manufacturer of medical instruments, there were times when they looked the other way, didn't ask questions. You had to, if you wanted the company to succeed. Her job was to protect the company from the legal risks of doing business, not to purge the world of dishonesty.

Magnus would never go to law school. He probably wouldn't even make it any further up the ladder in the police department.

A loser.

Which was why when a slim, well-dressed lawyer with whom

she had dealt the year before had bumped into her on the 'T' and asked her for a cup of coffee, she had said yes.

And why when he had called her to ask her out to dinner, she had also said yes.

His name was Richard Rubinstein. Cute, if a little too neat for her taste. Jewish, of course. She had googled him and discovered that he had just been made a partner of his downtown law firm. Which wasn't necessarily important, but did mean he wasn't a loser. And unlike almost everyone else she knew, he didn't know Magnus, had never even heard of Magnus, didn't know that she had had a boyfriend for the last three years.

She was going to enjoy herself. But not with Magnus's earrings.

She unfastened them, replaced them with a pair of simple pearls, and headed out into the warm evening.

From a car parked across the street, Diego watched her. Checked a photograph on his lap. It was the same girl all right.

By the way she was dressed she was going out for a while. That would give him plenty of time to sneak into the building and then into her apartment without being seen.

There was still the problem of the lone cop sitting in his patrol car right outside the building. But if Diego knew anything about cops the guy would be getting hungry.

Sure enough, once the woman disappeared down the street, the patrol car started up and pulled out.

Time enough to grab a pizza or a burger before the girl returned.

Diego got out of his car and crossed the street.

Magnus walked back to his new place in Thingholt from police headquarters. He needed the exercise and the fresh air. And you could at least say this for the air in Reykjavík, it was fresh.

His mind was buzzing with the day's events. It was way too early to tell, but according to Professor Moritz, there was nothing in the translation of *Gaukur's Saga* to suggest it was a forgery. The professor was clearly desperate to believe that the saga was authentic, but he admitted that if anyone could forge a saga, Agnar could.

Which raised another interesting possibility. Perhaps Steve Jubb had somehow discovered that the document Agnar was trying to sell him for so many millions of dollars was a fake, and he had killed him because of it.

Magnus still wasn't convinced that Ingileif was telling the whole truth. But she had seemed much more sincere when he had spoken to her that afternoon. And he had to admit that he found her mixture of vulnerability and determination attractive.

He smiled when he remembered Officer O'Malley's wise words of advice when Magnus started on the job: 'Just because a girl has a nice ass, it don't mean she's telling the truth.'

There was no doubt Ingileif had a nice ass.

Steve Jubb wasn't going to give them anything, especially if he was as guilty as Magnus thought he was. They needed to get on a plane to California and talk to Isildur. Threaten him with a conspiracy to commit murder rap and let him sing. Magnus could do that, he was sure he could.

'Magnus!'

He was in a little street not far from Katrín's house, quite high up the hill. He turned to see a woman he vaguely recognized walking hesitantly towards him. She was about forty, short reddish hair, a broad face with a wide smile. Although the hair was a different colour, her face reminded him strongly of his mother. Especially here, so close to the house in which he had grown up.

She stared at him closely, frowning. 'It is Magnus, isn't it? Magnus Ragnarsson?' She spoke in English.

'Sigurbjörg?' It was a bit of a guess on Magnus's part. Sigurbjörg was his cousin on his mother's side of the family. The side that he had hoped to avoid in Reykjavík.

The smile broadened. 'That's right. I *thought* it was you.'

'How did you recognize me?'

'I noticed you walking along the street. For a second I thought you were my father, except you're a whole lot younger and he's in Canada. Then I realized it must be you.'

'We haven't met for what, fifteen years?'

'About that. When you came to Iceland after your father's death.' Sigurbjörg must have seen Magnus grimace. 'Not an enjoyable trip for you, I seem to remember.'

'Not really.'

'I apologize for Grandpa. He behaved appallingly.'

Magnus nodded. 'I haven't been to Iceland since.'

'Until now?'

'Until now.'

'Let's get a cup of coffee and you can tell me all about it, eh?'

They walked down the hill to a funky café on Laugavegur. Sigurbjörg ordered a slice of carrot cake with her coffee, and they sat down next to an earnest man with glasses who was plugged in to his laptop.

'So you came back from Canada?' Magnus said. 'Weren't you in graduate school?'

'Yes. At McGill. Actually, I had just finished when I saw you. I stayed on in Iceland. Got a law degree: I'm a partner in one of the law firms here. I've also picked up a husband and three kids.'

'Congratulations.'

'Dad and Mom are still in Toronto. Retired, of course, now.'

Sigurbjörg's father, Magnus's Uncle Vilhjálmur, had emigrated to Canada in the seventies and worked as a civil engineer. Like Magnus, Sigurbjörg had been born in Iceland but spent most of her childhood in North America.

'And you? I had no idea you were in Iceland. How long have you been here?'

'Only two days,' Magnus replied. 'I stayed in Boston. Became a cop. Homicide detective. Then my chief got a call that the National Police Commissioner of Iceland wanted a body to come over here and help them. He picked me.'

'Picked you? You didn't want to come?'

'Let's say I had mixed feelings.'

'After your last visit?' Sigurbjörg nodded. 'That must have been rough. Especially just after your dad died.'

'It was. I was twenty and I had lost both parents. I wasn't handling it well – I was drinking. I felt alone. After eight years I had almost fit in the States and suddenly it felt like a foreign country again.'

'I know what you mean,' said Sigurbjörg. 'I was born in Canada, but my family are Icelanders and I live here. I sometimes think everywhere is a foreign country. It's not really fair, is it?'

Magnus glanced at Sigurbjörg. She was listening. And she was the one member of his family who had shown any sympathy during that awful couple of days. She was the one he had felt closest to, perhaps because of their common North American experiences, perhaps simply because she had treated him like a normal human being.

He wanted to talk.

'I needed some kind of family, other than just my brother Óli. All Icelanders do, you know that. It might be OK for Americans to live out their lives alone, but it wasn't for me. I had lived with Grandpa and Grandma for a few years and I guess I thought they would welcome me back after what had happened. I thought they'd have to. And then they rejected me. More than that, they made me feel like *I* was responsible for Mom's death.'

Magnus's face hardened. 'Grandpa said Dad was the most evil man he had ever known and he was glad he was dead. That brought back all the pain of those last years before Dad took me away with him to America. I was glad to leave and I swore I'd never come back.'

'And now you're here,' said Sigurbjörg. 'Do you like it?'

'Yes,' said Magnus. 'I guess I do.'

'Until you met me?'

Magnus smiled. 'I do remember how sympathetic you were to me, even if the rest of the family wasn't. Thanks for that. But do me a favour. Don't tell them I'm here.'

'Oh, they can't do anything to you now. Grandpa must be eighty-five, and Grandma's not much younger.'

'I doubt they've mellowed in their old age.'

Sigurbjörg smiled. 'No, they haven't.'

'And, from what I remember, the rest of the family was just as hostile.'

'They'll get over it,' said Sigurbjörg. 'Time has passed.'

'I don't see why they were so angry,' Magnus said. 'I know my father left Mom, but she made his life hell. Remember, she was an alcoholic.'

'But that's the whole point,' said Sigurbjörg. 'She only became an alcoholic after she discovered the affair. And it was from that that everything else followed. Your father leaving. Her losing her job. And then that awful car crash. Grandpa blames your father for all that, and he always will.'

A noisy group of two men and a woman sat down next to them and began to discuss a TV programme they had seen the night before.

Magnus ignored them. His face had gone blank.

'What? What is it, Magnus?'

Magnus didn't reply.

'Oh my God, you didn't know, did you? Nobody told you!'

'What affair?'

'Forget I said anything. Look, I've got to go.' She began to stand up.

Magnus reached out and grabbed her hand. 'What affair?' The anger surged through his voice.

Sigurbjörg sat down again and swallowed. 'Your father was having an affair with your mother's best friend. She found out about it, they had a god-awful row, she started drinking.'

'I don't believe you,' Magnus said.

Sigurbjörg shrugged.

'Are you sure it's true?'

'No, I'm not,' said Sigurbjörg. 'But I suspect it is. Look, there must have been other problems. I used to really like your mother,

130

especially before she started drinking, but she was always a bit neurotic. Given her parents, that's hardly surprising.'

'It is true,' Magnus said. 'You're right, it must be. I just find it hard to believe.'

'Hey, Magnus, I'm really sorry you heard this from me.' Sigurbjörg reached out and touched his hand. 'But I've got to go now. And I promise I won't tell the grandparents you're here.'

With that, she ran away.

Magnus stared at his coffee cup, still a quarter full. He needed a drink. A real drink.

It wasn't far to the bar he had drunk in the night before, the Grand Rokk. He ordered a Thule and one of the chasers all the other guys at the bar were drinking. It was some kind of kummel, sweet and strong, but OK if gulped down with the beer.

Sigurbjörg had just turned his world upside down. The whole story of his life, who he was, who his parents were, who was right and who was wrong, had just been inverted. His father had never blamed his mother for what had happened, but Magnus had.

She had driven away his father. She had ignored Magnus through drink and then abandoned him through death. Ragnar had heroically rescued his sons, until he had been cruelly murdered, possibly by the wicked stepmother.

That was the story of Magnus's childhood. That was what had made him who he was.

And now it was all false.

Another beer, another chaser.

For a moment, a calming moment, Magnus flirted with the idea that the affair was a fiction invented by his grandfather to justify his hatred of his father. One part of him wanted to go along with that idea, to try to live the rest of his life in denial.

But in his time in the police department Magnus had seen enough squalid family disintegrations to know that what

Sigurbjörg had told him was all too plausible. And it would explain the depth of his grandfather's hatred.

He had assumed that his father's refusal to blame his mother for the mess she had made of all their lives was nobility on his part. It wasn't. It was a recognition that he was partly responsible. Wholly responsible?

Magnus didn't know. He would never know. It was a typical family mess. Blame all over the place.

But it meant that his father was a different man than he thought he was. Not noble. An adulterer. Someone who abandoned his wife when she was at her weakest and her most vulnerable. Magnus had known all along that if he really thought about it he would have realized that his father must have started his affair with Kathleen, the woman who became his stepmother, while she was still married to someone else. So Magnus hadn't really thought about it.

It was true that Icelanders had a more relaxed view of adultery than the prudish Americans, but it was still wrong. Something that lesser mortals might dabble with, but not Ragnar.

What else had he done? What other flaws had he concealed from his sons? From his wife?

Magnus's beer was still half full, but his chaser was empty. He caught the shaven-headed barman's eye and tapped the glass. It was refilled.

He felt the liquid burn his throat. His brain was fuzzing over pleasantly. But Magnus was not going to stop, not for a long time. He was going to drink until it hurt.

That was how he drank in college, after his father died. He got wildly horribly drunk. And the following morning he would feel wretched. For him, that was half the reason why he drank, the feeling of self-destruction afterwards.

He had lost most of his friends then, other than a few hardened drinkers like himself. His professors were dismayed, he went from close to the top of his classes to scraping along the bottom. He almost got thrown out of the university. But no matter how hard he tried, he didn't quite manage to destroy his life totally.

Unlike his mother, of course. She had succeeded very well.

It was a girl who pulled him out of it, Erin. Her patience, her determination, her love, that made him realize not that he was destroying himself – he knew that already, that was the point after all – but that he didn't want to destroy himself.

After college she had gone her way, teaching in inner-city schools in Chicago, and he had gone his. He owed her a lot.

But now he wanted to drink to his mother. He raised his beer glass. 'To Margrét,' he said.

'Who's Margrét?' said a tall man in a black leather jacket, on the stool next to him.

'Margrét's my mother.'

'That's nice,' said the man, with a slur. He raised his beer. 'To Margrét.' He put down his glass. He nodded towards the beer in front of Magnus. 'Bad day?'

Magnus nodded. 'You could say that.'

'You know they say that drink doesn't solve anything?' the man said.

Magnus nodded.

'That's balls.' The man laughed and raised his glass.

Magnus noticed for the first time that chess sets were glued upside-down to the ceiling. Huh. That was kind of cool.

He looked around the bar. The patrons were all ages and sizes. They carried on a desultory conversation interrupted with bursts of chuckles and wry laughter. Many were unsteady on their feet and inaccurate with their gestures and back-slapping. At one end of the bar two college-age American girls were perched on stools, entertaining a succession of loquacious Icelanders. At the other end a thin man with grey hair sticking out under a flat cap suddenly burst into a rendition of a tune from Porgy and Bess in a mellifluous baritone. '*Summertime – and the livin' is ea-easy ...*'

Good singers, these Icelanders.

Another beer. Another chaser. The anger dissipated. He began to relax. He struck up conversations with the men on either side. With the American girls, although he put on a heavy Icelandic accent for their benefit. He thought that was pretty funny. In fact, he thought he was pretty funny. He played a game of chess and lost.

Another beer. Another chaser. Two chasers. How many chasers did that make? How many beers? No idea.

Eventually it was time to go home. Magnus lifted himself off his stool and bade an emotional goodbye to his new buddies. The room lurched wildly. The guy with the flat cap briefly became two guys with flat caps, before resolving himself into a single individual again.

Boy, was Magnus drunk. Drunker than he had been for a long time. But it felt good.

He strode out of the bar and straightened up in the cold night air. It was way past midnight. The sky was clear, stars twinkled icily above him. A three-quarter moon was reflected in the bay below. He took a deep breath.

He liked Reykjavík. It was an innocent little town, and he was glad of that. He would do his part to keep it that way.

He was proud to be one of Reykjavík's finest.

There was no one on the streets. The contrast between a Sunday and a Saturday night in Reykjavík was marked. But as he headed up the hill towards home, Magnus spotted a cluster of three men in an alley. The tableau was so familiar.

Drugs.

Magnus scowled. Low-lifes in Toytown.

He would sort them out. 'Hey!' he shouted, and headed down the alley. 'Hey! What are you doing?'

The guy selling the drugs was small and dark, possibly not even Icelandic. The guy doing the buying, was taller, wiry, with a woolly hat. He had a friend, a great big Nordic block with short blonde hair and a tiny little blonde beard. Bigger even than Magnus, and showing off bulging biceps under a black T-shirt on this cold night.

'What has it got to do with you?' said the drug pusher. He said it in English, because Magnus had hailed him in English.

'Give that to me,' said Magnus, holding out his hand and swaying. 'I'm a cop.'

'Piss off,' said the pusher.

Magnus lunged at him. The guy ducked and struck him in the chest. But there was no power in it and Magnus laid him out with a single blow to the jaw. The Nordic hulk grabbed Magnus and tried to drag him down to the floor, but Magnus shook him off. For a few moments the adrenaline overcame the alcohol, and Magnus landed two good blows, before getting an arm lock on the big guy. 'You're under arrest!' he shouted, still in English.

The pusher was on the ground, moaning. The thin guy with the woolly hat started running.

'Get the hell off me,' growled the hulk in Icelandic.

He swung round and crashed backwards into the wall, crushing Magnus. Magnus let go. The big guy turned and struck Magnus twice, once in the head and once in the stomach, but Magnus dodged the third blow and hit him with an uppercut.

The big guy reeled. Another crunching punch from Magnus and he went down.

Magnus stared at the pusher who was pulling himself to his feet. 'You're under arrest too.'

But then the alley started to sway and spin. The blow to his stomach did its stuff, and Magnus doubled up to retch. He tried to stand up straight, but he couldn't. He swayed. Staggered.

The little guy was about to run, when he saw the state that Magnus was in. He laughed and head-butted him in the face.

Magnus dropped.

He lay on the cold tarmac for a while. Seconds? Minutes? He didn't know.

He heard sirens. Good. Help.

Rough hands picked him up. He tried to focus on the face in front of him. It was a cop wearing the uniform of the Reykjavík Metropolitan Police.

'They went that way,' said Magnus, in English. Waving indeterminately.

'Come with us,' said the cop and pulled Magnus over to the waiting car, with its lights flashing.

'I'm a police officer,' said Magnus. 'Look, let me show you my badge.' All this still in English.

The patrolman waited while Magnus pulled out his Commonwealth of Massachusetts driver's licence from his wallet.

'Come on,' said the cop.

Then Magnus threw up all over the patrolman's shoes.

CHAPTER SIXTEEN

DIEGO TURNED ON the light. The two naked bodies entwined on top of the bed froze, but only for an instant.

Then the man leaped off the woman, twisted and sat up, all in one athletic movement. The woman opened her mouth to scream, but stopped when she saw the gun.

Fortunately, there was no way that either of them could know that there was only one bullet in the cylinder of the revolver.

Diego chuckled.

It was pretty funny. He had positioned himself in an armchair in the living room, gun drawn, out of line of sight of the door. He'd waited there happily all evening. Then *two* people had come in.

Diego decided to wait. Surprise them when they turned around. But he'd never got the chance!

The guy jumped the girl right away. And she seemed happy with that. For a moment it looked as if Diego was going to get a show right there on the living room floor, but then the woman led the guy into the bedroom. And neither of them even saw him!

He decided to wait until they had taken off whatever clothes they were going to take off. Naked was good, as far as he was concerned. Then he slipped through the open door into the bedroom, and watched the action in the dim glow of the streetlights outside for a few seconds.

Now they were both blinking in the glare of the electric light.

'You!' Diego jabbed the revolver at the man. 'In the bathroom!

Now! And if I hear a sound I'll come right in there and pump your skinny ass full of bullets.'

The guy needed no more prompting. He was out of the bed and in the bathroom with the door shut in an instant.

He moved over towards the woman. Colby.

Nice body. A bit thin, but nice firm tits.

She saw where he was looking. 'Do what you want,' she said. 'Just do it.'

'Hey, all I want is a little talk,' said Diego. 'I ain't gonna touch you, as long as you talk to me.'

Colby swallowed, her eyes wide.

In a swift movement, Diego grabbed her hair with one hand and jammed the revolver in her mouth with the other. 'Where's Magnus?'

'Who?' The woman was barely audible.

'Magnus Jonson. Your boyfriend.' He smiled and glanced at the bathroom. 'Or one of your boyfriends. Looks like you're the kind of girl that needs several men to keep you happy.'

'I ... I don't know.'

Diego pulled the trigger. Click.

A strangled sob from Colby.

Diego explained the rules of his version of the Russian roulette game. He just loved that bit, loved watching the eyes of his victims. The fear. The uncertainty. Perfect.

'OK. I'll ask you again. Where is Magnus?'

'I don't know,' said Colby. 'I swear it. He said he was going away somewhere and he couldn't tell me where.'

'Did you guess?'

Colby shook her head.

Diego spotted weakness. 'You guessed, didn't you?'

'N-no. No, I swear I didn't.'

'Thing is, I ain't believing you.'

He pulled the trigger again.

Click.

'Oh, God.' Colby slumped backwards, trying to sob with the barrel of a gun crammed into her mouth.

Diego loved this game. 'You guessed. OK. So now I'm gonna guess,' said Diego. 'Is he in state?'

Colby hesitated and then shook her head.

'All right. In the country then?'

'No.'

'We talking Mexico?'

A shake of the head.

'Canada?'

Another shake.

Diego was rather enjoying this. 'Is it hot or cold?'

No answer.

He squeezed the trigger.

Click.

'Cold. It's somewhere cold.'

'Good girl. But I give up now. My geography ain't that good. Where's he at?'

Another click. The game wasn't strictly fair. Although Colby didn't know which chamber the bullet was in, Diego knew it was in the last. That's how he liked to play the game. It really would be too bad to blow her brains out before he had gotten the answer he wanted.

'OK. OK. He's in Sweden. I don't know where in Sweden. Stockholm, I guess. It's Sweden.'

'You're just a thick-headed Icelandic drunk, aren't you?'

With difficulty Magnus focused on the red face of the National Police Commissioner in front of him. His mouth was dry, his head was pounding, his stomach growling.

'I'm sorry, sir.' He would call his superior officer 'sir'. Screw Icelandic etiquette.

'Do you do this often? Is this a once-a-week thing for you? Or perhaps you hit the bottle every day? I didn't read anything about this on your file. You broke a few rules from time to time, but you never showed up for duty intoxicated.'

'No, sir. It's been years since I got that drunk.'

'Then why did you do it?'

'I don't know,' Magnus said. 'I got some bad news. Personal news. It won't happen again.'

'It had better not,' said the Commissioner. 'I have an important role in mind for you, but that role demands that my officers should respect you. Within three days you have made yourself a laughing stock.'

The night was a blur, but Magnus could remember the laughter. The desk sergeant had heard about the new hot-shot detective over from America and had thought it highly amusing that this man was now in his drunk tank. As had the patrolmen who had arrested him. And the other uniformed officers coming off duty. And the next shift coming on.

They had had the kindness to drive him back to his house. He had passed out in the car, but vaguely remembered Katrín getting his clothes off and putting him to bed.

He had woken up a few hours later with his head exploding, his bladder full and his mouth dry. He crawled back into the police station at about ten o'clock. The rest of the detectives grinned and whispered as he sat at his desk. Within a minute Baldur had told him with a thin smile that the Big Salmon wanted to see him.

'I am very sorry I have let you down, Commissioner,' Magnus repeated. 'I do appreciate what you have done for me here, and I am sure I can help.'

The Commissioner grunted. 'Thorkell seems to think you have made a good start. How is the Agnar Haraldsson case going? I heard about the discovery of the saga. Is it genuine?'

'Possibly, but we don't know yet for sure. It looks like the Brit Steve Jubb was trying to buy it from Agnar. There was a problem, they had a dispute, and Jubb killed him.'

'Jubb still isn't talking?'

'Not yet. But there's this guy Lawrence Feldman who goes by the Internet alias of Isildur, who seems to have financed the deal.

We know where he lives. If I put some pressure on him, I'm sure he'll talk.'

'So why don't you?'

'He's in California. Baldur won't authorize it.'

The Commissioner nodded. 'Can you work today, or do you need to take the day off sick?'

Magnus suspected that this wasn't a kind offer from a concerned superior. It was a direct question of his commitment.

'I can work today.'

'Good. And don't let me down again. Or else I will send you straight back to Boston and I don't care who is after you.'

Ingileif watched as Professor Moritz carefully carried the envelope containing the old scraps of vellum to his car outside while a female colleague took the bigger seventeenth-century volume. A couple of uniformed police officers and the young detective called Árni danced around in attendance.

She had expected to feel relief. She felt nothing of the kind. She was drowning, drowning beneath a wave of guilt.

The secret that her family had kept for so many generations, hundreds and hundreds of years, was disappearing out of the door. It had been an astounding achievement to keep it so quiet for so long. She could imagine her ancestors, fathers and eldest sons, huddled over a peat fire in their simple turf-roofed farmhouse, reading the saga over and over to each other during the long winter nights. It must have been difficult keeping its existence from extended family, neighbours, in-laws. But they had succeeded. And they hadn't sold out. A farmer's life in Iceland during the last three centuries was extremely precarious. Even when they had endured unimaginable poverty and starvation, they hadn't taken the easy way. They had needed the money more than her.

What right did she have to cash it in now?

Her brother, Pétur, had spoken the truth when he had urged her not to sell. And he hated the saga even more than she did.

She looked around the gallery. The objects on display – the vases, the fish-skin bags, the candle-holders, the lavascapes – were truly beautiful. But did they matter so much?

The police said that the saga would be needed for evidence. They would keep its existence quiet while the investigation was still under way. But eventually everyone would know. Not just Icelanders, but the whole world. Tolkien fans from America, England, the rest of Europe would want to find out everything about the document. Every corner of the secret would be raised to the glare of global publicity.

Eventually, she would probably be allowed to sell the saga. In the open, under the glare of publicity, she would no doubt get a handsome price, if the Icelandic government didn't somehow manage to confiscate it from her. If she could just keep the gallery going for a few months longer, it might survive.

Until Agnar's death, keeping the gallery open was the most important thing in her life. Now she appreciated how wrong she was.

The gallery was going bust because she had made a poor business judgment. The *kreppa* made matters worse, but she should never have trusted Nordidea. She was to blame and she should have taken the consequences.

Outside, the professor and the police climbed into their cars and drove off. Ingileif felt trapped in the tiny gallery. She grabbed her bag, switched off the light and locked up. So what if she lost a sale or two that morning?

She walked down the hill, her mind in incoherent turmoil. She soon reached the bay, and walked along the bike path which ran along the shore. She headed east, towards the solid block of Mount Esja, its top smothered in cloud. The breeze skipping in from across the water chilled her face. The sounds of Reykjavík traffic merged with the cries of seagulls. A pair of ducks paddled in circles a few yards out from the red volcanic pumice that served as a sea wall.

She felt so alone. Her mother had died a few months before, her father when she was twelve. Birna, her sister, wouldn't care or understand. She would be sympathetic for a few minutes, but she was too self-absorbed, stuck in her nice house and her bad marriage and her bottles of vodka. She had never been interested in *Gaukur's Saga*, and after their father died she had picked up their mother's hostility to the family legend. She had told Ingileif she couldn't care less what Ingileif did with it.

Ingileif knew she should speak to Pétur, but she couldn't bring herself to do it. He had hated the saga with a passion for what he thought it had done to their father. Yet, even he had believed that it would be wrong to sell. She had assured him that Agnar would be able to do a deal while keeping the secret safe, and only then had Pétur reluctantly agreed. He would be angry with her now, and justifiably so. Not much sympathy there.

He must have read about Agnar's murder in the papers, but he hadn't been in touch with her yet. Thank God.

It was ironic. She had been determined not to let her father's death screw her up like it had screwed up the other members of her family. She was the sane, down-to-earth one, or so she thought.

And now poor Aggi had been murdered. Foolishly she had tried to hide the existence of the saga from the police. As a plan, that was never going to work. And even now she was hiding something.

She glanced down at her bag. Where she had slipped the envelope just before the police came to take away the saga. The *other* envelope.

She recalled the big red-haired detective with the slight American accent. He was trying to catch the man who had murdered Agnar, and she had some information that would be certain to help him. It was far too late to try to keep it quiet, the police would find out in the end. The betrayal had been committed, the mistake had been made, the consequences were playing themselves out. There was nothing she could do to put the saga back in its safe.

She stopped in front of the Höfdi House, the elegant white-timbered mansion where Gorbachev had met Reagan when she was six years old.

She dug the detective's number out of her purse, and punched it into her mobile phone.

Colby was waiting on the sidewalk outside the bank when it opened. Walked straight in to the cashier, first in line, and withdrew twelve thousand dollars in cash. Then she drove to an outdoor equipment store and bought camping gear.

When the thug with the gun had left her apartment she had been too scared to scream. Richard hadn't been any help: he had scurried out of the bathroom muttering how his legal career was too important to be caught up with criminals, and she should rethink her friendships. She had watched dully as he had scrambled to get into his clothes and left her. He forgot his jacket.

Tough.

She was glad she hadn't told the thug about Iceland. It had been a close call, she had been so scared that she had almost given it away, but the change to Sweden at the last minute was inspired. Magnus had told her that he used to have the nickname 'Swede', and that had stuck in her brain.

The thug had believed her. She was sure of it.

She hoped it would take him and his friends some time to realize their mistake, but she wasn't going to hang around. She certainly wasn't going anywhere near Magnus. Now she took Magnus's warnings seriously. She wasn't taking any risks with credit cards, or hotels or friends. No one would know where she was.

She was going to disappear.

From the camp shop she went to the supermarket. Then, with the trunk full of supplies, she drove west. Her plan was eventually to head north, to Maine or New Hampshire or somewhere, and to lose herself in the wilderness. But first she had something to do. She pulled off the highway in the suburb of Wellesley. She found an Internet café, grabbed a cup of coffee.

The first e-mail was to her boss, telling him that she was not going to be at work and she couldn't explain why, but he shouldn't worry. The second was to her mother, saying more or less the same thing. There was no way to phrase it so that her mother wouldn't drive herself demented with panic, so Colby didn't even try.

The third was to Magnus.

CHAPTER SEVENTEEN

IT WAS NO more than a ten-minute walk from police headquarters to the Höfdi House, where Ingileif had asked to meet Magnus. He was feeling a little better after the sausage he had picked up from the coffee shop in the bus station on his way back from the Commissioner's office, but he still needed to do all he could to clear his head.

He felt so stupid. His apology to the National Police Commissioner had been sincere; he appreciated all the man had done for him, and Magnus had let him down. His fellow detectives had initially appeared to be in awe of him; now they would just think he was a joke. Not a good start.

He was also scared. Alcoholism ran in families. If there was a gene for it, he suspected that he had it. It had been a very close call in college. And learning about his father's infidelity had disturbed something deep inside him. Even now, with his ears ringing with the consequences of his stupidity, part of him just wanted to take a detour to the Grand Rokk and buy a beer. And then another. Of course it would screw everything up. But that was why he wanted to do it.

This was dangerous. Somehow he had to cram what Sigurbjörg had told him back in its box.

Throwing himself into the Agnar case would help. He wondered what it was that Ingileif wanted to speak to him about. She had sounded tense on the phone.

He didn't trust her. The more he thought about it, the more

likely it seemed that the saga was a forgery drawn up by Agnar. Ingileif was his accomplice, to add authenticity. Their relationship had been very close, perhaps it still was very close, the ballet-dancing literature student notwithstanding.

The Höfdi House stood all alone in a grassy square between two busy roads that ran along the shore. A solitary figure was perched on a low wall beside the squat white building.

'Thank you for coming,' Ingileif said.

'No problem,' said Magnus. 'That's why I gave you my number.'

He sat next to Ingileif on the wall. They were facing the bay. A steady breeze rolled small clouds through the pale blue sky, their shadows skittering over the sparkling grey water. In the far distance Magnus could just make out the glacier of Snaefellsnes, a white blur floating above the sea.

Ingileif was tense, sitting bolt upright on the wall, shoulders back, forehead knitted in a frown accentuating the nick in her eyebrow. She looked like so many other girls in Reykjavík, slim, blonde with high cheekbones. But there was something about her that set her apart, a determination, a purposefulness, a sense that despite the doubts and worries that were obviously troubling her, she knew what she wanted and was going to get it, that Magnus found appealing. She seemed to be debating with herself whether or not to tell him something.

He sat in silence. Waiting. He saw that there was also a small scar on her left cheek. He hadn't noticed that before.

Eventually she spoke. Someone had to. 'You know this place is haunted?'

'The Höfdi House?' Magnus looked over his shoulder at the elegant white building.

'Yes. The ghost is a young girl who poisoned herself after she was convicted of incest with her brother. She scared the wits out of the people who used to live here.'

'Icelanders have got to learn to be a little braver about ghosts,' said Magnus.

'Not just Icelanders. It used to be the British consulate. The consul was so terrified that he demanded that the British Foreign Ministry allow him to move the consulate to another address. Apparently she keeps turning the lights on and off.' Ingileif sighed. 'I feel quite sorry for her.'

Magnus thought he detected a quiver in her voice. Odd. Most ghosts had had a tough time in life, but still. 'Is that what you wanted to speak to me about?' he asked. 'You want me to check it out? All the lights seem to be off at the moment.'

'Oh, no,' she replied, smiling weakly. 'I just wanted to find out how the investigation was going.'

'We're making progress,' Magnus said. 'We need to track down Steve Jubb's accomplice. And we haven't verified the authenticity of the saga yet.'

'Oh, it's authentic.'

'Is it?' said Magnus. 'Or is it an elaborate hoax dreamed up by Agnar? Is that why he was killed? Steve Jubb found out he was being taken for a ride?'

Ingileif laughed. The tension seemed to flow from her body. Magnus waited for her to finish.

'Well?' he said.

'I'd love you to be right,' Ingileif said. 'And I can see why you might think that. But, of course, I *know* it's genuine. It has over-shadowed my whole life, and that of every member of my family for generations.'

'So you say.'

'Don't you believe me?'

'Not really,' Magnus said. 'You don't have a great track record for telling me the truth.'

The smile disappeared. Ingileif sighed. 'I don't, do I? And I can see how from your point of view you have to consider the possibility that it's a forgery. But your lab guys will do tests on it, carbon-14 or whatever, and they'll tell you how old the vellum is. And the seventeenth-century copy.'

'Maybe,' said Magnus.

Ingileif's grey eyes looked straight at his. For a moment Magnus found it unsettling, but he held her gaze. 'I want to show you something,' she said.

She rummaged in her bag and pulled out a yellowing envelope.

She handed it to Magnus. A British stamp, same king as last time, and the same handwriting.

'This is the reason I asked you to meet me. I should have shown it to you yesterday, but I didn't.'

Magnus opened the envelope. Inside was a sheet of notepaper.

Merton College
Oxford

12 October 1948

Dear Ísildarson

Thank you for your extraordinary letter. What an astonishing tale! The part I found the most amazing was the inscription 'The Ring of Andvari' in runes. One never knows with the Icelandic sagas. They are so realistic, yet the scholarly fashion is to dismiss them as fiction. Yet here is the very ring, at least a thousand years old, that appears in Gaukur's Saga! After the discovery of his farm buried under all that ash, the saga has much more credence than I originally gave it.

I would have loved the opportunity to see the ring, to hold it, to touch it. But I think you were absolutely right to return it to its hiding place. Either that or take it to the mouth of Mount Hekla yourself and toss it in! It would be altogether wrong to hold up the evil magic of the ring to scientific archaeological testing. And please do not worry, I will not mention your discovery to anyone.

I have at last brought the Lord of the Rings to its conclusion after 10 years of toil. It is a vast sprawling book, which will probably run to at least 1200 pages, and one of which I am very proud. It will be difficult to produce in these hard times

when paper is so scarce, but my publishers remain enthusi-
astic. When it is eventually published, as I hope it will be, I
will be sure to send you a copy.

With best wishes,
Yours sincerely,

J.R.R. Tolkien

'This says your grandfather found the ring,' Magnus said.

Ingileif nodded. 'It does.'

Magnus shook his head. 'It's incredible.'

Ingileif sighed. 'No it's not. It explains everything.'

'Explains what, exactly?'

'My father's obsession. How he died.'

'What do you mean?'

Ingileif stared out to sea. Magnus watched her face closely as she wrestled with her emotions. Then she turned to Magnus, moisture in the corners of his eyes. 'I think I told you my father died when I was about twelve?'

'Yes.'

'He was looking for the ring. It always seemed absurd to me that an educated man should be so convinced that it still existed. But of course he *knew*. His own father must have told him.'

'But not told him exactly where it was hidden?'

'Precisely. My father started searching right after my grand-father died. My guess is that Grandpa had forbidden him to look for it. Dad used to spend days scouring the area around the Thjórsá Valley in all weathers. And then one day he never came back.'

Ingileif bit her lip.

'When did you find this letter?' Magnus asked.

'Very recently. After I had approached Agnar. He had already seen the first letter from Tolkien, the one written in 1938, which I showed you yesterday. But he asked me if I could find any more evidence, so I went back to Flúdir and looked through my father's papers. There was a bundle of letters from Tolkien to Grandpa, and this was one of them.'

'Did you tell Agnar?'

'Yes.'

'I bet he was excited.'

'He drove straight over to Flúdir to see me. And the letter.'

Magnus took out his notebook. 'What day was that?'

'It was Sunday last week.' She did a quick mental calculation. 'The nineteenth.'

'Four days before he was killed,' said Magnus. He remembered Agnar's e-mail to Steve Jubb saying that he had found something else. And Jubb's text message to Isildur suggesting more or less the same thing. Something valuable. Could it have been the ring?

'Do you have any idea where the ring is?'

Ingileif shook her head. 'No. There is that part in the saga about the ring being hidden beneath the head of a hound. There are all kinds of strangely shaped outcrops of lava that could be hounds when looked at from certain directions. That was what my father was looking for. Presumably my grandfather found the cave and my father didn't.'

'What about Agnar? Did he have any idea where it might be?'

Ingileif shook her head. 'No. He asked me, of course. He was very aggressive about it. I more or less threw him out.'

'So, as far as you know, the ring is still hidden in a small cave somewhere?'

'I think so,' said Ingileif. 'You still don't believe me, do you?'

Magnus examined the upright precise handwriting. It looked real. But of course if it had been written by a careful forger it would look real. He glanced up at Ingileif. She seemed to be telling the truth, unlike her previous two conversations with him when she had been lying badly. Of course she could have feigned her earlier awkwardness to lull him into thinking she was telling the truth this time, but she would have to be a consummate actress to pull that off. And very cunning.

Could he believe that the ring in *Gaukur's Saga* had really survived?

It was tempting. There was great scholarly debate about how historically accurate Iceland's sagas really were. Most of the people and many of the events mentioned in them had really existed, but then there were also passages that were obviously pure invention. Whenever Magnus read them, the matter-of-fact style and the realistic characters lulled him into suspending disbelief until he felt medieval Iceland was almost close enough to touch.

The homicide detective in him resisted the temptation. First of all, Magnus couldn't even be sure that the saga itself was authentic. And even if it was, then the ring could be fictional. And even if a gold ring had existed, it would probably be either buried under tons of ash, or long since have been found and sold by a poor shepherd. The whole thing was unlikely. Highly unlikely. But speculation was pointless. It didn't really matter what Magnus thought: what mattered was what Agnar believed, and Steve Jubb and Isildur.

For if a true *Lord of the Rings* fanatic thought he had a chance of getting his hands on the ring, the One Ring, then he might be tempted to kill for it.

'I don't know what I think,' said Magnus. 'But thank you for telling me. Eventually.'

Ingileif shrugged.

'Of course, it would have been better if you had come out with all this up front.'

Ingileif sighed. 'It would have been better if I had never let the damn saga out of my safe in the first place.'

CHAPTER EIGHTEEN

THE CANTEEN WAS almost full. Officer Pattie Lenahan looked around for someone she knew, and saw Shannon Kraychyk from Traffic, sitting alone at the table in the back of the room next to a bunch of civilian geeks from the computer department. She carried her tray over.

'How you doin', Shannon?'

'I'm doin' good. Other than my dumb-ass sergeant giving me a hard time because we're behind on our quota for this month. Like there's anything I can do about it! What am I supposed to do if Boston's citizens suddenly decide they're all gonna respect the speed limit?'

Pattie and Shannon traded grumbles happily for a while until Shannon excused herself and left Pattie alone with the rest of her chef's salad.

The geeks were talking about a case the previous year. Pattie remembered it. The kidnapping of a woman in Brookline by her next door neighbour; it had dominated the newspapers and the station gossip for a couple of weeks.

'I haven't seen Jonson around here recently,' one of them said.

'Haven't you heard? He's been disappeared. He's a witness on the Lenahan case.'

'You mean Witness Protection Programme?'

'I guess.'

'I heard from him the other day.' Pattie glanced quickly at the speaker. A Chinese guy, small, talked real fast. 'Sent me an e-mail out of the blue. He wanted me to check out an e-mail header for him, same as in the Brookline case.'

'Did you nail it?'

'Yeah. It was nowhere near as difficult. Some guy in California. He made no real attempt to hide the IP.'

The conversation moved on and Pattie finished her salad. She got herself a cup of coffee and took it back to the squad room.

Uncle Sean's arrest had caused a big stir in her family. It was hardly surprising, everyone in her family were cops, had been for three generations, and none of them was a bad one, especially not Uncle Sean. That was the problem with the department, it was all bound up in rules and regulations, in cops snooping on cops. Cops like Magnus Jonson.

Pattie wasn't entirely sure she agreed with the family consensus. It seemed to her that Uncle Sean was accused of something pretty serious. And she had never really trusted him: he was just a little too glib, too flaky. She didn't know Magnus Jonson; but what she did know was that you didn't rat out a fellow cop. Ever.

Should she tell her father what she had heard? He, at least, was a straight guy. He'd know what to do, whether to tell anyone else.

And besides, if she didn't tell him and he ever found out, he would have her hide.

Better tell him.

The noise was appalling. Magnus and Árni were sitting at the back of a long low room, deep underground, listening to a group of teenage no-hopers called Shrink Wrapped. They were playing a bizarre mixture of reggae and rap, with their own Icelandic twist. Original, perhaps, but painful. Especially in combination with Magnus's malingering hangover. He had thought that food and fresh air had taken care of his headache, but now it was back with a vengeance.

Magnus had dutifully returned to the station to fill Baldur in on his interview with Ingileif. Baldur shared Magnus's scepticism that the ring in the saga did really exist, but he understood his point that the promise that it might would fire up Steve Jubb and the modern-day Isildur, as well as Agnar.

Baldur had sent one of his detectives to Yorkshire to search Steve Jubb's house and computer, although they were having trouble getting a search warrant from the British authorities. A hot-shot criminal lawyer from London had popped up from nowhere to raise all kinds of objections.

Another sign that there was big money somewhere in the background of this case.

'This your kind of music, Árni?' Magnus asked.

Árni looked at him with contempt. Magnus was relieved. At least the boy had some taste. He knew very little about Icelandic bands himself, but had recently formed a fondness for the ethereal Sigur Rós. A far cry from this bunch.

The band stopped. Silence, wonderful silence.

Pétur Ásgrímsson stood up from his chair in the middle of the floor and took a few paces towards the band. 'Thanks, but no thanks,' he said.

There were cries of protest from the five blond teenage rap'n'reggae stars. 'Come back next year, when you have refined things a little,' he said. 'And lose the drummer.'

He turned towards his visitors and pulled up one of the chairs lining the back of the room. He was a tall, imposing figure with a spare frame but square shoulders, and Ingileif's high cheekbones. His cranium, shaved smooth, bulged above his long thin face. His grey eyes were hard and intelligent, swiftly assessing the two policemen.

'You've come to speak to me about Agnar Haraldsson, I take it?'

'Are you surprised?' Magnus asked.

'I thought you would have been here earlier.'

There was a hint of rebuke in the comment, an accusation that they were a little slow.

'We would have been if your sister had only told us the full story up front. Or if you had contacted us yourself.'

Pétur raised his fair eyebrows. 'What would I have to say?'

'You knew that Ingileif was trying to sell *Gaukur's Saga* through Agnar?'

Pétur nodded. 'Much against my will.'

'Did you ever meet him?'

'No. Or at least not recently. I think I might have bumped into him a couple of times when Ingileif was a student. But not since then. I was quite clear that I would play no part in the negotiations over the saga.'

'But you would take your share of the sale proceeds?' Árni asked.

'Yes,' said Pétur simply. He looked around his nightclub. 'Times are tough. The banks are getting difficult. Like everyone else, I borrowed too much.'

'Is this your only club?' They were in the depths of Neon, on Austurstraeti, a short shopping street in the centre of town.

'No,' Pétur replied. 'This is my third. I started with Theme on Laugavegur.'

'Sorry, I don't know it,' said Magnus. 'I've been away from Iceland a long time.'

'I thought from your accent you were American,' Pétur said. 'It was the most popular place in Reykjavík a few years ago. I spent a few years in London on the edges of the music scene there, learning the trade you could say, but when Reykjavík was setting itself up as the Ibiza of the north I thought I had better come home. Theme was just a small café, but I squeezed in a dance floor and got lucky. It became *the* place to go, and because it was so small, everyone had to queue outside. There's no one happier than a seventeen-year-old Icelandic girl wearing a crop top, shivering outside a club at three o'clock in the morning in the snow.'

'What happened to it?' Magnus asked.

'It's still going, but it's much less popular than it used to be. I saw that coming, so I opened Soho, and now Neon.' Pétur smiled. 'This town is fickle. You have to stay one step ahead or you get trampled.'

Pétur exuded confidence. *He* wasn't going to get trampled.

'Have you read *Gaukur's Saga?*' Magnus asked.

'Read it? I think I know it off by heart. I certainly used to.'

'Your sister said you have no interest in it.'

Pétur smiled. 'That's certainly true now. But not when I was a boy. My father and grandfather were obsessed, and they passed that obsession on to me. Have you read it?'

Magnus and Árni nodded.

'I adored my grandfather, and I loved the stories he told me about Ísildur and Gaukur and Ásgrímur from when I was little. I was groomed to be the keeper of the saga, you see, the keeper of the secret. And it wasn't just *Gaukur's Saga* that interested me, it was all the others.'

'Did you know that your grandfather found the ring?' Magnus asked.

Pétur frowned. 'My sister told you about that? I didn't know she even knew about it.'

Magnus nodded. 'She turned up a letter from Tolkien to your grandfather Högni, which mentioned that Högni had found the ring.'

'And replaced it,' said Pétur. 'He put it back, you know.'

'Yes, the letter said that too.' Magnus studied Pétur. There was no doubt that the mention of the ring had disconcerted him. 'So why aren't you still obsessed with the saga?'

Pétur took a deep breath. 'My father and I argued about it, or about the ring, just before he died. You see my grandfather didn't trust my father after he had revealed *Gaukur's Saga* to the whole family. He wasn't supposed to do that, it was supposed to be just me, the eldest son.'

A hint of bitterness touched Pétur's voice. 'So Grandfather decided to tell me of the existence of the ring a few months before *he* died. He impressed upon me the importance of leaving the ring undisturbed. He scared the living daylights out of me. He persuaded me that if I, or my father, were to find the ring and take it from its hiding place then a terrible evil would be unleashed throughout the whole world.'

'What kind of evil?' Magnus asked.

'I don't know. He wasn't specific. In my imagination it was some kind of nuclear war. I had just read *On the Beach* by Nevil Shute – you know, the story about survivors of a nuclear war in Australia – and it scared me witless. But the day after my grandfather died, my father set out on an expedition to Thjórsárdalur to find the ring. I was furious. I told him he shouldn't go, but he wouldn't listen.'

'You didn't go with him?'

'No. I was away at high school in Reykjavík. But I wouldn't have gone in any case. My father was close friends with the local pastor. As soon as my grandfather died, my father told him all about *Gaukur's Saga*, and the ring. It was something else I was upset about: letting the secret out to someone outside the family. The pastor was an expert on folk legends and the two of them discussed where the ring might be. So they went off on expeditions together.

'My mother didn't like them going off, either. She thought all this Ísildur and Gaukur and magic ring stuff was very weird. I honestly don't think my father told her anything about it until after they were married and it was too late.'

He smiled. 'Of course they never found it.'

'Do you believe it exists?' Árni asked, wide eyed.

'I did then,' Pétur said. 'I'm not at all sure now.' A note of anger crept into his voice. 'I don't think about the ring or the damned saga at all now. My stupid father went off into the hills when a snowstorm was forecast and blundered over a cliff. Gaukur and his ring did that. It didn't need to exist to kill him.'

'What about your sister, Ingileif?' Magnus asked. 'Was she involved in all this?'

'No,' said Pétur. 'She knew about the saga, of course, but not about the ring.'

'Do you see much of her?'

'Now and again. After my father died I drifted away from the family. Ran away, more like. I couldn't handle it. All the ring stuff;

it seemed to me that it had killed him. And I felt that I should have stopped him from looking for the ring, like my grandfather told me to. Of course, there was nothing I could do, I was only fifteen, but at that age you sometimes think you have more power than you really do.

'I dropped out of high school, went to London. Then, after I came back, I started to see Ingileif a bit. She was angry with me: she thought I had abandoned our mother.' Pétur grimaced. 'I guess she was right.'

'Do you know if she was still involved with Agnar?'

'I doubt it very much,' Pétur said. 'But he was the natural person for her to go to when she wanted to sell the saga.' His eyes narrowed. 'You don't suspect her of killing him, do you?'

Magnus shrugged. 'We are keeping an open mind. She wasn't altogether straight with us when we first spoke to her.'

'She was just trying to cover up her mistake. She should never have tried to sell the saga, and she knew it. But Ingileif is honest through and through. It's inconceivable she killed anyone; she's incapable of it. I'm actually very fond of her, always have been. She'd do anything for her friends or her family. She was the one of the three of us who looked after Mum at the end, when she was dying of cancer. You know the gallery is in trouble?'

Magnus nodded.

'Well, that's why she needed the money from the saga. To pay out her partners. She blames herself. I told her not to worry too much about it; it's business. A venture goes wrong, you drop it, pick yourself up, and go on to something else. But she doesn't think that way. Everyone is going bust in Iceland these days.'

The door to the club opened and three more musicians came in, lugging big bags of musical instruments and electronics. This lot were a little older, a little hairier.

'I'll be with you in a minute,' Pétur said to them. Then, turning back to Magnus and Árni, 'Ingileif's had a tough life. First her father, then her stepfather, then her mother, all on top of losing her business.'

'Stepfather?' Magnus asked.

'Yeah. Mum married again. A drunken arsehole called Sigursteinn. I never met him, it all happened when I was in London.'

'They separated?'

'No, he got drunk in Reykjavík. Fell off the harbour wall and killed himself. A good thing all round from what I have heard. Mum never got over it, though.'

Magnus nodded. 'As you say, tough for her. And for you.'

Pétur shrugged. 'I ran away from it all. Ingileif stayed to do what she could. She always did.'

'And your other sister? Birna?'

Pétur shook his head. 'She's pretty much screwed up.'

'Thank you, Pétur,' Magnus said, getting to his feet. 'One last question. What were you doing the night Agnar died?'

At first Pétur seemed taken aback by the question, but then he smiled. 'I suppose that's something you have to ask?'

Magnus waited.

'What day was that?'

'Thursday the twenty-third. The first day of summer.'

'The clubs were busy that night. I spent the evening moving from one to the other. Now if you will excuse me, I have some music to listen to. I just hope these guys are better than the last lot.'

CHAPTER NINETEEN

Á RNI DROVE MAGNUS out towards Birna Ásgrímsdóttir's house in Gardabaer, a suburb of Reykjavík.

Magnus's headache was getting worse. 'Check out Pétur's alibi, Árni,' Magnus said.

'Is he a suspect?' Árni said, surprised.

'Everyone's a suspect,' Magnus said.

'I thought you were certain Steve Jubb killed Agnar.'

'Just do it!' Magnus growled.

They drove through the grey suburbs. 'By the way, I heard back from the Australian Elvish expert,' Árni said. 'He figured out what *kallisarvoinen* means.'

'And what's that?'

'It's Finnish. Apparently Tolkien liked the Finnish language, found it interesting. A lot of Quenya words come from Finnish as does much of the grammar. Our friend wondered whether Jubb and Isildur might have used Finnish vocabulary when there wasn't an existing Quenya word. So he looked up *kallisarvoinen* in a Finnish dictionary.'

'And?'

'It means "precious".'

'Precious? That's the word Gollum used for the ring in *Lord of the Rings*.'

'That's right.'

Magnus recalled the SMS from Steve Jubb. *Saw Agnar. He has kallisarvoinen.* 'So Steve Jubb thought that Agnar had the ring,' he said. 'That's what he wanted to sell for five million bucks.'

'We haven't found an old ring amongst Agnar's stuff,' Árni said.

'Perhaps Steve Jubb took it,' Magnus said. 'After he killed him.'

'And did what with it? We didn't find it in his hotel room.'

'Hid it perhaps.'

'Where?'

Magnus sighed. 'God knows. Or perhaps he mailed it back to Isildur in California. No one remembered Steve Jubb mailing a package at the Post Office, but he could easily have slipped a ring into an envelope and dropped it in a mail box.'

'But Jubb sent the text message to Isildur *after* he had come back from seeing Agnar. That suggests that Agnar still had it, or at least Jubb thought he had.'

Magnus saw Árni's point.

'Do you really think that Agnar found the ring?' Árni said. 'He only heard about it on Sunday. The e-mail was sent on Tuesday. People have devoted years to looking for it and haven't found it. Unless it was a fake?'

'That would be just as hard to arrange in a hurry. Harder. Faking a thousand-year-old ring is a major job. And you can bet that Isildur wouldn't shell out five million bucks without checking out what he was buying pretty thoroughly.'

'You're not suggesting it's real?' said Árni. 'That the ring that Gaukur took from Ísildur survived?'

'Of course not,' said Magnus irritably. But then, as he had just pointed out, it was hard to see how the ring could be a fake. Perhaps it was an older fake, the work of Ingileif's grandfather? Patience. All would become clear in time.

Chastened, Árni was silent for a minute. 'So what do we do?' he asked eventually.

'Tell Baldur. Look for likely hiding places. See if we've missed anything.' Magnus glared at Árni. 'Why didn't you tell me this earlier?'

'I only got the response this morning.'

'You could have told me back at the station.'

'Sorry.'

Magnus turned away to look out of the window at the grey boxes. He was lumbered with an idiot. And he wished his headache would go away.

Birna Ásgrímsdóttir lived in a new concrete house with a bright red roof in a new development. Each house had its patch of lawn, together with optimistically planted saplings. Expensive SUVs littered the driveways. Wealthy. Comfortable. Soulless.

Birna herself was softer, rounder and older than Ingileif. She had big blue eyes and pouting lips. She could have been attractive, but there was something sagging and sloppy about her. Two lines pointed downwards from the corners of her mouth. She was wearing tight, bulging jeans and a bright orange top.

When she saw Magnus, she smiled, her eyes lingering over his body before moving up to his face.

'Hello,' she said.

'Hello,' said Magnus, disconcerted despite himself. 'We are from the Metropolitan Police. We have come to ask you about the murder of Professor Agnar Haraldsson.'

'How nice,' said Birna. 'Come in. Can I get you something to drink?'

'Just coffee,' said Magnus.

Árni nodded. 'Me too,' he said, his voice a little hoarse. This woman had presence.

They sat in the living room, waiting for the coffee. The furniture was new and characterless, and the room was dominated by a truly massive television, on which was some daytime American TV show in English that Magnus vaguely recognized. Satellite.

Dotted around the living room were photographs. Most of them were of a stunning blonde girl of about eighteen wearing swimsuits and various sashes. Birna. A younger Birna. There were also a couple of pictures of a suave, dark-haired man wearing the uniform of Icelandair.

Birna returned with the coffee. 'I'm sorry, I don't think I can help you much, but I'll try.'

'Did you ever meet Agnar?'

'No, never. You know about the family saga, I take it?'

'Yes, yes we do.'

'Well, Ingileif was handling all the negotiations. She did ask me whether I objected to her selling the thing, and I told her I didn't give a toss.'

'Did she tell you how the negotiations were progressing?'

'No. In fact I haven't spoken to her since then.'

'Did she mention a ring?'

Birna laughed out loud. 'You don't mean Gaukur's ring?'

'It seems that your grandfather found it sixty years ago, but then he hid it again. Agnar may have found it more recently, or he may have claimed he did.'

'Don't be ridiculous,' Birna said. 'If there ever was a ring it was lost centuries ago. Let me tell you something,' she said, leaning forward towards Magnus. He could smell some kind of alcohol on her breath. In his current state it was all he could do not to recoil. 'That ring and that saga are just trouble. It's all a load of bullshit. Don't believe a word of it. I tell you Ingileif should have sold the damn thing, especially if she could have done it in secret.'

'Are you and Ingileif close?'

Birna leaned back in her chair. 'That's a good question. We were once, very. After my father died my mother married again, and I had some trouble with my stepfather. Even though she was two years younger than me, Ingileif helped me a lot. Got me through it. But after that, we kind of drifted apart. We lead different lives now. I married a jerk, and Ingileif does her designer stuff.'

'Trouble with your stepfather?'

Birna looked at Magnus again, this time at his eyes, as if deciding whether to trust him. 'Is this relevant to your investigation?'

Magnus shrugged. 'It might be. I won't know until you tell me.'

Birna pulled out a packet of cigarettes, and after offering one to Magnus and Árni, lit up.

'I was fourteen when my father died. I was a pretty girl.' She nodded towards the photographs. 'My mother got it into her head that I should become Miss Iceland. She became obsessed with it. As bad as Dad and his saga. I think it might have been a way of trying to deal with his death, putting it out of her mind. Of course it didn't work.'

She smiled. 'I never managed better than third, but Mum and I tried really hard. In the middle of all that, she married Sigursteinn, who was some kind of car dealer from Selfoss. I could tell the minute I met him that Sigursteinn fancied me. It took him less than a month after he got married before he, well ...' she took a deep drag of her cigarette. 'Well, he raped me really. I didn't think that at the time, but it *was* rape. He wanted sex with me, I was scared of him. It happened. Lots of times.'

'Ingileif found out, caught us at it, and she went crazy. She went at him with a broken bottle, but in the end it was she who was cut. Have you noticed she has a little scar on her eyebrow? And on her cheek?'

Magnus nodded.

'Well, that was Sigursteinn. Ingileif told Mum, who didn't believe her. There was the most almighty family row. Ingileif was thrown out of the house, I was too scared to say anything. Then, three months later, Sigursteinn was on a business trip to Reykjavík when he fell into the harbour. I was so relieved.'

'How did your mother react?'

'She was totally distraught. She went as far as accusing Ingileif of killing him, which was just stupid. Then I told her exactly what he had done to me, and eventually she believed it.' Birna stared, her big blue eyes unblinking. 'That pretty much mucked up our family.'

'I can imagine,' said Magnus.

'Ingileif went away to Reykjavík. In recent years she started speaking to Mum again. She spent a lot of time with her just before she died.'

'And you?'

Birna blinked. 'Oh, I married Matthías and have lived a perfect life of happiness ever since.'

Magnus ignored the sarcasm. 'And Pétur?'

'He missed all this. He came back to Reykjavík a couple of years later. We see each other occasionally. But whenever we do I get the impression he feels sorry for me. Can't think why.'

God, what a family, Magnus thought. His own was bad enough. He remembered Ingileif's quavering voice when she had told him about the ghost of the girl accused of incest at the Höfdi House. No wonder she felt sorry for her. She was thinking of Birna.

'One last question. Where were you last Thursday night? The first day of summer?'

Birna laughed again. 'You can't be serious? You don't think *I* killed the poor man, do you.'

'Just answer the question.'

Birna hesitated. 'Do I have to?'

Magnus knew what was coming next. He was beginning to get used to the sex life of Icelanders. 'Yes, you do. And we will have to check out whatever you tell us. But we will do it discreetly, I can promise you. And it won't come up in any eventual trial, unless it is relevant to the prosecution.'

Birna sighed. 'Matthías was in New York. Probably in bed with a flight attendant.'

'And you?'

'I was with a friend named Dagur Tómasson. He's married as well. We spent the night in a hotel in Kópavogur. It's anonymous and as discreet as you can get in Iceland.'

'Which one?'

'The Merlin.'

'And can we have his address?'

'I'll give you his mobile phone number,' said Birna. 'It's nothing serious,' she continued, staring straight at Magnus. The corners of her mouth twitched upwards. 'I don't like to restrict myself to any one man.'

'I think she likes you,' said Árni five minutes later as he was driving Magnus back to station.

'Shut up,' growled Magnus. 'And check out the hotel. But somehow I suspect *that* alibi will hold up.'

CHAPTER TWENTY

BALDUR LISTENED CLOSELY as Magnus explained his theory that Agnar was trying to sell the ring from *Gaukur's Saga* to Steve Jubb and the modern-day Isildur.

'So what are you suggesting?' he said, when Magnus had finished. 'We go over Agnar's house again, looking for a mythical ring that has been lost for a thousand years? Do you know how absurd that sounds?' The expression on Baldur's long face verged on contempt. 'You were brought here to bring us some big-city homicide experience. Instead you start mumbling about elves and rings like the most superstitious Icelandic grandmother. You'll be saying the hidden people did it next.'

Magnus's foul mood deepened. He knew that Baldur was trying to needle him, and he fought to control his anger.

'Of course I don't believe that the ring is really a thousand years old,' Magnus said. 'Look. We know Steve Jubb murdered Agnar. But since he won't tell us why, we need to figure it out for ourselves. We also know that Agnar was trying to sell a saga – we've both seen it. It exists.'

Baldur shook his head. 'All we've seen is a hundred and twenty pages that was spat out of a computer printer two weeks ago.'

Magnus leaned back. 'Fair enough. Maybe the saga is a forgery. Maybe there is a ring, but it's a fake too. If anything, that would create a bigger motive for Steve Jubb to kill Agnar. We still need to find it.'

'The thing is, I'm not sure that Steve Jubb did murder Agnar.'

Magnus snorted.

'I've just interviewed him again. He wouldn't tell me anything about sagas or rings. But he did deny he murdered Agnar.'

'And you believe him?'

'Yes, actually. My hunch is he's telling the truth.'

'Your hunch?'

Baldur found a sheet of paper in the pile on his desk. 'Here's a report from the forensics lab.'

Magnus scanned it. It was an analysis of the soil samples on Steve Jubb's size forty-five shoes.

'It shows that there were no traces of the kind of mud on the path from the summer house down to the lake shore, or the mud on the shore itself.'

Magnus read the report, his mind buzzing. 'Maybe Jubb cleaned his shoes. Thoroughly.'

'There *was* soil from the area right in front of the summer house. So he was at the front that evening, but not at the back. And he didn't clean his shoes.'

'Perhaps he changed into boots? Ditched them afterwards?'

'We'd have found footprints in or around the house,' Baldur said. 'And that's pretty unlikely, isn't it?'

Magnus stared at the piece of paper, not reading the words, just trying to figure out how Jubb could have dragged the body down to the lake without getting mud on his shoes. He found it impossible to believe that Jubb's presence at the summer house that evening was just coincidence.

'Someone else moved Agnar,' Baldur said. '*After* Steve Jubb had left. And it's quite probable that someone else killed him.'

'Did you find footprints near the lake?'

Baldur shook his head. 'Nothing useful. It had rained overnight. And the scene was well and truly compromised. The kids, their father, the paramedics, the police officers from Selfoss. They left footprints all over the place.'

'An accomplice then,' said Magnus.

'Like who?' Baldur said.

'Isildur. This Lawrence Feldman guy.' As soon as he said it Magnus regretted it.

Baldur spotted the flaw immediately. 'You contacted Isildur two days later, and he replied from a computer located in California.'

'An Icelandic accomplice. There are *Lord of the Rings* fans in this country.'

'There is no record of any Icelandic number on Steve Jubb's mobile phone, apart from Agnar's. We know that Steve Jubb never left his hotel from the time he arrived in Reykjavík in the morning to the time he went out to Lake Thingvellir late afternoon. None of the hotel staff recalls anyone visiting him at the hotel.'

'Someone could have gone directly to his room without stopping at the front desk.'

Baldur just raised his eyebrows.

'Don't tell me you're going to spring him?' Magnus asked.

'Not yet. And I'm not ruling him out as a suspect. But we need to widen the investigation. Look at the more real-world circumstances.' Baldur counted them off on his fingers. 'Agnar saw a lover and a former lover in the weeks before he died. His wife was seriously angry about his infidelity. He had big money problems. He bought drugs. Maybe he had debts we don't know about? Maybe he owed his dealer money? Someone else was there that night and we need to find out who.'

'So it's just a coincidence he was negotiating this deal with Jubb and Isildur?'

'Why not?' said Baldur. 'Look. We shouldn't rule out this saga deal completely. If you like, you can focus on that. But there are plenty of other things for the rest of the team to look at.'

'I'm sure if I went to California I could get Isildur to—'

'No,' said Baldur.

Several time zones to the west, it was early morning in the woods of Trinity County, Northern California. Isildur looked out of his study over the little valley towards the waterfall tumbling down

170

from the bare rock face opposite. The morning sunlight glistened off the rain-washed greenery. In the garden he could see the life-sized shapes of Gandalf, Legolas and Elrond, bronze sculptures he had commissioned at great expense from a San Francisco artist.

It was a beautiful spot. He had bought it with a fraction of the money he had made from selling his share in 4Portal the year before. He had been looking for a hideaway in the woods to concentrate on his projects and had found the perfect place. Alpine mountains on three sides, a small winding road on the fourth leading down through forests to the nearest very small town ten miles away.

It was a place where he could think.

He had named it Rivendell, naturally, after the sanctuary that the Fellowship of the Ring had rested in. He remembered when he had first read of Rivendell, when he was seventeen, and he had had a clear vision in his mind of the place, surrounded by woods, mountains, running water, peace, tranquillity.

This was it.

He had been working on two projects. The one that had taken most of his time was his attempt to coordinate the collation of an online dictionary of two of Tolkien's Elvish languages, Quenya and Sindarin. The project had turned out to be much more frustrating than he had thought. Tolkien had never laid down hard and fast grammar rules and vocabulary, so there were many differing inter-pretations of the two languages. Isildur knew that: the whole point about his dictionary was that it would be flexible enough to deal with the different dialects that had grown up over time. Trouble was his collaborators were not of a flexible frame of mind.

The project had descended into acrimony and abuse. He had hoped that as the provider of the money he would have the final say. It turned out that he was indeed a unifying figure: the authority they all loved to hate.

His other project was to try to track down *Gaukur's Saga*. He had first become aware of it a few years before, through an Internet forum. He had put together a Danish academic who had discovered echoes of the lost saga in an eighteenth-century letter he had turned up, with Gimli, an Englishman whose grandfather had studied at Leeds University under Tolkien. The details were frustratingly vague, but Isildur was willing to spend big money to flesh them out.

And he did all this from the computer in his study at Rivendell.

He had never been overseas. He had been brought up in New Jersey, and spent all his vacations as a child with his family on the Jersey Shore. He had majored in electrical engineering at Stanford in California, and spent his career in Silicon Valley. He was a gifted programmer, intuitive, focused, able to make connections. 4Portal was his second venture, a company that developed software for advertising portals on cell phones. It was spectacularly successful, and Isildur's six per cent share had been converted to many millions when he and his more commercial minded partners sold out.

The plan was that after a year or so in Rivendell, he would go back to the Valley and try something else.

Once he had *Gaukur's Saga* in his possession. And the ring.

The last few weeks had been a rollercoaster ride of rising expectations and disappointments. First, the message from Agnar that he had found the saga. Then, a couple of weeks later that he had actually found Ísildur's ring. Gimli's excited reports that the saga might indeed be real and that there was a deal to be done, and then it had all gone wrong.

Agnar was dead. Gimli was in jail. The police had the saga.

And the ring was out there, somewhere in Iceland, and he had no way of knowing where.

Isildur had done what he could from Rivendell. He had procured the best legal representation for Gimli. But it was becoming clear that if he was to find the ring, he would have to go to Iceland himself.

He had a passport, ordered before a planned trip to New Zealand to see where the movies were made. He had abandoned the trip at the last minute in a fit of nervousness. Had gotten as far as the airport, but never made it on to the plane.

That nervousness had to be overcome.

He turned to his computer screen and called up a travel website.

Magnus spent the rest of the day talking to the police officers who had searched the summer house and Agnar's house, as well as Steve Jubb's hotel room. No sign of anything resembling a ring.

He went to see Linda, Agnar's wife at her house in Seltjarnarnes. She tolerated his intrusion with barely concealed irritation. She was tall and thin with blonde hair and a drawn face. With a baby and a toddler to look after, she was barely holding things together.

She was an angry woman. Angry with her husband, angry with the police, angry with the bank, the lawyers, the fridge door that wouldn't shut properly, the broken window that Agnar hadn't got fixed, angry at the great big enormous hole in her life.

Magnus felt for her, and for her two children. Whatever Agnar's sins, whatever his infidelities, he hadn't deserved to die.

Yet another family blown apart by murder. Magnus had seen so many over the course of his career. And he did all he could for each and every one of them.

Of course she hadn't seen any bloody ring. He searched the house for possible hiding places, but found nothing. At eight o'clock he left, taking the bus back to the centre of Reykjavík. He hadn't yet been allocated the use of a police-owned car, and he had left Árni behind.

His conversation with Baldur had shaken him. He understood Baldur's point, that was the trouble. He couldn't figure out how Steve Jubb could have murdered Agnar and disposed of his body without getting his feet dirty.

But he just couldn't accept that Jubb had gone to see Agnar about a secret multi-million dollar deal, and then Agnar had been murdered for some totally unrelated reason a couple of hours later.

His intuition told him that just didn't make sense. And, like Baldur, he trusted his intuition.

He stopped off at the Krambúd convenience store opposite the

Hallgrímskirkja, and bought himself a Thai curry to heat up. When he got back to Katrín's house, he shoved it in to the microwave.

'How are you feeling?'

He turned around to see the landlady of the house making her way to the refrigerator. She was speaking English. She took out a *skyr* and opened it.

'So so.'

'Quite a night last night.'

'Thank you for getting me into bed,' said Magnus. He meant it, although he would rather have avoided the subject. He had had enough humiliation for one day.

'No problem,' said Katrín smiling. 'You were very sweet. Just before you went to sleep you gave me a cute little smile, and said "You're under arrest." Then you fell asleep.'

'Oh, Jeez.'

'Don't worry. You will probably have to do the same for me one day.'

She leaned back against the fridge, eating her yoghurt. She had a couple fewer studs in her face than she had the first night Magnus had met her. She was wearing black jeans and a T-shirt emblazoned with an image of a wolf's jaws. The microwave pinged and Magnus extracted his dinner, tipped it out on to a plate, and began to eat. 'I don't usually get that drunk.'

'I really don't mind. Just as long as you are careful where you throw up. And you clean it up afterwards.'

Magnus grimaced. 'I will. I promise.'

Katrín examined him. 'Are you really a policeman?'

'Matter of fact I am.'

'What are you doing in Iceland?'

'Helping out.'

Katrín ate some more of her *skyr*. 'You see, the thing is, I don't like my little brother spying on me.'

'I'm not surprised,' said Magnus. 'Don't worry. I'm not officially a signed-up member of the Reykjavík Metropolitan Police. I'm not going to tell anyone what you're up to.'

'Good,' said Katrín. 'I saw you going into Ingileif's gallery yesterday.'

'Do you know her?'

'A bit. Is she suspected of something?'

'I can't really tell you that.'

'Sorry. Just curious.' She waved her spoon in the air. 'I know! Is it Agnar's murder?'

'I really can't say,' Magnus said.

'It is! A friend of mine went out with him when she was at university. I saw him the other day in a café, you know. The Café Paris. With Tómas Hákonarson.'

'Who's he?' Magnus asked.

'He has his own TV show. *The Point* it's called. Gives politicians a hard time. He's quite funny.'

They ate in silence for a minute. Magnus knew he should write the name down, but he was too tired, he couldn't be bothered.

'What do you think of her?' he asked.

Katrín put down the yoghurt and poured herself some orange juice. Magnus noticed that there was a tiny blob of *skyr* on the ring jutting out of her lip. 'Ingileif? I like her. Her brother's a bastard, though.'

'Why's that?'

'He won't let me sing in his clubs any more, that's why,' said Katrín, anger in her voice. 'He owns the hottest places in town. It's not fair.'

'Why did he ban you?'

'I don't know. I had some really successful gigs. It's only because I missed a couple, that's all.'

'Ah.' From what he had seen of Pétur he wasn't surprised that he was tough on unreliable acts.

'I like her, though.'

'Ingileif?'

'Yeah.' Katrín lit up a cigarette and sat down opposite him. 'I've even bought some of the stuff in her gallery. That vase, for instance.'

She pointed to a small twisted glass vase with a dirty wooden spoon in it. 'Cost a bomb, but I kind of like it.'

'Do you think she's honest?' Magnus asked.

'Is that a cop talking?'

Magnus shrugged.

'Yes, she is. People like her. Why? What's she done?'

'Nothing,' Magnus said. 'Do you know Lárus Thorvaldsson?'

'The painter? Yes, a little. He's a friend of Ingileif's too.'

'A good friend?'

'Nothing serious. Lárus has lots of girls. You know where you are with him, if you see what I mean. No hassle.'

'I think I do,' said Magnus. It was pretty clear that Katrín knew him in much the same way Ingileif did.

Katrín looked at him closely. 'Are you asking that as a cop, or do you have some other interest?'

Magnus put down his fork and rubbed his eyes. 'I really don't know.' He picked up his empty plate, rinsed it off and stuck it in the dishwasher. 'I need sleep. I'm going to bed.'

CHAPTER TWENTY-ONE

BALDUR SEEMED TO have a new lease of energy at the morning meeting as he doled out tasks to his detectives. He passed on the report from the forensics lab about the mud on Steve Jubb's shoes, and explained that they needed to widen their investigation. Speak to everyone they had interviewed one more time. Interview new people: anyone who might conceivably have seen another visitor to Agnar, the people who sold Agnar drugs, his students, his former girlfriends, his colleagues, his friends, his wife's friends, neighbours, everyone.

There was some discussion with Rannveig about providing the British police with the paperwork they required to grant a search warrant for Jubb's house and computer. The detective Baldur had sent to Yorkshire had spoken to Jubb's neighbours. Jubb was a bit of a loner, often on the road with his lorry. His passion for *The Lord of the Rings* was well known. A former girlfriend, now married to someone else, said he was an intelligent man, obsessive, but not violent in the least. No help there, no leads.

Throughout all of this, Baldur did not look at Magnus once.

Until after the meeting, when he beckoned Magnus to follow him to his office. He slammed the door behind him.

'I do *not* like being undercut!'

'What do you mean?'

'I mean that I don't like you going to the Commissioner behind my back and telling him we should be sending people to California.'

'He asked my opinion. I gave it to him,' said Magnus.

'This is exactly the wrong time to divert resources away from the main thrust of the investigation.'

'When do I go?' asked Magnus.

Baldur shook his head. 'You're not going. Árni is on his way. He left last night.'

'Árni! Alone?'

'Yes. I can't afford to spare more than one detective.'

'What about me?'

'Oh, you are far too valuable,' said Baldur, his voice laden with irony. 'Besides, Árni has a degree from the States. And he speaks good English.'

'And what should I do?'

'You can look for a ring,' Baldur said, smiling grimly. 'That should keep you busy.'

As soon as he was back at his desk, Magnus called Árni. The young detective was at JFK, waiting for his connecting flight to San Francisco. Although it was very early morning in New York, Árni sounded wide awake. He was really excited. Magnus just managed to calm him down enough to suggest a line of questioning for Isildur. Threaten him with conspiracy to murder unless he explained what Steve Jubb was really doing in Reykjavík.

Árni seemed to take it in, although Magnus had little confidence in his ability to get Isildur to divulge anything he didn't want to.

'By the way,' Magnus asked, 'did you check out Birna and Pétur's alibis yesterday?'

'They're good,' said Árni. 'I checked with Birna's lover and the hotel in Kópavogur. I also spoke to the managers at Pétur's three clubs. They all saw him on that night.'

Magnus wasn't surprised. But he knew how important it was in an investigation to check and double check everything. 'Well, good luck,' he said.

'Can I bring you back anything?'

'No, Árni. Just a full confession from Lawrence Feldman.'

Magnus turned to his computer and logged on. He was convinced that Baldur was wrong to downplay the importance of Isildur or Lawrence Feldman or whoever the hell he was. He would continue looking for the ring, or a ring, and hope that Árni came back with something useful.

He checked his e-mails.

There was one from Colby.

Magnus,

Last night one of your big ugly friends broke into my apartment and attacked me. He put a gun in my mouth and asked me where you were. I said you were in Sweden and he went away.

He scared the shit out of me.

I'm gone. They won't find me. You won't find me. No one knows where I am, not my family, not my friends, not the people at work, not the cops, and I'm definitely not telling you.

Magnus, you have screwed up my life and nearly gotten me killed.

Rot in hell wherever you are. And don't ever EVER talk to me again.

C.

There was a short e-mail accompanying it.

Hello Magnus,

Sorry about the delay in forwarding this – I was out of the office yesterday. I'm checking it out.

Agent Hendricks

Magnus stared at the screen. Emotions flooded over him, leaving him gasping for air. Drowning.

Anger at the scumbag who had done this to Colby. At Williams for not protecting her. At Colby herself for not understanding that it wasn't his fault.

Anger with himself for letting it happen.

Guilt, because of course it *was* his fault.

Powerlessness, stuck in Reykjavík, thousands of miles away.

Guilt again, because in the last twenty-four hours he had thought very little about Colby, had almost forgotten her when she was in the greatest of danger.

He slammed his fist hard on his desk. There were only a couple of detectives in the room, but they both turned to stare.

At least Colby hadn't said where he really was. Although at this point he didn't care. At this point he thought of jumping on a plane to Boston, finding Pedro Soto personally and blowing him away. Why should he lurk cowering away in Iceland? He wasn't a coward.

He tapped out an angry e-mail to Deputy Superintendent Williams, via Agent Hendricks, telling him what had happened and asking him where the hell the protection that he had promised Magnus was.

If the Boston PD couldn't protect Colby, then Magnus would fly over and do it himself. It wasn't as if he would be allowed to do anything useful in Iceland.

Ingileif waited in Mokka, toying with a latte. She liked the café, one of the oldest in Reykjavík, on the corner of Skólavördustígur and Laugavegur. Small, wood panelled and cosy, it was famous both for its waffles and for its clientele: artists, poets and novelists. The walls acted as a kind of rotating art exhibition for local artists, changing once a month. In March it had been her partner from the gallery's turn.

There was a newspaper lying on the table, but she didn't pick it up. It had been a good afternoon – she had sold six vases worth several hundred thousand krónur. But she had also had an awkward conversation with one of her partners about the delay in payments due from Nordidea.

She hadn't exactly lied, but she hadn't exactly told the truth, either.

The whole business with the saga and Agnar's death had made her think again about her father. She could clearly remember the last morning she saw him. He had been walking out of the house with his rucksack when he had paused, turned and kissed her goodbye. She could remember what he was wearing – his blue anorak, his new lightweight hiking boots. She could remember the smell of him, the mints he used to like to suck. She also remembered her feelings of irritation towards him because he had forbidden her to sleep over at her friend's house the night before. She hadn't really forgiven him that dreadful morning.

There were all those questions now swirling around the death of Agnar, but there had been very few about her father. In Iceland, a man stumbling to his death in a snowstorm was an all too common occurrence, a feature of Icelandic life over the centuries.

Perhaps there should have been more questions. Perhaps there should be more questions now.

'Hi, Inga!'

The other patrons of the café stared at the man who addressed her, but only for a couple of seconds, before returning to their conversations and their newspapers. Icelanders were proud of their ability to let famous people get on with their lives in public. Although of course there was only one truly famous Icelander, and that was Björk, but the people of Reykjavík let her go as she pleased in their town.

'Tómas! How good to see you!' She stood up and kissed him on the cheek.

'Hang on a moment,' said the man. 'Let me get myself a coffee. Do you want another?'

Ingileif shook her head and her companion went up to the

counter to order a double espresso. His features were very familiar to Ingileif: the round glasses, the buck teeth, the bulging cheeks, the thinning brushed-back mousy hair. Partly, it was true, this familiarity was from seeing him once a week on TV, but it was also the result of a childhood spent together.

He returned to her table. 'How's things?' he said. 'I went into your gallery the other day. I missed you, but you have some lovely stuff. It must sell well.'

'It does,' said Ingileif.

'But?' Tómas had noticed the doubt in her voice. He was perceptive like that.

'Too well,' Ingileif admitted. 'Our biggest customer went bust last month and they owe us a lot of money.'

'And the bank isn't being much help?'

'You're right there. A couple of years ago they were throwing money at us, and now they can't get it back fast enough. They gave us one of those foreign currency loans that just keeps on growing.'

'Well, good luck with that,' said Tómas. 'I'm sure you will thrive.'

'Thank you,' Ingileif smiled. 'How about you? Your show seems to be going very well. I love the way you skewered the British Ambassador last week.'

Tómas smiled broadly, his cheeks bunching up like a squirrel's. 'He deserved it. I mean, using anti-terrorist legislation to grab our country's biggest bank. It was bullying, pure and simple. How would the British like it if the Americans did the same thing to them?'

'And that banker the week before. The one who paid himself a four-million-dollar bonus three months before his bank went bust.'

'At least he had the grace to come back to Iceland to face the music,' Tómas said. 'But that's the problem, you see. I won't get any more bankers on the show for a while, or ambassadors for that matter. I have to tread a fine line between being disrespectful to please the viewers and not being too aggressive so that I scare the guests away.'

He sipped his espresso. Fame suited him, Ingileif thought. She had always liked him, he had a warm approachable sense of humour, but he used to be a bit shy, lacking in self-confidence. Now he was a household name, some of that shyness had disappeared. Not all of it though. That remained part of his charm.

'You heard about Agnar Haraldsson?' Tómas asked, peering at Ingileif closely through his glasses.

'Yes,' she said simply.

'I remember you and he had a bit of a thing going.'

'We did,' Ingileif admitted. 'Big mistake. Actually, it was probably only a little mistake, but a mistake none the less.'

'It must have been a bit of a shock? His death. I mean I was shocked and I scarcely knew the guy.'

'Yes,' said Ingileif, her voice suddenly hoarse. 'Yes, it was.'

'Have the police been in touch?'

'Why should they be?' Ingileif asked. She could feel herself reddening.

'It's a big case. A big investigation. They have, haven't they?'

Ingileif nodded.

'Are they getting anywhere? Hasn't there been an arrest?'

'Yes. An Englishman. They think he was involved in some dodgy deal with Agnar. But I don't think they have much evidence to prove it.'

'Had you seen him recently?'

Ingileif nodded again. Then when she saw Tómas's raised eyebrows, she protested. 'No, not that. He's married, and he's sleazy. I have better taste than that.'

'I'm glad to hear it,' said Tómas. 'You're way out of his league.'

'That's so kind of you to say,' said Ingileif with mock politeness.

'So what were you talking to him about?'

For a second Ingileif considered telling Tómas all about the saga. It would all come out in the open soon anyway, and Tómas was such an old friend. But only for a second. 'Why do you want to know?'

'I'm curious. It's been all over the papers.'

'It's not for your show, is it?'

'Good God, no.' Tómas saw his denial wasn't strong enough. 'I promise. Look, I'm sorry if I have been too direct with my questions. It's become a habit.'

'It must have,' said Ingileif. Tómas had always had the ability to get people to confide in him. He seemed harmless and he seemed interested. But something told Ingileif to be careful. 'Just a social call,' she said. 'Like this.'

Tómas smiled. 'Look, I have to go. I'm having a party on Saturday, do you want to come?'

'Will it be as wild as your parties used to be?' Ingileif said.

'Wilder. Here, let me give you the address. I moved a few months ago.' And he took out a business card emblazoned with the logo of RUV, the state broadcaster, and wrote down his home address, somewhere on Thingholtsstraeti.

As he left the café, drawing one or two surreptitious stares after him from the customers, Ingileif couldn't help asking herself a simple question.

What the hell was all that about?

Vigdís accepted the cup of coffee and began to sip it. It was her fifth of the day. Interviewing people in Iceland always involved lots of drinking coffee.

The woman opposite her was in her late thirties, wearing jeans and a blue sweater. She had an intelligent face and a friendly smile. They were sitting in a handsome house in Vesturbaer, a smart area of Reykjavík just to the west of the city centre. The family Range Rover blocked the view to the quiet street outside.

'I'm sorry to take more of your time, Helena,' Vigdís began. 'I know you have answered plenty of questions from my colleagues. But I would like to go through everything that you can remember from the day of the murder, and the couple of days before. Any tiny little detail.'

It was Helena and her family who had been staying in one of the other summer houses on the shore of Lake Thingvellir and whose children had found Agnar's body. After speaking to Helena, Vigdís planned to visit her husband in the office of his insurance company on Borgartún.

'By all means. I'm not sure there is much else I can tell you.'

But Helena frowned as she finished the sentence. Vigdís noticed it. 'What is it?'

'Um … It's nothing. It's not important.'

Vigdís smiled, coaxing. 'Don't worry about that,' she said. She showed Helena the pages of her notebook, covered with neat handwriting. 'This book is filled with unimportant stuff. But just a little of it will turn out to be very important.'

'My husband didn't think we should mention it.'

'Why not?' asked Vigdís.

Helena smiled. 'Oh, well, you decide. Our five-year-old daughter, Sara Rós, told us this story at breakfast yesterday. My husband is convinced it's a dream.'

'What was the story?' asked Vigdís.

'She says that she saw two men playing in the lake at night.'

'Lake Thingvellir?'

'Yes.'

'That sounds interesting.'

'The thing is Sara Rós makes up stories. Sometimes it's to get attention. Sometimes it's just for fun.'

'I see. Well, I think I should speak to her. With your permission, of course.'

'All right. As long as you bear in mind that she might have made the whole thing up. You'll have to wait until she gets back from kindergarten.'

'No,' said Vigdís. 'I think we had better talk to her now.'

The kindergarten that Helena's daughter attended was only a few hundred metres away. The principal grudgingly gave up her office to Vigdís and Helena and went to fetch the girl.

She was a typical Icelandic five-year-old. Bright blue eyes, pink cheeks and curly hair that was so blonde it was almost white.

Her face lit up when she saw her mother and she curled up next to her on the sofa in the principal's office.

'Hello,' said Vigdís. 'My name is Vigdís and I am a police officer.'

'You don't look like a policeman,' said Sara Rós.

'That's because I am a detective. I don't wear a uniform.'

'Do you come from Africa?'

'Sara Rós!' her mother interjected.

Vigdís smiled. 'No. I come from Keflavík.'

The little girl laughed. 'That's not in Africa. That's where the airport is when we go on holiday.'

'That's right,' said Vigdís. 'Now, your mummy said you saw something last week at your summer house by the lake. Can you tell me about it?'

'My daddy says that I am making it up. He doesn't believe me.'

'I believe you,' said Vigdís.

'How can you believe me when you haven't heard what I am going to say?'

Vigdís smiled. 'Good point. I tell you what. You tell me the story, and I'll tell you whether I believe you or not at the end.'

The girl glanced at her mother, who nodded. 'I woke up and it was the middle of the night. I wanted to go to the toilet. When I came back I looked out of my window and I saw two men playing in the lake just outside the professor's house. They were splashing about a bit. Then one of them got tired and fell asleep.'

'Were they both splashing?'

'Hm,' said the little girl, thinking hard. 'No they weren't. One of them was splashing and the other one was all floppy.'

'And did the man fall asleep in the water, or on the lake shore?'

'In the water.'

'I see. What did the other man do?'

'He got out of the lake and then he got in his car and he drove away.'

'Did you see what the man looked like?'

'Of course not, silly. It was dark! But I think he had his clothes on, not a swimming costume.'

'What about the car? Did you see the colour of the car?'

The girl giggled. 'I said it was dark. It was night time. You can't see colours in the dark.'

'Are you sure about this?'

'Yes, I am quite sure. And I know it's true because I saw the man asleep in the lake the next day when Jón and me went down there to play. Except then he was dead.' The little girl went quiet.

'Did you tell anyone about this?' Vigdís asked.

'No.'

'Why not?'

'Because nobody asked me.' She looked straight at Vigdís with her bright blue eyes. 'Well, I told you my story. Do you believe me?'

'Yes,' said Vigdís. 'Yes, I do.'

CHAPTER TWENTY-TWO

MAGNUS TOOK A last look around Room 208, trying to place himself in the shoes of Steve Jubb. Where would he hide something as small as a ring?

He couldn't think of anywhere. He had been over every inch of the room, and he was leaving quite a mess. He didn't care. Relations between the Reykjavík Metropolitan Police and the management of the Hótel Borg had taken a bit of a dive over the last couple of hours. The management had been upset at Magnus's insistence that the current occupant of the room, a German businessman, should be turfed out an hour before he was ready to check out. So had the businessman.

The cleaner, a young Polish woman, was more helpful. She was quite certain that she hadn't seen a ring, or anything that might contain a ring, as she had told the police a few days before. Unfortunately for Magnus, she seemed a reliable, observant girl.

The ring definitely wasn't there. Árni's interpretation of Jubb's text message to Isildur was probably right – Jubb hadn't taken it, but Jubb thought Agnar had it.

Next stop, the summer house on Lake Thingvellir. Again.

Magnus took the stairs down to the lobby. His thoughts drifted back to Colby. Was he serious about flying back to Boston?

At least he would be doing something. But finding Pedro Soto would be difficult. Killing him even more difficult. Magnus would be much more likely to give Soto the opportunity to finish him off. That would solve Soto's problems, take the pressure off the

Lenahan trial, keep his narcotics import and distribution businesses going.

What about finding Colby and protecting her? That, too, might be difficult. Colby had sounded determined to disappear. She was a capable woman: when she was determined to do something she usually did it. She would be hard for Magnus to find. And for the Dominicans. But if Magnus charged around looking for her, he ran the risk of leading the Dominicans right to her.

Like it or not, Magnus's best shot at hurting Soto and protecting Colby was to lie low, stay in Iceland, and testify at Lenahan's trial.

He handed the key card to the receptionist. As he was leaving the hotel, he passed a small man with a scruffy beard coming in, wheeling a suitcase behind him. The man was wearing a green baseball cap proclaiming 'Frodo Lives'.

Magnus held the door open.

'Oh, er, thank you very much, sir,' the man said, nervously. The language was English, the accent American.

'No problem,' said Magnus.

The Hótel Borg shared a square with the Parliament building, the site of the weekly Saturday afternoon demonstrations over the winter. As Magnus walked across it towards the police-department silver Skoda that he had signed out that morning, he wondered about the cap. Strange, he had never thought about *Lord of the Rings* memorabilia before. Was he going to be stopped short by every Gollum or Gandalf T-shirt he came across? Were there really that many of them?

No. There weren't.

He turned on his heel and returned to the lobby in time to see the elevator door closing behind the wheeled suitcase.

'What was the name of the guest who just checked in?' he asked the receptionist.

'Mr Feldman,' she said. Then, glancing at her computer screen. 'Lawrence Feldman.'

'Which room?'

'Three-ten.'

'Thank you.'

Magnus gave Feldman a minute to get himself into his room and then took the elevator up to the third floor. He knocked on the door of Room 310.

The man answered.

'Isildur?' said Magnus.

Feldman blinked. 'Who are you?'

'My name is Sergeant Detective Jonson. I'm working with the Reykjavik Metropolitan Police. Can I come in?'

'Er, I guess so,' said Feldman. His suitcase and his jacket were on the bed, together with the baseball cap. Magnus could hear the sound of the lavatory cistern refilling from the bathroom.

'Take a load off,' said Magnus, indicating the bed. Feldman sat on it, and Magnus pulled out the chair behind the desk.

Feldman looked tired. His brown eyes were quick and intelligent, but rimmed with red blood vessels. His skin was a waxy pale underneath the scrappy beard.

'Just flown in?' Magnus asked.

'You followed me in from the airport?' said Feldman. 'I guess you knew I would check in at the Borg.'

Magnus just grunted. Feldman was right, they should have known there was a good chance that he would show up in Iceland sooner or later. They should have been checking the airports. And the Hótel Borg was the natural place to stay. But Magnus decided not to explain to Feldman that it was just dumb luck that he had spotted him.

He thought about Árni, currently high over the Midwest on his way to California. It was all he could do not to smile to himself.

'Should I get a lawyer here?' Feldman asked.

'Good question,' said Magnus. 'There's no doubt you're in deep shit. And if this was the States, then I would definitely advise it. But here? I don't know.'

'What do you mean?'

'Well, here they can lock you up for three weeks if they think you're a suspect. That's what happened to Steve Jubb. He's in the top-security jail at Litla Hraun now. I could easily send you in there with him, if you don't cooperate. I mean we're looking at conspiracy to murder.'

Feldman just blinked.

'These Icelandic places are tough. Full of these big blond beefy Vikings. Oh, don't worry, they'll like you. They like little guys.' Feldman shifted uncomfortably on the bed. 'A lot of them are shepherds, you know, stuck up on a hillside all alone with a flock of sheep. They break the law – rape, incest, indecent acts with herbivores, that kind of thing. They get caught. They go to prison. No women, no sheep. What's a big blond Viking guy going to do?' Magnus smiled. 'That's where you come in.'

For a moment Magnus thought he had gone too far, but Feldman seemed to be buying it. He was tired, disoriented, in a foreign country.

Of course Magnus had absolutely no idea what conditions at Litla Hraun were really like. Knowing Iceland he rather suspected that the warders brought the prisoners hot cocoa and slippers every night as the inmates watched the latest soap on TV and knitted themselves scarves.

'So, if I talk to you now, you'll guarantee you won't send me there?'

Magnus looked directly at Feldman. 'That kinda depends on what you tell me.'

Feldman swallowed. 'I didn't have anything to do with Agnar's murder. And I really don't think that Gimli did either.'

'OK,' said Magnus. 'Let's start from the beginning. Tell me about Gaukur's ring.'

'I like to call it Isildur's ring,' said Feldman. 'I changed my on-line nickname to Isildur when I first heard the story.'

'What was it before?' Magnus asked.

'Elrond. The lord of Rivendell.'

'All right. So tell me about Isildur's ring.'

'I first heard about it three years ago. A Danish guy, Jens Pedersen, popped up on one of the websites saying he had found a letter from a poet who was an old friend of Árni Magnússon in Copenhagen. The poet had read *Gaukur's Saga*. There were a couple of sentences about Ísildur's quest to throw the ring into Mount Hekla.

'Now, this Danish guy was an academic doing his PhD thesis on the poet. He wanted some help from the forum to see if there was any link between *Gaukur's Saga* and the *Lord of the Rings*. Of course, we all went wild: he didn't know what had hit him. I tried to contact him directly to pay him to do more research on this saga. I think I tempted him at first; he said he had been in touch with a Professor of Icelandic at the University of Iceland named Agnar Haraldsson, who had given him some help about Gaukur and his lost saga. But then he went quiet.' Feldman sighed. 'I think he thought I was some kind of weirdo.'

Magnus let that ride. 'Have you heard from him recently?'

Feldman shook his head. 'No, but I know where he is.'

Magnus raised his eyebrows.

Feldman explained. 'He finished his PhD and is now teaching history at a high school in a town in Denmark called Odense. I'm in touch with one of his students.'

'What? A high-school student? How old is he?'

'Seventeen, I think. He's a big LOTR fan.'

There was something distinctly creepy about Lawrence Feldman being able to recruit a Danish schoolboy over the Internet to spy for him. In fact, there was something distinctly creepy about Lawrence Feldman.

'So how does Steve Jubb fit into this?' Magnus asked.

'Gimli? I met him through the same forum. He mentioned a story his grandfather had told him. Apparently he was a student at Leeds University in the 1920s and was taught by Tolkien, who was a professor there. One evening he had been drinking beer with an Icelandic fellow student and Tolkien. The Icelander was a bit drunk and began telling Tolkien about *Gaukur's Saga*, about the Ring of Andvari being found by a Viking called Ísildur and how Ísildur was told to throw it into Mount Hekla. The story made a big impression on Gimli's grandfather, and on Tolkien, apparently.

'Thirty years later, when he read *Lord of the Rings*, the grand-father was struck by the similarity of the stories.'

'Did he write any of this down?'

'No. He told Gimli about it when Gimli first read *The Hobbit*. Of course it fascinated him, and that's why Gimli became a *Lord of the Rings* fan. I checked the grandfather out. His name was Arthur Jubb and he was a student at Leeds in the 1920s. Tolkien was a professor there and set up a Viking Club where they all seem to have gotten drunk and sung songs. But there's nothing in Tolkien's published correspondence about the saga. Have you seen the two letters to Högni Ísildarson?'

'Yes.'

'Then you'll know why. Tolkien had promised to keep the family saga secret.'

Magnus nodded.

'So I teamed up with Gimli. I don't like to travel. Matter of fact this is my first time outside the States, but Gimli's a smart guy, and being a truck driver, he travels all the time. So I said I would provide the funding, and he would do the legwork and we would find *Gaukur's Saga*.

'Gimli's grandfather never told him the name of the Icelandic student, so Gimli started out going to Leeds to look for it. No luck.'

'I'd have thought the university would keep records.'

'Bombed in World War Two, apparently. So then Gimli went to Iceland. Saw Professor Haraldsson, who was interested but couldn't help very much. We'd kinda drawn a blank. Until a month or so ago, when Professor Haraldsson got in touch with Gimli. A former student had approached him with *Gaukur's Saga* and wanted to sell it. You can imagine how excited Gimli and I were, but we had to give Haraldsson time to translate it into English.'

'How much was he asking?'

'Only two million dollars. But the deal was that the saga would have to be kept a secret. I kinda liked that idea. So we set a date for Gimli to fly to Iceland to see Haraldsson. Gimli went to meet him at the summer house on Lake Thingvellir, where he read the saga. But they couldn't agree on a final price, and the professor didn't actually have the original saga with him. So Gimli came back here to the hotel.'

'From where he sent you an SMS?'

'That's right. I called him back and we figured out a strategy for how we were going to negotiate for the saga. He was going out to meet Agnar again the next day, but the next thing Gimli heard the professor was dead and he was a suspect for murder.'

'What about the ring?'

'The ring?' Feldman said. He was trying to feign innocent surprise, but failing badly.

'Yeah, the ring,' said Magnus. 'The *kallisarvoinen*. Your precious. It's a Finnish word. We figured that out. And Agnar wanted five million bucks for it.'

Feldman sighed. 'Yes, the ring. The professor said he knew where it was and he could get it for us, but it would cost us five million.'

'So he didn't have it at the summer house?'

'No. He gave Gimli no idea where it might be. But he was confident he could get hold of it. For the right amount of money.'

'Did you believe him?'

Feldman hesitated. 'We *wanted* to believe him, of course. That would have been the coolest discovery in history. But we knew we were wide open to being ripped off. So I started to work on lining up an expert to examine the ring once we got a hold of it. Someone who would keep quiet about it afterwards.'

'Steve Jubb never saw it?'

'No,' said Feldman.

Magnus leaned back in his chair and studied Feldman.

'Did Jubb kill the professor?'

'No,' said Feldman immediately.

'Are you sure?'

Feldman hesitated. 'Pretty sure.'

'But not absolutely positive?'

Feldman shrugged. 'That wasn't part of the plan. But I wasn't there.'

Magnus accepted the validity of the point. 'How well do you know Jubb?'

Feldman looked away from Magnus, out of the window at the naked branches of the trees in the square, and the top of the statue of a distinguished nineteenth-century Icelander. 'That's a difficult question to answer. I've never met him or spoken to him. I don't know what he looks like, what he sounds like. But on the other hand I've been communicating with him online for the last couple of years. I know a lot about him.'

'Do you trust him?'

'I did,' said Feldman.

'But now you are not so sure?'

Feldman shook his head. 'I genuinely don't believe that Gimli killed the professor. There would be no reason to, and we never discussed anything like that. Gimli never struck me as being violent. People get aggressive online when they are anonymous, but Gimli never was. He thought flaming was plain dumb. But I can't be one hundred per cent sure he's innocent, no.'

'So you came to Iceland to help him?' Magnus asked.

'Yeah,' said Feldman. 'To see what I can do. We've been communicating through the lawyer, Kristján Gylfason, but I wanted to do what I could myself.'

'And look for the ring,' Magnus said.

'I don't even know if there *is* a ring,' said Feldman.

'But you want to find out,' said Magnus.

'Are you going to arrest me?' Feldman asked.

'Not for the moment, no,' said Magnus. 'But I'll take your passport. You're not leaving Iceland. And let me tell you something. If you do find a ring, whether it's a real one or a hoax, I want to know about it, know what I'm saying? Because it's evidence.' Feldman recoiled from Magnus's stare.

Magnus doubted he had the authority to confiscate Feldman's passport, but he also doubted that Feldman would know that. 'And if I catch you withholding evidence, you'll definitely be spending some nights in an Icelandic jail.'

CHAPTER TWENTY-THREE

INGILEIF WAS ABSORBED in her drawing, her eyes flicking from her emerging design to the piece of tanned fish skin in front of her. It was Nile perch – the scales larger than the salmon she often used, the textures rougher. It had a wonderful light blue, translucent colour. She was designing a credit-card holder, always a popular item.

Ingileif didn't work in the gallery on Tuesday afternoons, her partner Sunna, the painter, was minding the store. She had plenty to worry about, but it felt good to lose herself in the design process for an hour or two. She had spent a year in Florence after she had graduated from university learning how to work with leather. When she returned to Iceland she had attended the Academy of Arts where she experimented with fish skin. Each skin was different. The more she worked with the material, the more possibilities she saw.

The bell rang. Ingileif lived in a tiny one-bedroom flat on the upper floor of a small house in 101, not too far from the gallery. The bedroom was her studio and occasional guest room – she slept in the living area. The flat was stark: Icelandic minimalist with white walls, lots of wood and not much clutter. Despite that, it was cramped, but it was all she could afford in Reykjavík 101, the central postal area. And she didn't want to live in one of those soulless apartments in the suburbs of Kópavogur or Gardabaer.

She went downstairs to the front door. It was Pétur.

'Pési!' She felt a sudden urge to throw herself into her brother's arms. He held her tight for a few moments, stroking her hair.

They broke apart. Pétur smiled at her awkwardly, surprised at her sudden show of affection. 'Come on up,' she said.

'I'm sorry I haven't been in touch,' said Pétur.

'You mean since Agnar's murder?' She flopped back on to the white counterpane on her bed, leaning back against the wall. Pétur took one of the two low chrome chairs.

He nodded.

'In a way I'm glad you haven't,' Ingileif said. 'You must be so angry with me.'

'I told you you shouldn't have tried to sell the saga.'

Ingileif glanced at her brother. There was as much sympathy as anger in his eyes. 'You did. And I'm sorry. I wish I hadn't: I need the money.'

'Well, you'll get it now,' said Pétur. 'I assume you'll still be able to sell it?'

'I don't know,' said Ingileif. 'I haven't asked. I don't care about the money any more. The whole thing was just a big mistake.'

'Have the police been round?'

'Yes. Lots of times. And you?'

'Once,' Pétur said. 'There wasn't much I could tell them.'

'They seem to think an Englishman killed Agnar. The guy who was acting for the American *Lord of the Rings* fan who wanted to buy the saga.'

'I haven't seen anything in the news about the saga,' Pétur said.

'No. The police are keeping its existence quiet while the investigation is proceeding. They've taken it away for analysis. The detective I spoke to seemed to think it's a forgery, which is ridiculous.'

'It's no forgery,' said Pétur. He sighed. 'But they'll make it public eventually, won't they? And then the world's press will be all over it. We'll have to give interviews, talk about it, see it on the cover of every Icelandic magazine.'

'I know,' said Ingileif. 'I'll do all that if you like. I know how much you hate the saga. And this is all my fault, after all.'

'That's kind of you to offer,' Pétur said. 'We'll see.'

'There's something else I should show you,' Ingileif said. She fetched her bag from behind the door and handed Pétur Tolkien's letter. The second one, the one written in 1948.

He opened it and read, frowning.

Ingileif had been expecting more of a reaction. 'This shows that Grandpa actually found the ring.'

Pétur looked up at his sister. 'I knew that.'

'You knew it! How? When?'

'Grandpa told me. And he told me that he wanted the ring to remain hidden. He was worried that Dad would look for it once he died and he wanted me to stop him.'

'Why didn't you tell me?' Ingileif asked.

'It was another one of our family secrets,' Pétur said. 'And after Dad died, I didn't want to talk about it. Any of it.'

'I wish you *had* stopped him,' Ingileif said.

Anger flared in Pétur's eyes. 'Don't you think I do? I beat myself up about that for years. But what could I do? I was in high school in Reykjavík. Besides, I was his son, I couldn't tell him what to do.'

'No, of course not,' said Ingileif quickly. 'I'm sorry.' They sat in silence for a moment, Pétur's anger subsiding.

'I've been wondering recently, since I found this letter, wondering about Dad's death,' she said.

'What do you mean?'

'Well, he went off with the pastor to look for the ring. Maybe they found it?'

'No. We have no reason to think that.'

'I should ask him.'

'Who? The pastor? Don't you think he would have told us if they had found anything?'

'Maybe not.'

Pétur closed his eyes. When he opened them, they were moist. 'Inga, I don't know why thinking about Dad's death affects me like this, but it always does. I want to forget it. I have tried so hard over the years to forget it, but I never seem able to. I just can't stop thinking that it's all my fault.'

'Of course it wasn't your fault, Pési,' Ingileif said.

'I know that. I *know* that.' Pétur dabbed his eye with a finger. It was strange for Ingileif to see her brother, usually so composed and aloof, so upset. He sniffed and shook his head. 'Or else I think it's that damned ring. When I was a kid I was obsessed with it, scared of it. Then when Dad died I thought it was a load of bullshit and I wanted nothing to do with it.'

He stared angrily at his sister. 'And now? Now I wonder whether it hasn't destroyed our family. Reached out from that moment a thousand years ago when Gaukur took it from Ísildur on the summit of Hekla, reached out to destroy us: Dad, Mum, Birna, me, you.'

He leaned forward, his moist eyes alight. 'It doesn't need to exist anywhere but in here.' He tapped his temple with his finger. 'It is lodged in the minds of all of us, all our family. That's where it does its damage.'

Vigdís parked her car on one of the small streets leading down towards the bay from Hverfisgata, and she and Baldur jumped out. The renewed questioning at the university had turned up something. A uniformed officer had interviewed one of Agnar's students, a dopey twenty-year-old, who had remembered someone asking around at the university for Agnar on the day he had died. The student had mentioned to the man that Agnar had a summer house by Lake Thingvellir and that he sometimes spent time there. Why the student hadn't reported this before wasn't clear, to the student or to the police, although he didn't have a good explanation as to what he was doing on the university campus on a public holiday. The police let that drop.

No, the man hadn't given his name. But the student recognized him. From TV.

Tómas Hákonarson.

He lived on the eighth floor of one of the new blocks of luxury apartments that had sprouted up in the Skuggahverfi, or Shadow District, along the shore of the bay. He answered the door, bleary eyed, as if he had just been woken up.

Baldur introduced himself and Vigdís, and barged in.

'What's this about?' asked Tómas, blinking.

'The murder of Agnar Haraldsson.'

'Ah. You'd better take a seat then.'

The furniture was expensive cream leather. The view of the bay was spectacular, although at that precise moment a dark cloud was pressing down on the darker sea. Only the lowest hundred feet or so of Mount Esja was visible, and there was no chance of seeing Snaefellsnes glacier in the gloom. To the left, tall cranes dithered above the unfinished national concert hall, one of the casualties of the *kreppa*.

'What do you know?' Tómas asked.

'I'd rather ask you what you know,' Baldur said. 'Starting with your movements on Thursday the twenty-third. Last Thursday.'

Tómas gathered his thoughts. 'I got up late. Went out for a sandwich for lunch and a cup of coffee. Then I drove over to the university.'

'Go on.'

'I was looking for Agnar Haraldsson. I asked a student who said that he might be at his summer house by Lake Thingvellir. So I drove up there.'

'At what time was this?' Vigdís asked, her notebook out, pen poised.

'I got there about four o'clock, I think. I don't know. I can't remember precisely. Can't have been much before three-thirty. Might have been a bit after four.'

'And was Agnar there?'

'Yes, he was. I had a cup of coffee. We chatted a bit. And then I left.'

'I see. And what time did you leave?'

'I don't know. Once again, I didn't look at my watch. I was there about three-quarters of an hour.'

'So that would make it four forty-five?'

'Or thereabouts.'

Baldur was silent. Tómas held his silence too. Vigdís knew the game: she was motionless, pen poised. But Tómas wasn't saying any more.

'What did you chat about?' Baldur asked, eventually.

'I wanted to discuss a possible television project on the sagas.'

'What kind of project?'

'Well, that was the trouble. I didn't have a specific idea. I was kind of hoping that Agnar would provide that. But he didn't.'

'So you left?'

'That's right.'

'And then what did you do?'

'I came back home. Watched a movie, a DVD. Had a drink. Well, I had several drinks actually.'

'Alone?'

'Yes,' said Tómas.

'Do you often drink alone?'

Tómas took a deep breath. 'Yes,' he said again.

Vigdís looked around the flat. Sure enough there was an empty whisky bottle in the bin. Dewar's.

'And was this the first time you had met Agnar?' Baldur asked.

'No,' said Tómas. 'I had bumped into him once or twice in the past. I suppose he was my saga contact.'

Baldur's long face was impassive, but Vigdís could feel the excitement in him. Tómas was talking nonsense, and Baldur knew it.

'And why didn't you come forward before?' Baldur asked, gently.

'Um. Well, you see, I didn't see anything about the murder in the papers.'

'Oh, don't give me that, Tómas! Your job is to keep up with the news. The papers have been full of it.'

'And ... I didn't want to get involved. I couldn't see that it was important.'

At this Baldur couldn't maintain his composure. He laughed. 'Right, Tómas. You are coming with us to the station, where you had better think up a better story than that bullshit. I would suggest the truth; that usually works. But first I want you to show me what clothes you were wearing on that day. And the shoes.'

CHAPTER TWENTY-FOUR

'YOU CAN'T RELEASE Steve Jubb!' Magnus almost shouted.

Baldur stood in the corridor outside the interview room, facing him. 'I can and I will. We don't have the evidence to hold him. We *know* that there was someone else there that night after Steve Jubb had driven back to Reykjavík. Someone who dumped Agnar into the lake once it got dark.'

'According to a four-year-old girl.'

'She's five. But the point is all the forensic evidence backs that up.'

'But what about her parents? Surely they would have heard another car going past their house after nine-thirty?'

'We checked. They went to bed early. Their bedroom is at the back of the house. And they were busy.'

'Busy? Busy doing what?'

'Busy doing what married people sometimes do when they go to bed early.'

'Oh.'

'And now we have another suspect.' Baldur nodded towards the door where Tómas Hákonarson was just beginning a marathon interview session.

Magnus looked in. A man with round glasses, thinning hair and chubby cheeks was sitting smoking a cigarette, watched closely by Vigdís. The famous television personality.

'And has he confessed?'

'Give me time,' Baldur said. 'His fingerprints match the unidentified set we found in the house. We're analysing his clothes and his boots now. For the moment his story is that he came and went *before* Steve Jubb arrived. Jubb arrived at about seven-thirty that evening and the neighbours were out all afternoon, so it's just about possible that Tómas came and went without them seeing him. But if you thought Jubb was lying, you should see this guy. His story is shot full of holes. We'll break it.'

'Don't you think what I told you about Lawrence Feldman and Steve Jubb trying to buy a ring from Agnar changes things?'

'No,' said Baldur, firmly. 'Now, I have some work to do.'

Magnus went back to his desk in intense frustration. What really bugged him was the possibility that Baldur might be right and he wrong. Baldur was a good cop who trusted his intuition, but then so was Magnus. Which was why it would be so galling if Baldur's hunches proved to be correct and his were not.

He knew he should take a deep breath, keep an open mind, let the direction of the inquiry follow the evidence as it emerged. But the trouble was, the more he looked into the saga and ring deal, the murkier it got. And the higher were the stakes for those involved.

When it came right down to it, Tómas Hákonarson had the opportunity but as yet not the motive. Isildur and Gimli, as they liked to call themselves, had motive aplenty.

The seat opposite Magnus was empty – Árni was still up in the air. Magnus called his cell phone and left a message on his voice-mail to tell him that Isildur was in Reykjavík and he may as well come home.

Poor guy.

He switched on his computer and checked for an e-mail. There was one from Deputy Superintendent Williams, a long one by his standards.

Williams apologized for the failure to protect Colby. He claimed there was a patrol car outside all night, but they didn't see anything. There was no trace of Colby herself, although she had told her boss and her parents that she was going away for a while.

There had been questions asked around Schroeder Plaza, the headquarters of the Homicide Unit, questions about Magnus disguised as gossip. Friends of Lenahan; friends of friends of Soto. There was no doubt that Soto's gang was after Magnus.

The kid Magnus had shot had died. The inquest into his death and that of his older partner was going to be delayed until after the Lenahan trial.

But the big news was the Lenahan trial itself. The judge had finally grown impatient with the delay tactics of the defence and had denied their motions to subpoena thousands of e-mails from the police department. That, combined with the surprise collapse of another murder trial which left a hole in the judge's docket, meant that it was likely that the trial would begin sometime the following week. Magnus would be called as a witness as early as possible: the FBI hoped that as soon as he testified, Lenahan would talk. The Feds would send Magnus details of his flight as soon as they had decided them. The destination airport was still under discussion, but it wouldn't be Logan. The FBI would be there in force to meet him and take him to a safe house.

Magnus tapped out a reply saying it would be good to be home. Which was true. He felt that the value he was adding to the Icelandic police force was precisely zero. Baldur's estimate would be negative.

He thought about Colby, and smiled. Good for her. If the Boston police couldn't find her, that was a good thing. If she really wanted to hide, she could do it.

He wrote a quick e-mail to her, telling her to let him know she was OK, if she got the opportunity. That was the best he could hope for.

His thoughts turned to the case. He hated the idea of dropping it, leaving it to Baldur to clear up.

OK, if he was right and Baldur was wrong, that meant the case turned on the saga and the ring. Especially the ring. Leave aside the question of whether this was really the ring that was taken from a dwarf who fished in the shape of a pike a couple of millennia ago. That wasn't important. What was important was that Agnar thought he knew where a ring was, and Feldman wanted that ring. Badly.

So where was it?

As he had pointed out to Árni, it seemed unlikely that Agnar could conjure up a fake thousand-year-old ring in a couple of days. Which meant either that someone else had it, Ingileif for example, or that Agnar had figured out where he could find it.

Magnus didn't think Ingileif had the ring. All right, he didn't *want* to believe that Ingileif had the ring, but he knew he should keep the idea open as a possibility.

Unless someone else had it. Magnus had no idea who.

What if Agnar had figured out where it was hidden? Magnus had read *Gaukur's Saga*: there were not enough clues in there to lead anyone to the ring. But Agnar was an expert on medieval Icelandic literature. He no doubt knew of dozens of folk tales and legends which might hold clues, cross-references.

Then Magnus remembered the entry in Agnar's diary for Hruni. Not Flúdir, Hruni. Vigdís had interviewed the pastor there, the pastor Pétur had told Magnus about, Dr Ásgrímur's friend. Magnus recalled her report: the pastor had had nothing much of interest to say.

Magnus needed to go to Hruni. But first he wanted to speak to Ingileif. He wanted to find out more about the ring, and the pastor.

And, damn it, he wanted to see her.

He walked to the gallery and arrived just before closing time, but Ingileif wasn't there. Her partner, a striking dark-haired woman, told him she was probably working at home. He had her home address from the initial interview and it only took him ten minutes to walk there.

Her first reaction when she saw him on her doorstep seemed to be pleasure, her smile was wide and warm, but a moment later it was clouded by doubt. But she invited him in.

'How are you getting on in Iceland?' she asked 'Met any nice girls yet?'

'Not yet.'

'I'm offended.'

'Present company excepted of course.'

'Of course. Have a seat.'

Magnus sat in a low chrome chair and accepted a glass of wine. A cello was propped up against the wall, dominating the small room. In an apartment this tiny a violin might have been a better choice of instrument, Magnus thought. Or a piccolo.

'I didn't know you were allowed to drink on duty,' Ingileif said as she handed the glass to him.

'I'm not sure I am on duty,' said Magnus.

'Really?' said Ingileif, raising her eyebrows. 'I didn't realize this was a social call.'

'Well, it's not a formal interview,' Magnus said. 'I want your help.'

'I thought that's what I had been doing,' Ingileif said. 'Helping the police with their inquiries. Except I admit I wasn't very helpful at first.'

'I want to talk to you about the ring. I need to figure out where it is. Who has it.'

'I have no idea, I told you that,' Ingileif said. 'It's stuffed in some tiny niche in the rocks somewhere in the Icelandic wilderness.'

'Agnar thought he had found it,' Magnus said. 'Or at least he thought he knew where it was. It wasn't just the saga he was trying to sell to Lawrence Feldman, it was the ring too.'

Magnus explained the contents of the text message Steve Jubb had sent to Feldman the night Agnar had been murdered, and Feldman's conviction that Agnar knew where the ring was.

'So somebody has it?' Ingileif asked.

'Possibly,' Magnus said.

'Who?'

'The most obvious candidate is you.'

Ingileif exploded. 'Hey! You said you wanted my help. I would have said if I had it. I know I didn't tell you everything earlier, but I've given up on the saga, and the damned ring. So if you don't believe me, take me away and interrogate me. Or torture me. You are American, aren't you? Do you want to try out some water-boarding on me?'

Magnus was taken aback by the vehemence of her denial. 'It's true I have lived in America for a while. But I'm not going to torture you. In fact, I'll just ask you. Do you know where the ring is?'

'No,' Ingileif said. 'Do you believe me?'

'Yes,' Magnus said. He knew that as a professional detective he should still doubt her, but a professional detective wouldn't have been drinking a glass of wine in her apartment. He had given up on being a professional detective, at least while he was in Iceland. He just wanted to find out who killed Agnar.

She seemed to calm down. 'Sorry,' she said. 'About the water-boarding dig.'

'Will you still help me?'

'Yes.'

'Your brother told me that your father confided in the local pastor. That the two of them worked on theories of where the ring might be hidden. Can you tell me something about this pastor?'

'I didn't know anything about my grandfather finding the ring at that stage, but I did know that Dad planned several hiking trips around Thjórsárdalur with the pastor to look for it. So, what can I tell you about Reverend Hákon?'

She paused, gathering her thoughts. 'He's strange. I mean there are plenty of eccentric country priests in Iceland, but Hákon is one of the strangest. A lot of my friends were scared of him, scared and fascinated at the same time. He used to mess with their heads.'

'But not yours?'

'No, he was always straightforward with me, because of my father, I think. He's clever, he fancies himself as an intellectual. He's very interested in Saemundur the Learned – you know, the guy who kept on cheating the devil. And of course he knows everything about the legend of the Hruni dance.'

'Have you seen him recently?'

'He officiated at my mother's funeral at the end of last year. He didn't do a bad job, actually. He definitely has presence.' She finished her wine. 'Do you want another glass?'

Magnus nodded. Ingileif went to the fridge to retrieve the bottle and refilled their glasses.

'I've been thinking a lot about my own father's death this week, after what happened to Agnar. I know it's Agnar's murder you are investigating, but I wonder whether Dad's death was all that it seemed.'

'What happened?'

'Dad and the pastor were going on a two-day expedition, with tents, up in the hills to the west of the River Thjórsá. It's pretty barren up there, and there was still some snow on the ground. I never found out exactly where they went – presumably they were checking out some local caves or hound-shaped chunks of lava.'

Ingileif took a gulp of her wine. 'On the second day they were on their way back when a snowstorm blew up out of nowhere. I say out of nowhere, it had been forecast, but the previous day had been clear and sunny, I remember it. They got lost on the moor, and Dad stumbled over a cliff. He fell about fifteen metres on to some rocks. The pastor climbed down. He says he thought Dad was badly injured but still alive. He hurried off as quick as he could to find help, but he got lost in the snowstorm. Six hours later he found a sheep farm and grabbed the farmer. By the time they got back to the cliff, Dad was dead: fractured skull, broken neck. In fact, they think he probably died within a few minutes of the fall.'

'I'm sorry,' said Magnus. 'My father died when I was twenty. It's rough.'

Ingileif smiled quickly. 'Yes, it is. And although you think you have come to terms with it, you never really do. Especially when something like this happens.'

'Do you think he was pushed?' Magnus asked.

'By Reverend Hákon? You mean, they both found the ring and the pastor pushed my father over the cliff to take it from him?'

Magnus shrugged. 'You just said it. What do you think?'

'I don't know,' Ingileif said. 'The pastor and my dad were good friends. My dad had lots of friends, he was good with people, but Reverend Hákon wasn't. I think Dad was probably the only true friend he really had. After Dad died the pastor sort of withdrew into himself and became really weird. His wife left him a couple of years later. No one in the village blamed her.'

'Or it could simply be the reaction of someone who had just murdered his best friend,' said Magnus. 'I think I should go and see the Reverend Hákon tomorrow.'

'Can I come?' Ingileif asked.

Magnus raised his eyebrows.

'It's hard to explain,' Ingileif said. 'I need to find out what really happened to my father. It was a long time ago and I've tried to bottle it all up, but there are so many questions that I don't have the answers to. Agnar's murder has brought them all back. I've just *got* to find those answers if I'm going to get on with my life. Do you understand?'

'Oh, I understand,' said Magnus. 'Believe me, I understand. I sometimes think I spend every day trying to answer those kinds of questions about my own father.'

He considered her request. It was certainly not part of the standard investigative procedure to take one witness along to interview another, just to satisfy her curiosity. 'Yes,' said Magnus, smiling. 'That would be fine.'

Ingileif returned his smile. There was a silence that was and was not uncomfortable.

'Tell me about your father,' Ingileif said.

Magnus paused. Drank some wine. Glanced at the woman opposite him, her grey eyes warm now. It wasn't standard investigative procedure. But he told her. About his early childhood, his parents' separation, his own move to America to join his father. About his stepmother, his father's murder and his failed attempts to solve it. And then about his recent discovery of his father's infidelity.

They talked for an hour. Perhaps two hours. They talked a lot about Magnus, and then they talked about Ingileif. They finished the bottle of wine and opened another.

Eventually Magnus got up to leave. 'So you still want to come with me to Hruni? To see the Reverend Hákon?'

'I'd like to,' said Ingileif, with a smile.

'Good,' said Magnus, putting on his coat. Then he froze. 'Wait a minute!'

'What?'

'This pastor. This Reverend Hákon. Does he have a son?'

'Yes. As a matter of fact I saw him only this morning. He's an old friend of mine.'

'And what's his name?'

'Tómas. Tómas Hákonarson. He's a TV presenter now. He's quite famous: you must know him.'

'Yes,' said Magnus. 'As a matter of fact, I do know him.'

The street was cold and damp after the warmth of Ingileif's flat. There was a light drizzle and a steady fresh breeze pushed the moisture against Magnus's cheeks.

He knew he should go home, but Ingileif lived not far from the Grand Rokk.

Just one beer.

As he made his way along the higgledy-piggledy little streets, Magnus pulled out his phone. He should call Baldur, tell him that the man he had in custody was the son of the pastor who had accompanied the doctor in his search for the ring seventeen years before.

He didn't have Baldur's home number or the number for his cell phone. But if he called the station they could pass on the message.

Screw it. Magnus slipped his phone back in his pocket. It's not as if Baldur would care. He wouldn't actually *do* anything with the information. Magnus would tell him the following day, when he had actually spoken to the Reverend Hákon.

His phone rang. It was Árni.

'I've just arrived in San Francisco,' he said. 'I got your message.' The disappointment flowed unhindered the thousands of miles from California.

'Sorry about that, Árni. I saw Isildur this morning at the Hótel Borg.'

'Did he give you some good information?'

'Yeah, he did. Not that your boss would care.'

'Why? What's happened?'

'He's made another arrest. Some guy called Tómas Hákonarson.'

'Not from *The Point*?'

'That's the guy.'

Árni whistled down the phone. 'So what shall I do now?'

'I guess you'd better come home. Your plane will probably turn right around and head back to New York. You'd better check they got a seat for you on it.'

'Oh, shit,' said Árni. 'It feels like I've been on the plane for days already. I don't think my body could stand another flight that long.'

Don't be such a wimp, Magnus thought. But he took pity on his new partner. 'Or you could just check into a hotel and listen to my message first thing tomorrow morning.'

'Good idea. I'll do that. Thanks, Magnús.'

'No problem.'

'And Magnús?'

'Yeah?'

'Keep at it. Don't give up. You'll get there.'

'Night, Árni.'

As Magnus switched off his phone he thought about Árni's last comment. He was pleased to be going home. But he didn't like giving up. He hated the idea that he would leave Iceland with Agnar's murder unsolved. To be brutally honest, he hated the idea of Baldur solving it just as much. Árni was right, he shouldn't give up. He was looking forward to going to Hruni the next day with Ingileif. There was her father's death to explain as well.

There was so much to explain. With a kind of weary inevitability, his mind drifted back to his own father's death.

He paused outside the Grand Rokk and strode towards the pool of light emanating from the bar. The warmth of the chatter and the alcohol seeped out into the little front yard.

He went in.

Magnus was in a tight spot. He had already wasted three of the bad guys, but there were another two out there, at least. He was packing a Remington shotgun and a three fifty-seven magnum. The docks were dark. He heard a rustle.

He turned, saw a gun poke out from behind a container and loosed off two rounds from the Remington. A figure rolled out on to the tarmac, dead. Two more figures jumped him from close quarters; he shot one and then a message flashed up in the bottom corner of the screen. SHOULDER WOUND. He had to drop the gun. The grinning face of a hoodlum appeared in the screen, followed by the business end of an MP5. 'Make my day,' the guy said and the screen went orange and then black.

GAME OVER.

Johnny Yeoh swore and pushed his chair back from the screen. He had been playing Magnus's career for five hours straight. Kopz Life was his favourite game, and he always called himself Magnus. That guy was just so cool.

Johnny wondered whether he should take the plunge and apply to join the police department for real. He was certainly smart enough. And he thought of himself as good under pressure. Sure, he wasn't exactly big, but if you packed the right piece, what did that matter?

The buzzer sounded. He checked his watch: half-past midnight. He suddenly realized how hungry he was. He had ordered the pizza forty-five minutes before, although thanks to his total absorption in the game, it felt like only ten.

He buzzed the pizza guy into his building, and a minute later unlocked his apartment door to let him in.

The door slammed open and Johnny found himself pinned up against the wall of his living room, a revolver shoved down his throat. A light brown face with cool eyes stared at him, inches away. Johnny's own eyes hurt as he crossed them, trying to focus on the gun in his mouth.

'OK, Johnny, I got one question for you,' the man said.

Johnny tried to speak, but he couldn't. He didn't know whether it was the fear or the metal pressed on his tongue.

The man withdrew the gun so that it was an inch away from his mouth.

Johnny tried to speak again. No sound. It was the fear.

'Say what?'

This time Johnny squeezed out some words. 'What do you want to know?'

'You done some work for a cop by the name of Magnus Jonson?'

Johnny nodded vigorously.

'You found the address of some guy in California he was looking for?'

Johnny nodded again.

'How about you write that down for me, man?' The guy glanced around the room. He was tall, slim, with a smooth face and hard brown eyes. Eyes which alighted on some paper and a pen. 'Over there!'

'I need to check my computer,' Johnny said.

'Go right ahead. I'll be watching you. So don't go typing no messages to nobody.'

Intensely aware of the gun in the back of his head, Johnny Yeoh went over to the desk and sat in front of his computer. He clenched his buttocks, trying desperately hard to stop his bowels moving. He wanted to pee too.

Within less than a minute he had found Lawrence Feldman's address. He wrote it down: his hand was shaking so badly it took him two attempts, and even then the words were illegible.

'Did Jonson say where he's at?' the guy asked.

'No,' said Johnny, turning to look up at the man, his eyes wide. 'I didn't speak to him. He sent me an e-mail.'

'Where'd it come from?'

'I don't know.'

'Sweden?'

'I don't know.'

'Then look!' The gun was crammed into his skull.

Johnny called up his e-mail folder and found the one from Magnus. The truth was he hadn't checked the address. The domain name was *lrh.is*. Where the hell was that? A country beginning with 'IS'. Isreal? No, that was '.il'. 'Iceland, perhaps?'

'Hey, I'm asking you.'

'All right, all right. I'll check.' It took Johnny less than a minute to confirm that the domain was indeed in Iceland. The Icelandic police to be precise.

'Now, Iceland ain't in Sweden, is it?'

'No,' said Johnny.'

'Is it near Sweden?'

'Not really,' said Johnny. 'I mean it's in Scandinavia but it's right in the middle of the Atlantic Ocean. A thousand miles away. Two thousand.'

'All right, all right.' The man with the gun grabbed the scrap of paper and backed off towards the door. 'You know, you ain't no fun, man.'

Then the gunman did something very strange. He looked Johnny Yeoh right in the eye. Put the revolver to his own temple. Smiled.

And pulled the trigger.

CHAPTER TWENTY-FIVE

THE PASTOR CARRIED the newspaper he had just bought from the shop down in Flúdir into his study. There was a short article on page five about the investigation into Agnar's murder. It sounded as if little real progress had been made since the initial arrest of the Englishman. The pastor smiled as he remembered how he had so disconcerted the black policewoman. But he shouldn't be complacent. The police were making a plea for any witnesses who had seen anyone at all driving down to that part of the shore of Lake Thingvellir on the First Day of Summer to come forward.

That worried him.

He thought about making a phone call, but he knew the best thing to do was to stay calm, and stay quiet. There was no reason why the police should pay him another visit, but he would be wise to be prepared nonetheless.

He glanced at the pile of books on his desk, and the exercise book open at the page he had left off working the night before. He should get back to the life of Saemundur. But he couldn't dispel the anxiety the article in the newspaper had awakened. He needed some comfort.

He put down the paper and examined his small CD collection on the bottom shelf of a long bookshelf, and selected one. *Led Zeppelin IV*. He slipped it into his CD player and turned up the volume.

He smiled when he remembered the time fifteen years before when he had shouted at his son for listening to devil worship, and then how he had surreptitiously listened to the music himself when his son was away at school. He liked it; it was somehow apt. He stood for a moment, closed his eyes and let the music wash over him.

After a couple of minutes he left the house and crossed the fifty yards over to the church, nestled beneath the rocky crag. Heavy, insistent chords rang out of the parsonage behind him, echoing off the rocks behind, swirling around the valley.

The church was bright and airy inside. The sunlight streamed in through the clear glass windows. The ceiling was painted light blue and decorated with gold stars, the walls were cream wooden planks and the pews were painted pink. The pulpit and the small electric organ were made of blond pine. He walked towards the altar, draped with red velvet. Behind it was a painting of the Last Supper.

On mornings like this, some of his congregation claimed that they could feel God in the church. But only the pastor knew what was really hidden in there.

Beneath its finery, the altar was actually a tatty old pine cupboard, inside which were piles of old copies of the *Lögbirtingablad*, official notices going back several decades. The pastor reached under the pile to the right of the cupboard. His fingers felt for the familiar round shape.

The ring.

He drew it out and pulled it on to the fourth finger of his right hand, where it fitted snugly. The pastor had big hands, he had been a good handball player in his youth, yet the ring was not too tight. It had been made for the fingers of warriors.

And now it belonged to the pastor of Hruni.

Baldur ignored Magnus in the morning meeting.

He was amassing a case against Tómas Hákonarson. No one had seen Tómas come home that evening, either when he said he did at around five or six o'clock, or much later. There was little obvious sign of mud on the trainers Tómas said he had worn that night, but then they had been soaked the previous Saturday when he had walked through puddles wearing them. The lab was working on a more thorough examination, and attempts to match the fibres on his socks with three still-unexplained fibres from the summer house.

Tómas himself had asked for a lawyer and was sticking to his story, refusing to admit how unconvincing it sounded.

During the whole meeting, Baldur never directed a single comment to Magnus, nor asked his opinion, nor gave him any tasks in the investigation. And all this was watched by Thorkell Holm.

Screw Baldur.

Magnus's head hurt. He had had quite a bit more than one beer in the Grand Rokk the night before, but had managed to go easy on the chasers. He was suffering from more of a thick head than a full blown hangover. But it was enough to put him in an uncooperative mood.

Magnus would tell Baldur all about Tómas's father in his own good time. When he had spoken to the pastor himself.

Lawrence Feldman sat in the back seat of the black Mercedes four-wheel-drive and surveyed the prison buildings ahead of him. He was in the car park of Litla Hraun. The buildings themselves weren't too bad, white, functional, surrounded by two layers of wire fencing. But the landscape surrounding them was bleak: flat, bare and brown, stretching across to the mountain slopes to the north. To the south lay the wide grey expanse of the Atlantic Ocean. At least there was some sunshine on this side of the pass.

The journey from Reykjavík, only an hour away, had been exhilarating, as they drove up through the lava field into the clouds. Feldman thought he could well have been in Middle Earth, perhaps on the edge of Mordor, the home of the Dark Lord Sauron. There was no grass, no greenery, or not the greenery of home. Weird lichens and mosses, some of them a bright lime colour, some grey, some orange, clung to the rock. Patches of snow stretched up the mountainsides into the clouds. To the side of the road, plumes of steam rose up from the ground.

Mordor. Where the shadows lie.

A large black bird swooped down and alighted on a fence post only feet from the car. It opened its beak and croaked accusingly. It cocked its head on one side and seemed to be staring right at Feldman with one eye. A raven. The damn bird was weirding him out.

Feldman had elected to remain in the car, while Kristján Gylfason, the lawyer he had hired to represent Gimli, had gone into the prison to fetch him. The stories the big red-haired policeman with the flawless American accent had told Feldman about the prison still unsettled him.

A man emerged from a nearby building. He was a big guy, six-foot six, with long fair hair, a beard and a barrel chest, wearing blue overalls, and he was coming right towards the Mercedes. One of those depraved shepherds Feldman had heard about, no doubt. Feldman reached for the door lock, and was relieved to hear the comforting electronic clicks as he depressed it. The guy in the overalls caught sight of him in the car, gave him a curt nod and a wave, and climbed into a Toyota pick-up.

At last he saw the smooth besuited figure of Kristján emerge from the prison entrance, accompanied by a big man in a blue tracksuit, his stomach protruding in front of him. Feldman reached over, unlocked the door and pushed it open.

'Gimli!'

Gimli flopped into the back seat with a grunt. 'How you doin'?' he said.

Feldman hesitated. This was the first time he had ever met Gimli in the flesh, but he felt he knew him so well. He was overcome with emotion. He leaned forward clumsily to give him a hug.

Gimli sat still. 'Steady on, mate,' he said. He had a pronounced Yorkshire accent.

Feldman broke away.

'How was it?' Feldman asked. 'In there? Was it really bad?'

'It were all right. Food's OK. Mind you, the telly in this country is crap.'

'What about the other prisoners? Did they treat you OK?'

'Didn't talk to them,' Gimli said. 'I kept meself to meself.'

'That was wise,' said Feldman. He looked closely at Gimli, trying to figure out if he was lying. Feldman would understand if he didn't want to be too specific about his prison experiences.

Gimli shifted uncomfortably under Feldman's stare. 'Thanks for your help, Lawrence. With Kristján and everything.'

'Not at all. And please call me Isildur. I'll call you Gimli.'

Gimli turned towards Feldman, raised an eyebrow and shrugged. 'Fair enough. I didn't tell them anything, you know. Although they seemed to have figured a lot of it out theirselves. They found out about the saga, and the ring, for instance, but it weren't me what told them.'

'Of course not,' said Feldman, instantly guilty about how much he had told the police under much less pressure.

Kristján started the car and drove out of the prison grounds and back towards Reykjavík. Feldman was glad to get out of there. He glanced at his companion. Jubb was bigger than he imagined: because of his nickname Feldman had assumed someone shorter. But this Gimli shared a tough solidity with his namesake from Middle Earth. A good partner.

'You know, Gimli, we might have missed *Gaukur's Saga*, but we could still find the ring. Do you want to help me?'

'After all that's happened here?' Gimli asked.

'Of course, I'd understand if you didn't,' said Feldman. 'But if we found it, we could share it. Split custody of it. Seventy-five, twenty-five.'

'What do you mean?'

'I mean you get to keep it twenty-five per cent of the time. Three months in every year.'

Gimli stared out of the window at the brown plain. He nodded.

'Well, I've gone through so much, I may as well get something from it.'

'Deal?' Feldman held out his hand.

Gimli shook it. 'How do we start?'

'Did Agnar give you any indication at all where the ring might be?'

'No. But he was pretty confident he could get his hands on it. Like he knew where it was.'

'Excellent. Now, when the police questioned you, did they ask you about anyone in particular?'

'Yes, they did. A brother and sister. Peter and Ingi-something Ásgrímsson. I'm pretty sure they must be the ones who were selling the saga.'

'All right. All we have to do is find them. Kristján? Can you help us?'

'I haven't been listening to your conversation,' said the lawyer.

'We need to track down a couple of people. Can you help?'

'I don't think that would be wise,' said Kristján. 'If I need to defend you in the future, the less I know the better.'

'I get it. Then can you recommend a good investigator? Someone who is willing to bend the rules a bit to find out what we need?'

'The kind of investigators we use would never do that kind of thing,' Kristján said.

Feldman frowned.

'So who would you *not* recommend, then?' asked Steve Jubb. 'You know, who should we steer clear of?'

'There's a man called Axel Bjarnason,' said Kristján. 'He's well known to stray on the wrong side of the law. I would stay well clear of him. You'll find his name in the phone book. Under "A", we list people under first names in this country.'

It took Magnus a while to requisition a car for the journey to Hruni, and it wasn't until after lunch before he rolled up outside the gallery on Skólavördustígur to pick up Ingileif. It would take a little less than two hours to get to Hruni, but there should be time to get there, speak to the pastor and return to Reykjavík that evening.

She was wearing jeans and an anorak, her blonde hair tied back in a ponytail. She looked good. She also looked pleased to see him.

They drove out of Reykjavík under a broad dark cloud, the suburbs of Grafarvogur and Breidholt, a lesser grey, stretching out beside them. As they climbed up the pass to the south-east, lava and cloud converged, until suddenly they crested the final rise and a broad flood plain sparkled in the sunshine beneath them. The plain was scattered with knolls and tiny settlements, and bisected by a broad river, which ran down to the sea, through the town of Selfoss. Closer by, steam rose in tall plumes from the boreholes of a geothermal power station. Immediately below were the vegetable greenhouses of Hveragerdi, heated by spouts of hot water shooting up from the centre of the earth. There was a touch of sulphur in the air, even inside the car.

A thin band of white edged the black cloud hovering above them. Ahead, the sky was a pale, faultless blue.

'Tell me about Tómas,' Magnus said.

'I've known him for about as long as I can remember,' Ingileif said. 'We went to elementary school together in Flúdir. His parents separated when he was about fourteen, and he moved with his mother to Hella. He's totally different to his father, a bit of a joker, charming in his way, although I never found him attractive. Quite smart. But his father was always disappointed in him.'

She paused as Magnus manoeuvred around a particularly steep bend down the hill, swerving slightly to avoid a truck coming up the other way.

'We drive on the right in this country,' Ingileif said.

'I know. We do in the States too.'

'It's just you seem to prefer the middle of the road.'

Magnus took no notice. He was in perfect control of the car.

'Tómas bummed around after university for a bit,' Ingileif continued. 'Then did some journalism and suddenly fell into this show he does: *The Point*. He's perfect for it. The producer who spotted him must be a genius.'

'When was that?'

'A couple of years ago. I think it's gone to his head a bit. Tómas always liked to drink, do drugs, but his parties have the reputation for being pretty wild.'

'Have you been to any?'

'Actually, no. I haven't seen much of him recently, until yesterday. But he asked me to go to one on Saturday.'

'I wouldn't buy yourself a frock for that one.'

'No,' said Ingileif. 'I hear he might be double booked.'

'You say you saw him yesterday?'

Ingileif described her meeting with Tómas in Mokka, and his cryptic questions about the Agnar case.

'How does he get along with his father?' Magnus asked.

'Well, I don't know about now. But it always used to be the classic relationship between an over-demanding father and a son who is constantly trying to please and never quite succeeds. Tómas tried to rebel, dropping out, the parties and so on, but he never quite managed it. He always felt his father's disapproval deeply. I'm sure he still does.'

'So he might do his father a favour? A big favour?'

'Like murdering someone?'

Magnus shrugged.

Ingileif thought about it for a few seconds. 'I don't know,' she said in frustration eventually. 'I can't imagine he would. I can't imagine that anyone would murder anyone else. That kind of thing just doesn't happen in Iceland.'

'It happens everywhere,' said Magnus. 'And it's happened here. To Agnar.'

They were now on the floor of the plain, driving on a long straight road that cut through fields of knotted brown grass. Every mile or so, a farmhouse or a little white-and-red church perched on top of a hillock, a green patch of home meadow laid out neatly in front of it. Sheep grazed, most still shaggy with the winter's wool, but the prevalent animal was the horse, sturdy animals, barely bigger than ponies, many a golden chestnut colour.

'So, back in America, are you a tough-guy cop with a gun like you see on TV?' Ingileif asked. 'You know, chasing the bad guys around the city in sports cars?'

'Cops get irritated as hell by the TV shows, they never get it right,' said Magnus. 'But yes, I do have a gun. And the city is full of bad guys, or at least the areas I end up working in.'

'Doesn't it depress you? Or do you get a thrill out of it?'

'I dunno,' said Magnus. It was always hard to explain being a cop to civilians. They never quite got it. Colby had never gotten it.

'Sorry,' said Ingileif, and she turned to look out of the window.

They drove on. Perhaps Magnus was being unfair to Ingileif. She had made an effort to understand him the night before.

'There was a girl I knew in college, Erin. She used to go down into Providence to work with the kids there. It was a real tough place back then. I went with her, partly because I thought what she was doing was good, mostly because I thought she was the most beautiful girl in the college and I wanted to get her into bed.'

'How romantic.'

'Yeah. But she *did* do a lot of good. She was great with the kids, the boys drooled over her, and the girls thought she was cool too. And I helped out.'

'I bet all the girls thought you were cool as well,' Ingileif said with a grin.

'I managed to fight them off,' said Magnus.

'And did you worm your evil way into this poor girl's bed?'

'For a while.' Magnus smiled at the memory. 'She was genuinely a very good person. One of the best people I've ever met. Much better than me.

'Every time she met a screwed up kid who was dealing drugs or knifing his neighbours, she saw a scared little boy who had been abused and abandoned by his parents and by society.'

'And you?'

'Well, I tried to see it her way, I really did. But in my world there were good guys and bad guys, and all I saw was a bad guy. The way I saw it, it was the bad guys who were ruining the neighbourhood and corrupting the other kids in it. All I wanted to do was stop the little punk from ruining other people's lives. Just like my life had been ruined by whoever killed my father.'

'So you became a cop?'

'That's right. And she became a teacher.' Magnus smiled wryly. 'And somehow I think she has made the world a better place than I have.'

'Do you still see her?'

'No,' said Magnus. 'I visited her once in Chicago a couple of years after we left college. We were very different people by then. She was still gorgeous, though.'

'I think I'd agree with you,' Ingileif said, turning towards him. 'About the bad guys.'

'Really?'

'You sound surprised?'

'I guess I am.' Erin certainly hadn't agreed with him. Neither had Colby for that matter. Policemen always felt lonely on that point, as if they were doing the jobs no one else wanted to do, or even wanted to admit needed doing.

'Sure. You've read your sagas. We Icelandic women are constantly nagging our menfolk to get out of bed and go and avenge their family honour before lunch time.'

'That's true,' said Magnus. 'I've always loved that in a woman, especially on a Sunday morning.'

They drove on in silence. Over the cantilevered bridge at the River Ölfusá and through the town of Selfoss.

'How long are you staying in Iceland?' Ingileif asked.

'I thought it was going to be several months. But now it looks like I will have to go back to the States next week to testify at a trial.'

'Are you coming back afterwards?'

'Not if I can help it,' said Magnus.

'Oh. Don't you like Iceland?' Ingileif sounded offended. Which was hardly surprising; there is no easier way to offend an Icelander than to disparage their country.

'I *do* like it. It just brings back difficult memories. And my job at the Reykjavík CID isn't working out that well. I don't really get along with the boss.'

'Is there a girlfriend back in Boston?' Ingileif asked.

'No,' said Magnus, thinking of Colby. She was an *ex*-girlfriend if ever there was one. He wanted to ask Ingileif why she had asked him that, but that would sound crass. Perhaps she was just curious. Icelanders asked direct questions when they wanted to know answers.

'Look, there's Hekla!'

Ingileif pointed ahead towards the broad white muscular ridge that was Iceland's most famous volcano. It didn't have the cone shape of the classic volcano, but it was much more violent than the prettier Mount Fuji, for example. Hekla had erupted four times in the previous forty years, through a fissure that ran horizontally along the ridge. And then, every couple of centuries or so, it would come up with a big one. Like the eruption of 1104 that had smothered Gaukur's farm at Stöng.

'Do you know that around Boston they sell Hekla cinnamon rolls?' Magnus said. 'They're big upside-down rolls covered in sugar. Look just like the mountain.'

'But do they blow up in your face at random intervals?'

'Not that I'm aware of.'

'Then they're not real Hekla rolls. They need a bit more violence in them.' Ingileif smiled. 'I remember watching Hekla erupt in 1991. I was ten or eleven, I suppose. You can't quite see it from Flúdir, but I had a friend who lived on a farm a few kilometres to the south and you got a great view of it from there.

'It was extraordinary. It was January and it was night time. The volcano was glowing angry red and orange and at the same time you could see a green streak of the aurora hovering above it. I'll never forget it.'

She swallowed. 'It was the year before Dad died.'

'When life was normal?' Magnus asked.

'That's right,' said Ingileif. 'When life was normal.'

The volcano loomed bigger as they drove towards it, and then they turned to the north and lost it behind the foothills that edged the valley. With two kilometres to Flúdir, they came to a turn-off to Hruni to the right. Magnus took it, and the road wound through the hills for a couple of kilometres, before breaking out into a valley. The small white church of Hruni was visible beneath a rocky crag, surrounded by a house and some farm buildings.

They pulled up in the empty gravel car park in front of the church. Magnus climbed out of the car. There was a spectacular view to the north, of glaciers many miles away. Plovers dived and swirled over the fields, calling as they did so. Otherwise there was silence. And peace.

They approached the rectory, a large house by Icelandic standards, white with a red roof, and rang the doorbell. No answer. But there was a red Suzuki in the garage.

'Let's check inside the church,' suggested Ingileif. 'He is a pastor after all.'

As they walked through the ancient graveyard, Ingileif nodded towards a line of newer stones. 'That's where my mother is.'

'Do you want to look?' said Magnus. 'I can wait.'

'No,' said Ingileif. 'No, it feels wrong.' She smiled sheepishly at Magnus. 'I know it doesn't make sense, but I don't want to involve her in all this.'

'It makes sense,' said Magnus.

So they continued on to the church and went in. It was warm and really quite beautiful. It was also empty.

As they made their way back to the car, Magnus caught sight of a boy of about sixteen moving around the barn next to the rectory. He called out to him. 'Have you seen the pastor?'

'He was here this morning.'

'Do you know where he might have gone? Does he have another car?'

The boy noticed the Suzuki parked in the garage. 'No. He could have gone for a walk. He does that sometimes. He can be out all day.'

'Thank you,' said Magnus. He checked his watch. Three-thirty. Then turning to Ingileif: 'What now?'

'You could come back to our house in the village,' she said. 'I can show you the letters from Tolkien to my grandfather. And my father's notes about where the ring might be. Although I doubt they will be much help.'

'Good idea,' said Magnus. 'We'll come back here later.'

CHAPTER TWENTY-SIX

AUSTURSTRAETI WAS ONLY a block away from the Hótel Borg. Isildur was reassured by the two men beside him, the big trucker from England and the wrinkled Icelandic ex-policeman. When Gimli had suggested a sum to Axel Bjarnason, he had been eager to drop everything to help them, although Gimli suspected that the private investigator didn't have much to drop. He had short grey hair, sharp blue eyes and a weather-beaten face, and he looked more like a fisherman than a private investigator, not that Isildur had ever employed a private investigator before.

He clearly knew his town, though. He had recognized Pétur Ásgrímsson's name immediately and had only required a few seconds to check that Ingileif's gallery was where he thought it was. He was at the Hótel Borg less than a quarter of an hour later.

Isildur was nervous, scared even. He was in a strange country, and Iceland was a *very* strange country. Someone had been murdered and there was a chance that the murderer was the man walking along beside him. Isildur didn't like to think too hard about that; he had decided not to ask Gimli right out whether he had killed the professor.

But the danger added to the thrill. It was a long shot: perhaps the police would get to the ring first. Perhaps the ring was a fake all along. Perhaps no one would ever find it. But there was a chance, a real chance, that Isildur might end up the owner of the actual ring that had inspired *The Lord of the Rings*, that had been carried to Iceland by his namesake a thousand years before.

That was cool. That was seriously cool.

The main entrance to Neon was just a small door on the street, but Bjarnason led them around the back. There another door was propped open by a couple of crates of beer. A young man was carrying in some cases of vodka.

Bjarnason stopped him and rattled something in Icelandic. That was one weird language. Isildur wondered to himself which Middle Earth language would sound like it. Possibly none of them: Quenya was Finnish-influenced and Sindarin was derived from Welsh. Perhaps Icelandic was just too obvious for Tolkien – no fun.

The boy led them downstairs past a vast dance floor to a small office. There a tall man with a shaved head was in earnest discussion with a red-haired woman in jeans and a Severed Crotch T-Shirt.

'Go ahead,' said Bjarnason to Isildur. 'I'm sure he speaks English.'

'Mr Ásgrímsson?' said Isildur.

The man with the shaved head looked up. 'Yes?' No hint of a smile. His smooth skull bulged alarmingly.

'My name is Lawrence Feldman and this is my colleague Steve Jubb.'

'What do you want? I thought you were in jail?' Ásgrímsson said.

'Steve was always innocent,' Isildur said. 'I guess the cops finally figured that out.'

'Well, if you want the saga, the police have it. And when they have finished with it, there is no way we are selling it to you.'

Ásgrímsson was aggressive, but Isildur stood up to him. He was used to people trying to push him around, people who underestimated the programmer whose talents they needed to make their business work.

'That's a topic for a later day. We want to speak with you about a ring. Isildur's ring, or perhaps you prefer Gaukur's ring.'

'Get out of my club now!' Ásgrímsson's voice was firm.

'We'll pay well. Very well,' said Isildur.

'Listen to me,' said Ásgrímsson, his eyes burning. 'A man has died because of that stupid saga. Two men, if you include my father. My family kept it a secret for centuries for a reason, a good reason as it turns out. It should still be a secret, and it would have been if I had had my way. But the reason it isn't is you – your nosing around, your flashing dollars everywhere.'

He took a step closer to Isildur. 'You've seen what the result is. Professor Agnar Haraldsson is dead! Don't you feel guilty about that? Don't you think you should just get the hell out of Iceland and fuck off back to America?'

'Mr Ásgrímsson—'

'Out!' Pétur was shouting now, his finger pointing to the exit. 'I said, get out!'

The pastor was sweating in the unseasonably warm sun. It was a glorious day and he had already walked about seven kilometres. He was in a high valley, uninhabited even by sheep this early in the year. A brook ran down from the snow-covered heath at the head of the valley. All around him snow was melting, trickling, dribbling, seeping over the stones and into the earth. Most of the grass that had been revealed in the last few days was yellow, but by the side of the brook there was a patch of rich green shoots. Spring. New nourishment for this barren land.

All around birds chirped and warbled in the sunshine.

He took a deep breath. He remembered when he had first come to this valley, as the newly arrived pastor of Hruni, how he had felt that this is where God lived.

And at that moment, he believed it again.

Over to the left, along the side of the valley, were some rocky crags. He turned off the path, what little there was of it, and squelched through the yellow grass towards them. He took out his notebook.

He needed to find a good hiding place.

Tómas's arrest as a suspect for the murder of Agnar Haraldsson had been on the lunch time news on the radio. Top story, hardly surprising, given Tómas's celebrity. The moment he heard it the pastor knew he had to find a new place to hide the ring.

He paused and examined it on the fourth finger of his right hand. It didn't look a thousand years old. That was the thing with gold – it didn't matter how old it was, if you polished it carefully it looked new. Or newer.

There were scratches and scuffs. But the inscription in runes engraved on the inside was still legible, just.

He remembered when he and Ásgrímur had found it in that cave. Well, it was hardly a cave, more like a hole in the rock. It was the greatest, the most profound moment of his life. And of Ásgrímur's of course. Even if it was just about his last.

It was miraculous that the hole had not been submerged in any of the volcanic eruptions of the previous millennium, especially the big one that had smothered Gaukur's farm. But then the ring dealt in miracles.

He had worn it on and off now for nearly twenty years. He loved it, he worshipped it. Sometimes he would just sit and stare at it, the music of Led Zeppelin or Deep Purple swirling around him, wondering at its history, its mystery, its power. Andvari, Odin, Hreidmar, Fafnir, Sigurd, Brynhild, Gunnar, Ulf Leg Lopper, Trandill, Ísildur and Gaukur, they had all owned it. And now it was his. The pastor of Hruni.

Extraordinary.

But although it gave him a tremendous feeling of exhilaration, of power, every time he put it on, over time his disappointment had grown. The pastor thought of himself as a pretty extraordinary man, and he had assumed that the ring had chosen him because of his knowledge of the devil and of Saemundur. But although he had thrown himself into his studies, nothing had happened. Nothing had been revealed to him. The way to power and domination had not appeared.

But how could it, when he locked himself up in the hills at Hruni? He had assumed that it was his duty to keep the ring in the

shadows of Mount Hekla, which was after all only forty kilometres away as the raven flew. But keep it for whom? He had
always assumed that his son was worthless, far too lightweight and
superficial to make any use of the ring. But perhaps he might make
something of his life after all. He was already a celebrity in Iceland.
It was unlikely that an Icelander could go out into the wider world
and make a name for himself, but perhaps Tómas could.

With the help of the ring.

The pastor scrabbled around in the rocks looking for a niche
similar to the one in which he had originally found the ring seventeen years before. He would have to be very careful to make clear
notes of where he had hidden it, or else it might be lost for another
ten centuries.

But maybe he shouldn't conceal it? The ring had not revealed
itself to him and Dr Ásgrímur merely to be removed from the
world again. It was making an entrance into the affairs of men.

It wanted to be discovered.

The hiding place in the altar at Hruni church wasn't the best. A
determined police team, or anyone else for that matter, could find
it there. But it was the *right* place.

The pastor took off the ring and grasped it in his hand. He
closed his eyes and tried to feel what the ring was telling him.

It *was* the right place.

He turned on his heel and began walking back towards Hruni
at a brisk pace. He checked his watch. He would be lucky to be
home by nightfall.

Ingileif's house, or rather her family's house, was on a bank over-
looking the river that ran through Flúdir. Flúdir itself was a
prosperous village with a convenience store, an hotel, two schools,
some municipal buildings and a number of geothermally powered
greenhouses – Ingileif said it had the best farming in Iceland. But
no church: the parish church was at Hruni, three kilometres away.

Although the village itself wasn't up to much, the view was spectacular. To the west was the valley of the glacial River Hvítá, with its ancient settlement at Skálholt, the site of Iceland's first cathedral, and to the north were the glaciers themselves, thick slabs of white running a dead-straight horizon between mountain peaks.

Hekla was out of sight, behind the hills to the south-east.

The house was a single-storey affair, cosy, but large enough for a family of five. Magnus and Ingileif spread out the contents of several cardboard boxes on the floor of Ingileif's mother's bedroom. There were indeed a dozen letters from Tolkien to Högni, Ingileif's grandfather, which had only come into her father's possession after Högni's death. Ingileif showed Magnus a first edition of *The Fellowship of the Ring*, the first volume of *The Lord of the Rings*. Magnus recognized the handwriting of the inscription inside: *To Högni Ísildarson, one good story deserves another, with thanks and all good wishes, J.R.R. Tolkien, September 1954.*

They studied a folder of notes and maps, most of which were in Dr Ásgrímur's handwriting, which showed guesses of where the ring might be hidden. There were also notes and letters from Hákon, the pastor. They dealt with various folk tales he had researched. There were several pages on the story of Gissur and the troll sisters of Búrfell, which was a mountain close to Gaukur's farm at Stöng. There was also a mention of a story about a shepherd girl named Thorgerd who ran off with an elf.

'Do you have elves in America?' Ingileif asked.

'Not as such,' said Magnus. 'We got drug dealers, we got pimps, we got mobsters, we got crooked lawyers, we got investment bankers. No elves. But if we ever do have any problems with elves in the South End, I know right where to come for help. We could do an exchange with the Reykjavík Metropolitan Police.'

'So you didn't hear any stories about them when you were a kid?'

'Oh, yes, especially when I was living with my grandparents in Iceland. My dad was more into sagas than elves and trolls. But I do remember asking him about them.' Magnus smiled at the memory. 'I guess I was fourteen. We were hiking in the Adirondacks. That was my favourite thing, hiking with my dad. My brother wouldn't come, so it was just me and him. We spoke nothing but Icelandic to each other for a whole week. We talked about everything.

'I can remember exactly where we were, on the shore of Raquette Lake. We were eating a sandwich sitting on a rock that looked like a troll. Dad told me how the Icelanders would have invented a long involved story about it. Then I asked him whether he believed in elves.'

'And what did he say?'

'He kind of dodged the question. So I pressed him on it. He was a mathematician, he spent all his life dealing in proofs, there was no proof that elves existed.

'So he gives me a long lecture about how although there is no proof that elves exist there is equally no absolute proof that they don't. So science can't answer the question. He said although he didn't believe in elves, he was too much of an Icelander to deny their existence, and if I ever lived in Iceland I would understand.'

'And now you live in Iceland, do you believe in them?'

Magnus laughed. 'No. What about you?'

'My grandmother saw hidden people all the time,' Ingileif said. 'Back in a rock near the farm where my mother was born. In fact a hidden woman came to her the night before my mother's birth. They were planning to call Mum Boghildur, but the hidden woman said that unless my grandmother named her Líney the baby would die young. So that's how my mother became Líney.'

'Better than Boghildur,' said Magnus. 'The hidden woman had taste.'

'Here, look,' said Ingileif, pointing to a map with notes and arrows scrawled across it. 'This is where they were heading for the weekend my father died.' A cave was marked near a stream about ten kilometres away from the abandoned Viking farm at Stöng.

Ingileif's cell phone rang. As she answered Magnus could hear an agitated male voice, although he couldn't hear it well enough to recognize it.

'That was my brother,' Ingileif said when the call was over. 'Apparently the two foreigners who were trying to buy the saga showed up at Neon. An American and an Englishman. They were asking about the ring. Pétur sent them packing.'

'You'd think they would have the sense to leave all that alone.'

'That's certainly Pétur's opinion,' said Ingileif. 'He warned me they'll be looking for me too. He doesn't want me to tell them anything.'

'Will you?'

'No. And they're not buying the saga at any price, if we ever do get the chance to sell it. Pétur is adamant about that, and I agree with him.' She checked her watch. 'It's nearly seven o'clock. The pastor should be back by now. Shall we go and check?'

They drove back up to Hruni, but there was no answer when they rang the doorbell. The pastor's car was still in the garage. They looked up around the hills and the valley to see if they could spot a solitary walker. The sun, lower now, produced a soft, clear light, that seemed to pick out every detail of the landscape, and lit the snow on the distant mountains with a pinkish glow. A pair of ravens whirled in the distance, their croaking borne over the grassland by the breeze. But there was no sign of a human being anywhere.

'What time does it get dark?' Magnus asked. 'Nine-thirty?'

'I don't know,' said Ingileif. 'About that, I guess. It's getting later and later these days.'

'Are you hungry?'

Ingileif nodded. 'I know a place in the village we can get something to eat.'

'Let's do that. We can come back here afterwards.'

'And then drive back to Reykjavík?'

Magnus nodded.

'We could do that,' said Ingileif. 'Or ...' She smiled. Her grey eyes danced under her blonde fringe. She looked delectable.

'Or what?'

'Or we could see him in the morning.'

Magnus woke with a start. He was sweating. For a moment he didn't know where he was. He looked across the room at an unfamiliar window, blue-grey moonlight behind the thin curtains.

A hand touched his forearm.

He turned to see a woman lying in bed next to him. Ingileif.

'What is it, Magnús?'

'A dream, that's all.'

'A bad dream?'

'Uh huh.'

'Tell me about it.'

'No, it's OK.'

'Magnús, I want to know about your bad dreams.' She pulled herself up on one elbow, her breasts shadows in the weak light seeping in from the curtains. He could make out a half smile of concern. She touched his cheek.

So he told her. About the dream, the 7-Eleven, O'Malley, the dopehead. And about the alleyway, the garbage cans, the fat bald guy, and the kid, the kid who Williams had said had just died.

She listened. 'Do you get these dreams a lot?'

'No,' Magnus said. 'Not until very recently. That second shooting.'

'But they were trying to kill you, weren't they, those two men?'

'Oh, yeah. I don't feel guilty about it at all,' said Magnus. 'At least, not while I'm awake.' He slammed his fist into the mattress. 'It doesn't make any sense. I don't know why I let it bother me.'

'Hey, you killed someone,' Ingileif said. 'You were absolutely right to do it, you had no choice, but you feel bad about it. You wouldn't be human if you didn't, and you *are* human, even if you think you are a big tough cop. I wouldn't like you if you weren't.'

And she snuggled up into his chest. He pulled her tightly to him.

They kissed.

He stirred.

Afterwards she fell right back asleep. But Magnus couldn't. He lay still, on his back, staring up at the ceiling.

She was right about the dreams, of course. He should expect them, accept them. The idea lulled him.

But then he thought of Colby, hiding out somewhere, God knows where, fearing for her life. Shouldn't he feel guilty about her?

He glanced over to Ingileif, her eyes closed, breathing gently in and out through half-open lips. Even in the gloom he could make out the nick in her eyebrow.

Colby had made it pretty clear that there was little chance of salvaging their relationship. In fact, a one-night-stand with a beautiful Icelandic girl was a perfectly sensible way to get over her. Much better than getting blind drunk and winding up in jail. Trouble was, looking at Ingileif lying beside him, it didn't feel like a one-night stand at all. He really liked her. *Really* liked her.

And for some stupid reason that made it a much worse betrayal of Colby.

After driving back from Hruni they had stopped at the only hotel in Flúdir. It turned out to have a very good restaurant. They had eaten a long leisurely dinner, watching the valley of the Hvítá submerge into darkness in front of them. They had walked back to Ingileif's house along the smaller river that ran through the village, and then they had wound up in Ingileif's childhood bedroom.

He smiled at the memory.

He was being ridiculous. He had been in Iceland for less than a week, and already he was beginning to understand that the Icelanders had a more casual attitude to sex than he was used to. He was just like, what's-his-name, the painter, Ingileif's alibi. Sure she liked him, just like she liked *skyr* or strawberry ice cream. Maybe less.

He had to be careful here. Sleeping with a witness was a definite no-no in America, and somehow he doubted that Baldur would be impressed if he ever found out. And could he be entirely sure that she was innocent?

Of course he could.

But the detective in him, the professional, whispered something else.

CHAPTER TWENTY-SEVEN

THIS TIME, THE pastor of Hruni was in.

He came to the door, an imposing man with a large bushy beard and big black eyebrows. He frowned when he saw Magnus, but his expression changed when his eyes rested on the detective's companion.

'Ingileif? Goodness me, I haven't seen you since your poor mother's funeral. How are you, my child?' The pastor's voice was a pleasant rich baritone.

'I'm very well,' said Ingileif.

'And to what do I owe this pleasure?'

Magnus spoke up. 'My name is Magnús Ragnarsson and I am attached to the Reykjavík Metropolitan Police. I'd like to ask you a few questions, if I may. May we come in?'

The pastor pulled together his mighty eyebrows. 'I was expecting a visit from you,' he said. 'I suppose you had better come through.'

Magnus and Ingileif took off their shoes and followed the pastor through a hallway thick with the aroma of freshly brewed coffee. He led them into a study, crammed full of books. In addition to a desk, there was a sofa and an armchair covered in worn chintz fabric. Ingileif and Magnus perched next to each other on the sofa, while Hákon took the chair. Magnus was surprised to notice a small collection of CDs tucked among the books, including Pink Floyd, Black Sabbath and Led Zeppelin.

No sign of any coffee. Which was pretty rude in Iceland. You always gave your guests coffee and cakes, especially if you had some brewing.

Hákon addressed Ingileif. 'I must confess I was expecting another visit from the police. But I don't understand why you are accompanying them?'

'Ingileif is concerned about the death of her father,' Magnus said.

'Ah, I see,' said the pastor. 'It is natural to have questions, especially since you were so young when the tragedy happened. Although I still don't see why you would want to ask them now. And in the presence of the police.'

'You know we have your son in custody?' Magnus said.

'Yes, I heard it on the radio. You have made a mistake there, young man. A terrible mistake.' Deep-set eyes glowered at Magnus. Although an imposing man, the Reverend Hákon seemed younger than Magnus imagined. There was some grey around his temples, and some lines along his forehead, but he looked closer to forty than to sixty.

'He is being interviewed at Police Headquarters in Reykjavík right now,' said Magnus. 'And I'm sure that my colleagues will want to talk to you once they have finished speaking with him. But in the meantime, tell me what happened on the trip you and Dr Ásgrímur took the weekend he died.'

The pastor took a deep breath. 'Well, there was a police investigation of course, and I spoke to them at length. I'm sure you could look up the file. But to answer your question. It was early May. Your father and I had worked throughout the winter on a project.' He glanced inquiringly at Ingileif.

'Magnús has read *Gaukur's Saga*,' said Ingileif. 'And he knows that my grandfather claims to have found the ring and hidden it again.'

This information caused the pastor to pause a moment while he collected his thoughts. 'Well, in that case you know as much as me. Using my knowledge of folklore, together with the clues in the saga, such as they are, we drew up a list of three or four possible hiding places for Gaukur's ring. This was our second trip of the season, and it was a glorious day. We didn't check the weather forecast, although we should have done, of course.

'A few years before, I had read an old nineteenth-century history of Icelandic folklore, in which I stumbled across a little-known local legend about a ring hidden in a cave guarded by a troll. It was a variation on the old story of a shepherd girl meeting a hidden man or an elf and going off with him, despite the opposition of her family. That theme is quite common in these stories, but the ring was unusual. The location of the cave is identified in the story, so we took a tent and hiked out there.'

Magnus recognized the story of Thorgerd from the pastor's old notes in the doctor's papers at Ingileif's house.

The pastor sighed. 'It was more of a hole in the rock, really. And there was nothing in it. We were disappointed and we camped about a mile away, by a stream. It snowed in the night – you know, one of those sudden storms you get in May that come out of nowhere – and it was still snowing when we got up. We took down our tent and headed home. The snow thickened, it became difficult to see. Your father was walking a few metres ahead of me. We were both tired, I was just staring at the ground in front of me, one step at a time, when I heard a cry. I looked up and he had disappeared.

'I realized that we were on the rim of a cliff, and he had slipped over. I could see him about twenty metres down, lying at an odd angle. I had to move a fair distance along the cliff top to find a route down, and even then it was very difficult in the snow. I slid and fell myself, but my fall was cushioned by the snow.'

The pastor paused and fixed Ingileif with his deep-set dark eyes. 'When I found your father he was still alive, but unconscious. He had hit his head. I took off my own coat to keep him warm, and then rushed off to find help. Well, "rushed" is hardly the word for it in the snowstorm. I should have taken it more slowly: I got lost. It was only when the snowstorm ceased that I saw a farm in the distance. I was *very* cold by then – remember I had given my coat to your father.'

'The farm was Álfabrekka?'

'That's right. There were two farmers there, a father and a son, and they both came back with me to look for Ásgrímur, while the farmer's wife called mountain rescue. By the time we got to your father, he was dead.' The pastor shook his head. 'When the rescue team eventually arrived they said he had been dead for a while, but I still wish I hadn't got myself lost in the storm.'

'Did the police find any evidence that the doctor's death wasn't accidental?' Magnus asked.

'Of course not!' the pastor protested, his voice booming. 'You can check on the file. There was never any doubt about that.' The pastor glared at Magnus, commanding him to accept his assertion. Magnus didn't flinch. He would make up his own mind.

He was beginning to understand what Ingileif had meant when she said the pastor was creepy. The man had an aura of power about him that reached out towards Magnus, urging him to bend to his will.

It was a power that Magnus was determined to resist.

'Did you continue looking for the ring after my father's death?' Ingileif asked.

The pastor turned to her and relaxed slightly. 'No. I let all that drop. I must confess it was fun working on the puzzle with your father, but once he had died then I lost all interest in the ring. Or the saga.'

Magnus glanced at the walls. There were three different prints of a volcano erupting. Hekla. 'So how do you explain those?'

'I have made quite a study of the role of the devil in Icelandic ecclesiastical history,' said Hákon. 'Hekla was known throughout Europe as the mouth of hell. That, as you can imagine, intrigues me.'

He paused. 'I must admit that from that point of view, *Gaukur's Saga* is very interesting. As far as I am aware it is the earliest mention of Hekla in that role. And also the first recorded ascent of the mountain. Until now we thought that no one dared climb Hekla until 1750. But of course Ísildur and Gaukur were climbing it before the big eruption of 1104, so perhaps it wasn't quite so frightening then.'

'You spoke to my colleague a few days ago about a visit here by Professor Agnar Haraldsson,' Magnus said.

'That's true.'

'And what did you tell her he wanted to speak to you about?'

The pastor smiled, a mass of wrinkles appearing around his eyes. 'Ah, I wasn't entirely honest with your colleague. I take the confidences of my parishioners very seriously.' He looked pointedly at Ingileif.

'So what did Agnar really talk to you about?'

'*Gaukur's Saga*, of course. And the ring.' The pastor pulled at his beard. 'He told me that Ingileif had asked him to act for the family in the sale of the saga.' He frowned at Ingileif. 'I must admit that I was quite shocked by this. After all the years that the family had successfully kept the saga a secret. Centuries even.'

Ingileif reddened at the admonition from her pastor.

'I hardly think that's for you to judge,' said Magnus. 'In fact, you should have told my colleague the truth first time around. It would have saved a lot of people a lot of time.'

'Ásgrímur was a very good friend of mine,' said Hákon sternly. 'I know what he would have wanted me to do.'

'What you did was obstruct a murder inquiry,' said Magnus. 'Now. Did Agnar have something specific to ask you?'

'Ingileif had just discovered the letter to her grandfather from Tolkien which referred to the discovery of the ring. Agnar came straight here and asked me much the same questions as you did just now. I gained the very strong impression that he wanted to try to find the ring himself. Of course, I couldn't help him.'

'How did he behave?' Magnus asked.

'Agitated. Excited. Aggressive in his questioning.'

'Did you tell him anything you didn't tell us?' Magnus asked.

'Absolutely not.'

Magnus paused, examining the pastor. But the man wasn't about to say any more. 'See, the day after he saw you, Agnar sent a message which implied that he knew where the ring was.'

'Well, he certainly didn't seem to know when I saw him.'

'Did you tell him where you looked for it that day in 1992?'

'No. He asked, but I told him I couldn't remember. But of course I can.'

Ingileif showed the pastor the map that she had found among her father's papers. 'Is that the place?'

Hákon peered over. 'Yes, that's it. And there's the farm, Álfa-brekka. I suppose I could have told Agnar where it was, wasted his time. I'm sure the ring is not there. At least it wasn't there seventeen years ago, and I doubt it could have got there since.'

'Are you certain it wasn't there?' Magnus asked. 'I wonder if Agnar discovered clues to the location somewhere else and found something you missed.'

'I'm absolutely certain,' said Hákon. 'Believe me, Ásgrímur and I scraped every inch of the cave, and it wasn't very big.'

'Did your son know anything about this?' Magnus asked.

'Tómas? I don't think so. He was, what, thirteen at the time? I didn't tell him about the saga or the ring either then or afterwards. Did you, Ingileif?'

'No,' said Ingileif.

'Then why was he speaking to Agnar the day he died?' Magnus asked.

Hákon shook his head. 'I don't know. I had no idea they knew each other.'

'Interesting coincidence, don't you think?'

Hákon shrugged. 'Maybe. I suppose so.' Then he leaned forward, his eyes boring into Magnus. 'My son is not a killer, young man. Remember that.'

'God that man gives me the creeps,' Ingileif said as they drove back towards Reykjavík.

'Was he always like that?'

'He was always weird. We didn't go to church much, but when we did his sermons always used to scare the wits out of me. Lots of fire and brimstone, the devil behind every rock. As you can imagine, hearing that sort of thing while you are actually sitting in Hruni church is pretty frightening for a kid.'

She laughed to herself. 'I remember one Monday morning, after one of his services, I gave back the hair clip I had "borrowed" from the girl I sat next to in class. I was so scared I was going to be swallowed up by the earth or struck by a bolt of lightning.'

'I can imagine that.'

'So, Mr Detective, was he telling the truth?'

'I don't think so. We know he lied to Vigdís about Agnar. I'm pretty sure he was lying about Tómas. He must have told him about the saga and the ring; why else would Tómas be talking to Agnar? It's good I got him to deny that. Bad decision on his part.'

'Why's that?'

'Because when I get Tómas to admit that he heard about the saga from his father, we will have caught Hákon out in another lie. From then on he'll be struggling to keep his story straight. What did you think?'

'I think he killed my father. And I think he's got the ring. Couldn't you search his house?'

'We'd need a search warrant.'

'Are you going to get one?'

'Possibly.' Magnus would have loved to do that. But he would have to persuade Baldur, and that would not be easy. Not until he had broken Tómas's story. He was looking forward to getting back to police headquarters to interview him.

'Can we drop by that farm that Reverend Hákon went to for help?' Ingileif asked. 'Someone there might remember something.'

'I'd like to get back as soon as possible to interview Tómas.'

'I understand. But it might shed some light on my father's death.'

Magnus hesitated.

'Please, Magnús. You know how important it is to me.'

'What was the name of the farm? Álfabrekka. He showed us on that map.'

'That's right. We'd have to go up Thjórsárdalur.'

'But that would be fifty kilometres out of our way, there and back.'

'At least.'

Magnus knew he should tell Baldur about his interview with Hákon as soon as possible. And he wanted to do that in person rather than over the phone so he would be able to confront Tómas himself.

He glanced at Ingileif. It was true, he did know how important her father's death was to her.

'OK,' he sighed. 'Get the map out and tell me where to go.'

CHAPTER TWENTY-EIGHT

A S THE AIRPLANE began its descent into Keflavík Airport, Diego licked his lips. He was nervous. It wasn't the hit, he was looking forward to that. And it wasn't flying, he had been on many airplanes. But he had never been to Europe before. Spain he could have handled, Italy maybe, but Iceland?

From what little he had been able to find out about it, it was one weird country.

He was expecting snow and ice, Eskimos and igloos. The cold he could probably cope with. Since the age of fifteen he had lived in the town of Lawrence, about twenty miles north of Boston. It got pretty cold there in winter.

The cold had been one hell of a shock when he had first arrived in the States, aged seven. His family were from the town of San Francisco de Macorís in the Dominican Republic. They had crossed the hundred-mile Mona Passage to Puerto Rico by boat, and with fake ID purchased there flew to New York. They spent several years in Washington Heights in Upper Manhattan, where his father had plied his trade as a mule. He got caught, went to prison, died there ten years later. His mother had taken Diego and his two sisters up to where her cousin lived in Lawrence.

There, Diego had begun his narcotics career in logistics, before taking up an enforcement role, at which he was very successful. He wasn't quite as gratuitously violent as some of Soto's other enforcers, but he was smart, and often that counted for more. He was certainly the best guy to go find a Boston cop among a bunch of Eskimos and off him.

They landed, and were out of the plane in no time. Immigration control wasn't a problem, the official glanced quickly at Diego's fake US passport and stamped it. Then in the arrivals hall he looked for and found a sign saying *Mr Roberts*. The guy holding it was stocky, with close-cropped brown hair and what sounded a bit like a Russian accent, although actually he was Lithuanian. He led Diego out to the car park and a Nissan SUV.

There had been very little time to prepare for Diego's trip. But Soto had managed to find out from his wholesale suppliers who the big guys in drugs in Iceland were, and to make an introduction. They were Lithuanians, which was some kind of country in Russia, and they would help him.

He looked out over the black wasteland. No snow. Certainly no igloos. And not even a goddamned tree. The place already gave him the creeps.

After half an hour or so of driving, they pulled up in the parking lot of a Taco Bell. Sweet. Diego insisted on getting himself a burrito, even though it was early. When he returned to the car, there was another man waiting for him in the back seat. Thirties, also short-cropped hair, small blue eyes.

'My name is Lukas,' he said, by way of introduction, in a strong accent that wasn't quite the Russian that Diego knew from Boston.

'Joe,' said Diego, shaking the proffered hand.

'Welcome to Iceland.'

'Have you got the piece?'

Lukas hesitated and then pulled a Walther PPK out of a black shoulder bag. Diego examined it. It looked like a PPK/S but it had a blue-steel finish. Some European model, perhaps. It was in good condition. Serial number filed off. Not a revolver, but this job would be bang bang and outta there.

'Be careful with this,' the Lithuanian said. 'There are no handguns in Iceland. This one was bought in Amsterdam and smuggled in.'

'Other than the cops. They got guns, surely?'

'Cops don't have guns either. Except at airport.'

Diego smiled. 'Man, that's cool. And the ammo?'

Lukas handed it to him.

'How about the getaway?'

Lukas reached into his bag and took out a mobile phone. 'Take this. The first name on the address list is "Karl". Call that when you want to get out. If you are for real, say "Can I speak to Óskar?" Got that? Otherwise we think cops have you and you are on your own.'

'What happens then?'

'We'll meet your car. Get you out of Iceland.'

'Will it be quick?'

'It will be very quick. Trust me, we don't want you caught. And if you do get caught, don't tell them we help you. We don't want start war with police.'

'I get it,' said Diego. 'So where do I find Magnus Jonson?'

'You know what he looks like?'

'Uh huh.'

'Then I suggest you hang around outside police headquarters until you see him.'

'Oh, great. Can you ask some questions for me, man? Find out where he lives?'

'No,' said Lukas. 'If you shoot policeman on the streets of Reykjavík it will be big deal. Very big deal. If they learn we have been asking questions about cop there will be big trouble for us. You understand?'

'I guess so,' said Diego.

'Good. Now we take you to hotel and then you go to small airport in centre of city to hire car. There is bus station opposite police headquarters. I suggest you go there to watch.'

Árni was exhausted. It was amazing how sitting in one place for so long could be so tiring. He was very glad to be back in Iceland, although his body clock was completely confused.

He had been really looking forward to interviewing Isildur. He had planned all kinds of clever strategies to prompt him to finger Steve Jubb as the murderer. And he had hoped to see a bit of California – the drive to Trinity County had promised to be spectacular. He might even have got to see some giant redwoods. As it was he hadn't even made it in to San Francisco, spending the night at an airport Holiday Inn and the following morning organizing the flight back, via Toronto.

He had never been to Canada before. Not impressed.

The only good thing was that he was whipping through *The Lord of the Rings*. He was on page 657 and going strong. It was a great book. And all the more interesting for having read *Gaukur's Saga*.

Keflavík Airport was crowded – all the flights from North America arrived back in Iceland at the same time. Árni ignored his compatriots stocking up at the duty free shop and went straight through immigration and customs. As he came through the door into the main concourse, he spotted a man he recognized, Andrius Juska, stocky with short hair, a foot soldier in one of the Lithuanian gangs that sold amphetamines in Reykjavík. Árni only recognized him because he had tailed him for three days a couple of months before, while he was helping out the Narcotics Squad.

The 'yellow press', as Iceland called its popular newspapers, had whipped itself into a bit of a frenzy over Lithuanian drug dealers, seeing them on every street corner. The truth was that the majority of drugs in Iceland were sold by Icelanders. But the Police Commissioner in particular was concerned about the possible future spread of foreign drugs gangs, the main candidates being Scandinavian motorcycle gangs, and the Lithuanians. There was as yet no sign of Latino gangs, or Russians, but the police were all on the lookout for them.

Juska was holding up a welcome sign for a Mr Roberts. Árni slowed his pace to a saunter. As he did so a slim man with light brown skin approached the Lithuanian. From the reticence with which they greeted each other, it was clear that they had never met before.

Árni let his bag slip from his fingers, and then knelt down to pick it up. The two men were speaking English, the Lithuanian's accent was heavy, the other man's was American. Not educated American, street American. Árni took a good look. The man was about thirty, wearing a black leather jacket, and he looked as if he could handle himself. He most certainly did *not* look like your typical American tourist in Iceland.

Interesting.

'Battle of Evermore' rang out through the study as Hákon sat in his chair, eyes shut. The ring was on his finger as Led Zeppelin's music washed over him.

He was excited. The more he thought about it, the clearer he understood his role in the plans of the ring. Sadly, he was not to be the one through which the ring would unleash its power on the world. But he *had* been chosen as the catalyst by which the ring would escape from a thousand years in the Icelandic wilderness and make its way back into the centre of the world of men.

An important role indeed.

The murder of Agnar, the arrest of Tómas, these were not everyday events. The police were getting closer, but now that did not worry the pastor unduly. It was preordained.

He listened to the haunting mandolin: '*Waiting for the angels of Avalon*'. His thoughts returned to who it was who would be chosen to bear the ring after him. Tómas perhaps? Unlikely, the more he thought of it. Ingileif? No. Although she had always been a strong-willed girl, she was the last person he could imagine being corrupted. The big red-haired detective? Possible. He had an American accent and he exuded an aura of power and capability.

For a moment Hákon wondered whether he should just give the detective the ring. But no, he couldn't bring himself to do that.

The phone rang. The pastor turned down the music and answered. The conversation didn't take long.

When he had finished, he glanced again at the ring. Should he replace it in the altar, or should he take it with him?

Events were picking up pace.

He turned off the stereo, grabbed his coat and went out to the garage, the ring still firmly on his finger.

A few kilometres south of Flúdir, Magnus and Ingileif came to the mighty Thjórsá. This was the longest river in Iceland, carrying cold green-white water in a torrent from the glaciers in the centre of the country south towards the Atlantic Ocean. They turned left, following the road up the valley towards Gaukur's old farm of Stöng.

The river glistened in the sunlight. On the left, scattered farms and the occasional church nestled in the lee of the crags, many of them still covered in snow. Ahead, to the right, loomed Hekla. That morning the summit was draped with cloud, darker than the white puffs which smattered the rest of the pale sky.

At Ingileif's direction, Magnus turned off the road and along a dirt track, winding up through the hills and into a small valley. His police-issued Skoda strained to maintain traction: the road was in poor condition and in places very steep. After a bone-rattling eight kilometres they finally came across a small white farm with a red roof nestling in the hillside at the head of its own little valley. Beneath the farm the obligatory lush green home meadow stretched down to a fast-flowing stream. The rest of the grass in the valley lurked brown and lacklustre, where it wasn't still covered in snow.

Álfabrekka.

'"How fair the slopes are",' Ingileif said.

Magnus smiled as he recognized the quotation from *Njáls Saga*. He finished it: '"Fairer than they have ever seemed to me before".'

As they pulled into the farmyard, a thin, sprightly man in his mid-fifties marched towards them, wearing blue overalls.

'Good morning!' he said, smiling broadly, his body almost quivering with the excitement of receiving visitors. 'How can I help you?'

Bright blue eyes shone out of a pale and wrinkled face. Tufts of grey hair peaked out of his woolly cap.

Ingileif took the lead, introducing herself and Magnus. 'My father was Dr Ásgrímur Högnason. You may remember him. He fell to his death near here in 1992.'

'Oh, yes, I do remember that, very clearly,' the farmer said. 'You have my sympathy, even so many years later. But let's not stand around out here. Come inside and have some coffee!'

Inside, the farmer's father and mother greeted them. The father, an impossibly wizened man, stirred himself from a comfortable armchair, while the mother busied herself with coffee and cakes. A stove warmed the living room, which was chock full of Icelandic knick-knacks, including at least four miniature Icelandic flags.

And a giant high-definition television screen. Just to remind them that they were truly in Iceland.

The younger farmer who had greeted them did most of the talking. His name was Adalsteinn. And before they could ask him any questions he told them about his parents, the fact that he himself was single, the fact that the farm had been in the family for generations, and particularly the fact that farming these days was tough, very tough indeed.

The coffee was delicious, as were the cakes.

'Adalsteinn, perhaps you could tell me what happened the day you found my father?' Ingileif interrupted.

Adalsteinn launched into a long description of how a frozen pastor had come to the door, and how he and his father had followed the pastor back to the place where Ásgrímur had fallen. The doctor was definitely dead and very cold. There were no signs of a struggle or foul play, it was quite clear where he had fallen. The police hadn't asked any particular questions suggesting they suspected anything other than an accident.

During all this, the farmer's mother added certain helpful embellishments and corrected the odd detail, but the old man sat in his chair, silent, watching and listening.

Magnus and Ingileif stood up, and were taking their leave when he spoke for the first time. 'Tell them about the hidden man, Steini.'

'The hidden man?' Magnus looked sharply at the old man and then at the younger farmer.

'I will, Father. I'll tell them outside.'

Adalsteinn ushered Magnus and Ingileif out into the yard.

'What hidden man?' said Magnus.

'Father has seen the *huldufólk* all his life,' Adalsteinn said. 'There are a few who live around here, according to him. Have done for generations. You know how it is?' His friendly face examined Magnus, looking for signs of disdain.

'I know how it is,' said Magnus. Álfabrekka meant 'Elf Slope' after all. There was some discussion in Iceland as to the precise differences between elves and hidden people, but this place was probably teeming with both races. What should he expect? 'Go on.'

'Well, he says he saw a young hidden man scurry by on the far side of the valley an hour before the pastor arrived.'

'A hidden man? How does he know it wasn't a human?'

'Well, he and my mother decided it was a hidden man, because the pastor was wearing an old gold ring.'

'A ring?'

'Yes. I didn't see it, but they took off his gloves to get his hands warm, and he was wearing it.'

'And what has that to do with hidden people?'

Adalsteinn took a deep breath. 'There is an old local legend about a wedding ring. Thorgerd, the farmer's daughter of Álfa-brekka, was tending her sheep on the high pastures when she was approached by a handsome young hidden man. He took her away and married her. The farmer was angry, searched for Thorgerd and killed her. Then he chased after the hidden man. The hidden man concealed the wedding ring in a cave guarded by the hound of a troll. The farmer went to look for the ring but the troll killed him and ate him. Then there was a great eruption from Hekla and the farm was buried in ash.'

Magnus was impressed by how far *Gaukur's Saga* had been mangled over the generations. The basic elements were still there, though: the ring, the cave, the troll's hound. 'So your father thinks that the hidden man was looking for the pastor?'

'Something like that.'

'And what do you think?'

The farmer shrugged. 'I don't know. He told the police, who didn't take any notice. No one else had seen a young man on the hills. There was no reason for a young man to go out in a snowstorm. I don't know.'

'Do you mind if we go back and ask your father about the hidden man?'

'Be my guest,' said the farmer.

The old man was still in his armchair while his wife was tidying up the coffee cups.

'Your son tells me that the pastor was wearing a ring?'

'Oh, yes,' said the old man's wife.

'What kind of ring?'

'It was dark, dirty but you could see it was gold under the dirt. It must have been very old.'

'It was the hidden man's wedding ring,' said the old man. 'That's why his friend was killed. He stole the hidden man's wedding ring. Fool! What did he expect? I'm surprised the pastor wasn't killed as well, although he was half dead when he came to our door.'

'Did you see the hidden man clearly?' Magnus asked.

'No, it was snowing. I caught no more than a glimpse of him, really.'

'But you could tell he was young?'

'Yes. By the way he moved.'

Magnus glanced at Ingileif. 'Could he have been thirteen?'

'No,' said the old man. 'He was taller than that. And besides, remember he was married. Thirteen was too young for a hidden man to get married, even in those days.' He stared at Magnus with eyes full of certainty.

*

'Tómas was tall at the age of thirteen, one of the tallest in our class,' Ingileif said. 'Probably one metre seventy-five, something like that.'

They were driving fast down the Thjórsárdalur back towards Reykjavík.

'So he could have been out there with them that day,' Magnus said.

'You would have thought that the police would have discovered that, wouldn't you?'

'Maybe not,' said Magnus. 'Country police. No reason at all to think that a murder had been committed. I will dig out the files. They're probably at Selfoss police headquarters.'

'I *knew* Hákon had the ring!' Ingileif said.

'It certainly sounds like it. Though I still find it difficult to believe the ring actually exists.'

'But the farmers saw it on his finger!'

'Yes, just before they saw an elf.'

'Well, I don't care what you believe. I believe Hákon killed my father and took the ring! He must have done.'

'Unless it was Tómas who killed him?'

'He was only thirteen,' said Ingileif. 'He wasn't that kind of kid. Whereas Hákon ...'

'Well, if Tómas didn't kill your father, he would have witnessed it. It sounds like I have plenty to talk to him about.'

'Can't we just go back to Hruni and search Hákon's house?'

'We need a warrant. Especially if we're going to find evidence we plan to use at trial, which it sounds like we might. That's why I've got to get back to Reykjavík.'

They were going pretty fast. The surface of the road along the edge of the river was excellent, but there were some bends and wiggles. Magnus sped over the crest of a small hill, and almost hit a white BMW four-wheel-drive coming at him the other way.

'That was close.' He glanced over to see Ingileif's reaction to his driving.

She was sitting bolt upright in her seat, frowning slightly.

Her phone rang. She answered quickly, glanced at Magnus, mumbled '*Já*,' two or three times, and hung up.

'Who was that?' Magnus asked.

'The gallery,' Ingileif answered.

Magnus took Ingileif directly to her apartment in 101.

'Will I see you tonight?' she said as she got out of the car. 'I could cook you dinner.' She smiled.

'I don't know,' said Magnus. 'I'm bound to be working late on the case.'

'I don't mind,' said Ingileif. 'We can eat late. I'll be eager to hear what's happening. And well ...' she hesitated, blushing. 'It would be nice to see you.'

'I don't know, Ingileif.'

'Magnús? Magnús, what is it?'

'There's this girl. Colby. Back in Boston.'

'But I asked you if there were any girls! You told me there weren't.'

'There aren't.' Magnus tried to get his thoughts in order. 'She's an ex-girlfriend. Definitely an ex-girlfriend.'

'Well then?'

'Well ...' Magnus was floundering. Ingileif was standing on the pavement watching him flounder. Her smile was long gone.

'Yes?'

'Am I just like Lárus?'

'What!'

'I mean, am I just a, you know, someone to see, when you feel like ...'

'When I feel like a fuck? Is that what you're trying to say?'

Magnus sighed. 'I don't know what I'm trying to say.'

'Look, Magnús. You're going back to the States in the next few days. I would like to spend as much time as possible with you before you go. It's simple. If you have a problem with that, just tell me, and I won't waste my time. Do you have a problem with that?'

'I ...'

'Don't bother answering, because come to think of it, maybe I have a problem myself.' She turned on her heel.

'Ingileif!'

'Men are such jerks,' she muttered as she stalked back to her flat.

CHAPTER TWENTY-NINE

'**N**OT ANOTHER FUCKING elf!'
Baldur stared at Magnus in disbelief. Magnus had dragged him out of the interview room where he was still working on Tómas. He was unhappy to be interrupted, but reluctantly led Magnus along to his office. He listened closely as Magnus described his interview with the Reverend Hákon and with the sheep farmers, but began to lose patience once Magnus related the old man's story about trolls and rings and the hidden man he had seen.

'I'm supposed to be the old-fashioned one around here. And then I have to listen to this elf and troll bullshit!'

'Obviously, it wasn't an elf,' said Magnus. 'It was Tómas. He was a tall thirteen-year-old.'

'And the ring? Are you trying to tell me that the pastor was wearing an ancient ring belonging to Odin or Thor or someone?'

'I don't know whether the ring is authentic,' said Magnus. 'And frankly, I don't care. The point is that seventeen years ago a small group of people did think it was important. Important enough to kill for.'

'Oh, so now we're solving another crime, are we? A death in 1992. Except this wasn't a crime, it was an accident. There was an investigation: we know it was an accident.'

Magnus leaned back in his chair. 'Let me talk to Tómas.'

'No.'

'I spoke to his father.'

Baldur shook his head. 'Vigdís should have spotted they were father and son.'

'Hákon isn't such an uncommon name,' Magnus said. 'We must have interviewed dozens of witnesses; I'll bet at least five of them have the same first names as someone else's last name. She didn't know Tómas had spent his childhood in Flúdir, so there was no obvious connection.'

'She should have checked,' Baldur insisted.

Baldur might have had a point, but Magnus didn't want to dwell on it. 'I can tell Tómas the farmers saw him in the snowstorm. I can convince him that we know he was there.'

'I said, no.'

They sat in silence, staring at each other. Then Magnus smiled. 'I know you and I haven't started out very well together.'

'You can say that again.'

'But just give me twenty minutes. You can be there too. You'll know if we're making progress, if there's an opening. If I get nowhere, then we've lost twenty minutes, that's all.'

The corners of Baldur's lips were turned down, scepticism was written all over his long face. But he was listening.

He took a deep breath. 'OK,' he said. 'Twenty minutes. Let's go.'

Tómas Hákonarson looked exhausted, as did his lawyer, a mousy woman of about thirty.

Baldur introduced Magnus. Tómas's tired eyes assessed him.

'Don't worry, I don't want to talk to you about Agnar,' Magnus began.

'Good,' said Tómas.

'It's another murder I want to discuss with you. One that took place seventeen years ago.'

Tómas was suddenly awake, his eyes focusing on Magnus.

'Know whose murder I'm talking about?'

Tómas remained motionless. Magnus felt that he wasn't trusting himself to speak. A good sign.

'That's right,' he said. 'Dr Ásgrímur. Seventeen years ago your father pushed Dr Ásgrímur off a cliff. And you witnessed it.'

Tómas swallowed. 'I don't know what you are talking about.'

'I've just come back from Hruni where I interviewed your father. And I went to Álfabrekka and spoke to the farmers who helped him go back and find Dr Ásgrímur. They saw you.'

'They can't have done.'

'They saw a thirteen-year-old boy sneak by their farm in the snow.'

Tómas frowned. 'That wasn't me.'

'Wasn't it?'

'Anyway. Why would my father kill the doctor? They were friends.'

Magnus smiled. 'The ring.'

'What ring?'

'The ring you went to talk to Professor Agnar about.'

'I have no idea what you are talking about.'

Magnus leaned forward. He spoke in a low urgent voice, only a fraction above a whisper. 'You see, the farmers saw your father wearing an ancient ring. We *know* that your father pushed Dr Ásgrímur off a cliff and took the ring. You witnessed it and ran away.'

'Has he admitted it?' Tómas asked.

Magnus could see that the instant he had uttered it, Tómas regretted his question, with its implication that there was something to admit.

'He will. We are going to arrest him shortly.'

He paused, watching Tómas as he fiddled with the empty coffee cup in front of him. 'Tell us the truth, Tómas. You can stop protecting your father. It's too late for that.'

Tómas glanced at his lawyer, who was listening intently. 'OK.'

'Talk to me,' said Magnus.

Tómas took a deep breath. 'I wasn't there,' he said. 'I don't know who your farmer witness saw, but it wasn't me.'

Magnus was tempted to argue, but held his tongue. Best to coax out the entirety of Tómas's story and then pick holes in it.

'I don't even know for sure whether my father did kill him, I really don't. But I do know that he has the ring, Gaukur's ring.'

'How do you know?' Magnus asked.

'He told me. About five years later, when I was eighteen or so. He said that he was looking after it for me. He told me the whole story of the ring, how it was the very same ring of Andvari from the *Volsung Saga*, about how Ísildur had taken it back to Iceland and how Gaukur had killed his brother for it, and had then hidden it. He showed it to me once.'

'So you've actually *seen* it?'

'Yes.'

'Did he tell you how he got it?'

Tómas hesitated. 'Yes. Yes, he did. He said that he and Dr Ásgrímur found it that weekend, and that Dr Ásgrímur was wearing it when he fell off the cliff. He said that he had taken it off Dr Ásgrímur's finger.'

'While he was lying dying at the bottom of the cliff?'

Tómas shrugged. 'I guess so. I don't know. It was either then, or when he came back for him with the farmers and found him dead. But it would have been quite difficult to take the ring then, I would expect.'

'Didn't that shock you?'

'Yes, it did.' Tómas swallowed. 'My father was always a bit strange. But he became much stranger after the doctor died. I was scared of him, in awe of him. I still am, if the truth be told. And, well ...'

'Yes?'

'Well, I wouldn't be surprised if he had done something awful like take a ring off a dying man's finger.'

'What about killing that man?'

Tómas hesitated. Magnus glanced at Tómas's lawyer. She was listening intently, but letting him speak. As far as she was concerned her client was going some way towards exonerating himself.

Baldur was also listening closely, letting Magnus get on with it.

Tómas took a deep breath. 'Yes. Like killing the doctor.'

'Did he admit he had done that?'

'No, not at all. Never.'

'But you suspect he did?'

'Not at first,' said Tómas. 'It didn't occur to me. I had always believed my father about everything. But then the suspicion did begin to nag at me. I hoped it wasn't true, but I couldn't help asking myself, what if Father had pushed the doctor?'

'Did you confront him?'

'No, absolutely not.' It was clear that the last thing on earth Tómas would do was confront his father. 'But one day I overheard something. It was Father talking to my mother, this was several years after they had separated. It was Birna Ásgrímsdóttir's wedding. Father was officiating. They were talking about how messed up Birna was. Father said something like: "It's hardly surprising when her father was murdered."

'I don't know whether Mother noticed. She didn't say anything. I could tell Father had realized he had made a mistake by the way he glanced at her immediately. I don't think he knew I was listening.'

'That's not exactly hard evidence,' Magnus said.

'No,' Tómas admitted.

Which was no doubt why Tómas had told them. Magnus still wasn't convinced that Tómas wasn't there and hadn't witnessed the whole thing. But he'd come to that later.

'All right. So why were you visiting Agnar?'

'Can I have some water?' Tómas asked.

Magnus nodded. To Magnus's surprise Baldur went to the door to ask for some. A minute later a police officer returned with a plastic cup and a jug.

Tómas drank gratefully. Gathering his thoughts.

'Agnar approached me. We knew each other vaguely, we'd met at parties, had one or two mutual friends, you know how this town is?'

Magnus nodded.

'We met at a café.'

'Café Paris,' Magnus said, remembering his conversation with Katrín, about her seeing them together.

Tómas frowned in surprise.

'Go on,' Magnus said.

'Agnar said that he had been approached by a wealthy American to buy Gaukur's ring. I acted dumb, but Agnar went on. He said that he had just come back from Hruni, where he had spoken to Father. He said that although Father denied he had the ring, Agnar was sure he was lying.'

'Did he say why?'

'He did. It was ridiculous.' Tómas smiled to himself. 'He said it was because Father looked much younger than his age. In *Gaukur's Saga* the warrior who bears the ring, Ulf something, is actually ninety, but looks much younger, and Agnar's theory was that the same thing was happening to Father, he wasn't getting any older.'

'I see what you mean,' said Magnus. 'That is a little weird.'

'I know. The problem was I laughed at him. It was a problem because right then Agnar could tell I knew what he was talking about.'

'But you didn't actually admit it?'

'No. Then he claimed that Father must have murdered Dr Ásgrímur. Obviously, I said that was wrong. But Agnar persisted. He seemed very sure of himself. Basically, he tried to blackmail me. Or us.'

'How?'

'He said that unless Father sold him the ring – and Agnar promised he would pay a high price – then he would go to the police and tell them, I mean you, about the ring and about Dr Ásgrímur's murder.'

'So what did you do?'

'I called Father. I told him what Agnar had said.'

'How did he take it?'

'He wasn't having any of it. We agreed how absurd it was that Agnar should think that Father had murdered Dr Ásgrímur. But, of course, Father knew I knew he had the ring. He said we should call Agnar's bluff. So I went to look for him. I went to the University first, and then a student said he was at a summer house on Lake Thingvellir. I actually knew the house, I interviewed Agnar's father there a few years ago. You know he was a cabinet minister?'

Magnus nodded.

'So I drove out to Lake Thingvellir. I told Agnar that my father had no idea what he was talking about. I urged him to drop the blackmailing.'

'Urged?' said Magnus. 'Or threatened.'

'Urged. I pointed out that if Agnar went through with it, his clients almost certainly wouldn't get the ring. I kind of admitted I knew that Father had it.'

'What did Agnar say?'

'He looked at me for several seconds, thinking. Then he suggested that if Father was too stubborn to give up the ring of his own accord, I should steal it from him. That way I would keep him out of jail.'

'What did you say?'

'I said I would think about it.'

Magnus raised his eyebrows.

'Agnar had a point. I knew Father would never give up the ring, but I didn't want him to go to jail. I knew where Father kept it, and it would be easy to take it and sell it to Agnar.'

'So did you?'

'Steal the ring? No. I drove straight home, and sat down and thought about it. In the end I decided to tell Father what Agnar had suggested. I called him that evening.'

'And what did your father say?'

'He was angry. Very angry.'

'With you?'

'With Agnar and with me. He was upset that I had as good as admitted that he had the ring. He didn't seem at all grateful that I had stood by him, that I had called him instead of taking the ring myself.' There was anger in Tómas's voice. 'He lost it, basically.'

'So what did you do?'

'I was wound up. I had a drink or two to calm myself down.' Tómas winced. 'I ended up drinking most of a bottle of whisky. I woke up late the next morning, still not sure what to do. Then I heard about Agnar's death on the radio.'

Tómas swallowed.

'What's the timing on all this?' Magnus asked. 'When did you get home from Lake Thingvellir?'

'About half-past five or so. Like I told your colleague.' Tómas's eyes flicked towards Baldur.

'And what time did you call your father?'

'About half an hour later, maybe an hour.'

'So that's about six, six-thirty.' The obvious question framed itself in Magnus's mind. 'So your father could have gone to Lake Thingvellir later that night? To shut Agnar up?'

Tómas didn't answer.

'Well?'

'I have no idea,' he said. But it was quite clear that the thought had occurred to him too.

'One other question,' said Magnus. 'Where does your father hide the ring?'

CHAPTER THIRTY

'WELL DONE,' SAID Baldur as they left the interview room and walked rapidly towards his office. He didn't smile, he didn't even look at Magnus, but Magnus knew he meant it.

'Shall we go arrest Hákon?' Magnus asked.

'We'll get the Selfoss police to arrest him and bring him here for interview,' said Baldur. 'They'll get there more quickly. And I'll ask them to search for that damned ring.' He paused as he reached the door to his office. 'I'd like you to join me when they bring Hákon in.'

'While you're talking to the Selfoss police, can you ask them to check their reports on Dr Ásgrímur's death in 1992?' Magnus asked.

Baldur hesitated, and then nodded curtly.

When Magnus got back to his own desk, Árni was there, looking exhausted.

'How's the Gubernator?' Magnus asked.

'Very funny. I hear things have been happening back here.'

'Baldur's just sending the Selfoss police to arrest the pastor of Hruni now.'

'Do you think he killed Agnar?'

'Him or Tómas,' said Magnus. 'We'll find out which pretty soon.'

'So Isildur and Steve Jubb are innocent?'

'Looks like it,' said Magnus. And he explained all that had happened while Árni had been thirty-five thousand feet up in the air.

Magnus was expecting to wait three hours before Hákon was brought in, but it was less than an hour before Baldur strode into the room, his face like thunder.

'He's gone,' he said.

'Has he taken his car?' Magnus asked.

'Of course he has.'

'And the ring?'

'Gone as well. If it ever existed.'

It had been a frustrating twenty-four hours for Isildur. He was beginning to have his doubts about Axel, the PI he had hired. Pétur Ásgrímsson had been spectacularly unhelpful, his sister Ingileif seemed to have disappeared off the face of the earth and Axel hadn't succeeded in finding out very much from his supposed contacts in the police. Tómas Hákonarson was under arrest for the murder of Agnar, there was evidence that he had been at Lake Thingvellir on the night in question, but the police were dismissing rumours of magic rings as mythology.

Morons!

He and Gimli were waiting in the Hótel Borg for a call from Axel. In separate rooms. Despite the fact that they had formed such a close bond in the virtual world, in the real one they had little in common. Isildur was rereading the *Volsung Saga* and Gimli was watching repeats of a handball match. He had explained that whenever he went to a foreign country he liked to watch the local sports on TV.

Isildur's cell phone rang. He checked the caller ID. It was Axel.

'I've found her,' the PI said.

'Where is she?'

'At her apartment.'

'Great! Let's go talk to her.'

'I'll pick you up in five minutes.'

Isildur summoned Gimli and they waited outside the hotel. The square was empty, other than the pigeons. The parliament building squatted on the south side, a tough building made of blackened stone. It was slightly smaller than the branch of Isildur's local bank in Trinity County, and stood next to what must have been the tiniest cathedral in the world.

Axel drew up in his old banger and they crammed inside. They were soon outside Ingileif's building. Once again, Isildur took the lead and rang the bell.

A pretty blonde woman answered the door with half a smile.

'Hi,' said Isildur, confident by now that a young Icelander would speak English. 'My name's Lawrence Feldman. I'm the guy who was all set to buy your saga. Can we come in?'

The half smile disappeared. 'No you may not,' said Ingileif. 'Go away. I want nothing to do with you.'

'I would still be willing to pay a very good price for the saga, Miss Ásgrímsdóttir.'

'I'm not going to discuss it with you.'

Isildur persisted. 'And if by any chance you know of the where-abouts of the ring itself, I will pay you for that information. Or for the ring, if you have it.'

'Fuck off,' said Ingileif in crisp English, and slammed the door in his face.

'Funny. That's exactly what her brother said,' said Gimli with a chuckle.

But Isildur did not see the funny side. He had been hoping for a breakthrough from Ingileif. In his experience, if you waved enough money, you could usually get what you wanted.

But not necessarily in Iceland, it seemed.

They crossed the street, back to the car.

'What now?' asked Gimli.

'Do you know much about electronic surveillance, Axel?' Isildur asked.

'What do you mean?'

'Listening devices. Bugging phones, that kind of thing.'

'That's illegal,' said Axel.

'So is jaywalking, and we just did it. All that matters is that you don't get caught.'

'Actually, jaywalking isn't illegal in Iceland,' Axel said.

'Whatever,' said Isildur. 'I want to know what that woman knows. And if she's not going to tell us, we're going to have to figure it out for ourselves.'

'I guess so,' said Axel.

'There's obviously a risk attached to it. Which means you deserve to get paid extra. For the risk.'

'I'll see what I can do.'

Árni drove back to his apartment. He was dog tired, too tired really to drive. He almost ploughed into the back of a van that stopped suddenly at a light.

His mind drifted over the case and what Magnus had told him. There was something that wasn't quite right, something nagging at his brain. It wasn't until he was actually in his apartment and making himself a cup of coffee that he realized what it was.

Oh, God. He'd made another mistake.

He was so tempted just to forget about it, crawl into bed, trust to Magnus and Baldur to figure everything out for themselves.

But he couldn't. He had some people to talk to. And he had to talk to them right away. If he was lucky, he would be proved wrong. He probably *was* wrong after all, he usually was. But he had to check.

He needed caffeine first. As soon as he had finished his coffee he grabbed his jacket and headed back out to his car.

Diego was not happy.

He had spent the bulk of the day knocking around the Hlemmur bus station, directly opposite police headquarters. He hadn't seen Magnus go in or out of the building. But then he didn't know for sure that Magnus wasn't in there, because in addition to the two entrances at the front, he was pretty sure there was an entrance in back, where the parking lot was.

Plus he stuck out like a sore thumb. This country was so goddamned *white*. Not Caucasian, not creamy brown, but honest-to-goodness white. The people were so blonde their hair was almost white as well. No sign of a tan anywhere, and certainly not any brown skin.

Diego was used to blending in. If you thought about it, you would probably say he looked Hispanic, but he could have been Arabic or Turkish or even Italian with a tan, or a mixture of all of the above. In any American city he fit right in. Even when he had offed that stockbroker in the cute little town on Cape Cod, he hadn't really turned heads. There were people that looked like him in every community in the US.

But not here.

Where were the goddamn Eskimos? They had black hair and brown faces. But they sure as hell didn't live in this country.

This was stupid. He evaluated his options. He had called the police headquarters to ask if a Magnus Jonson worked there. He did, in the traffic department. But Diego was pretty sure that wasn't the Jonson he was looking for.

So what was the next step? He could just walk in and ask if there was an American cop working at the station. He guessed that was the kind of thing that would have gotten around; if the guy he talked to didn't know the answer he could probably find it out easily enough. Problem was, Jonson would hear someone had been asking about him. Diego didn't want to tip off the target.

He could go back to the Lithuanians. He knew they had been paid well by Soto to help him out. He understood that in a small place like this they wanted to make sure that they weren't associated with the hit, but surely they could put him in touch with a third party that could help him? A PI or a crooked lawyer. Someone who spoke Icelandic. Someone who was whitey-white.

He didn't have much time. Jonson could be on a plane back to the States at any moment. Once there it would be easy for the Feds to keep him safe for the few days until the trial.

He was sitting in the coffee shop at the station, on his fifth or sixth cup, his eyes flicking between the two front entrances.

A big guy came out. A big guy with red hair.

That was him!

Diego left the half-empty cup of coffee and almost skipped out of the bus station.

To work.

Magnus headed up the hill towards the Grand Rokk. It was eight-thirty and he had the impression he wasn't needed at the station any more that evening.

Baldur had been furious. Any positive thoughts he had held earlier about Magnus had been dispelled. Why hadn't Magnus called Baldur as soon as he realized that Hákon was Tómas's father? Why hadn't he stayed with Hákon at Hruni and waited for reinforcements to arrest the pastor?

Why had he let Hákon get away?

While the rest of the Violent Crimes unit ran around like idiots, Magnus was left standing around with nothing to do. So he left.

The barman recognised him and poured him a large Thule. A couple of the regulars said hello. But he wasn't in the mood for chat, however friendly. He took his beer to a stool in the corner of the bar and drank it.

Baldur had a point, of course. The reason that Magnus had waited until he returned to Reykjavík before telling him what Hákon had said was hardly noble. It was so that he and not Baldur would crack Tómas's story.

Which he had done. He had solved the case. Discovered not only who had killed Agnar, but also what had happened to Ingileif's father. The moment of victory had been sweet, but it had only lasted an hour.

There was a chance that Hákon had just driven out on an errand and he would be back in an hour or so. Or that he would be caught by the police. He was an easy guy to spot, it was a small country, or at least the inhabited parts of it were. Magnus wondered whether Hákon would hide in the backcountry, like the outlaws in the sagas, living on berries while he dodged the law.

A possibility.

There was no doubt about it, Magnus had screwed up.

At least that meant that the National Police Commissioner wouldn't demand that he stay in Iceland for the full two years that he had originally expected. They would be glad to be rid of him next week.

And he would be glad to go.

Wouldn't he?

It was true what he had said to Ingileif, the memories of his early life in Iceland were painful, made more so by the chance meeting with his cousin. And clearly things were not going well with Baldur. But there were things he liked about his brief time in Iceland. He did have an affinity with the country. More than that – it was a loyalty, a sense of duty. The pride that Icelanders felt for their homeland, their determination to work their butts off to make the place function, was infectious.

The Commissioner's idea to recruit someone like Magnus wasn't a bad one. The police officers he had met were smart, honest, hard working. They were good guys, even Baldur. They just lacked experience in big-city crime and that was something he knew he could help them with.

And then there was Ingileif.

He had no desire to go back to Colby, and he was quite sure that she had no desire to go back to him.

But Ingileif.

He had really screwed that up. She had a point, their relationship was more than a quick roll in the hay. How much more, Magnus didn't know, and neither did she, but that didn't matter, he shouldn't have made it matter.

He ordered another beer.

He would try again. Say he was sorry. He wanted to see her

again before he went home. She might just tell him to get lost, but it was worth the risk. There was nothing to lose.

He gulped down half his beer and left the bar.

Diego had found himself a good spot, in the smokers' tent pitched outside in the front yard of the Grand Rokk. He had strolled in to get himself a beer at the bar, and had seen the big cop alone with his drink, absorbed in his own thoughts.

Perfect.

There was one problem; Diego's car was still parked a couple of blocks from the bus station. He had followed Jonson on foot. There was no way that he was going to carry out the hit in daylight. He needed darkness to make good his escape.

But it was still light. He checked his watch. It was nearly nine-thirty. What was with this country? It was still only April, back home it would have gotten dark hours ago.

So he would follow Jonson. If he was still on the streets when darkness eventually fell he would do it then, otherwise he would follow him home and break in in the small hours of the morning.

Then he saw the big cop walk purposefully out of the bar, past the tent and out on to the street.

Diego followed.

Finally, it was getting dark, or at least dusk. Not quite dark enough. But if Jonson had a long walk before he got home, there might be a chance to do something. Diego would rather pump a couple of shots into Jonson's head on a quiet street than lumber around in a strange house, with God knows who else there.

Magnus made his way to Ingileif's house. There was a light on upstairs in her apartment. He hesitated. Would she listen to him?

There was only one way to find out.

He rang the bell at the side entrance of the house, which was where the stairs led up to her flat.

She answered the door. 'Oh, it's you.'

'I've come to say I'm sorry,' Magnus said. 'I acted like a jerk.'

'You did.' Ingileif's face was cool, almost expressionless. Not hostile, but certainly not pleased to see him.

'May I come in?' he asked.

'No,' said Ingileif. 'You did act like a jerk. But your basic point was correct. You are leaving Iceland in a couple of days. It doesn't make sense for us to get more emotionally involved with each other.'

Magnus blinked. 'I understand that. It was what I told you, after all, but much less tactfully. But …?'

Ingileif raised her eyebrows. 'But?'

Magnus wanted to tell her that he really liked her, that he wanted to get to know her better, that it might not make sense but that it was the right thing to do, he knew it was the right thing to do. But her grey eyes were cold. No, they said. No.

He sighed. 'I'm very glad I met you, Ingileif,' he said. He bent down, kissed her quickly on the cheek and turned into the gathering gloom.

Árni sat in his car, parked illegally just outside Eymundsson's Bookshop in Austurstraeti, and called the station. Magnus had left for the evening. Then he called Magnus's mobile number. No reply – the phone was switched off. So then he called his sister's house.

'Oh, hi Árni,' Katrín said.

'Have you seen Magnús?'

'Not this evening. But he might be in. Let me check.' Árni tapped his fingers on the dashboard while his sister looked in Magnus's room. 'No, he's not here.'

'Any idea where he might be?'

'How the hell should I know?' Katrín protested.

'Please, Katrín. Where does he go in the evening, do you know?'

'Not really. Wait, I think he goes to the Grand Rokk sometimes.'

'Thanks.' Árni hung up and drove rapidly up to the Grand Rokk. He was there in two minutes.

He had to speak to Magnus. He had checked. He *had* made a mistake. He knew who had killed Agnar.

He stopped the car in the street right outside the bar and ran in. He flashed his badge at the barman and asked if he had seen Magnus. He had. The big man had left fifteen minutes before.

Árni jumped back into his car and headed up the hill towards the Hallgrímskirkja. He stopped at a junction. A man crossed in front of him wearing a baggy hooded sweatshirt. The man was fairly tall, slim, with brown skin, walking determinedly. Árni knew him from somewhere.

He was the guy in the arrivals hall at Keflavík Airport. The American who had been met by the Lithuanian drug dealer.

It was a quiet road. The Hispanic guy had increased his pace to a brisk walk. He lifted up his hood.

As Árni crossed the junction heading uphill, he glimpsed Magnus shambling slowly further along the street, head down, deep in thought. Árni was tired. It took him a couple of seconds to realize what was happening. He braked, slammed the car into reverse, and sped backwards down the hill. He crashed into a parked car, threw open the door and jumped out.

'Magnús!' he shouted.

Magnus spun around when he heard the sound of smashing metal. So did the Hispanic guy.

The guy was only twenty metres away, maximum. He was gripping something in the front pocket of his sweatshirt.

Árni charged.

He saw the Hispanic's eyes widen. He saw him pull the gun out of his pocket. Raise it.

Árni launched himself into mid air just as the gun went off.

Magnus saw Árni leap out of his vehicle, heard him shout, saw him run towards the tall figure in the grey hoodie.

He rushed forward just as Árni bowled the man over. He heard the sound of a gunshot, muffled by Árni's body. The man rolled away from Árni, and turned towards Magnus. Raised his gun from a prone position.

Magnus was about twenty feet away. No chance of reaching the man before he pulled the trigger.

There was a gap between two houses on his left. He jinked and dived through. Another gunshot and a ricochet of a bullet off metal siding.

Magnus found himself in a back yard, other back yards ahead and to one side. He turned right and leapt at a six-foot-high fence. Swung his body over just as another shot rang out.

But Magnus didn't want to run away from this guy.

He wanted to nail him.

A floodlight burst into life, dazzling Magnus. This yard backed on to a more prosperous looking house. Magnus searched for somewhere to hide.

Before it had erupted, Magnus had noticed that the floodlight was a couple of feet forward from the fence bordering the next yard along. He ran directly towards it, reached the fence and crouched down. He was in deep shadow. No chance of the man seeing him through the dazzling light.

The man appeared on top of the fence and dropped down. He paused to listen. Silence.

Magnus was breathing hard. He swallowed, trying to control it, to make sure he didn't make a sound.

The man stood stock still, peering around the garden. Magnus had realized he had made a mistake. The guy had heard the silence. Heard the lack of running footsteps.

He knew Magnus was in the yard.

Magnus's plan had been to catch the guy as he ran through the yard, grabbing him from behind. That plan wasn't going to work.

For a second the man looked straight at Magnus. Magnus stayed motionless, praying that his theory about the light would hold. It did.

Cautiously the man examined a shrub. Then another. Then he stood still again, listening.

The floodlight was motion-activated. No motion, no light. It went out.

Magnus knew he had a second or two before the man's eyes adjusted to the darkness. He also knew that if he ran straight, the man would shoot at the sound and he would take a bullet. So he ran a couple of paces forward and jinked to the left, a fullback slicing through the defence.

A shot rang out, the flame from the barrel illuminating the man's face for a fraction of a second.

The man moved his gun to the right, pointed it straight at Magnus, aiming high.

So Magnus dived low, a football tackle directly at the man's knees. Another shot, just a little too high, and the man went down.

Magnus wriggled and lunged for the hand holding the gun. He grabbed the barrel, and twisted it up and towards the man. Another shot and the sound of broken glass from the house. A satisfying snap and a cry as a thumb broke, jammed in the trigger guard. The man's free hand reached over Magnus's face grappling for his eyes. Magnus bucked and wrenched the gun away, rolling back and on to his feet.

He jabbed the gun into the man's face.

He wanted to pull the trigger; he wanted so badly to pull the trigger. But he knew it would lead to all kinds of problems.

'Get up!' he shouted in English. 'Stand up, or I'll blow your head off!'

The man slowly raised himself to his feet, his eyes on Magnus, breathing heavily.

'Get your hands up! Move over here!'

Magnus could hear shouting in the house. 'Call the police,' he yelled in Icelandic.

He pushed the man along the side of the house and out on to the street, and shoved him against the wall, his face pressed against the corrugated metal. Now he had a problem. He wanted to tend to Árni, but he couldn't risk leaving the man uncovered.

He considered once again blowing the guy's brains out. He was tempted.

Bad idea.

'Turn around,' he said, and as the guy turned towards him, he transferred the gun to his left hand and whacked the man with a blow to the jaw with his right.

The pain shot through Magnus's hand, but the man crumpled. Out cold.

Magnus knelt down beside Árni. He was still alive, his eyelids were fluttering and his breath was coming in short gasps. There was a hole in his chest, there was blood. But there wasn't that horrible wheezing sound of a sucking chest wound.

'It's OK, Árni. You'll be fine. Hang in there, buddy. You're not hit too bad.'

Árni's lips began to move.

'Shh,' said Magnus. 'Quiet now. We'll get an ambulance here in no time.'

Someone had called the police, he could hear the sirens coming closer.

But Árni's lips continued to move. 'Magnus. Listen,' he whispered, in English.

Magnus moved his head close to Árni's face, but he couldn't quite make out what Árni was trying to say, just the last word, which was something like 'Bye'.

'Hey, no need to say goodbye now, Árni, you're gonna make it, you're the Terminator, remember?'

Árni moved his head from side to side and tried to speak again. It was too much for him. The eyes closed. The lips stopped moving.

CHAPTER THIRTY-ONE

MAGNUS JUMPED INTO the police car that led the ambulance to the National Hospital, lights flashing, sirens blaring. It took less than five minutes. He was elbowed away by paramedics pushing Árni through corridors and double hospital doors. The last Magnus saw of his partner was his feet speeding towards the operating room at the stern of the gurney.

He was shown into a small waiting room and began pacing, a television mumbling in the background. Uniformed police officers bustled about.

A woman with a clipboard asked him about next of kin. He wrote down Katrín's name and address. Then he called her.

'Oh, hi, Magnus, did Árni find you?' she asked in English.

'Yeah, he found me.'

Katrín could tell from the tone of his voice that something was wrong. 'What's up?'

'I'm at the hospital. Árni's been shot.'

'Shot? He can't have been shot. This is Iceland.'

'Well, he was. In the chest.'

'Is he OK?'

'He's not OK, no. But he *is* alive. I don't know yet how bad it is. He's in surgery now.'

'Did it have something to do with you?'

'Yes,' said Magnus. 'Yes, it did have something to do with me.'

As he ended the call, he thought about exactly what it had had to do with him. It *was* his fault that Árni had been nearly killed. It was he who had led a Dominican hit man to Iceland, armed with a gun and primed to fire it.

It should have been him in there on the operating table.

'Damn, Árni!' He smashed his fist against the wall. A flash of pain ran through his hand, still sensitive from where it had connected with the punk's jaw. OK, Árni wasn't used to being around criminals with guns, but a Boston cop would never have done what he had done. There were lots of options. Drive the car straight at the guy. Drive up to Magnus and put the car between him and the punk. Just honk the horn, roll down the window and yell. All of those would have worked better than sprinting full speed at an armed man.

And, of course, if this was any normal country and Árni had been carrying a gun, he could simply have drawn it and shouted a challenge.

But even if he wasn't smart, Árni was brave. And if the hit man had just been a split-second slower, Árni's headlong rush might have worked. But the Dominican had been fast, and Árni had taken a bullet for Magnus.

The Police Commissioner had recruited Magnus to control the spread of big-city violence to Reykjavík. But all he had done was lead it right into the heart of the city, the heart of the police department.

Mind you, he had already come across plenty of unusual deaths in Iceland. Dr Ásgrímur, Agnar, Ingileif's stepfather.

Katrín burst in. 'How is he?' she asked.

'I don't know. They haven't said anything yet.'

'I've called Mum and Dad. They are on their way.'

'I'm sorry,' Magnus said.

Katrín was a tall woman. She looked him straight in the eye. 'Did you shoot him?'

'No.'

'Well, then you have nothing to be sorry about.'

Magnus gave her a small smile and shrugged. He wasn't about to take this moment to argue with an Icelandic woman.

A doctor appeared, mid-forties, confident, competent but concerned. 'Are you next-of-kin?' she asked Katrín.

'I'm Árni's sister, yes.'

'He's lost quite a lot of blood. The bullet's still in there, right next to the heart. We're going to go in and get it out. It will take a while.'

'Will he be OK?'

The doctor looked Katrín in the eye much the same way she had just looked at Magnus. 'I don't know,' she said. 'He's got a chance. A good chance. Beyond that I can't say.'

'OK, don't waste time here,' Katrín said. 'Get on with it.'

Magnus was sure that Iceland had competent doctors. But he was worried that they would have little experience with gunshot wounds. Back home, at Boston Medical Center, they spent much of their Friday and Saturday nights plugging up bullet holes.

He decided not to mention this to Katrín.

There was a commotion outside the waiting room and Baldur strode in. Magnus had seen Baldur angry before, but never this angry.

'How is he?' he asked.

'They're operating on him now,' Magnus said. 'The bullet's still in there somewhere and they're trying to fish it out.'

'Will he make it?'

'They hope so,' said Magnus.

'He'd better,' said Baldur. 'Now I've got some questions for you.' He turned to Katrín, disapproval all over his face. Although Katrín wasn't in full regalia, there was a sprinkling of metal sticking out of her face. 'Can you excuse us?'

Katrín frowned. Magnus could see she had taken an instant dislike to the policeman, and was not in the mood to be pushed around.

'Let's leave her here,' said Magnus. ' She has as much right to be here as we do. More. We can do this outside.'

Baldur glared at Katrín. Katrín glared back. They moved out into the corridor.

'Do you know why one of my police officers was shot?' Baldur said, his face only a few inches away from Magnus.

'Yes.'

'Well?'

'I'm a witness in a big police corruption trial in Boston. Some people there want me dead. Dominican drug traffickers. That's why I came here. Looks like they found me.'

'And why didn't you tell me about this?'

'The Police Commissioner thought that the fewer people who knew, the less chance there would be of a leak.'

'So *he* knew about it?'

'Of course.'

'If Árni dies, so help me I'll ...' Baldur hesitated as he tried to think of a convincing threat.

'I've apologized to Árni's sister, and I will apologize to you,' Magnus said. 'I'm sorry that I led the hit man over here. I'm bad news. I should go.'

'Yes, you should. Starting now. I want you to leave this hospital, you can't do anything more here. Go back to the station and make a statement. They're waiting for you.'

Magnus didn't have the strength to argue. He badly wanted to stay and see how Árni was doing, but in a way Baldur was right. He was a distraction. He should go.

He put his head into the waiting room. 'I've got to leave now,' he said to Katrín. 'Let me know if there's news, one way or the other.'

'The bald Gestapo officer sent you home, did he?'

Magnus nodded. 'He's a little wound up. Understandably.'

'Huh.' Katrín seemed unimpressed. 'I'll call you when there's news.'

Magnus slept badly. No dreams, thank God, but he kept on expecting the phone to ring. It didn't.

He got up at six and called the hospital. He didn't want to ring

Katrín's cell phone in case she had managed to snatch some sleep and he woke her. They had completed the operation and extracted the bullet. Árni had lost a lot of blood, but he was alive. They were cautiously optimistic, with the emphasis on cautiously. But Árni was still unconscious.

Magnus walked down the hill to the police station. It was a grey, windy, dull Reykjavík day. Cold, but not very cold.

There were two or three detectives in the Violent Crimes room. He nodded to them and they smiled and nodded back. Although he was prepared to shrug off hostility, he was glad that it didn't seem to be present.

Vigdís came over with a cup of coffee. 'I expect you need this.'

'Thank you,' Magnus said with a smile. And then: 'Sorry about Árni.'

'It wasn't your fault,' Vigdís said.

'Do we know who the shooter is?'

'No. He has a US passport, but we're pretty sure it's a fake. He's not talking.'

'He's a pro. He won't.' Magnus had given the detective who had taken his statement the night before all the information he could, including whom to contact in the Boston PD. It had been made very clear that Baldur didn't want him to interview the Dominican.

'They might send another one, you know?' Vigdís said. 'Another hit man.'

'It will take them a day or two before they realize things have gone wrong and they get someone else over here. And I'll be gone soon.'

'Keep your eyes open,' said Vigdís. 'Now you haven't got Árni around to watch out for you any more.'

Magnus smiled. 'I will.' Vigdís was right. He was probably OK for twenty-four hours, but he ought to think of a place to lie low until he flew back to the States.

'If you need any help with anything, just ask, OK?'

'OK. Thanks.'

As Vigdís left, Magnus turned to his computer. He needed to tell the FBI and Williams what had happened himself. But before he began to type there was an incoming e-mail, direct, not via the FBI.

Hey Magnus,

There's something I really ought to tell you. A guy broke into my apartment a couple of nights ago and shoved a gun in my mouth. He wanted to know where you were. I kinda told him about the Reykjavík police domain name on your e-mail address.

I feel real bad about this. I haven't told the department, but I figured you needed to know so you could keep a look out for trouble.

Johnny Yeoh

Anger flared in Magnus. He hit the reply key and began typing, but after a couple of words he stopped. He couldn't really blame Johnny. The gun was real, the threat was real, if Johnny hadn't told the man what he wanted to know he risked getting his head blown off.

Although he could have warned Magnus sooner.

Magnus was really most angry with himself. He shouldn't have breached the simple protocols that the FBI had set up. There was a reason they didn't want him sending e-mails directly to anyone in the States. Turned out it was a very good reason.

He deleted the half-written e-mail and replaced it with a simple 'thanks for letting me know'. Johnny Yeoh would be in big trouble anyway, not for talking to the gangster, but for not reporting the fact that he had immediately. And all that would come out in good time.

Magnus composed an e-mail to Williams describing what had happened the night before, omitting for the moment the information that Johnny Yeoh had pointed the Dominicans to Iceland.

He was aware of a figure sitting in Árni's chair opposite him. Snorri Gudmundsson, the National Police Commissioner of Iceland. The Big Salmon himself.

He had expected a summons to the Commissioner's office at some point. He hadn't expected a visit.

'How are you doing, Magnús?' the Commissioner asked.

'Hard to put into words,' said Magnus. 'I feel bad about Árni.'

'Don't,' said the Commissioner. 'I knew that your life was under threat. I knew that there was a chance that they would come looking for you. I didn't think that one of my officers would get shot, but I was wrong, and that's my responsibility, not yours.' The Commissioner sighed. 'Thank God he's going to live.'

'Are they sure?' Magnus asked.

'Not a hundred per cent, but it's looking better by the hour.'

'He's a brave man,' Magnus said. 'A very brave man.'

'He is.'

'Look, Snorri, I meant to tell you. I heard from my chief the other day. The trial in Boston has been moved up to next week. I'll have to fly over and testify.'

'That's good.'

'I guess I won't be coming back.'

'I guess you will.' The Commissioner's bright blue eyes twinkled.

Magnus raised his eyebrows in surprise.

'We discussed this when you arrived. I want you here for two years.'

'Yes, but after all that's happened ...'

'We got a result in the Agnar case. We know who the murderer is, all we have to do now is find him. From what I've heard, you were important in solving the case.'

'What you've heard? Not from Baldur, surely?'

'No. From Thorkell.'

'He can't be very pleased about his nephew getting shot up.'

'He's not. But he doesn't blame you. And if he blames me, he's not saying.'

'What about Baldur? I'm sure he would love it if I went back to the States and never came back.'

'You leave Baldur to me.'

'I don't know,' said Magnus. He had assumed that he would be done with Iceland within a matter of days. And he had assumed he would be very happy with that state of affairs.

'You're coming back,' said the Commissioner, getting to his feet. 'You have a moral obligation. That's important to me, and I think that's important to you.'

As Magnus watched the Commissioner leave the room, two thoughts were uppermost in his mind.

The first, the most insistent, was whether he should indeed stay in Iceland.

The second, lower key, nagging, was that he wasn't as sure as the Commissioner that the case was solved.

Ten minutes later, Baldur prowled into the room.

'What are you doing here?' he growled when he saw Magnus.

'It's where I work. At least for now.'

'We don't need spectators here. Have you made your statement?'

'Last night.'

'Then go home and stay home where we can get hold of you if we need you to add to it.'

'Have you found the Reverend Hákon?' Magnus asked.

'Not yet. But we will. He can't get out of the country.'

'Have you looked at Stöng? Or Álfabrekka?'

'Why should we do that?'

'We know that the ring has an enormous influence over Hákon. He's a strange man, a romantic in his way. Where would he run to? I'm sure you're watching all the obvious places, the airports, his relatives if he has any. But he might go somewhere that's important to the ring. Somewhere like Stöng. Or the cave where the ring was originally found. I think the map Dr Ásgrímur drew is still in my car.'

Baldur just shook his head. 'If you think I am going to divert scarce resources into the middle of nowhere to satisfy your idiotic notions of what a ring "thinks" then ...' He trailed off in frustration. 'Forget it. Go home.'

CHAPTER THIRTY-TWO

B UT MAGNUS DIDN'T go home. He signed out a car and drove out towards Gaukur's abandoned farm at Stöng. The further east he drove the worse the weather became. A grey damp cloud had settled on Iceland, and he was driving through it. Even once he dropped down from the lava fields on to the broad plain around Selfoss, visibility was poor. Horses looked miserably out of sodden fields towards the road. Every now and then a church or a farm would loom out of the mist on a little knoll.

There was certainly no sign of Hekla, not even as he turned up the road that ran along the banks of the River Thjórsá.

He had no idea whether he really would find anything at Stöng or Álfabrekka. But he sure as hell didn't want to hang around Reykjavík doing nothing. He had tried to put himself inside the pastor's strange mind. It was difficult to do, he couldn't pretend that he understood the man, but he thought his hunch wasn't bad as hunches went.

He thought about the Police Commissioner's request that he stay on in Iceland. It was more of a command, really.

He was sure that once back home he could persuade Williams to let him remain in Boston. But the Commissioner's appeal to Magnus's sense of honour was shrewd. The Icelandic police had provided him with sanctuary. One of them had almost given his life to save Magnus's. The Commissioner had a point; he did owe them.

When he had first arrived in Iceland he had immediately felt the urge to return to the violent streets of Boston. But perhaps

Colby was right, what kind of life was that, anyway? Solve one murder, look for the next. A frantic, never-ending search to discover who he was, to make sense of his past, of his father's murder, of himself.

There was a good chance the answers to those questions didn't lie in Boston, but here, in Iceland. If he wanted, he could try to continue running away from his Icelandic past, from his family. But he would be running away from himself. He would spend his life running, moving from dead body to dead body in the South End. Perhaps if he stayed in Iceland for a couple of years he could begin to answer those questions, to find out who he really was.

And even who his father was. For the last few days he had successfully crammed Sigurbjörg's disclosure that his father had been unfaithful to his mother back into its box. But it wouldn't stay there quietly for the rest of his life. That knowledge was part of him now. Just like his father's murder, it would haunt him.

Although he was driving through a short straight stretch of road, Magnus braked.

His father's murder.

That puzzle had tormented him wherever he went, whatever he did. The police hadn't found the murderer and neither had he, no matter how hard he had tried. But perhaps they had all been looking in the wrong place. Perhaps he should look in Iceland.

As soon as he thought of the idea, Magnus tried to dismiss it. He knew how much anxiety pursuing that line of thought would cause him, how he could become swallowed up in yet more fruitless investigation. But the idea, once thought, couldn't be unthought.

His mother's family hated his father and now he knew why, Sigurbjörg had told him. They blamed him for destroying her. They wanted revenge.

The answer was in Iceland. The answer to everything was in Iceland.

*

Pétur watched the small team of Poles go at his car, scrubbing, washing, polishing. He had overcome the urge to pay them double to do a good job; he didn't want them to remember him. The fact his BMW four-by-four was white helped. It meant it was easier to spot any dirt they left. He decided that he would go at it himself once they had finished.

Pétur usually kept a cool head, but he had almost missed the dirt. If the police had stopped by his apartment the night before and impounded his car, their forensics people would have been able to tell where he had been the previous afternoon.

And the problem with a white BMW four-by-four was that it stuck out, even in the land of expensive four-by-fours. Inga had certainly noticed it: his eyes had met hers for a fraction of a second as he had sped past her the day before.

Which was why he had called her mobile immediately and asked her not to mention it.

He hoped she hadn't said anything. He hoped to God she hadn't said anything.

Searching for comfort, his hand closed around the object stuck deep in the warm pocket of his coat.

A ring.

The ring.

But Ingileif hadn't told anyone. She had been surprised when she had seen Pési driving up the Thjórsárdalur, she couldn't think of any reason why he should be there. But her instinct was not to mention it to Magnus. She didn't know why.

She told herself it wasn't important, and indeed, why should it be important? But she didn't go the further step of asking herself why, if it wasn't important, she hadn't said anything.

She was frustrated by Magnus's behaviour. She liked to think that she had a pretty down-to-earth view of sex and relationships. Despite what Magnus implied, she didn't jump into bed with every man she fancied. There might be the odd night with Lárus, but everyone knew there was nothing in the odd night with Lárus. Or everyone in Reykjavík did anyway.

She had liked Magnus. And she had trusted him. Then suddenly he had pulled a girlfriend out of nowhere and more or less called her a slut.

Jerk.

The problem with the sudden deterioration in their relations was it made it more difficult for her to find out from Magnus whether Hákon really had killed her father, or indeed whether it was Tómas. She thought it unlikely that it was Tómas, but she didn't *know*.

She did know someone who would. Tómas's mother.

Her name was Erna, and Ingileif trusted her. She was a small woman with blonde curly hair, who had originally come from a village in the West Fjords where she had met Hákon when he had been serving as a priest there. Ingileif remembered the way Erna used to look up to her husband, not just literally, for Hákon was almost half a metre taller than his wife, but also how she seemed to submit to his will. But Erna was basically an honest, kind, sensible woman who had ensured that Tómas hadn't grown up an emotional wreck. It must have taken a lot of courage for her to leave her husband when she did, but it was definitely a wise decision.

She would know which of her son or her husband had killed the doctor. She would know.

So Ingileif drove her old Polo out to Hella, a town about fifty kilometres to the south of Flúdir, which is where she knew Erna lived with her second husband.

The drive was unpleasant in the fog, but at least there wasn't much traffic on the road. She listened to the news on the radio, hoping for more information about Tómas, or possibly the arrest of the Reverend Hákon. There was none of that. But there was something about shots being fired in 101, a policeman being wounded and taken to hospital and an American citizen being held by the police.

For a moment, a dreadful moment, Ingileif thought that the policeman was Magnus. But then they named him as Detective Árni Holm and she breathed again.

She was absolutely sure Magnus was involved somehow, though. Perhaps he was the American citizen they had locked up.

Hella was a modern settlement that lined the bank of the West Ranga river, the next one along after the Thjórsá. Ingileif had looked up Erna's address from the national phone-directory website: her house was a single-storey building only thirty metres from the river, surrounded by a green garden. Ingileif had no idea whether Erna would be out at work, after all most Icelandic women had a job, but when Ingileif rang the doorbell, Erna answered.

She recognized Ingileif immediately and ushered her in. Erna's blonde hair was still blonde, but dyed nowadays, and she had put on weight. But her blue eyes still twinkled when she saw Ingileif, although they swiftly clouded again with worry. 'Have you heard the dreadful news about Tómas?' she said, as she busied herself in the kitchen organizing coffee.

'I have,' said Ingileif. 'You can hardly miss it. It's all over the papers. Have you seen him?'

'No. The police won't let me. I've spoken to his lawyer on the phone. She says that the police don't have enough evidence to prove anything. I didn't even know he *knew* this Agnar fellow. Why on earth would he murder the man? The lawyer said that it all had something to do with a manuscript the professor was trying to sell. Here, Ingileif, let's go through and sit down.'

The sitting room boasted a large picture window opening out on a view of the river, barely visible through the mist. Ingileif remembered that Erna's husband was a manager in one of the local bank branches. He had obviously done well. Ingileif wondered, in the way that Icelanders had since the *kreppa*, whether the man had granted himself a hundred per cent mortgage in the boom times.

'It has to do with our family, Erna. And with your husband.'

'Oh. I feared as much.'

'The manuscript is an old saga that had been in my family for generations. *Gaukur's Saga*. Did Hákon ever mention it to you?'

'Not directly. But that's what he spent so much time discussing with your father, isn't it?'

'That's correct. And when my mother died at the end of last year—'

'Oh, yes, I'm so sorry about that. I would have gone to the funeral if I could.'

'Yes. Well, after she died, I decided to sell the saga, through Professor Agnar. And the police think that it was for this saga that Agnar was killed.'

'I see. But I still don't understand what this has to do with Tómas.'

Except that Ingileif could see in Erna's face that she was beginning to understand.

'It all goes back to my father's death.'

'Ah. I thought it might.' Erna was wary now.

'I'm sure that the police will ask you questions about it soon. Perhaps today,' said Ingileif. 'And I promise I won't tell them what you tell me.' This promise was easier to make now that Magnus had made an idiot of himself. 'But I want to know what happened to my father. I *need* to know.'

'It was an accident,' said Erna. 'Hákon witnessed it. A terrible accident. There was a police investigation and everything.'

'Did your husband tell you what he and my father were doing that weekend?'

'No. He was very secretive about all that, and frankly I wasn't interested. They were researching something, I've no idea what.'

'Did he ever mention a ring?'

'A ring? No. What kind of ring?'

Erna seemed genuinely puzzled. Ingileif took a deep breath. The questions were going to get more painful, there was no way of avoiding it.

'It was a ring that was mentioned in *Gaukur's Saga*, the manuscript the professor who was murdered was trying to sell. You see, the police believe that my father and your husband found the ring that weekend.'

Erna frowned. 'He never mentioned it. And I never saw a ring. But it is just the kind of thing that would fascinate him. And there was *something*. Something hidden in the altar in the church. I saw him sneak in there several times.'

'Did you ever look to see what it was?' Ingileif asked.

'No. I told myself that it was none of my business.' Erna shuddered. 'But the truth is I didn't want to look. I didn't want to know. Hákon had rather unconventional interests. I was scared about what I might find.'

'The police think that my father may have been killed for the ring,' said Ingileif.

'By whom?' said Erna. 'Not by Hákon, surely?'

'That's what they think.' Ingileif swallowed. 'That's what I think.'

Erna looked shocked. Shock turned to anger. 'I know that my ex-husband is eccentric. I know that all sorts of strange stories are told about him in the village. But I am absolutely sure he didn't kill your father. Despite all his fascination with the devil, he wouldn't kill anyone. Ever. And ...'

A tear appeared Erna's eye.

'And?'

'And your father was the only true friend Hákon ever had. Sometimes I think, well I *know*, that Hákon was fonder of him than of me. He was quite broken up by your father's death. It almost destroyed him.' She sniffed and dabbed her eye with her finger. 'He started behaving even more strangely, neglecting his parish duties, listening to Tómas's dreadful music. He became impossible to live with after that. Impossible.'

Ingileif realized she would get no further on the subject of Hákon. She would leave grilling Erna to the police. She still thought Hákon had killed her father, but she was convinced that Erna didn't, and she didn't feel the need to argue with her.

'But what has all this got to do with Tómas?' Erna asked.

'The police think he was there with Hákon and my father. The sheep farmers who Hákon went to for help saw him. Or at least they saw a boy, who the police think was Tómas.' Ingileif didn't want to confuse the issue with talk of hidden people.

'Oh, that really is too absurd,' said Erna. 'Do they think *Tómas* killed Dr Ásgrímur? But he was only twelve then!'

'Thirteen,' said Ingileif. 'And yes they do think he was there. He might have witnessed what happened at the very least.'

'That's ridiculous,' said Erna. 'It must have been someone else.' And then her eyes lit up. 'Wait a minute. It can't have been Tómas!'

'Why not?'

'Because he was with me that weekend. In Reykjavík. He was singing in the Hallgrímskirkja with the village choir. I went to listen. We stayed with my sister in Reykjavík that Saturday night.'

'Are you sure?'

'Oh, I'm quite sure. We didn't get back until Sunday evening. I can remember seeing Hákon when we arrived home. He had only just got back from the hills. He was in a terrible state.' She smiled at Ingileif. 'You see. My son is innocent!'

The three men were squashed into Axel's car, parked a hundred metres down the road from the house which Ingileif had entered. Axel was at the wheel, Isildur was in the back, and Gimli was in the passenger seat, a computer opened on his lap. With expense no object, Axel had planted four bugs on Ingileif when he had broken in in the small hours of the previous night. One in her bag, one in her coat, one in her studio bedroom – that had been the trickiest – and one in the car. The bug in the car doubled as a tracking device, and the location of the car was flashing on the GPS map on the computer.

The tracker had allowed them to follow Ingileif at a safe distance all the way from Reykjavík to Hella. They had driven by the house at which she had stopped and then parked out of sight. The bug in the coat was transmitting loud and clear, but in

Icelandic, through a receiver which was plugged into the laptop. Axel mumbled half-translations as he listened, but they were frustratingly incomplete.

When Axel started muttering about a ring, Isildur couldn't contain his impatience to find out more, but Axel refused to explain further, not wanting to miss any of the conversation.

As soon as Ingileif left the house, Isildur asked Axel for a translation.

'Shouldn't we follow her?' said Axel.

'We can catch her up later. The tracker will show us where she is. I want a full translation, and I want it now!'

Axel pulled the computer off Gimli's lap and tapped some keys. The conversation was recorded on the computer's hard drive. He went through the whole thing slowly and methodically.

Isildur was beside himself with excitement. 'Where's this church?' he demanded. 'The place where the ring is hidden?'

'I don't know,' said Axel. 'The nearest church to Hella is a place called Oddi. It's not far.'

'It sounds like they were neighbours when Ingileif was young,' said Gimli. 'This Hákon is obviously Tómas Hákonarson's father. Do we know where he was born? Where he grew up? Or for that matter where Ingileif grew up? It might not have been Hella. It sounded to me as if this Erna woman had moved out, or moved away.'

'Google him,' said Isildur. 'You got Google in Iceland, right?'

'Google who?'

'Tómas Hákonarson. If he's a big star in this country, there will be a bio on him somewhere.'

Axel called up the search engine, tapped out some words, clicked and scrolled. 'Here he is. He was born in a village in the West Fjords, but was brought up in Flúdir. That's not too far from here.'

'Well, let's go to Flúdir church, then!' said Isildur. 'Get a move on!'

Axel handed the laptop back to Gimli and started up the car.

'Hruni is the nearest church to Flúdir,' said Axel. 'This man must be the pastor of Hruni.' He grinned.

'What's so special about that?'

'Let's just say it fits.'

CHAPTER THIRTY-THREE

A S MAGNUS DROVE up the valley of the Thjórsá towards Mount Hekla, lurking behind the cloud somewhere to the south-east, the landscape became progressively bleaker. Grass gave way to black rock and mounds of sand, like the detritus of a massive abandoned coalfield. The river flowed past the rounded lump of stone several hundred feet high known as Búrfell, home to trolls in the old folk tales. Just beyond, the road crossed a smaller river, the Fossá, a tributary of the Thjórsá, but still powerful, and Magnus came to a junction and a sign. Well, two signs. One said *Stöng*. The other *Road Closed*.

Magnus turned. It wasn't a road. It wasn't even a track. There were twists, turns, steep hills, sharp drops. At one point the road was nothing but black sand. Mist swirled around Magnus as he cajoled his car through the blackened terrain. Below and to the left, the Fossá surged. Fingers of snow reached down from the mountains above, and indeed the road would have been completely impassable a couple of weeks earlier, before the snow had melted. Once or twice, Magnus debated turning back. But of course Hákon's four-wheel-drive would have had an easier time of it.

Then he rounded a bend and saw it. The red Suzuki. It was parked on a brief stretch of road fifty feet above the river. Magnus pulled up next to it and checked the plate. Definitely the Reverend Hákon's vehicle.

He turned off his engine and climbed out of his car.

The damp air hit his nostrils. After the whine of his own car engine and the clanking of stones and rock against the chassis, everything seemed quiet, damply quiet. Except there was a low roar, the sound of water rushing by below.

Somewhere in the fog a duck quacked. Odd to hear the sound of a living thing in that landscape.

Magnus walked over to the Suzuki. Empty. He tried the door handle. Unlocked. No keys in the ignition.

He looked around. Visibility was only a couple of hundred feet. He couldn't see Hákon. Mist swirled around the pinnacles of twisted lava all about Magnus, odd grotesque shapes, volcanic gargoyles. Under his feet was black grit and chips of obsidian, rock melted into black glass deep within the earth and then spewed out on to the very spot where he stood.

Perhaps Hákon had abandoned the car here to walk on to Stöng on foot? A possibility, Magnus could not see far enough along the road to evaluate its quality. But Hákon was an Icelander and he was driving a four-wheel-drive. He was unlikely to give up that easily.

The man was crazy, Magnus knew that. He could have set out on a long hike to God-knows-where over the bleak landscape. To the cave near Álfabrekka, perhaps? To Mount Hekla? He could be away for days.

Magnus looked around the Suzuki for footprints. There were some, but they were muddled. He moved away from the vehicle in expanding circles, but the ground was too hard to betray which direction Hákon might have gone. He did find something of interest, though.

Tyre marks. About thirty feet away from the Suzuki on a small patch of soft ground. Another car had parked there. But when?

Magnus had no idea of the last time it had rained at that particular spot. It had been beautiful in the Thjórsárdalur when he and Ingileif had driven to Álfabrekka the previous day. It was possible that it might not have rained since then. Or it could have rained twenty minutes before.

He debated whether to drive on to Stöng. He recalled the abandoned farm from his childhood. It lay in a small patch of green by a stream. But first he had to report what he had seen to Baldur.

He pulled out his phone. No signal, which was hardly surprising. And there wasn't a police radio in the car.

So he decided to drive back towards the main road until he found a signal to make the call.

After a bone-shattering two kilometres, his phone, which he had placed on the seat beside him, began to ring.

He pulled over and picked it up. He couldn't drive with only one hand on that road.

'Hi, Magnús, it's Ingileif.'

'Hello,' said Magnus, wary, yet pleased that it was her.

'Are you OK?'

'Yes, I'm fine.'

'It's just I heard on the radio this morning that there had been a shooting. A police officer was in hospital. An American had been arrested. I assumed one of the two was you.'

'Yeah, it happened right after I went to your place last night. My partner Árni was shot. I got the guy who did it.'

'And he was after you?'

'He was after me.'

There was a brief silence. Then Ingileif spoke again. 'I've just been to see Erna, Tómas's mother. She lives in Hella.'

'Oh, yes?'

'She is sure that Tómas didn't kill my father. He couldn't have been there. He was singing with the village choir in the Hallgrímskirkja in Reykjavík that weekend.'

'Or so she says. She is his mother, remember?'

'That can be checked, though, can't it? Even seventeen years later?'

'Yes, it can,' admitted Magnus. Ingileif was right. It was an unlikely lie. 'What did she say about Hákon?'

'She's certain that he didn't kill Dad either. But she doesn't have any evidence.'

'I think we can safely ignore that,' Magnus said.

'I suppose so,' said Ingileif. 'But she did sound convincing. She also told me where Hákon hides the ring.'

'In the altar in the church?'

'How do you know?'

'Tómas told me yesterday.'

'Have you found him? Hákon?'

Magnus looked back up the road. 'No. But I did find his car a few minutes ago. On the road to Stöng. He must have gone on a hike or something. Or met someone. I found another set of tyre tracks nearby.'

There was silence at the other end of the phone. For a moment Magnus thought the connection had been dropped. The signal was still poor. 'Ingileif? Ingileif, are you there?'

'Yes, I'm here. Bye, Magnús.'

And she was gone.

Pétur was under his car, wiping the chassis with a cloth. He had driven home from the car wash, grabbed a cloth and a bucket and then parked in a residential street a kilometre away. He didn't want his neighbours to see him washing his car so carefully.

His phone, stuffed in his jeans pocket, rang. He rolled out from under the BMW and answered it.

'Pési? It's Inga.'

He scrambled to his feet. He need to gather his wits for this conversation.

'Inga! Hi! How are you?'

'Why didn't you want me to say I saw you yesterday?'

'You were with that big cop, weren't you?'

'Yes. We had just been to see the sheep farmers who went to look for Dad with Hákon. Pési, I am pretty sure that Dad was killed. It wasn't an accident.'

Pétur realized she had given him the opportunity to go on the offensive. 'I thought we had agreed to leave all that alone,' he said. 'Why were you talking to the cops about it? What could it achieve?'

'Pési, where were you going yesterday?'

Pétur took a deep breath. 'I can't say, Inga. I'm sorry. Don't ask me any more.'

'That won't do, Pési. I need to know what's going on here. Were you going to meet Hákon? On the road to Stöng?'

'Look, where are you now?'

'Just outside Hella.'

'OK. You're right. You do deserve an explanation. And I'll give you one, a full one.'

'Go on, then.'

'Not over the phone. We need to do this face to face.'

'OK. I'll be back in Reykjavík this afternoon.'

'No, not here. You remember where Dad used to take us for picnics? The spot he said was his favourite place in Iceland?'

'Yes.'

'OK, meet me there. In, say, an hour and a half.'

'Why there?'

'I often go there, Inga. It's where Dad is. I go there to talk to him. And I want him to be there when I talk to you.'

There was silence on the other end of the phone. Ingileif would know that such sentimentalism was unlike Pétur, but then she also knew how much their father's death had affected him.

'OK. An hour and a half.'

'See you then. And promise me you won't say anything to the police. At least until after I've had a chance to explain things.'

'I promise.'

Now he had a signal, Magnus called Baldur.

'I've found Hákon's car,' he said, before the inspector had a chance to hang up on him.

'Where?'

'On the road to Stöng. There's no sign of him. And it's too misty to see very far.'

'Are you there now?' barked Baldur.

'No. I had to go back down the road a couple of kilometres until I could get a signal to call you.'

'I'll send a team up to look at it.'

'And to search for him,' said Magnus.

'That won't be necessary.'

'Why not? Have you found him?'

'Yes. At the bottom of the Hjálparfoss. A body was discovered there by a power worker half an hour ago. A large man with a beard wearing a clerical collar.'

Hjálparfoss was a waterfall only a kilometre or so from the turn-off to Stöng. Magnus had seen a sign to it. The powerful river below him, the Fossá, flowed into it.

'He could have jumped,' said Baldur.

'I don't think so,' said Magnus. 'I saw tyre tracks next to the Suzuki. He was pushed.'

'Well, don't go back to the scene,' said Baldur. 'I don't want you taking any further part in this investigation. I'm on my way to Hjálparfoss and you had better not be there when I arrive.'

Magnus felt the urge to snap back. He had had the hunch that Hákon had driven to Stöng. He had found the car. But he held his tongue.

'Glad I could be of assistance,' he said, and hung up.

Well, almost held his tongue.

It would take Baldur at least an hour, probably more like two to get to Hjálparfoss from Reykjavík, which gave Magnus plenty of time.

He drove steadily down the track to the main road. The foot of Búrfell emerged eerily out of the mist ahead. The turn-off to Hjálparfoss was a much better track, but still through black heaps of rock and sand. After a few hundred metres, the waterfall itself appeared, two powerful torrents of water divided by a basalt rock, tumbling into a pool. A police car with lights flashing was parked down by the bank of the river below the waterfall, and a small group of three or four people were clustered around something.

Magnus parked next to the police car and introduced himself. The officers were friendly and stood back to let him take a look at the body.

It was Hákon, all right. Badly battered by his journey down the river and over the waterfall.

Magnus looked at the pastor of Hruni's fingers.

They were bare.

CHAPTER THIRTY-FOUR

MAGNUS DROVE BACK towards Reykjavík. The Thjórsá, which had sparkled the day before, flowed broad and ominously grey down towards the Atlantic Ocean.

This changed things. This definitely changed things.

It looked very much as if someone had killed Hákon. It wasn't Tómas, he was locked up safe and sound. So who was it?

Steve Jubb and Lawrence Feldman?

Since he had arrived in Iceland, Magnus had heard about a lot of people who had suffered sudden death over the years. Not just Agnar and now Hákon. But also Dr Ásgrímur. And even Ingileif's stepfather.

Too many in such a peaceful country to be a coincidence.

Another fall. Another drowning.

Dr Ásgrímur had fallen to his death. That was supposed to be an accident. Agnar had been hit over the head and then drowned. Even Ingileif's stepfather had fallen into Reykjavík Harbour, hitting his head and drowning.

That was it. It was that death that had raised doubts at the back of Magnus's mind earlier when he was talking to the Commissioner.

It was a classic MO, a *modus operandi*, a means of killing for which a murderer showed a preference. Even the smartest killers often stuck to the same familiar method.

There were only two people who were linked to *all* these deaths. A brother and a sister. Pétur and Ingileif.

308

Magnus dismissed Ingileif. But Pétur?

He had alibis. He was at high school in Reykjavík when his father had died. But perhaps he had been able to get out that weekend without anyone knowing? Perhaps he was the hidden man that the old farmer had seen? He was supposed to have been in London when his stepfather had been killed, but he could easily have flown back to Reykjavík for a couple of days without anyone knowing. If he had heard of what the man had done to his sister, Birna, he might have been moved to take revenge. Especially if he had killed before.

But what about Agnar's murder? Pétur had an alibi for that. He was at his clubs all night, Árni had checked it out.

Magnus slammed his palm on the steering wheel. Árni! That was what he had been trying to say before he lost consciousness after he was shot. Not 'Goodbye' but 'Alibi'. He was trying to tell Magnus about an alibi. Pétur's alibi.

Magnus could imagine what had happened. Árni had been round each of Pétur's three clubs and had received assurances that Pétur had been seen there at some point on the evening of the murder. He hadn't cross-checked times, drawn up a precise time-line of exactly where Pétur was and when during that night. It was just the kind of sloppy mistake he would make. But, to be fair to him, it was also the kind of thing he would feel guilty about later.

Pétur had made sure he was seen in the early part of the evening and then driven up to Lake Thingvellir, arriving after nine-thirty when Steve Jubb had left. Perhaps he waited for an hour or so after he had killed Agnar until it was completely dark, before carrying him down to the lake. That would explain the signs of flies on the body in the summer house. Then, of course, he would still have time to get back to his clubs in the early hours of the morning, while they were still hopping.

Four deaths. And Pétur was responsible for all of them.

Magnus accelerated towards Reykjavík. He wanted to call Ingileif. Of course she was Pétur's sister, her first loyalty was to him. But she wouldn't shield a murderer. Or would she?

Magnus called her number. 'Ingileif? It's me, Magnús.'

'Oh.'

'Where are you?'

'I'm on the road to Flúdir.'

The road from Hella to Flúdir passed the turn-off up the Thjórsá valley not far ahead of Magnus.

'I need to talk to you. I'm pretty close. If you pull over and tell me where you are, I'll find you.'

'I can't, Magnús, I have an appointment.'

'It's important.'

'No, I'm sorry, Magnús.'

'It's very important!'

'Look, if you want to arrest me, arrest me. Otherwise let me go about my business.'

Magnus realized he had pushed too hard, but he was none the less surprised by her evasiveness.

'Ingileif, where's Pétur?'

'I don't know.' Suddenly the voice was quieter, less belligerent. She was lying.

'Where are you going?' Magnus asked.

Silence.

'Are you going to meet him?'

Ingileif hung up.

A police car screamed by, lights flashing, speeding upstream to reinforce the officers gawping at the pastor's body.

Magnus remembered the way Ingileif had suddenly stiffened on that very same road the day before. As though she had seen something. Perhaps the driver of a passing car? Pétur?

If she had seen him, then the information that Hákon's car had been found would make her think. Think along the same lines that Magnus had just been following. Like Magnus she would want to talk to Pétur. She was going to meet him now.

In Flúdir. If she was telling the truth about that.

Magnus called Ingileif back. As expected, she didn't pick up the phone. But he left her a message that Hákon's body had been found downstream from his car. If she was meeting her brother, that was something she needed to know.

He carried on driving. It was still a few kilometres to the junction where he could turn left for Reykjavík or right for Flúdir. But first he needed to tell Baldur about Pétur.

He called his cell phone. No reply. The bastard wasn't picking him up.

He tried Vigdís. She, at least, would listen to him.

'Vigdís, where are you?'

'At police headquarters.'

'I need you to go arrest Pétur Ásgrímsson.'

'Why?'

Magnus explained. Vigdís listened, asking one or two pertinent questions. 'Makes sense to me,' she said. 'Have you told Baldur?'

'He won't take my call.'

'I'll speak to him.'

Magnus's phone rang again a minute later.

'He won't do it.' It was Vigdís's voice.

'Won't do what?'

'Authorize me to arrest Pétur.'

'What!'

'He says it's too early to leap to conclusions. He hasn't even seen the body yet. There have been too many early arrests made in this investigation.'

'It's only because I suggested it,' Magnus said bitterly.

'I can't comment on that,' said Vigdís. 'But I do know I can't arrest Pétur if my chief told me not to.'

'No, of course not, Vigdís. I'm putting you in a difficult situation.'

'You are.'

'The thing is, I think he's going to meet his sister. I *think* she's on to him. I'm worried that if they do meet, he might try to keep her quiet. Permanently.'

'Aren't you jumping to a few too many conclusions there?'

Magnus frowned. He was concerned about Ingileif. Vigdís might be right, perhaps he was stretching to a conclusion too far, but after what had happened to Colby, Ingileif's safety worried him. Worried him big time.

'Maybe,' he admitted. 'But I'd rather jump to too many than too few.'

'Look. I'll see if I can find Pétur at his clubs or at his house. Then I'll follow him if he goes anywhere. OK?'

Magnus knew Baldur would be very unhappy when he found out what Vigdís was doing. 'Thanks,' he said. 'I appreciate it.'

Magnus approached the junction. With Vigdís looking for Pétur in Reykjavík, Magnus could afford to concentrate on Ingileif.

He turned right for Flúdir.

Pétur could barely see Lake Thingvellir in the gloom ahead of him. It was just over a week since he had last been there. A week in which plenty had happened. A week in which he had lost control.

Everything had been ruined that day seventeen years ago when his father had died in the snowstorm in the hills above Thjórsárdalur. Since then, his entire life had been spent trying to limit the damage.

He had tried removing himself: from the whole Gaukur saga thing; from his family; from Iceland. That had worked to some extent, although he could never remove his father's death from his heart, his soul. He thought about it every day. For seventeen years he had thought about it every single fucking day.

But the misery had reached some kind of equilibrium, until Inga had opened up the question of the saga again. Pétur had tried to tell her not to sell it. He should have been more persuasive, *much* more persuasive. Inga's and Agnar's assurances that it would be possible to keep the sale secret had never had credibility.

It was all Inga's fault.

He was nervous about meeting her now. He would explain everything, explain it so she could understand. He knew she looked up to him as a reliable big brother. That was precisely why she had been so angry with him when he had abandoned her and her mother and the rest of the family. Perhaps that would mean that she would understand why he had killed Sigursteinn. That man had deserved to die because of what he had done to Birna.

Agnar would be harder to explain. As would Hákon. But Pétur had had no choice. There was no other way. Inga was smart, she would understand that.

He was losing control. He had covered his tracks well with Agnar. Not so well with Hákon. And with Inga?

He hoped to God that she understood. That she would keep quiet. Because if she didn't. What then?

Pétur fumbled in his pocket for the ring. He felt a sudden urge to examine it. He pulled over to the side of the road and killed the engine.

Silence. To his right was the lake, a deep grey. Cloud obscured the island in the middle of the lake, let alone the mountains on the other side. In the distance he heard the sound of a car, growing louder, passing with a whoosh of air and then diminishing.

Silence again.

He examined the ring. Hákon had kept it in very good shape. It didn't *look* a thousand years old, but then gold didn't necessarily. He peered at the inside rim. He could make out the shapes of runes. What was it they were supposed to say? *Andvaranautur.* The Ring of Andvari.

The ring. It was the ring that had destroyed his family. Once Högni had found it, they were doomed.

It had obsessed his father and caused his death. It had briefly obsessed Pétur before he had tried to put it behind him. It had obsessed Agnar and the foreign *Lord of the Rings* fans, and it had obsessed Hákon. No *possessed* Hákon.

Only his grandfather, Högni, had had the courage to put the ring back where it belonged. Out of reach of men.

Pétur had spent his whole life struggling against the power of the ring. He should face facts. He had lost. The ring had won.

Pétur slipped the ring on his finger.

If Inga refused to keep quiet, she would have to die. That was all there was to it.

Pétur checked his watch. An hour to go. He put his BMW in gear and headed on to the rendezvous with his sister.

Magnus drove fast to Flúdir. The driveway in front of Ingileif's house was empty. He jumped out of his car and rang the doorbell. Nothing. He stood back and examined the windows. No signs of life. It was a gloomy day, and if there was anyone inside they would have needed at least one light on.

Damn! Where the hell was she?

He looked around, searching for inspiration. An old man in dungarees and a flat cap was pottering about in the next door garden.

Magnus hailed him. 'Good morning!'

'Good afternoon,' the man corrected him.

'Have you seen Ingileif?' Magnus was quite sure that in a village the size of Flúdir, the man would know who Ingileif was, even if she hadn't lived there herself for years.

'You just missed her.'

'How long ago?'

The man stood up straight. Stretched. Took his cap off, displaying spiky grey hair. Examined Magnus. Put his cap back on. Scratched his chin. He wasn't necessarily that old, but from his face, Magnus could tell he had spent decades outside in the cold and rain. And he wasn't rightly sure whether to help this stranger.

'How long ago did she leave?' Magnus repeated.

'I heard you. I'm not deaf.'

Magnus forced a smile. 'I'm a friend of hers. It's urgent I find her.'

'About ten minutes ago,' the man replied eventually. 'She didn't stay long.'

'Which way did she go?'

'Couldn't say for sure.'

'What kind of car does she drive?' Magnus asked. He had no clue himself.

'Seems to me,' the man said. 'If you are her friend, you would know that.'

Magnus fought to control his impatience. 'This might sound melodramatic, but I believe she's in danger. I really need to find her.'

The man just grunted and turned back to his yard.

Magnus leaped over the fence, grabbed the old man's arm and twisted it behind his back. 'Tell me what kind of car she drives or I'll break it!'

The man grunted in pain. 'I won't tell you anything. Dr Ásgrímur was a good friend of mine, and I'm not going to help anyone harm his daughter.'

'Goddamn Icelanders!' Magnus muttered in English and threw the man to the ground. Stubborn bastards the lot of them.

He climbed back in his car. Where to? If she had driven back to meet Pétur in Reykjavík Magnus should have spotted her – he had kept an eye out for her among the drivers he had met coming the other way. There wasn't much to the north of Flúdir. But to the east was Hruni. Perhaps she had gone there. Either to meet Pétur, or to look for the ring.

The turn-off to Hruni was just to the south of the village. He sped the three kilometres in two minutes. As he expected there was a police car in the car park in front of the church, with a single officer reading a book in the front seat.

The book was *Crime and Punishment*. The policeman had nearly finished.

He recognized Magnus and greeted him.

'Have you seen Ingileif Ásgrímsdóttir?' Magnus asked. 'Blonde woman, late twenties?'

'No. And I've been here since eight this morning.'

'Damn!'

'Did you hear they think they've found Hákon's body?' the constable said.

'Yeah, I've seen it, at the bottom of Hjálparfoss. He's dead, there's not much doubt about that. But I'm worried about Ingileif. I think whoever killed the pastor is after her.'

'I'll radio in if I see her.'

'Can you call me on my cell?' Magnus said, giving the constable his number.

'You could ask those guys back there.'

Magnus turned. A car was parked by the side of the road over-looking the church and the rectory.

'Who are they?'

'Three men. One Icelander and two foreigners. I asked them what they were doing, they didn't have an answer, or not one that made any sense.'

Feldman and Jubb, Magnus thought. 'They're waiting for you to leave so they can search the church,' he said. 'But thank you, I'll go speak with them.'

He drove up to the car. There was a small Icelander in the driver's seat, with Jubb next to him and Feldman in the back. They looked distinctly uncomfortable to see Magnus.

Magnus got out of his own vehicle and approached theirs. The Icelander wound down his window.

'Hello, Lawrence, Steve,' Magnus said in English, nodding to the two foreigners.

'Afternoon, officer,' said Lawrence from the back seat.

'And you are?' Magnus asked the Icelander.

'Axel Bjarnason. I'm a private investigator. I'm working for Mr Feldman.'

'To do what?'

Axel shrugged.

'He's helping us with some research,' Feldman said.

Magnus was about to tell them they were wasting their time, the church had been thoroughly searched and there was no ring there, when he thought better of it. Let them spend all day on this godfor-saken heath in the mist.

'Have any of you seen Ingileif Ásgrímsdóttir?' he asked.

Axel's expression of patient disinterest didn't change. But he didn't answer the question. Jubb frowned.

'No, officer, we haven't,' Feldman said. 'At least not today. We tried to speak with her yesterday, but she wasn't real excited to see us.'

'I'm not surprised,' said Magnus. 'If you do see her, let me know.' He scribbled his number on to a piece of paper torn from his note-book and gave it to Feldman. 'The pastor has just been found. Murdered. I'm pretty sure the guy who did it is after Ingileif right now.'

Feldman took the card. 'We'll be sure to call you,' he said.

Magnus turned to look at the church, squatting beneath the crags in the mist. A raven descended out of the cloud and landed by the side of the road a few feet ahead. It strutted along, eyeing the two cars.

'Enjoy your day,' Magnus said, and jumped back into his vehicle. He sped off down the hill back to the main road.

He must have missed her coming the other way. Reykjavík. His best bet was Reykjavík.

CHAPTER THIRTY-FIVE

STEVE JUBB WATCHED the cop's car disappear over the hill. 'You know this isn't right.'

'What isn't right, Gimli?' Feldman said.

'For a start, my name isn't Gimli, it's Steve.'

'We discussed this before. We should use our nicknames.'

'No, Lawrence. My name isn't Gimli, it's Steve. Your name isn't Isildur, it's Lawrence. This isn't Middle Earth, it's Iceland. *Lord of the Rings* isn't real, it's a story. A bloody good story, but a story none the less.'

'But Gimli, the ring could be in that church! The ring from the *Volsung Saga*. The ring that Tolkien wrote about. Don't you realise how cool that is!'

'Frankly, I don't give a toss. That professor I spoke to only a week ago is dead. A vicar is dead. There's a nutter running around somewhere out there who's looking to kill a girl. A real live person, Lawrence, don't you get that?'

'Hey, look, it's got nothing to do with us,' said Feldman. He looked at Jubb suspiciously. 'Or does it?'

'What do you mean?'

'Well, did you kill the professor?' said Feldman.

'Don't be daft. Course I bloody didn't.'

'You say that, but I have no way of knowing whether you are telling the truth.'

'Look. That copper out there is looking for Ingileif. We know where she is. We should tell him.' Jubb took out his mobile phone. 'Give me his number.'

'No, Gimli. No.'

'Jesus Christ!' exclaimed Jubb. He jumped out of the car, flung open the door to the back and hauled Feldman out. The little man tried to cling on to the seatbelt but Jubb broke his grip. Jubb clenched his fist. 'Give me that number or I'll smash yer face in.'

Feldman cowered on the ground and handed the big Yorkshireman the scrap of paper bearing Magnus's number.

Jubb went round to the driver's side. 'Are you with me?' he asked Axel.

'The problem is, Steve, that bugging the girl's car wasn't strictly legal.'

Jubb didn't wait to argue. He leaned in, grabbed the private investigator, and flung him into the road. He jumped into the driver's seat and started up the engine. With Feldman and Axel hammering on the side of the car, he executed a quick three-point turn and sped off after the copper, striking Feldman a glancing blow on the legs with his bumper as he did so.

Magnus slowed as he reached the junction of the main road just south of Flúdir. His cell phone chirped.

'Hello?'

'This is Steve Jubb. Just wait where you are! I'm right behind you.'

'All right,' said Magnus. He *knew* Feldman and Jubb had known more than they were saying, although he was surprised that they had decided to tell him what. 'I'll be waiting.'

Magnus pulled over to the side. Within two minutes he saw the private investigator's car fly down the road towards him. It pulled in behind him, and Steve Jubb jumped out, carrying a laptop under his arm. Alone.

He climbed into the passenger seat next to Magnus.

'Hang on,' he said, switching on the laptop, and a receiver attached to it. 'This will tell us where Ingileif is.'

'Excellent,' said Magnus. He put the car into gear and turned left, towards Reykjavík. That was by far the most likely direction and he wanted to catch her up. 'Where are your friends?'

'Tossers,' muttered Jubb as he fiddled with the computer.

Magnus wasn't exactly sure what a tosser was, but he was prepared to take Jubb's word for it. 'Thanks for coming to get me.'

'I should have said something back there,' Jubb said. 'Should have told you everything back when you arrested me.' He clicked a couple of keys. 'Come on ...' he muttered.

'So you bugged her car?'

Jubb just grunted and carried on tapping at the keyboard. 'Here we are. She's north of here. Way north of here. Turn around.'

'Are you sure?'

'Course I'm bloody sure. Take a look.'

Magnus slowed and peered at the computer screen on Jubb's lap. It displayed a map of south-west Iceland, and it showed a round circle moving north along a road on the other side of Flúdir.

'Where the hell is she going?' Magnus asked. 'There's nothing up there, is there? Take a look at the map. There's one in the glove compartment.'

Jubb pulled out a map. 'You're right, there's not much north of here. A couple of glaciers, I think they are. The road goes right the way across the middle of the country.'

'It'll still be closed this time of year,' Magnus said.

'Wait a minute. There's something here. Gullfoss? Do you know what that is?'

'It's a waterfall,' said Magnus. 'A massive waterfall.'

Pétur pulled into the large car park. This early in the season, and in this weather, it was empty, apart from one tour bus.

He climbed out of his BMW. The enormous waterfall roared at him, unseen, from beyond the far side of the information centre. Tourists emerged along the pathway leading to the waterfall, cooing to each other about the majesty of what they had just witnessed. In five minutes they would be whisked away to the next stop on their tour, the geysers at Geysir, perhaps, or the Althing assembly grounds at Thingvellir.

Good, thought Pétur.

Rather than heading straight down towards the waterfall, Pétur turned left, upstream. There was now a maintained path leading up the low hill; in his childhood it had just been a narrow sheep track.

Just over the crest of the hill was a shallow hollow. It was here that Dr Ásgrímur had liked to take his family for a picnic on sunny days. Tourists usually walked to the foot of the falls, or halfway up, or followed the gorge downstream. The hollow, above the falls, offered some privacy, even in the height of summer. The grass and moss, soft and springy, made a comfortable spot to sit, when things were dry.

At the beginning of May, in the mist, things were very wet and there was no sign of anyone. It was only a couple of hundred metres to the car park, but there was no chance of being seen or heard above the din from there.

Pétur walked towards the river. The dull roar turned into a crescendo as the magnificent waterfall opened out beneath him. Its power was extraordinary. The Hvítá flung itself down into the gorge in two stages, at each throwing up a thick curtain of spray. The resultant tumult was known as Gullfoss, which means 'golden waterfall', because of the tricks of light that low sunshine could play on the fine moisture suspended above the cauldron. In the right conditions rainbows danced gold and purple over the falls.

On a clear day it was possible to see Langjökull, the 'Long Glacier' which produced all this water, crouching between the mountain peaks thirty kilometres to the north. But not today. Today, everything was covered in a grey shroud of moisture, spray and cloud merging into one.

Again, good.

Pétur stood and waited for Ingileif.

He was pleased with his choice of meeting place. Like the road to Stöng. Pétur had tempted Hákon out to that remote spot with a far-fetched tale of how he knew where the helm of Fafnir was hidden. He remembered the look of excitement and expectation on the pastor's face as he had approached him parked above the Fossá. Pétur had led the pastor down to the river, and then paused to let him pass. A blow on the back of the head with a rock, and the pastor had tumbled: it was all that Pétur had been able to do to stop him from falling straight into the water. He held him back just long enough to ease the ring off his finger, and then tipped him into the torrent. It could be weeks before his body was found, if ever.

That was another effect of the ring on people. It persuaded them to suspend their normal critical faculties, to believe the unbelievable. Pétur smiled. The irony that the pastor had fallen for the same ruse that had done for Gaukur a thousand years before pleased him.

Pétur stood, staring at the waterfall, and thought of his father. This place really did remind him of that sunny period before things had gone so wrong. Perhaps what he had said to Inga was true. Perhaps their father really was present.

Pétur shuddered. He hoped not. He wouldn't want his father to witness what might happen to Inga if she didn't promise to keep quiet.

Pétur wondered what the police would think when they found the pastor's body, or more likely his car. An accident? Suicide perhaps?

That was an idea. If the worst came to the worst, and Inga ended up in the waterfall, Pétur could claim she had killed herself. He had received a call from her. She was distraught, upset by feelings of betrayal at trying to sell *Gaukur's Saga*. She told him that she was going to Gullfoss. He feared suicide, and drove up to try to stop her. But he was just too late. He saw her jump.

That would explain his own presence at the waterfall. It would be close enough to the truth that he could carry it off.

He fiddled with the ring on his finger. They would almost certainly arrest him, and it would be hard to describe how he came to have the ring in his possession. Much better to hide it some-where before he raised the alarm.

But he was getting ahead of himself. As long as he managed to explain things properly to Inga, she would understand him, she would realize he had had no other choice.

Wouldn't she?

Magnus and Steve Jubb sped through Flúdir and into the farm-land beyond, dotted with domed greenhouses and emitting spirals of volcanic steam. The road soon ran alongside the Hvítá, in full spate.

'I've been a daft bugger,' Jubb said. 'Somehow I thought that Agnar croaking had nothing to do with me. I knew I was innocent but I hoped I could keep the existence of the saga and the ring secret. Seemed worth it then.'

'I thought you had killed the professor,' said Magnus.

'I know you thought that. But I also knew I hadn't. And I guessed you'd figure that out in the end.'

'Have you had any dealings with Pétur at all?'

'Never,' Jubb said. 'I hadn't met the bloke till the other day when I saw him with Lawrence Feldman. That man is weird, by the way. Clever. Rich. But weird.'

'And you're not?' said Magnus.

'There's nothing wrong in being a *Lord of the Rings* fan,' Jubb said defensively. 'What *is* wrong is when you let it blind you to what's going on in the real world.' He looked around at the extraordinary countryside flashing through the mist around them. 'Although sometimes I find it hard to believe that this country is part of the real world.'

'I know what you mean.'

Magnus's phone rang. Vigdís.

'I can't find Pétur at his house or at Neon. They haven't seen him there all day – they don't know where he is. I'm just going to check the other two clubs.'

'Don't bother,' said Magnus. 'He's heading to Gullfoss. He's going to meet his sister there. And then he's going to kill her.'

'Are you sure?'

Magnus hesitated. How sure was he? He had made mistakes earlier in this investigation. 'Yeah, I'm sure. Can you call in a SWAT team? What do you call it – the Viking Squad. The cloud's probably too low for a helicopter, but the sooner they get here the better.'

'We'll never get the Viking Squad approved,' said Vigdís. 'I will call Baldur. But you and I both know what he's going to say.'

'Damn it!' Magnus knew Baldur would ignore his request. 'Can you come yourself, Vigdís?'

A pause. 'All right. I'm on my way.'

'And bring a weapon.'

'I'll be there as quick as I can. Unarmed.' She hung up.

'Careful!' Steve Jubb flinched as he shouted the warning.

Magnus nearly swerved off the road as he took a bend too fast with only one hand on the wheel. As they were moving north, the road was already deteriorating. Stones slammed against the floor of the car like so many bullets.

'She's stopped at Gullfoss!' Jubb said, staring at his screen.

After careering over some foothills, they descended to cross a narrow gorge at a small suspension bridge and then found themselves on a better road speeding across flat moorland into the fog.

CHAPTER THIRTY-SIX

PÉTUR SAW THE familiar figure of his sister emerge from the gloom over the lip of the hollow. She walked in the same way she had when she was a girl – her coat was even the same colour. It brought back memories of those family picnics, before everything had been ruined. At twelve Inga had been really quite pretty, even when wearing her earnest glasses, but she had always been overshadowed by the stunning Birna. Pétur felt a sudden surge of affection for his little sister.

She wouldn't let him down. She couldn't possibly let him down. He raised a hand to greet her.

'Why the hell are we meeting here?' she said, shivering.

'It's the right place,' said Pétur gravely. 'It's the right place to talk about Dad.' This wasn't starting well.

'What I want to know is what you were doing driving up to Stöng yesterday. They found Hákon's car, you know. And his body at the bottom of Hjálparfoss.'

'I'll tell you about that. But I want to tell you about Dad first.'

'My God!' said Ingileif. 'You know how he died, don't you?'

Pétur nodded, meeting her eyes. They were anxious, questioning, but also angry.

'I was with them that weekend. With the pastor and Dad.'

'I thought you were at school.'

'I know. Dad wanted me to come with him on the expedition. He was convinced they would find the ring. I was in two minds about it. As I told you, I was dead against them taking the ring –

325

I remembered Grandpa's warnings. But in the end, he persuaded me.

'The trouble was, Mum had forbidden it. So we didn't tell her. I took the bus to Hella from Reykjavík and they picked me up there.'

'So Mum never knew?'

'No.' Pétur shook his head. 'We camped out on the hills and then the next morning we got to the cave. It wasn't really a cave, more of a hole in the lava. It took us three hours to find it, but it was Dad who discovered it. He was so excited!'

Pétur smiled at the memory. 'And who can blame him? It was amazing. There was this ring, covered in a small film of dust. It's not that it was shining or anything, you had to rub it to tell it was gold. But there was the proof that *Gaukur's Saga*, this story that had been passed down by all of our ancestors for all those years, was actually true.'

'But you and Dad always thought it was true, didn't you?'

'We believed,' said Pétur. 'We had faith. But anyone who has to believe or have faith rather than simply knowing, always has doubts. And to have those doubts dispelled ... Amazing.

'So I was caught up in the whole thing. But after a few minutes I told Dad we had to put it back. I talked about all the evil it would bring the world, how Grandpa had told me to make sure that Dad never took it. We had a major row. Dad looked to Reverend Hákon for support and he got it. I even tried to grab the ring off him, but he pushed me to one side.

'I had kind of ruined everything,' Pétur said. 'They walked on together and I followed twenty metres behind, sulking, you could say. Then the weather got bad. It was sunny one moment, the next it was snowing.

'I saw my chance. Dad was in front, the pastor next and then me. I slipped past the pastor and tried to grab the ring from Dad: I knew which of his coat pockets it was in. My plan was to run off into the snow and replace it in the cave. I was pretty sure I could outrun them in the snowstorm and they would soon give up.

'So Dad and I rolled around in the snow, then I pushed him and he fell, hitting his head on a rock.' Pétur gulped. The tears came into his eyes. 'I thought I had knocked him out, but he was dead. Just like that.'

'Oh, don't give me that! You pushed him over a cliff! He was found at the bottom of the cliff.'

'I didn't, I swear it. It was only a fall of a couple of metres. It was just the way he hit his head. On his temple – right here.' Pétur tapped his own shaved skull.

'So how do you explain the cliff?'

'Reverend Hákon saw what had happened. He took charge. I was a wreck after I saw what I had done. My mind was a blank. I couldn't say anything, I couldn't think anything. Hákon knew it was an accident. He told me to go, run away, pretend I was never there. So I ran.

'He pushed Dad over the cliff. Oh, he was dead then, that's for sure, the autopsy people got that wrong when they said he was alive for a few minutes. But Hákon covered for me.'

Ingileif put a hand to her mouth, her brow knitted in anguish. 'I can't believe it,' she said. 'So you were the elf the old sheep farmer saw?'

'Elf?' Pétur frowned.

'Never mind.'

Pétur smiled at his sister. 'It's true. I killed Dad. But it was a mistake. A dreadful, horrible mistake. If Hákon were alive he could tell you that.' He took a step forward. Took his sister's hands in his. Looked in her eyes – horrified, shocked, confused. 'Can you forgive me, Inga?'

Ingileif stood stunned for a moment. Then she backed off.

'It wasn't murder, Inga. Surely you understand that?'

'But what about Aggi? And the pastor? Did you kill them as well?'

'Don't you see, I had to?'

'What do you mean, you had to?'

'As you know by now, Hákon took the ring. When Agnar went

to see him, he guessed he had it. He accused Hákon of killing Dad and taking the ring. Hákon threw him out, of course, but then Agnar approached Tómas, tried to get him to act as an intermediary. He tried to blackmail Hákon through him.'

'But what did all this have to do with you?'

'Hákon had been good to me. He had kept me out of the police investigation completely. Until then, I had no idea what had happened to the ring, I had tried so hard not to think about it, or to ask questions about it, but it didn't exactly surprise me that Hákon had taken it from Dad. So, in the end, Hákon called me. He explained what was going on, that it looked like he would have to tell the truth about what had happened to Dad, unless I did something.'

'Did what?'

'He didn't say. But we both knew.'

'Oh, my God! You *did* kill Aggi!'

'I had to. Don't you see, I had to?'

Ingileif shook her head. 'Of course you didn't have to. And then you killed Hákon?'

Pétur nodded. 'Once his son was in jail and the police were after him, I knew the truth would come out.'

'How could you?'

'What do you mean, how could I?' Pétur protested, with a flash of anger. 'You were the one who insisted on putting *Gaukur's Saga* up for sale. If it hadn't been for that, all would be well.'

'That's bullshit. Yes, I made a mistake. But I had no idea what would happen. It was you! You who killed them!' Ingileif took a step back. 'OK, maybe you killed Dad by accident, but not the other two. Hang on – did you kill Sigursteinn as well?'

Pétur nodded. 'You have to admit he deserved it after what he had done to Birna. I flew back from London, met him in Reykjavík, bought him a few drinks.'

'And he ended up in the harbour?'

'That's right.'

'Who are you?' Ingileif said, her eyes wide. 'You're not my brother. Who are you?'

Pétur closed his eyes. 'You're right,' he said. 'It's this.' He took his hand out of his pocket. Showed her the ring on his finger. 'Here. Take a look.'

He slipped it off and handed it to her. It was his last chance. Maybe the ring would corrupt his sister just like it had corrupted him, his father, Hákon and all the others.

Ingileif stared at it. 'Is this it?'

'Yes.'

She closed her fist around it. Pétur felt an urge to grab it, but resisted. Let her have it. Let it do its evil magic with her.

'So, what are you going to do?' Pétur asked.

'I'm going to the police,' Ingileif said. 'What did you think I would do?'

'Are you sure?' said Pétur. 'Are you absolutely sure?'

'Of course I am,' Ingileif said. She glared at her brother. In addition to fear and shock, there was hatred there now.

Pétur's shoulders slumped. He closed his eyes. Oh, well. The ring was going to have its way. He had been foolish to think that this could end any other way.

He took a step forward.

CHAPTER THIRTY-SEVEN

MAGNUS PASSED A tour bus on its way out as he screeched into the parking lot. It was almost deserted. Two cars were parked next to each other – a big SUV and a much smaller hatchback, with a third a few feet away.

'That's Ingileif's,' said Jubb, pointing to the hatchback.

'Stay here!' shouted Magnus, as he leaped out of the car.

He ran across the parking lot and down some wooden steps. The waterfall opened up before him, a cauldron of roaring water. The path went to a ledge with an observation point halfway down the waterfall.

Nothing. No one. Just water. An unimaginable volume of water.

He looked up at the falls. The path stopped just short of them, all pretty much in his view. But downstream were more steps, a path, another parking lot, a gorge. Plenty of places to hide out of view.

Magnus ran down the steps towards the gorge.

'Pési? What are you doing?' Ingileif's eyes widened, but anger overcame fear. Pétur knew he would have a struggle on his hands. His sister wouldn't go quietly. He wished he had to hand a rock or some other blunt instrument to hit her with first. If he hit her hard enough with his fist, he might knock her out.

He swallowed. It was going to be very hard to strike Ingileif.

But ... But he had to.

He took another step forward. But then he saw some movement out of the corner of his eye. A couple with a tripod appeared over the lip of the hollow. One of them, a woman by her size and shape, waved. Pétur didn't acknowledge her but turned back to Ingileif, who hadn't noticed.

He would have to play for time, until they had gone.

'Do you want me to turn myself in?' he asked his sister.

'Yes,' she said.

'Why should I?' said Pétur.

For two minutes they continued a halting conversation, with Pétur watching the couple through his peripheral vision. He saw them set up the tripod, move it, and then take it down. Whether they had taken a picture of the falls or decided against the shot, Pétur didn't know. But he was relieved to see them disappear back over the rim of the hollow.

He took another step towards his sister.

Jubb didn't stay in the car. He looked around the car park, and then made his way to the information office. A middle-aged woman inside wished him a good afternoon in English, having sized him up as a foreigner.

'Have you seen two people here?' Jubb asked. 'A man and a woman? The man is bald, and the woman is blonde. Icelanders.'

'No, I don't think so. I did just speak to a German couple. The man had a woolly hat so I couldn't see if he was bald. But the woman had dark hair, I am sure of it. They were going to take photographs of the falls.'

'But no Icelanders?'

'No, I am sorry. Of course, I don't have a good view of the car park from here.'

'Thank you,' said Jubb.

As he stepped out of the information centre, he saw the German couple the woman had mentioned, walking down into the car park from the hill above, huddling together against the weather. The man had a tripod slung over his shoulder.

Jubb trotted over to them. 'Hello?' he called. 'Do you speak English?'

'Yes, I do,' said the woman.

'Have you seen a man and a woman up there? The man is bald and the woman is blonde?'

'Yes,' said the woman. 'Just over the top of this hill here.'

Jubb thought for a second. Should he run up there himself, or should he get Magnus?

Get Magnus.

He ran down from the car park towards the falls.

Pétur decided against hitting Ingileif, at least right away. He turned and sauntered over towards the edge of the gorge.

'Where are you going?' Ingileif called after him.

'To look at the falls.'

'Are you listening to me?'

'Yes, I'm listening.'

As he had hoped Ingileif followed. She was still arguing with him, pleading with him to give himself up. But she was keeping her distance.

Pétur paused, talked and then moved on again. This seemed to work. Finally he was within a few feet of the rim of the gorge. He had to shout to be heard.

Ingileif had stopped dead. She wasn't moving any further.

Then he saw in her eyes that she understood what he was doing – tempting her forward to her death. She took a few steps backwards and then turned and ran. Pétur lunged after her. His legs were longer, he was stronger, fitter, he caught her up, throwing her to the ground.

She screamed, but the scream was killed by the mist and the roar of the water. He pinned her to the grass, but she raised her right hand and scratched at his face.

Damn! That would be very hard to explain to the cops. He would think of something.

He hit her in the face. She screamed, but continued to writhe beneath him. He hit her again, harder. She lay still.

He swallowed. His eyes were hot with tears. But he had had no choice. He had never had a choice.

He dragged her over towards the rim of the gorge. That spot wouldn't quite work. Below the cliff a grassy slope dropped down to the water. It was steep, but not quite steep enough. He would have to go a few metres upstream.

He pulled her along a rough path, her legs and body knocking against bare rock. She seemed to be coming round. But he was nearly to a good spot; the top of a rock jutting out with a near vertical drop down to the river hurtling towards the falls.

The ring! She had the ring. Damn it. Perhaps she had dropped it when they had fought. Or perhaps it was in her pockets.

He lay her down. She groaned. He began to search her pockets.

And then, out of nowhere, a large shape flew through the air and bowled him over.

Magnus never heard Steve Jubb's shouts above the din of the waterfall. But he did pause and look back up the way he had come.

He saw the portly figure of Jubb wobbling down the path towards him, his arms waving.

Magnus ran. It was uphill and it was steep but he sprinted.

He usually kept himself very fit, running several miles a day if he could. In Iceland he hadn't had the chance, and already the edge was off his fitness. His heart was pounding and the breaths were hard to take. It was a steep path, but he took it as fast as he could.

'Up there!' Jubb said. 'Above the waterfall.'

Magnus didn't wait for more explanation but continued running uphill.

His chest felt like it was going to explode as he scrambled over the rim of the hill.

He saw them. Two figures, a few feet from the edge of the cliff, one lying on the ground, the other crouching over her.

Magnus ran faster downhill towards them. There was no chance of Pétur hearing him in all the noise, and he was concentrating too hard on Ingileif to see what was coming at him.

Magnus threw himself at Pétur and together they rolled to the cliff edge.

Pétur writhed, broke away, and hauled himself to his feet. He stood swaying on the edge of the cliff above the river.

Magnus stared at him, keeping his distance of a few feet. He had no desire to plunge over the cliff in a death-grapple with Pétur. Arrest was going to be difficult. For a start, Magnus didn't have any handcuffs with him. He didn't know what he would do if he managed to overpower Pétur – perhaps get Steve Jubb to sit on him for an hour until Vigdís showed up. Of course, if he hadn't been in some Mickey-Mouse country, he would have a gun, in which case things would be much simpler. As it was ...

As it was, Magnus could see Pétur sizing him up. Pétur was tall and rangy. But Magnus was big, and he knew he looked like he could look after himself. People usually didn't mess with Magnus.

Magnus heard a groan behind him. Ingileif. That was good news: at least she was alive.

'OK, Pétur,' Magnus said evenly. 'You had better give yourself up. There's no way out for you now. Come with me.'

Pétur hesitated. Then he glanced behind him, at the boiling river and the jagged rocks rising out of it. In a moment, he had turned and was gone.

Magnus took a few steps and looked over the rim. There was a kind of path, or rather a series of hand- and footholds that led down to some rocks on the edge of the river. He could see that it would just be possible to clamber along these, down almost at the level of the river, and to climb up again further upstream.

Magnus descended after Pétur. The spray had left the rocks extremely slippery, and Magnus had real trouble keeping his footing. Pétur was taking more risks, widening the gap. Magnus realized he would have been much better off keeping to the cliff top; he could probably have run upstream to the point Pétur was aiming for before Pétur reached it. It was too late now.

Magnus felt his footing slip. He grabbed hold of the rock with one hand. Below, the river rushed headlong to the top edge of the waterfall. The water was a beautiful deadly mixture of green and white.

Pure cold death.

Magnus hauled himself up with both arms and lay panting on the rock. He saw Pétur skip across three rocks barely five feet above the river. The man's balance was extraordinary.

But then Pétur slipped. Like Magnus he grabbed hold of the rock with one arm and held on. But unlike Magnus, he couldn't find a hold for his other hand. He dangled there, swinging, his legs bunched up beneath him, desperately trying to keep his feet out of the water, lest the river grabbed them and snatched him down.

Magnus leaped on to one rock. Another. His sense of balance was not as good as Pétur's. The rocks were about ten feet from the cliff edge now, out in the river.

This was stupid.

Pétur stared at him, his face wincing in agony at the effort of hanging on with one arm, his bald head dripping with moisture.

He couldn't hold on much longer.

Magnus turned. He could see Ingileif standing on the edge of the cliff shouting and waving. She was beckoning to him to come. Magnus couldn't hear what she was yelling above the roar, but he could see her lips. 'Leave him!' they seemed to be shouting.

Magnus turned back to Pétur. Ingileif was right. He watched the man who had murdered four people, including his own father, and who had just tried to murder his own sister, fight for his life.

Pétur's eyes met Magnus's. Pétur knew that Magnus had given up trying to reach him.

He closed his eyes, his grip slipped and he fell without a cry. His body was whisked along the top of the spate and over the rim of the waterfall.

Within two seconds he was gone.

CHAPTER THIRTY-EIGHT

MAGNUS SAW INGILEIF standing next to her brother's white BMW four-wheel-drive, with the snow-covered mountain rising above her.

He pulled up beside her and got out of his car.

'You're late,' she said. Her face was pink in the cold, her eyes shining.

'Sorry.'

'Never mind. I'm glad you came.'

Magnus smiled. 'I'm glad you asked me.'

'I thought you might have gone back to America.'

'Tomorrow. Although everyone in the police department thinks I've already left.'

'So where are you staying?'

'I can't really tell you.'

Ingileif frowned. 'I would have thought that by now you would have trusted me.'

'Oh, no. It's not that. Let's just say I've learned the hard way that the fewer people who know where I am the better.'

There was a remote possibility that Soto would send out a replacement for the hit man who had shot Árni, so the Police Commissioner had decided to let everyone think that Magnus had flown back to Boston. Actually, he had sent Magnus to stay with his brother at his farm an hour and a half to the north of Reykjavík. It was a beautiful spot, on the edge of a fjord, with outstanding views. And the Commissioner's brother and his family were hospitable.

Nobody had heard anything from Colby. That was a good sign. All she had to do was lie low for a couple more days.

'So, what do we do now?' Magnus said, staring up at Mount Hekla rising above them.

'Climb it, of course.'

'Dare I ask why?'

'What kind of Icelander are you?' Ingileif said. 'It's a lovely day, so we're going up a mountain. Don't you want to?'

'Oh, I'd like to,' said Magnus. 'Is it difficult?' He had borrowed boots from the farmer, and he was more or less properly dressed for the occasion.

'It's easy in summer. It will be more difficult now. This early in May there's still a lot of snow about, but we'll manage. Let's go.'

So they set off up the side of the volcano. It was a glorious day, the sky was clear and cold and there was already a magnificent view stretching out behind them. The snow lay on lava and pumice, and was actually easier underfoot than the black rock and stone. Magnus felt good. The air was crisp, the exercise was invigorating, and it was nice to have Ingileif beside him. Or ahead of him. She set a rapid pace, which Magnus was happy to follow.

'How's your friend?' she asked as they paused to catch their breath and admire the view. 'The one who was shot?'

'Árni is doing well, thank God. They say he's going to make a full recovery.'

'I'm glad to hear it,' Ingileif said. Ahead of them was the blackened valley of the River Thjórsá, and beyond that the broad plain through which the Hvítá ran. And beyond that more mountains.

'So you're going tomorrow?' Ingileif said.

'That's right.'

'Are you coming back?' There was something a little hesitant in the way she asked the question.

'I don't know,' said Magnus. 'At first I was dead set against it. But the Commissioner has asked me to stay. I'm thinking about it.'

And he was thinking about it, seriously. Partly he felt a sense of obligation – gratitude for what the Commissioner and Árni had done for him. But also the seed of suspicion that had planted itself in his mind on the road up the Thjórsárdalur three days before was nagging at him. The suspicion that the answers to his father's murder might lie in Iceland rather than the streets of Boston.

As he had anticipated, the seed had taken root. It was growing. It wasn't going to die away now.

'If it makes any difference,' Ingileif said. 'I'd like you to.'

She looked at him, smiling shyly. Magnus felt himself grinning back. He noticed the nick on her eyebrow, already so familiar. It was strange how he felt that he knew her so well, as though it was much longer than ten days since he had first interviewed her in her gallery.

'Yes. That makes a difference.'

She moved closer to him, reached up and kissed him, long and deep.

Then she broke away. 'Come on, we've still got a long way to go.'

As they ascended, the mountain became stranger. There was no single neat round cone at the top of Mount Hekla. Rather, a series of old craters from previous eruptions dotted the ridge. Sulphurous steam rose out of fissures, narrow cracks in the mountain. The snow became thinner, the bare patches more common. As Magnus put his hand on the bare black lava, he realized why. It was warm. Underneath, and not very far underneath, the volcano was bubbling away.

When they reached the top, the view was extraordinary, as Iceland stretched all around them: broad rivers, craggy mountains, slow, powerful glaciers.

'It's amazing to think of the three brothers climbing this a thousand years ago,' Magnus said. 'You know, Ísildur, Gaukur and Ásgrímur.'

'Yes.'

Magnus looked around. 'I wonder where the crater they were trying to throw the ring into was then?'

'Who knows?' Ingileif replied. 'My father used to fret about that. Needless to say, I first came up here with him. The mountain has rearranged itself many times since their day.'

'What are you going to do with the saga now? Are you going to sell it?'

Ingileif shook her head. 'We're going to give it to the Árni Magnússon Institute. But before then, I'm going to let Lawrence Feldman have it for a year in return for enough money to bail out the gallery. Birna will get her share, of course.'

'That's a neat idea.'

'Yes. It was Lawrence's, but it looks like everyone can live with that. I think he feels guilty.'

'As he should.' Magnus thought about all that had happened over the previous two weeks. He wondered whether they would ever find the ring. Pétur's body had not turned up yet, apparently it could be days or weeks before it would be spat out by the water-fall. He rather hoped that somehow the ring would stay there, at the bottom of Gullfoss.

But he couldn't say any of this to Ingileif. That was her brother down there, after all.

'Let's go,' Ingileif said. She set off down the mountain to the left of the path they had used on the way up. The snow was thin or non-existent, the ground was so warm. She skirted an old crater and stopped by a small spiral of steam, coming out of a crack in the ground.

'Careful!' Magnus said. The snow and lava on which she was standing looked precarious. There was a strong smell of sulphur in the air.

Ingileif pulled something out of her pocket.

'What's that?' asked Magnus.

'The ring.'

'The ring? I thought Pétur had it!'

'He gave it to me. I think he hoped it would change my mind.'

'But you didn't tell anyone that!'

'I know.'

Magnus was only a few feet from Ingileif. He longed to examine the ring, the cause of so much pain and anguish over the last couple of weeks. What did he mean, couple of weeks? The last millennium. 'What are you going to with it?'

'What do you think?' said Ingileif. 'I'm going to toss it into the mouth of hell, just like Tolkien suggested my grandfather do. Just like Ísildur wanted to do.'

'Don't do that,' said Magnus.

'Why not? It's the right thing to do.'

'Why not? Because it's one of the most significant archaeological discoveries this country has ever seen. I mean, is it real? Haven't you wondered that all along? How old is it? Did Högni or someone hide it eighty years ago? Or is it really centuries old? Or even older, perhaps it really did come from the Rhine at the time of Attila the Hun. Don't you see? These are fascinating questions, even without the Tolkien connection. And they can all be answered by archaeologists.'

'Oh yes, they are fascinating questions,' Ingileif said. 'I can tell you, it's made of gold. There is an inscription in runes scratched on the inside, although I haven't tried to decipher it. But whatever it is, it's evil. It has caused enough damage to my family. I'm getting rid of it.'

'No, Ingileif, wait.' Magnus felt an overwhelming urge to grab the ring from her.

Ingileif smiled. 'I wanted you to come up here with me to make sure I had the strength to do this. But now look at you.'

Magnus could see the ring between Ingileif's thumb and forefinger. He didn't know what it was exactly, whether it was ten years old or a thousand. But he knew she was right.

He nodded.

Ingileif bent down and tossed the ring into the fissure.

There was no thunder. No lightning. The sun shone out of the pale blue Icelandic sky.

Ingileif climbed back up to Magnus and kissed him quickly on the lips.

'Come on,' she said. 'Let's get going. If you're flying back to Boston tomorrow, we've got things to do and not much time to do them.'

Grinning broadly, Magnus followed her down the mountain.

AUTHOR'S NOTE

A reader putting down a book such as this might well ask how much of it is real and how much is invented. This question deserves an answer.

There really was a Gaukur. He lived at Stöng, a prosperous farm which was obliterated in the eruption of Hekla in 1104. Both the remains of the original building and the reconstruction a few miles away on the main Thjórsárdalur Road are well worth seeing. His death at the hand of his foster-brother Ásgrímur is mentioned in *Njáls Saga*. Gaukur had his own saga which is referred to in the fourteenth century *Mödruvallabók*, but it was never transcribed. The story that saga told remains unknown.

J.R.R. Tolkien taught Middle English at Leeds University from 1920 to 1925, where he instituted the 'Viking Club' with its beer and its Icelandic drinking songs. His letters show that after writing the first chapter of *The Lord of the Rings* at the end of 1937 he agonized for several months over how to continue the story and link it in with his earlier novel, *The Hobbit*. *Where the Shadows Lie* speculates upon a solution.

Iceland is a small country where everyone seems to know everyone else. It is quite possible that some of the characters in this book resemble real people. If so, such resemblance is completely coincidental.

I am thankful to the late Ólafur Ragnarsson and Pétur Már Olafsson for first introducing me to Iceland. It was after this visit that I became determined to write a book set in the country – an ambition that took me fifteen years to achieve. I should also like to thank Sveinn H. Gudmarsson, Sigrídur Gudmarsdóttir, Superintendent Karl Steinar Valsson of the Reykjavík Metropolitan Police, Ármann Jakobsson of the University of Iceland, Ragga Ólafsdóttir, Dagmar Thorsteinnsdóttir, Gautur Sturluson, Brynjar Arnarsson and Helena Pang for their time and assistance. Richenda Todd, Janet Woffindin, Virginia Manzer, Toby Wyles, Stephanie Walker and Hilma Roest made many helpful comments on the manuscript. I am grateful to my agents, Carole Blake and Oli Munson, and to my publishers, Nicolas Cheetham at Corvus and Pétur Már Ólafsson at Bjartur-Veröld, for all their help. And lastly I would like to thank my wife Barbara for all her patience and support.